Praise for Adam Brookes

Night Heron

"The must-read thriller of the year." —*NPR Books*

"*Night Heron* is a fascinating portrait of the dangerous complexities of spying in a restricted country, the competing agendas driving international intelligence, and China's startlingly varied social realities. A must-read for fans of espionage and smart global fiction in general."
—*Booklist* (starred review)

"Outstanding fiction debut…Brookes [is] a thriller writer to watch." —*Publishers Weekly* (starred review)

"*Night Heron* is a wonderfully cinematic novel—I felt myself visually transported into every scene, watching the action unfold—that also immersed me in the sounds and smells and feel of China, all the while telling a rich, complex espionage story. A remarkable accomplishment."
—Chris Pavone, interna̶̶̶̶̶̶̶̶̶̶̶̶̶̶̶̶ author of *The Expats*

"A top-notch̶̶̶̶̶̶̶̶̶̶̶̶̶̶̶ *Heron* already places̶̶̶̶̶̶̶̶̶̶̶̶̶ today's spy novelists." —*Washington Post*

"Engrossing and compelling."
—*Los Angeles Review of Books*

"Fans of the international espionage genre will inhale this fast tale in a few suspenseful breaths."
—*Library Journal*

"The pace is frenetic and Brookes does a wonderful job with both the high-tech world of cyber intelligence and survival on Beijing's gritty, smog-smothered streets. Highly recommended." —*The Bookseller*

"One of the best and most compulsively readable spy fiction debuts in years." —*Kirkus*

Spy Games

"[Adam Brookes] does an excellent job of keeping the action moving and the tension high, making *Spy Games* a difficult book to put down....Brookes has separated himself from the pack: I've read a lot of very good China books by excellent journalists, but I've never before stayed up far too late on a work night to finish one, unwilling to go to sleep until I knew how it ended." —*Los Angeles Review of Books*

"A rich, can't-put-it-down thriller.... Terrific." —Joseph Kanon

"A smarter or more exciting mystery likely won't be released this year." —*Kirkus* (starred review)

"Authentic, taut and compelling. Brookes is the real deal." —Charles Cumming

"Brookes shows that his impressive debut was no fluke, and readers will look forward to Mangan's next adventure." —*Publishers Weekly*

THE
SPY'S
DAUGHTER

By Adam Brookes

Night Heron
Spy Games
The Spy's Daughter

THE
SPY'S
DAUGHTER

ADAM BROOKES

www.redhookbooks.com

Redhook Books/Orbit
Hachette Book Group
1290 Avenue of the Americas
New York, NY 10104
hachettebookgroup.com

Originally published in Great Britain by Sphere in 2017
First U.S. Mass Market Edition: October 2017

Redhook is an imprint of Orbit, a division of Hachette Book Group.
The Redhook name and logo are trademarks of Hachette Book Group, Inc.

The publisher is not responsible for websites (or their content) that are not owned by the publisher.

The Hachette Speakers Bureau provides a wide range of authors for speaking events. To find out more, go to www.hachettespeakersbureau.com or call (866) 376-6591.

ISBNs: 978-0-316-50349-5 (mass market), 978-0-316-50350-1 (ebook)

Printed in the United States of America

OPM

10 9 8 7 6 5 4 3 2 1

For Susie, Anna and Ned

In the past, espionage activity was typically directed towards obtaining political and military intelligence. These targets remain of critical importance but in today's technology-driven world, the intelligence requirements of a number of countries are wider than before. They now include communications technologies, IT, energy, scientific research, defence, aviation, electronics and many other fields. Intelligence services, therefore, are targeting commercial as well as government-related organisations. They sometimes do this on behalf of state-owned or sponsored companies in their own countries.

MI5.org.uk

We are talking here of an elaborate, comprehensive system for spotting foreign technologies, acquiring them by every means imaginable and converting them into weapons and competitive goods. There is nothing like it anywhere else in the world. The system is enormous, befitting a nation of one point three billion, and operates on a scale that dwarfs China's own legitimate S&T enterprise.

Chinese Industrial Espionage, William C. Hannas, James Mulvenon and Anna B. Puglisi

Life is first boredom, then fear.

Philip Larkin

PROLOGUE

Great Falls, Maryland
The recent past

The sound of the shot made the outdoor diners at a nearby restaurant lift their eyes and turn, wondering, from their conversations. They looked across the parking lot, towards the trees. There, partly hidden by azalea bushes and undergrowth, a car rocked momentarily on its suspension. Startled birds rose in the warm air.

The first intrepid soul to leave his table and approach the vehicle was a former Marine of broad back and strong stomach. He picked his way past the vegetation and peered through the windscreen, then backed away shaking his head—whether in sorrow or disgust it was hard to say. A single body, he reported, male, in the driver's seat, the back of the head shot away, suggesting a self-inflicted wound. Blood all over the place. The hand holding the weapon was limp and curiously positioned, turned back on itself in the well between the seats.

The diners called their children to them. Some paid their bills and left hurriedly. The police and paramedics arrived, then a detective, then a forensic investigator from the Office of the Chief Medical Examiner. The male in the driver's seat was declared dead. The investigator picked his way around the car, leaned into it, made copious notes. Photographs were taken, and evidence bagged and tagged. Finally, the body was manoeuvred from the car and laid upon a gurney.

The dead man was of sixty-some years. He wore a well-cut suit and a silk tie for the day of his death. He appeared prosperous, trim, fit, lightly tanned. He wore a silver beard, trimmed close to the jaw. On his right wrist was an extremely expensive watch, a Breguet. This was odd, thought the forensic examiner, since it would suggest left-handedness, yet the weapon, a Sig .357, was in the right.

The forensic examiner pondered the strangeness of it all—out here on the edge of the city, in the trees, near a popular restaurant and a pretty canal, a place for day trips, for hikes; the suit and tie, the sense of orderliness and authority they hinted at. And as he did so, the FBI arrived, as he knew they would. For the man's identity—quickly established from his wallet and the federal government identification tag in his inside pocket—was already sending tremors through Washington, DC. He was, apparently, a senior official of the State Department—not a diplomat, but an intelligence analyst by the name of Jonathan Monroe. And when such people—the holders of security clearances that allowed them into the most secret compartments of this most secretive of cities—took their own lives, all the worst assumptions frothed and bubbled around their cadavers. Was it corruption? Sex? Was he coerced, compromised, cuckolded? Was he, God help us all, a spy?

Two FBI special agents waited politely to talk to him, and for a moment the examiner looked skyward at the circling birds, felt the sun on his face. Such a death was not uncommon in Washington: the pressure, the secrecy, the sheer viciousness of the place ate away at people.

But such a death was rarely uncomplicated.

PART ONE

The Possible

1

Beijing, China
The recent past

Granny Poon came in dry as a bone, this time.

She carried no handheld, no tracker. Nothing to leak a signal, however faint. She would leave no signature, no spoor. She would float through the digital medium like a dust mote in dark, quiet air.

She took a bus from the airport. She paid in cash and turned her face from the cameras that monitored her boarding. The bus crawled into the city and she watched the tower blocks creep past, the concrete rendered gold in the late summer sunlight.

Bone dry. Alone.

That was the way of it, she thought. She looked down at her hands, their liver spots, veins rising from the dry, papery skin. She wondered if this might, perhaps, be the last time.

Let's see what this stupid old woman can do.

The restaurant was packed with market traders and migrant workers, the air clattering and heavy with grease, the reek of sorghum spirit. They came here for the Shanxi food, the bowls of fatty lamb and shaved noodles. She had come in good time to watch from the scrubby park across the street, sitting still in the warm twilight, clutching a walking stick and her purse. She had made two passes before entering, tottering along the sidewalk in dark glasses, wheezing. Now she occupied a corner table. The waitress smiled at her, called her *ayi*, auntie, a sweet girl. She ordered Cat's Ear Noodles heaped with garlic bolts and tomatoes, the broth thick with cumin, laced with black vinegar. The girl caught her accent, the sibilant sing-song of the south, and smiled, tilting her head questioningly. Eileen Poon just nodded.

And now Eileen waited, and watched. She waited for a particular moment, one rapidly approaching, whose exact location in time had been determined months previously, perhaps years. She watched for the anomaly, the ripple on the surface of the crowd.

Not long now.

The girl came and placed before her a steaming bowl, plastic chopsticks wrapped in a napkin. A glass of tea. She picked at the noodles, letting the seconds tick down. She allowed her gaze to float and settle, float and settle.

Nothing.

Nothing but the bark and clatter of the restaurant, steam rising from the bowls and curling in the afternoon light, the ruddy-faced men leaning into their food, pouring the sorghum spirit from the little green bottles, tossing it back.

Time, now.

She laid her chopsticks down, got shakily to her feet, one hand leaning on the table, the other clutching her purse. The sweet waitress was there, asking if she needed anything.

"*Cesuo,*" she said. Toilet.

The girl gestured to the back of the restaurant, a

corridor. Eileen Poon tottered past the busy tables, down the corridor, past stacks of greasy chairs, an empty fish tank. The noise receded.

The door to the toilet was of plywood and stood half open. She went in, felt for a light switch, locked the door behind her and stifled her breathing against the ammonia stench. From a squat toilet a pipe snaked up the wall to the cistern. She took a pair of latex gloves from her purse and put them on. She ran her hand up and down the pipe, feeling behind it. Nothing there. She opened the toilet paper dispenser. Nothing. Beneath the hand washbasin, she found a cupboard. She opened it and ran her hands around the inside.

And just there, deep in the cupboard's filthy recesses, taped to the underside of the basin, a packet of White Rabbit milk candy.

Eileen worked the packet free, peeled the tape from it, and put it in a plastic bag. She threw the tape and the latex gloves into the toilet and put the plastic bag containing the candy in her purse.

She waited for a moment, steadied herself. She flushed the toilet and washed her hands, unlocked the door and made her way back down the corridor.

A little flutter of relief. Well, that's *that* part done, she thought.

Now the difficult part.

She emerged into the restaurant and stopped. The roar of talk and laughter and the rattle of crockery broke over her. She reached beyond the sound and the visual clutter. Was he here, the bringer of White Rabbit candy? Was he watching? Or she? She felt around the room for a gaze, for a look a little too laden with meaning, for the tilt down of the head, the turn away.

Nothing.

She walked slowly back to her table, sat, drank her tea.

The sweet girl brought her bill.

"You didn't like the noodles?" she said.

"Too much," said Eileen.

"I'm sorry," said the girl.

"*Mei shi.*" No matter. She raised her frail old hand, waved away the girl's concern. She peered at the bill and counted out yuan notes from her purse, her frugality on show. The girl smiled, waited patiently. Eileen put on her dark glasses and stood to leave—the egress protocol was complicated, calling for some quick street work and a weave through the subway system, alone. She took her stick and walked to the front door. The waitress was there, holding the door, lovely girl, saying, "*Manman zou.*" Go carefully.

Eileen stepped out of the restaurant into the warm evening. She stood on the sidewalk, fussing with her purse, her stick, scanning the street, the pavement, counting, watching: a boy in a Chicago Bulls cap, staring at his phone, moving slowly west; a silver SUV, and behind it a Yamaha motorbike, yellow, the boy riding it in a white T-shirt, moving quickly; a couple, deep in conversation, with shopping bags and a purple backpack.

And a man on a bench.

The very same bench, the one that afforded a clear view of the restaurant, that Eileen Poon had taken advantage of earlier in the day.

The man wore a cream, short-sleeved shirt and grey cotton slacks. He sat with his knees together. He held a folded newspaper in his lap, but looked straight ahead. His hair was grey and thinning and combed back from the forehead. Some oil or pomade may have been used.

Eileen Poon absorbed these details in an instant, fixed them in her mind.

And who are you?

She surveyed him from behind her dark glasses. Even

at this distance she saw that the hands that lay in his lap were small and smooth. His cheeks and chin were smooth, too, as if scrubbed with pumice. He evinced cleanliness. A fastidious man, this. One with well-kept nails, shiny shoes. He sat very still. And it was his stillness, she realised, that had drawn her eye to him. He sat as if in prayer, and his eyes were small, dark stones.

She looked both ways, made to cross the street. A bus drew up, obscuring her view of the park, the bench, the man. When it pulled out and away again, he was gone.

In her hotel room, later, after the streets and the subway and the sidewalks, Eileen Poon sat on the edge of the bed in darkness and removed her shoes, massaged her aching feet for a moment. The visage of the smooth-cheeked man lay fixed just behind her retina, and now she worked it deep into her memory.

During half a lifetime of secret work on behalf of Her Majesty's Government, Eileen had built within herself a vast mental vault peopled with places, faces, postures, gaits, voices, accents, atmospheres and encounters, every one of them specific and immediate to her, every one available for instant recall. For, when it came down to it, the practitioners of secret intelligence working along Asia's Pacific Rim were relatively few in number. Oh, the listeners and cyber sleuths and local security thugs numbered in the millions. But the professionals—the agent runners, the handlers, the watchers and the street artists—not so many. And Eileen, of anyone, could spot them. To Granny Poon the street artist—the finest in Asia, Hopko said—the skills of recall and connection were central to intelligence work, and her astounding capacity for both was the reason that the United Kingdom's Secret Intelligence Service had kept faith with the Poon family for forty years. Hopko valued Granny

Poon's gifts. *You're my eyes, Eileen*, she had once said. *You're my memory.*

But of Fastidious Man, Eileen found nothing.

She held the image of him in her mind, allowed it to drift and move. She made demands of it. Tell me why you sat on the bench, at that time, in that way. Tell me what it was in your look that hinted at awareness, of resources available to you. Tell me about intention, how it manifests in a person. Tell me why I know you, even though I don't. Tell me about White Rabbit milk candy.

She stood, walked to the desk, turned on the lamp and pulled the curtains closed. She went to her suitcase and took from it a second pair of latex gloves and a face mask, and put them on. She took also a rubber mat wrapped in cellophane. She unwrapped the mat and laid it on the desk. She walked to the bathroom, and took from her sponge bag a box containing a pair of nail scissors and a pair of tweezers, both in sterile wrap.

She sat at the desk, her purse before her.

Using the tweezers, she removed the bag containing the White Rabbit candy from the purse, then used the nail scissors to cut it open. With the tweezers, she took twelve pieces of candy from the packet, each individually wrapped in waxy red and blue paper, with twists at each end. She laid them out side by side on the mat. Carefully, she began to unwrap each one, delicately working the gobbets of chewy white candy from the paper.

When she reached the seventh, she knew she had found it. She felt its different density, the uniformity of its shape. She unwrapped the waxy paper. Inside, no milk candy, but a white plastic capsule, hard and smooth. Upon closer examination, the capsule revealed a join at its middle, as if it were in two parts. Eileen pulled gently and with a *snick* the two halves came away to reveal a foam centre, and encased in the foam was a tiny drive, no bigger than a finger nail. She held the drive in the tweezers for a moment, wondering.

Movement in the corridor.

Eileen looked around, towards the door, sitting very still. A burst of laughter, then nothing.

She listened. More movement, in a room down the corridor, perhaps.

Nothing there, she thought. Why so jumpy? Stupid old woman.

She pushed the drive back into its foam recess, clicked the two sides of the capsule together. She rewrapped the capsule in its candy wrapper, replaced it in the packet with the others, put the candy back in the bag, the bag back in the purse.

Just candy. In a purse.

This operation, she thought, had an austere feel to it. Very quiet, very deep. Very hard-edged. Just her, dry as a bone. Not even her sons. If Peter or Frederick had been with her they could have sniffed Fastidious Man, filmed him, listened to him, run him through the servers, found him out. She thought of the man's stillness, his unnatural posture.

From the street, the sound of a car accelerating, too aggressively, too fast.

She stood, pulled the curtain away from the wall a little, looked into the dark.

In nearly forty years on the street, Eileen Poon had learned the virtue of solid cover and pure nerve. She knew to brazen it out, not to run. Every little drama, every midnight flit, left unanswered questions in its wake, left chambermaids calling the shift manager, slack-jawed security officers reviewing the camera footage, accountants looking at your credit card. And soon someone notices. And then the someone starts paying attention, looking for patterns. And before you know it he's in your phone, your laptop, your apartment, watching you move, sniffing the air as you pass. Better to sit still, wait, move deliberately, calmly.

And yet. A packet of White Rabbit candy currently residing in her purse screamed, *Run. Now.*

She stood motionless and listened again, her stomach churning. Fear did not come often to her. Why tonight?

She picked up the phone and called room service.

"*Wei?* Yes. I want club sandwich. But no mayonnaise. You understand? No mayonnaise. Yes, lettuce, tomato, want. No mayonnaise. Mayonnaise give me irritable bowel. Also, Bloody Mary, large one."

She put down the phone, and went back to her purse, pulling out the packet of candy, feeling in it for the capsule. She put the capsule in a sterile evidence bag. She knelt by the curtains. They were heavy, floor length, of some dun-coloured material. Using the nail scissors, she unpicked two inches of hem, slipped the bag and capsule in, used a needle and thread to tack the hem, let the curtains fall.

By the time the food arrived, she had changed into a cotton nightgown and had donned a hairnet and sat on the bed, watching a Chinese news channel. A parade was planned, said the reporter. A grand military parade! Through central Beijing, past Tiananmen Gate, to mark the anniversary of China's great victory in the War of Resistance Against Japan. There would be twelve thousand goose-stepping troops, stealth fighters overhead. In preparation, the authorities were seeding clouds and setting monkeys to roam the city's parks. The monkeys were tasked with killing birds, though it was unclear to Eileen Poon why the birds might pose a security threat. "As the tanks roll down Beijing's central thoroughfare," said the reporter, "the people's unity will reach its peak."

The waiter pushed a little clinking trolley to her, and lifted a plastic cover to reveal her sandwich.

"Club sandwich. No mayonnaise," he said. "Bloody Mary."

He didn't meet her eye. She tipped him and he left quickly.

She ate the sandwich fast, tipped the Bloody Mary down the sink, turned the television and the lights off, listened. Waited. She badly wanted to smoke a beedi, one of the reeking Indian cigarillos she bought in bunches tied with string from the little store in Wan Chai.

The night spooled out endlessly. Fear slowed time down. She forced herself to think of her boys, back in Hong Kong awaiting her return, waiting to signal *She's back*. She thought of the hand-off to Hopko. Where would it be? Geneva? Bangkok? She thought of dropping the capsule into Hopko's waiting hand, her smile, the venal look that would frame her eye.

And the *fuss* Hopko would make of her. Hopko would take her for a nice dinner, and give her presents from London, the shortbread from Fortnum's for which Eileen had such a weakness. It would be just the two of them, nobody else. Because this operation—she didn't even have a codename for it—was theirs alone. Just Eileen Poon and Valentina Hopko. Twice she had been into Beijing in the last eight months at Hopko's order, dry as a bone each time. Twice she had cleared an old-fashioned dead drop loaded by an agent she never saw. Did Hopko even know who he was? This one is *special*, Eileen, Hopko had said. This one has the scent of *greatness* on him. And he's just for us, Eileen. Not even for your boys.

Restless, she puffed her pillows, smoothed her nightgown, sipped water to ease the dryness in her mouth, listened to the hiss of the air conditioning.

She had known other long nights. Nights when she

feared State Security was at the corner, on the street, at the door. Nights with her nerves writhing and sleep a distant, treacherous shore. Nights when nothing had happened, and when everything had happened. Nights long ago when numbers crackling across the shortwave frequencies told her *ABORT ABORT*, and she'd burned her passport and run through the backstreets of Chengdu or Semarang or Hanoi. Why such unease tonight?

Perhaps three times was enough. Perhaps it was time.

At four or so, she dozed, and at five she watched the grey light filter in from a crack in the curtains.

If they come, she thought, it will be now.

She got up and put on a pink shirt and tan hiking pants that reached halfway down her blue-veined calves, and a pair of sneakers. She stretched, pushed away the wheeze and shuffle of yesterday, and readied herself to move fast.

She thought of Fastidious Man, his smooth cheeks, his little hands. She wondered what it might be like to be touched by those hands. What they would feel like on her cheek, her waist, her breast. She wondered if, in a way, he was touching her now.

She knelt, extracted the capsule in its polythene bag from the hem of the curtain and returned it to the packet of candy, before packing it in her carry-on.

She stopped at the door to her room, listened, calmed herself.

An operation is a whisper, Hopko had once said to her. Don't make it an argument.

2

Sorong, West Papua, Indonesia

Mangan entered the shop through a ragged plastic shower curtain. The interior was all clutter. Half-refurbished laptops were strewn about, piles of boxes, cell phones, tablets. From behind the counter, the Javanese woman—toothy, powdered, hair in a bun—eyed him. Mangan was conscious of his own dishevelment: he was unshaven, his T-shirt hanging limply from his awkward, lanky frame, his jeans had gone baggy at the knees, and on his feet were flip-flops, on his back the scraggy backpack. The shop smelled of clove cigarettes and damp.

"You back again," said the woman.

"Yup," said Mangan.

"What you want this time?"

"Same as before," said Mangan.

She frowned.

"Phone card?" she said.

"Yes. Please."

She flicked an accusatory finger at him.

"You just buy. One week."

"I want another. The same. Pre-paid. No name."

She was giving him a stern look now.

"Why you want?"

"Is it important why?"

"You already have. Why you want one more?"

"I lost it. Now can I have another one?"

She paused, considering. He looked at her, and caught in her eye the tick of calculation. He realised that something was happening he didn't understand, a tinge of alarm bleeding into his chest, his stomach.

"What's the problem?" he said.

She shook her head, looked down.

"What's the problem?" he said again.

"No problem," she said.

She reached into a glass-fronted case behind her, and from a filthy tangle of cables, old phones and chargers, extracted an envelope. She handed it to him. He felt the hard little SIM card through the paper.

"Six million rupiah," she said. About four hundred U.S. dollars.

"Six?" said Mangan. "Why the price rise?"

She shrugged.

"What's changed since last week?" he said softly.

She pointed upward with her forefinger.

"Price go up." She wouldn't meet his eye. "You pay now."

Very alert now, he leaned across the counter, smiled, laid his hand on her forearm. He felt her tense under his touch.

"What's changed?"

She said nothing.

"I'll pay the price, and I won't come back here again. Okay? Just tell me."

She licked her lips.

"You. Problem."

"What? What problem?"

"Some people they come here. Ask about you."

"They asked about me? Who? What did they say?"

"They say if I have seen Inggris. Tall man. Hair red colour, like you."

"Did they know my name?"

"I don't know."

"What did you tell them?"

She shook her head, her finger-wagging gone now. He let his voice rise a little.

"What did you fucking tell them?"

"I say ... I say I see you. But I don't know where you go. Where you stay."

His hand was still on her forearm. He felt a prickling of his scalp.

"Who were they?"

"*Orang Cina.*" Chinese, the words coated in contempt. She paused. "They have photo. You."

"They showed you a photo?"

She nodded. He took back his hand. She was staring at the counter. He counted out notes from his wallet, dropped them in front of her. She reached out to take them, but he planted his finger on them, pinning them.

"The card," he said. "It's good?"

She nodded.

"It register, but name not true. Is okay."

He kept the money pinned to the counter.

"And now?"

She looked up at him.

"What?"

"You'll call them, won't you? The *orang Cina*. They told you to call them."

She blinked, then made a *what can I do* gesture, holding her hands out.

"If I not call, then ..."

"Then what?"

"They say they make trouble for me. For family. They say they tell polis, make big trouble." She was becoming agitated.

"Why did they come to you?"

She looked blank.

"They ask many place. Hotel, phone place, internet place."

Jesus Christ.

"Did they say anything else?"

She shook her head.

"What you do?" she said. "You are criminal? You are thief."

He took his finger off the rupiah notes, let her take them.

"I didn't do anything. I'm just a journalist. *Wartawan.*" He pointed at himself. "*Wartawan.*"

He let her take the money, pocketed the SIM card, and left.

3

Washington, DC

Patterson found the apartment on an online listing service, and she loved it immediately. It was off 18th Street, a tiny top floor with big windows in an elderly brick row house. An iron fire escape bore rows of plant pots. Below, a cobbled courtyard.

The owner seemed reluctant, worried about her lack of credit history, and when they met was visibly startled: the British accent on the phone didn't match the blackness of her person, apparently. In the end, the diplomatic passport prevailed, and the owner, a smooth, highlighted matriarch in beige, pushed the rental agreement across the table for her to sign.

Now Patterson sat on the bed in shorts and T-shirt, the windows open, allowing the sultry late-summer air to move a little. The walls were a clean, bright white, the floors of dark wood. I need some rugs, she thought, some colour. She walked to the kitchen and ran her hands over the stainless-steel fittings. She'd never lived anywhere like this.

And so, she reflected, began her period of exile and disgrace. No rap on the knuckles, more like a vicious backhander to the face, the Service's way of telling her: *You are a monumental, gold-plated fuck-up.* Hopko's way of telling her: *You are not ready for operations, nor will you be until you grow up.* So here she was. In a gorgeous flat, in a strange new city, where she was of interest, exotic almost. The tall, broad-shouldered black woman who spoke like an English army officer because she'd been one, who was *with the Embassy,* but whose role was never quite spelled out. Fascinating creature.

Could be worse, she supposed, even as it was humiliating and awful.

She stepped out onto the fire escape, looked across the rooftops. A low city. None of the caverns of New York or Chicago. And then, from beneath her, a mock-dramatic gasp, and a voice.

"Is it? I think it is!"

"It is!"

"Yes, it definitely is!"

"A neighbour!"

She looked down. Two of them, a man and woman, both in sunglasses and shorts. They had pulled cushions out onto the fire escape and were holding wine glasses and looking up at her.

The woman, white but tanned, with dirty blonde curls, raised her glass.

"Hail, neighbour. Come down and make yourself known."

"Yes, come on down." He was slender, paler, dark haired. He waved her down.

Patterson's immediate response was to pull back. *Who are they?*

They are two people sitting on a fire escape drinking wine, in a new place, a new city.

"Oh, well, hi," she said.

"Hi, yourself. Get on down here. Get a glass, Este."

"Comin' up." He crawled through their window and disappeared. Patterson started down the iron stairway.

"Nice apartment, huh. We were wondering when it was going to be let. It's been empty for weeks." She held out a hand. "I'm Emily."

"I'm Trish. And yes, it's a lovely flat."

The woman was looking at her over the top of her sunglasses.

"Este. Quick. This person appears to be something other than 'Murican."

The man was reappearing through the window clutching a wine glass. "I hear it. I hear it. Hi. I'm Esteban." He passed her the glass, and he gave her a quick, light smile that disarmed her.

"I'm Trish. And I'm British," she said. He was pouring wine for her.

"Welcome, British Trish," Emily said, holding up her wine glass. "What brings you to these shores?"

"I'm a diplomat. I'm with the British Embassy."

The two of them made *I'm impressed* faces at each other.

"Well, that raises the tone around here," said Esteban. "Which section?" He spoke as if he knew embassy geography intimately.

"Oh. Trade section."

"Riiiiight. You'll be busy. Won't she, Em?" He turned and gestured to Emily. "Em here is on the Hill, dubiously attached to a congressional committee with dubious oversight of trade agreements. Wouldn't you say, Em?"

"On the nail. We'll have plenty to talk about."

Shit.

"Well, terrific," she said. Both of them were looking at her. She sipped her wine. "What about you, Esteban?"

"Oh, K Street. But in a good way."

She decided to play it for a laugh.

"I have absolutely no idea what that means," she said. They did laugh, but it was polite. Emily spoke.

"It means he belongs to that class of bloodsuckers known as lobbyists. He loiters around the offices of congressmen and tries to influence them with flattery and favours and money. Fact-finding trips to Vegas, the Bahamas. Campaign contributions. Private jets. It's pathetic."

He was nodding, grinning. Emily went on.

"Though in Este's case, he's not looking for defence contracts or drilling rights, he's trying to get clean energy legislation passed, so perhaps he will escape the fiery pit of hell."

"I'm a shit in a good cause," said Este. "And it suits me, right, Em? Have you always been a diplomat?"

"No, I used to be a soldier, believe it or not," Patterson said.

"I can believe it," said Emily. "You look fit, tough." She clenched a fist, made a fierce face.

"Wow. Really? Did you serve in . . . ?" Esteban let the sentence hang. He doesn't know if it's polite to ask, she thought.

"Yes, yes," she said. "Three tours. Iraq and Afghanistan." She smiled. Both of them looked as if she'd announced a death in the family.

"That must have been . . . intense." Emily said. She spoke as if war were an alternate universe, incomprehensible.

"Yes, it was. It was. Intense." She smiled again, not wanting to make a thing of it.

But, there, sliding through the space behind her eyes, was the road of yellow-brown dust, a boy on a moped. He was barefoot, and as he pulled away from her, he looked back with a smile and those eyes that just glowed, and then he was gone. She could hear the insect rasp of the engine, the gear changes, could feel the weight of her own body armour in the heat.

"Well, now look," Emily said, signalling a change of subject. "Let us come clean with you. We have a terrible ulterior motive in bringing you here and plying you with alcohol. Have some more wine, actually. Este." *Ulterior motive?* Esteban reached over and filled her glass. It was a lovely, crisp white from Oregon.

"I'm afraid so," said Este. "Do you want to ask her, or shall I?"

Patterson felt a jolt of irritation.

"The thing is," Emily was twisting her fingers into a knot, trying to look cute. She did look cute. Very, Patterson thought.

"The thing is..."

She looked cute and awkward. So did Esteban. *What the fuck do they want?*

Emily gave an exaggerated sigh.

"Do you think, just possibly, that we might implore you to...not wear your shoes in the apartment?"

What?

Esteban was looking at her with a mock-desperate expression.

"It's just, the previous guy, he stomped around up there in his shoes on those wooden floors and for us, it's like an earthquake down here," he said. "Like, showers of dust from the ceiling, and six thirty in the morning, stomp, crash. It was awful. And he wouldn't put any rugs down, and it was like, dude, seriously?"

"Yes, rugs. We'll buy you rugs. We'll take you to the best rug place and buy you rugs." Emily was starting to look worried; Patterson realised she had her flinty expression on, and forced her face into a smile.

"Of course. Good Lord. Of course. Shoes off. Absolutely. No problem."

Emily gave an exaggerated sigh of relief and ran her hand through those curls, and Este cracked a huge grin.

"I was thinking of getting some rugs, anyway," Patterson said. "The place needs some colour."

"I'm likin' this one," said Esteban.

"Oh, we're likin' this one a *lot*," said Emily.

Later, Patterson microwaved a pizza and sat by the open window in the hot dark, eating, watching, listening. A siren, a helicopter, snatches of speech, and the rustle of cicadas in the gingko trees, and beneath it all the city's sub-aural *thrum*.

The boy was still there, just on the edge of sight, bobbing along on his moped, the glowing coals in his eyes.

His presence brought a sour pain, right to the centre of her, somewhere between heart and gut, the pain a perfect alchemy of self-blame and sick regret. He was still there when she tried to sleep. *My habashi*, he used to call her in his reedy boy's voice. *My Ethiopian. My black woman.* And all she could do was to imagine laying down her weapon in the yellow-brown dust, shucking off her body armour and unlacing her boots, walking away.

4

Silver Spring, Maryland

Pearl had finished her calculus problems, prepared for the next day's class, cleaned out her backpack of crumpled paper, hairbands, leaking pens and candy-bar wrappers, tidied her room and put away her laundry, and in Pearl Tao's world such endeavours merited a pause, a moment on her bed wrapped in a fleece blanket, alone with her phone.

She needed the blanket because the air conditioning was on, and her father always set it at about ten below zero and her room turned into a walk-in refrigerator and she froze, so she pulled the blanket tight about her and snuggled in among her pillows and soft toys: a Tigger, a pink unicorn, an Elmo. It was evening, and low sunlight flooded the room, painting the walls a golden orange. The smell of her mother's cooking was drifting up the stairs.

She took a picture of herself, her face half out of shot, her tongue out, the blanket pulled up around her neck, the sunlight reflected in her glasses. She peered at the image. Her complexion was, well, as usual, the spattering of spots and welts on her pale skin, the breaking-out around the nose, pores like a lunar landscape. She had put her dreary, featureless hair up in a bun. Her mother urged her to wear make-up, but when she did her skin turned really volcanic. She sighed, and sent the picture to Cal, the phone emitting a crisp, metallic *ting* as it went.

She heard the front door closing. Her father was home. She looked up from her phone. Was he coming upstairs? No. She heard the murmur of her parents' conversation below her. They were speaking Mandarin, in their furtive way. She heard the scrape of the kitchen chair as he sat heavily, and her mother padding about, putting away his jacket and his briefcase and taking him tea that he'd blow on and sip noisily.

Ting.

It was Cal. A photo of him in his lab coat, holding a handwritten sign that read: *MUKBANG!!!! munchigirl!!* She texted back: new one?

For reals she does like a ton of hot sauce.

Pearl found herself smiling.

ok imma watch

She streamed the video. munchigirl was in her bedroom, as usual, somewhere near Shanghai, judging from the girl's accent. Somewhere out in Zhejiang, maybe? She wore a strappy top that showed her shoulders, and her eye make-up gave her that manga princess look. She had a little pout, and beautiful hair. On the table in front of her was a colossal bowl of rice, a stewed chicken, a pot of what looked like *hongshao rou,* red-cooked pork. munchigirl, deadpan, introduced all the dishes and talked briefly about their ingredients. She picked up a pair of chopsticks and set about the chicken, dunking each mouthful in scarlet chilli sauce and holding it out to the camera so the viewer could see. She was mostly silent, but held eye contact with the viewer, and each little murmur of appreciation—*Mmm, this is good. Ooh, so spicy*—brought a rush of likes and dislikes and comments skating across the screen. A lot of men seemed to want to marry her. She continued eating, unperturbed, holding Pearl's gaze. The scene felt intimate to Pearl, as if munchigirl were her friend or a sibling sitting across the table, sharing a meal, allowing her in. Pearl scrolled through it, a full hour of video. munchigirl ate all the food, and then signed off with a peace sign and a sing-song, *Bye-byeeeee*.

She texted Cal.

> lol how she not fat like a dumpster
> > I know right?
>
> u like her
> > mm yeah my type. Specially the false eyelashes

Cal loved these videos, considered himself an aficionado of the weird web. He watched hours of Ukrainian women brushing their hair, people getting put in plaster casts, community dancing.

> Wot u doing now
> > In lab finishing up. Hey come tomorrow after class.
>
> wait why?
> > something to show you!!!!!
>
> k
> > making baozi this Saturday. yum. Pork and jiucai.

Pearl felt a twinge of apprehension. Was that an invitation? She bit her lip and thought for a moment.

k. see you tmrow

She heard her mother's tread on the stairs, and clicked quickly away from Cal's texts. There was a tremulous tapping at her bedroom door.

"Dinner's ready."

Pearl watched the door.

"I'm not hungry," she said.

A pause.

"You should come and eat something."

"Ma, I'm not hungry, really."

Her mother tiptoed away.

They didn't come for Mangan straight away.

He made himself available, wandering about in public places, sitting at a roadside café eating grilled fish and *nasi goreng*, watching the street in the hot, clammy evening. He heard the call to prayer as the dusk came down, and felt for a moment taken out of himself, a momentary release from fear.

Mangan knew fear now as his natural condition. It was an acrid cloud in the pit of his stomach, rising, falling, expanding, contracting. He measured his experiences by it. He felt for it now, its sour pulse as he gnawed on the fish, picking the bones from his mouth.

When would they come?

Perhaps they would just watch.

He ordered another beer and the boy brought it, cold and dewy, and he held the bottle against his forehead for a moment, then took a long pull. He lit a clove cigarette and worked through his options.

Option one. Skip town. Move, make a hard target.

Staying still makes you vulnerable. Get somewhere safe, busy, crowded, anonymous. Kuala Lumpur, maybe. Singapore. Move.

But the harder you run, the harder they chase. Running just excites them.

Or.

Option two. Do what London keeps screaming at you to do. Get on a plane. *Come in, Philip. You did everything we asked, and we know how hard it's been. Oh, and we might have a few questions.* Hard questions, Mangan thought, to be administered by some very skilled, very hard men. He wondered where they'd do it. Not the swanky little mews house in Paddington where they normally kept him. Somewhere quiet, he thought, out in the dank English countryside. A place you can't see from the road, with fences and low brick buildings and a military policeman on the gate. *We are very patient, Philip, but we are going to need to talk to you.* He heard Hopko's voice and felt the uptick in anxiety that always accompanied it.

Or.

Option three. Do what the handlers tell you. Do what Patterson said, months, centuries ago, back in the Paddington house. When things have gone to shit, Philip, live your cover. Be who you are, or who your cover says you are. Sleep, eat, make a plan. Resoluteness and a good story, that's what you need.

They knew he was here, in Sorong. How? Some infestation on the laptop, firing off a digital flare each time he logged on? Impossible to tell. The phone? But he'd been living on burners, bought in damp stores down muddy side streets, places that sold supposedly untraceable SIM cards. *Just the sort of place they'd look, you idiot.*

Unless the woman had sold him, of course. *Here's someone interesting. Anxious, scruffy* bulé *paying top dollar for burners. Tall. Red hair. Green eyes. Can't miss him.* And someone had mentioned it to someone whose ears had pricked up and they'd mentioned it to someone else, and the knowledge of Mangan's whereabouts had floated, like a splinter on the tide, towards the gaping maw of Chinese intelligence.

For the last five weeks he had zig-zagged the length of the Indonesian archipelago—boats, small planes, then buses lumbering through lush forests, down red earth roads, shuddering to their appointed halts in tiny, forgotten villages where the barefoot men in sarongs held fighting cocks under their arms and stood and stared. He had slept in dingy hotels in out-of-the-way towns. He had lived his cover. *Philip Mangan, progressive journalist, liberated from the controlling exigencies of the corporate media, roams Asia mapping the marginal, narrating the unspoken.* He'd written obscure stories and posted them on the website. One on land use in Ambon. *Migrating Home: Displaced Muslims and Christians Struggle to Reconcile Claims to Land and Genealogy.* Another on the schooners that ply the routes between Indonesia's islands. *Crafting the Modern: the Pinisi Boats of the Archipelago.* He'd loved writing these pieces, had tried to make them true, despite their daft titles.

But for all the truth in the writing, the pieces themselves and the website on which he posted them were fictions. Fictions dreamed up, built and paid for by clever tech wallahs in the basement of VX. The fictions of cover.

At what point, he thought, do I also become a fiction? Or am I one already?

He stood unsteadily and dropped rupiah notes on the table, looked out cautiously into the twilight. The air smelled of kerosene, cigarette smoke and, running beneath, the sea. He walked through silent, darkening streets back to his hotel. He realised that at this particular moment he didn't care that much if they were watching or not. It came over him more frequently of late, this feeling. Often, alcohol helped bring it on. He'd be ducking, diving, watching his back, worrying about cover and comms, and it would just bubble up in him. *What's the point?*

In his room, he stripped and lay naked under the mosquito net in the darkness, smoking. Why not just do what London wanted? Why not come in? They'd question him, and he would cope. He would give them everything he had. China, Ethiopia, Thailand, everything that had happened over the last two years. How, blown, he had watched a truck driver bleed out in the cold night beside a highway, a stubby knife in his chest. How the man, as he died, had asked for his child.

How he'd once had a lover, but she'd been taken.

How his agent had died, sprawled in a casino bedroom on the banks of the Mekong River, foam at the mouth, skin mottling.

He'd tell them how it felt to lie. How it felt to be played. He'd tell them of his revulsion, and his compulsion, the rhyming contradictions of the self. Spy. Don't spy.

But they knew it all. And the fevered self-examination of a minor, blown agent in a hot and distant country wouldn't interest Hopko, or Patterson, or any of them.

What *would* interest them, back there in dank England, other than dissection of his operational carcass?

Well, one thing.

He had one thing to make Patterson sit straighter and lean into him, to bring Hopko's glittering gaze on him, to make him *matter*. And the thing? A tiny, smooth bead of possibility residing unspoken and silent just beneath the meniscus of memory. He reached for it as he lay there in the vile, fetid room, and there it was, hard and urgent.

Very desirable, this little bead of possibility.

And then, as if scenting his thoughts, they came.

5

It was around three. Mangan struggled up from the depths of alcohol-soaked sleep at the creak of a chair, the smell of something, someone. He sat bolt upright, blinking at the darkness, heart pounding. Beyond the mosquito net he could make out the orange glow of a cigarette. The someone was sitting at the little writing desk. The orange ember moved upward, glowed brightly for an instant, and Mangan heard the crackle of the burning tobacco. Then a long exhale, like a sigh.

Mangan tried to think of something to say or do.

"Who the fuck are you?" he managed.

The figure shifted on the chair a little.

"You're awake," it said. A man's voice.

"Get the fuck out of my room," said Mangan.

The seated figure said nothing for a moment and Mangan got the impression it might be deferring to another person. Was there more than one of them? He looked around, but could make out nothing through the mosquito net and the darkness.

"We're so sorry to disturb you," came the voice. English spoken by a non-English speaker, the pronunciation Asian, Chinese perhaps, but American inflected.

"The fuck you are. Get out." His mouth was dry, his words thick.

"What was said?" The voice was quiet, very assured.

"What?" said Mangan.

"What was said?"

Mangan made to get off the bed. He was still naked.

"Don't," came the voice. "Stay there."

Mangan swallowed. Were they armed?

"What was said, Mr. Mangan?"

"Fuck you. Get out." The words were starting to feel as if they belonged to another, as if someone else were speaking them. That's fear, he thought. Fear does that.

Another crackle and exhale.

"You have been a busy, busy man the last, what, year and a half, two years. Lots going on."

"I'm a journalist. What's it got to do with you?"

"What's it got to do with me? Well. Okay. Let's see. Couple of months ago you were hanging out with a slutty little Chinese colonel, right? That's got to do with us."

"No."

"This colonel was a little free with his confidences, am I right?"

"None of your fucking business who I hang out with."

"You know what happened to him? He got a little frisky with the birdie powder in some shitty casino up the Mekong someplace. What an asshole. They found him with a needle sticking out of his groin. You hear that?"

"Don't know what you're talking about."

"Sure. Well, the people I work for, they feel that this colonel talked a lot of shit to a lot of people. And, I'm sorry to say, they hold the opinion that he said some shit to you, Mr. Mangan."

The voice paused for a second, drew on the cigarette again, the orange glow.

"You are talking to the wrong person." It sounded weak, he knew.

"Really. The thing is, Mr. Mangan, the people I work for—"

Mangan found himself speaking over the voice.

"Who *do* you work for?"

There was a pause, as if the voice were displeased at the interruption.

"The thing is, the people I work for want to know what got said, Mr. Mangan. The colonel was very forthcoming to us before his needle episode. He talked *a lot*. Lots of detail. He told us about you, all your creeping around Asia, bits of Africa, pretending to be a journalist. We know about your communications, the darknet sites you use, all that stuff. And believe me, back home they know your name. We asked around, and they're like, what the fuck? Philip Mangan? The one who did nine kinds of crazy shit in Beijing two years ago? You're famous. Or blown. Yeah, you could call it blown. And they're like, so what did Colonel Slutski say to Mangan? When they were alone, dreaming up their little conspiracies, what got said?"

Mangan felt the polished bead, deep in his mind. Hard as a gemstone.

"This is bullshit. Now get out."

The voice was moving, approaching the bed. And there *was* another person in the room, to Mangan's right, also moving now. Mangan felt his own fingers digging into the mattress.

"Mr. Mangan, please don't tell me to get out. In fact, you tell me to get out one more time and we may have a frank disagreement, okay?"

The voice was standing at the end of the bed. Mangan could just make out his form through the mosquito net, his eyes.

The voice was quiet, matter-of-fact.

"Mr. Mangan, we don't do kidnapping or rendition or any of these things like your Service and the Americans and the Russians do. We don't grab people off the street and drug them and put them in a nappy and fly them off for a torture cruise. We don't blow them to pieces with drones. We don't put polonium in their tea. It's not in our playbook. Not yet, anyway. We like to think that we're smarter than that. So we prefer to ask you nicely, okay, to please tell us whatever the fuck it is you are doing."

The other figure, to his right, was standing very still. He tried to rally.

"What do you mean what I'm *doing*? I'm not *doing* anything. Now fuck off and leave me alone."

There was silence in the room. The voice stood still at the end of the bed. So did the other one, to Mangan's right. Then the voice spoke again, as if he'd decided to restrain himself. The tone was calm, but Mangan could feel anger running underneath it.

"Okay. Okay. So the colonel, before he shoots up, he has a little moment of defiance, right? Just a moment. He gets all brave. And he tells us he's done something. 'I've done something,' he says. 'What have you done?' we ask."

The *snick* of a lighter, and Mangan suddenly saw through the net, in the shocking light of the flame, a face. A young face, Asian featured, and, Mangan registered, absurdly handsome. A fine-boned, full-lipped, dimpled, doe-eyed treasure of a face. Then darkness again, the glowing tip of the cigarette, the visage fading at the back of Mangan's eye. The man spoke again.

"He says, the colonel, 'I've let something go.' He says, 'I've let it go on the wind. For them to use. And they'll find it and they'll fuck you with it.' That's what he says. He means us, right? My bosses. Me. We are the ones getting fucked in this scenario. But who is going to do the fucking? This, we do not know, because Colonel Slutski wouldn't tell us, and he had an appointment with a needle. Now what are we supposed to think?" He was feigning exasperation. "I mean, what?"

Mangan said nothing.

"Well, what we think is: it may be you. You. Maybe he told *you* something, and you are planning to use this one little thing to do the fucking. Some little thing. Maybe you don't even know what it was he told you. I mean, that's possible, right? He tells you something and you don't even know its significance. Sure, that's possible."

The ember arcing in the darkness, its pulse and hiss.

"But then . . . then we see you take off. Whoosh. You're gone. We see you, like, running all over the place, getting as lost as you can, all through Indonesia. Ending up in this shit hole. You're watching your back. You're buying burners. You're using all this encryption. And we think, Well, this guy is not moving like a journalist. This guy is moving like a spy."

Silence for a moment. Mangan was aware of the *chee-chat* of a gecko somewhere up in the rafters.

"So that's what we think. We think, Holy crap, Philip Mangan is pretending to be a journalist, as usual, but actually he still thinks he's a spy."

Mangan sensed that the person to his right—was it a man?—had come closer to the bed, was standing right next to the mosquito net. The voice was still talking.

"Which means that Philip Mangan has some *reason* to think he's a spy. Maybe he's got some *reason* to be all operational, some *reason* for all this—what do you call it?—*skulking*." An exhale. "So that's why we're here, Mr. Mangan. We would like to know what got said."

In Mangan's chest, corrosive fear. But in his mind, a signal.

The questions are wrong, he thought. They're not directed. They're reaching, but they don't know what for. They don't know what I know, or if I know anything. So they mean to intimidate.

So be intimidated.

"Look, I really, really don't know what you're talking about. I just…I just…whatever, okay? I'm sitting here with no clothes on and I don't know what the fuck you're talking about and just, please, leave me alone. Okay?"

The mosquito net to his right was pulled up roughly. He saw a pair of jeans, a black T-shirt on a muscled torso. And then a shower of white specks exploding in his eyes, and a concussive wave rolling through his face and head and he felt himself falling back, his head on the pillow, and blood in his mouth. The man had hit him, but how? With what? He raised his hands to his face and let out a sound he didn't recognise.

The voice came faster now, excited, turned on.

"So, really, if anything got said, Mr. Mangan, that we don't know about…I mean, you are not equipped for this, okay? You are not equipped for this. We are not here to hurt you, but you are doing this wrong. In way, way, way over your head. You should go away now. Go somewhere nice. Get a regular job. Get a girl. Get a dog." The voice was rising in pitch, tripping over its words. "And stay away from all the sluts, and all the spooks, and the drives that you don't know what they are or what's on them, and stay the fuck away from China. Really. Just fucking do that."

Mangan heard the sounds coming from his own mouth, a thick, nasal, moan. There was blood everywhere. He could feel it slippery and wet on his fingers. He could sense the second man looming over him. He stayed still.

One of them was speaking in Mandarin quietly, a little performance for Mangan's benefit.

"*Ta tingdong le ma?*" Has he understood?

"*Bu zhidao.*" Don't know.

"*Wo zai gei ta jieshi yi xia.*" I'll explain it to him again. Mangan tensed.

The second blow was harder, delivered with something the man was holding, something short and black, falling across the bridge of the nose, and sending everything into darkness for a moment, but then he was back, and the two men were still standing there looking at him.

"*Zhe yang ni jiu hui shale ta.*" You'll kill him like that.

The second man just sniffed and turned away. And they left.

6

Eileen Poon, carrying now, moved deftly across Beijing in a morning turned thick and grey. A taxi to Fangzhuang, a wander through a forest of high-rises, their tops lost in the haze, her carry-on bag rattling behind her. She walked past scrubby concrete parks, the old folk out stretching and chatting. Then the metro, so jammed with silent commuters she couldn't see a thing. She jabbed and shoved her way through, ducking, tacking. At a mall, she sat in a coffee shop where she ordered a hot chocolate, caught her breath and watched, sensed the flow of the crowd.

Nothing. She was sure of it.

At the train station, they were checking IDs. *Wujing* paramilitary police, armed, a dog with them, circling and whining. They had extra cameras, mounted on wheeled platforms, the cables snaking away.

She looked down, walked doggedly ahead, pulling her carry-on. A hand in a black glove stopped her.

"*Shenfenzheng.*" Identity card.

"I'm from Hong Kong," she said.

He said nothing, just held out his hand. He wore body armour, and had a stubby automatic weapon slung across his chest. She fussed in her purse, poking and riffling. He watched her. After an age, she pulled out her passport and the travel permit for China's mainland. He took them, turned them over, frowned.

"Where are you going?"

"Oh, Tianjin. My brother's niece is there and they've just had a baby, and it came three weeks early. Three weeks! And everything is chaotic. He was away at work—he fixes computers, he was in Anhui, I think. Anyway, he had to rush home and nothing is ready and it's *luanqibazao*—chaos in eight directions. So I'm going to go and see them and help. If they'll let me. Which they won't. She's got a face like a slapped arse, that woman. But you can't blame the baby, so—"

"What were you doing here in Beijing?"

"Meetings. Meetings. I have a business. Well, it's a family business." She opened her purse again, her fingers probing the pockets. She produced a card, thrust it at him. He took it and she jabbed a finger at it.

"Yip Lo Exports. That's us. We do plastic novelties. Party gifts, wristbands, hair notions, all sorts. Meetings with suppliers. We needed to talk about—" The policeman had looked away and was holding out her documents. She took them and put them deliberately back into her purse.

She stood there for a moment, fiddling with her bag, muttering, looking around as if trying to reorient herself, thinking of the cameras, the facial recognition software, the behaviour analysis. She pushed the thought of White Rabbit candy as far from her mind as she could, burying it deep beneath the contrivances of cover. She took hold of her carry-on, walked to the platform, and boarded.

The fastest train in the world to Tianjin—one last dog-leg—then a plane to Hong Kong. Easy now, she thought. I'm on my way, Val. Just for us.

TOP SECRET STRAP 2 BOTANY—UK EYES ONLY
ANNEXE B COPY 4/8
//REPORT
1/ (TS) Source FULCRUM addressed a letter to C/
FE. It is printed below in full.

Beijing
To: Controller, Far East and Western Hemisphere,
United Kingdom Secret Intelligence Service,
Vauxhall Cross, London

Dear Friends,

I am in a very precarious situation, and I must explain some things to you.

Three times now I have provide most valuable items to your Service, which can allow great and powerful understanding of my country's Deep State. Never forget this, my friends. I do not only give you information. I give you power. I give you some of my power.

I require that you are most careful with the materials provided to care of my safety. Distribution MUST be limited, number of people familiar with operation MUST be limited. I know you are most professional and you understand importance of this.

The items I choose to share with you are of utmost importance, and can show you that I am in very senior position, with great access to China's intelligence secrets. You can see this.

My situation is precarious because of anti-corruption campaign. Many senior officers, even Central Committee cadres, are arrested. This is very serious. I have nothing to fear for corruption accusations. But the atmosphere is very suspicious, investigators are everywhere. They check my records, my bank account. Even my wife's bank account is investigated! She is most upset and the life in my house is tense. My family are unable to understand the difficulty of my work, and are panic and flighty. I can make no mistakes now. We must be very careful in our contacts and I must rely to your professionalism.

This time, please find provided materials defining high-priority commercial targets in USA. As you know, tasking of my organs places emphasis on long-term growth and security of China's economy. Intelligence requirements include agent/cyber penetration of companies with expertise in following fields:

- Defence technology. Avionics. Night vision. Rail gun. UAV. Plasma stealth.
- Nanotechnology. Nano-manipulation and positioning technology. Scanning probe microscope. Nanolithography system.
- Genetics. Genetically modified organisms. Especially rice, wheat. Rice research Institute at Stuttgart, Arkansas, is high priority target.
- Transport. High-speed rail. Hyperloop. Silent propulsion. Space launch systems.
- Artificial intelligence. Machine learning algorithms. Evolutionary computation. Swarm intelligence.

A complete list of target companies is on this drive. All materials I send you are marked JUEMI/TOP SECRET and are most valuable. I choose these materials as ones which will most strengthen your understanding while not pointing to me directly.

Now for your kind suggestions made in your last communication:

1/ There can be NO meeting outside country. It is inconvenient. Travel to another country bring many questions from family and friends and government. I must say also that I will NOT reveal my identity to you. It is not necessary and most threatens my security.

2/ There can be NO electronic communication channels. Computer security here is very weak, very dangerous. Everything I do online, someone can see it. Everything is monitored. Our communications will stay like this, based on courier. Congratulations on excellent work of courier, by the way.

3/ I know you do not really place payment in a foreign bank account, except for accounting purposes. We do same thing. Anyway, I will NOT defect to you, so how would I ever receive the money? It is impossible. I have considered, and suggest you can send diamonds to me. This could be most useful.

Finally, it is most important you understand what are my MOTIVES, and act accordingly. I find my organisation very corrupt and many senior officers are not competent or professional. All the time, significant plans are crushed, great ideas ignored. I am shocked at how poor and bad the work standard is. Only a few officers like me can manage affairs properly, and I require you to help me. Give me successes, and I can strengthen my position and rise to significant leadership position here. You must do this as part of our bargain, my friends. I know you can make strong, professional suggestions.

Next communication will be in eight/8 weeks exactly, according to COWBELL protocol. Please reply to my points, and my thanks and best wishes to you,

Z

///END REPORT

7

Baltimore, Maryland

The drones, twenty-four of them, held steady in a perfect lattice formation. They hovered some five feet from the floor, whining, jittery, each correcting its position with a nervous tip of its rotors. They made Pearl think of dragonflies, or hummingbirds.

As she watched, the drones, without warning, burst into movement. They swung away from their positions in the lattice, arcing and sweeping inward again to form, this time, a long line two abreast. A moment's suspension in the air, and all twenty-four began to move in perfect unison, a ghostly, floating march through space. They moved towards an obstacle, two posts six feet high, the space between them only inches wide. The drone column approached the posts.

They'll not be able to, Pearl thought. The gap is too tight.

As she finished the thought, the first two drones sped up. One drone gave way to the other, and the lead drone, moving at speed now, flipped itself onto the vertical and posted itself elegantly between the two posts. It turned a full somersault before righting and hovering, then moving away at a sedate pace. The second drone followed, slicing through the gap and falling back into formation with its leader, and within half a minute all twenty-four were through and had returned to formation.

Pearl smiled and looked over at Cal, who mouthed, *No hands!* He held out both palms to show they were empty. The drones were stationary now, bobbing in the air, awaiting orders. Cal asked for different formations in three dimensions, the drones deciding for themselves how best to organise, each proceeding to its allotted place with what Pearl saw as intention and certainty. But one, she noticed, had drifted away from the formation and was moving towards the hangar wall. She looked at Cal, and pointed. He held up a *just-wait-a-moment* finger. She watched the solitary drone, alone now in space, pursuing some individual quest while the humming collective waited. The drone was losing height, and came to rest on a low black platform at floor level, just below where Pearl stood. Its rotors ceased turning, and it squatted, still now. On the platform, a red diode had lit, and Pearl realised that the drone had taken itself out of formation to charge its battery. And, she saw, the formation had rearranged itself to take account of the solitary drone's absence.

Cal was smiling. *Still no hands!*

And then the formation began lowering itself to the floor. The drones touched down, and all the rotors stopped, and the hangar fell silent.

"You like?" Cal shouted across to her. "They'll bring you tea. Make you noodles."

He jumped down to the hangar floor and picked one up, strolling over to her, his long-legged gait under the white lab coat. Why did he wear that coat? He reached up, handed the machine to her, smiling. She bent down and took it from him and held it in her hand. It was a beautiful thing, silver, its casing smooth and aerodynamic, its rotors slender and finely machined. It was warm from its flight, and she felt as if she were holding a living thing, as if there could be a heart beating inside. On its underside was a small claw-like apparatus.

"For payload," said Cal. "Could be a sensor. Could be a tool. Could be a weapon."

She raised her eyebrows, nodding.

"Throw it," said Cal.

"What?"

"Just throw it." He curled his wrist back and then released it, as if hurling something away into space.

She leaned out over the railing and threw it upwards, towards the ceiling, ten feet or more. The drone tumbled upward in the air, reached its apex and hung for a fraction of a second. As it began to fall the rotors buzzed into life and the little vessel righted and hovered, turning slowly on its own axis as if looking to orientate itself.

"Watch," said Cal.

The drone darted downward, to where the rest of the swarm sat immobile on the hangar floor. It circled for moment, and then landed at the same place in the formation it had occupied before Cal picked it up.

"We teach them to find their way home," he said.

"Teach?" she said, amused.

"Feels like teaching," he said.

She shook her head.

"No, it doesn't," she said.

"What does it feel like, then? It's more than programing."

She thought for a moment.

"It feels like imbuing them with something."

"With knowledge?"

"No. It'll be more than that."

He laughed.

"When? When will it be?"

She looked at him.

"When I'm done," she said.

He cocked his head to one side.

"And when will that be?"

She shrugged.

"We are all waiting, you know."

She smiled. He shifted his weight, put his hands in his pockets.

"Are you coming on Saturday?"

"Am I invited?" she replied, startled.

"Of course you're invited!"

"Oh. Well, I don't know. My dad..."

"It'll be nice. We're making *baozi*. There'll be people you know."

She looked regretful. "I just..."

"Pearl, you are nineteen. You are a junior." He was speaking gently, but she could tell he was exasperated.

"I know these things, Cal, but it's like..." She couldn't finish the sentence.

"Why's he like this? It's a party. With *baozi*. And physicists. And engineers. Chinese physicists and engineers, mostly. I mean, seriously. It'll be the least sexy thing that ever happened. The threat to your integrity is, like, so small as to be immeasurable in conventional mathematics. There is no scale where it is non-negligible. I mean, like, you'd have to use non-standard analysis."

He held up his forefinger and thumb in a pincer shape, one eye closed, to indicate something infinitesimally small. She laughed.

Cal's English name had been California Cheung, his parents hoping and plotting from their dank Hong Kong apartment that he would make it to sunny Stanford. Instead, here he was at Hopkins, in this tough, eastern town with its raddled streets and harsh winters. And he'd changed his name to Cal. Now he stood, tall, sallow, eyebrows raised, questioning. He was six years older than her, deep into his Ph.D. He was a study buddy, and a shoulder to lean on. He saw her, listened to her. He admired her; they all did, but he actually liked her, too, she felt. Maybe a little more, even. One day.

"Maybe I should invite your mom and dad, too. You could all come."

She put her hands to her cheeks.

"Oh my God, no. Please. That would be embarrassing."

"Why?"

"He'll interrogate everybody. And hand out business cards. And insist on doing the cooking. And it'll just be, like, ugh. And then he'll find someone whose great-grandparents were from the same province as his and he'll start singing songs or something."

"Which province is that, actually?"

"Shanxi. Like, real glamorous."

"Why's it glamorous?"

"Seriously, you are such a Hong Kong child. Everybody knows Shanxi is the total opposite of glamorous."

"Why, what's there?"

"Mountains. Coal. They make this great black vinegar."

Cal made a face of recognition.

"Ah! So that's what you smell of."

She felt a jolt of alarm.

"Wait. What?"

"I'm kidding."

"No, really, my whole house smells of it. It's entirely believable I stink."

Cal folded his arms. He seemed to want to make this a heart-to-heart. She wanted that, and didn't want it at the same time.

"So you won't come because you anticipate that he won't want you to come?"

She found herself folding her arms too, mirroring

him—neurologically interesting, she thought—and leaned against the railing.

"I just want to avoid having to negotiate the issue. It's exhausting."

"Tell me again why he won't let you come and live on campus? In a dorm? Like every college student ever?"

"They want me at home. I told you. And it's cheaper. By far."

"Cheap? *Cheap?* Pearl, you are on full scholarship *and* a corporate sponsorship. Money really should not be an issue here. I mean, seriously."

She shrugged, uncomfortable at where his questioning was going.

"Why do they want you at home? I mean, what purpose do you serve, do you think?"

She wasn't looking at him now, and had started to chew the inside of her cheek.

"I think it's more than serving a purpose. I'm their daughter, their only kid." She could see he was regretting his words.

"I'm sorry, I just meant...what need of theirs are you having to fulfil?"

She sighed. "I don't know, Cal. But he really wants me at home. And so does Mom. They feel like they have to nurture me, nurture this..."

"This thing you have."

"Yes."

"Your talent."

"I guess."

"Your genius."

"Oh, come *on.*"

"And do they? Nurture it?"

"Do you think they don't?"

He sighed now, looked down.

"I think you have a very rare ability, Pearl. *Very* rare.

You see stuff that the rest of us don't see. I'm, like, completely, insanely jealous of your ability. But you have to use it. You have to get out into the world. Get out of the comfort zone, let things happen to you, grow."

"The *comfort zone*? Seriously? Did you just say that?"

"What?"

"You'll have me *thinking outside the box* next."

"You know what I mean."

"No, I don't. You're talking in meaningless metaphors."

He shook his head. "I mean that you will not grow by sitting in your bedroom at home every night. You will grow by hanging with other young, very smart people. By talking to them. By navigating new things and new people and new places."

"Really? Listening to my roomie talk about her... whatever." She realised she had no idea what a roommate might talk about. "And doing my laundry? And going to frat parties? That's better for me? I don't just sit in my bedroom, Cal. I work. I think. It's quiet there. I achieve stuff." She paused for a moment. "And I write code for you," she said.

He frowned. That had hurt, as she knew it would.

"You code for all of us."

"I code, therefore I am," she said.

He was wondering what she meant by that, she could see.

"You got invited to a frat party?" he said.

"Maybe."

"Really?"

"No."

He held out a hand to her. She took it.

"I for one, would like to hang with you more, and not talk about drone swarms," he said.

"I feel like I don't know how to talk about anything but work."

"Which is *why* you should come and live on campus. Interesting things might happen."

"Yeah, right. Like what?"

"Jeez, Pearl. I don't know. Like, making spaghetti and staying up. Like, watching the movies of Zhang Yimou. Going for walks. Sailing on the bay. Roller derby. I don't know."

"What *is* roller derby, actually?"

"Exactly! We'll find out. Adventures in roller derby. Life awaits."

He was looking at her questioningly. He still held her hand.

"Cal, I sort of know what awaits, right? I live at home. I graduate. I go straight to work at Telperion. I do my Ph.D. Maybe then I can explore roller derby with you."

He sighed.

"Roller derby waits for no man," he said. He looked disheartened. He played with her hand. "What about the spaghetti part?"

"I can manage spaghetti. As long as my dad has, like, a month's advance warning."

She walked to her car, the little red Honda—her sanctuary, and the spoils of a fierce campaign of attrition waged against her parents. Her mother had insisted on driving her to campus and picking her up every afternoon all through her freshman year. Pearl had found it humiliating and infuriating, and demanded she be allowed to drive herself. Months of trench warfare followed, the advantage gained only when Pearl had threatened to move out altogether. Her parents had sullenly relented and a nine-year-old Civic with 76,000 miles on the clock appeared in the driveway. Pearl loved the car with a passion that surprised her, and made her wonder what else in life she was missing. What else she might be able to love.

She turned on WTMD, for its pithy indie rock. I-95 was slow, the traffic between Baltimore and Washington torpid in the hot afternoon, the sun blinding. She didn't mind the commute. She sat in the car's air conditioning, letting her mind wander. As she passed the National Security Agency on her left behind its screen of trees, the traffic loosened a little, and she headed for the Beltway.

She parked in the driveway, stepped from the car, and felt the heat wash over her. Her mother was standing at the front door.

"*Ni wan le,*" she said. You're late.

"I went to Cal's lab," she replied in English.

"You should call."

Pearl said nothing, shucked off her shoes, dropped her bag on the kitchen table. The house was cool and dim and smelled of cooking fat. And vinegar. Her mother was fussing at the fridge.

"You should call," she said again.

"I really don't have to call, Mom," Pearl said. "Sometimes…" She left the sentence hanging. Her mother put a glass of iced tea on the table in front of her.

"Why you go to Cal's lab?"

"Just to say hi. But he showed me the new swarm manoeuvre."

"He showed you?"

"Yup."

Her mother looked at her, expectant.

"Yes, it worked," said Pearl.

"So you can tell the company."

"I can tell the company."

"You tell them."

"I will."

"Smart girl."

"My piece of it was pretty small."

"You *tell* them. Your algorithm."

"I will, Mom."

Pearl picked up the iced tea and her bag, and hurried from the kitchen, her mother watching her. She climbed the stairs, her footfalls soft on the carpet, and went to her room. It was dark and cool, and the curtains were drawn. She stripped to her underwear, put on a *Doctor Who* T-shirt and plaid pyjama bottoms, and tied her hair in a ponytail, before settling down cross-legged at her desk. She turned on her laptop, the big one, and cleaned her spectacles as it booted up. She went to her email and tapped compose.

> Dear Dr. Katz,
>
> I just wanted to let you know the new swarm manoeuvre worked out pretty good. I watched it in the lab today with twenty-four nano-quadrotors. (This was the one used my trajectory definition and management algorithm.) The modified Bezier spline curve approach seems like it's a go (you said so!) for feasible trajectory planning, but I still think we got issues with computational efficiency.
>
> So, Telperion's summer internship program not entirely wasted on me!
>
> Yours,
>
> Pearl Tao

She hit send, and toggled over to her music. She filled the room with a wide, cool ambient track, and sat back, biting her nails. She read the email again, realised she sounded young and eager. Too late now, she'd sent it. Then, a reply.

> Dear Pearl,
>
> Way to go! That's great news, and all of us here at Telperion knew you would not be wasting the internship! Remember that we remain very concerned

about minimising execution times, which of course plays into the computational efficiency question. Keep at it, and we'll talk when you come down to see us next month.

We need to talk about your courses this semester. Thinking about the trajectory generation, have you signed up for Differential Geometry? And have you looked at the graduate course for Partial Differential Equations? Hope so. What else?

We also need to get going on your security clearance. I'm asking Carla at Telperion Integrity to contact you about this. She'll walk you through it.

Well done.

John K

PS Miriam tells me your stipend should have been in your account last week, but she hasn't had confirmation from you. Can you get back to her? Tks.

Way to go, Pearl. She brought up her online banking, and there it was. Twenty-seven thousand dollars to see her through the semester, placing her among the wealthiest undergraduates on the Johns Hopkins campus.

What do they think they are buying? she wondered. She could be done with Partial Differential Equations in a week, given the opportunity. But the company made her sit through the course. And as for the algorithm. It was fine as far as it went. It helped to govern the drones' movements, allowed them to decide as a group how they would plot a course based on incoming information from sensors, how they would plan their neat little flip between the posts.

But that was all. It was such a small thing.

There was a tapping at the door, and then her father was peering into the room, wearing his eager expression.

"So it worked?"

She looked straight ahead at her screen.

"Yes, Dad, it worked."

"All waypoints?"

"All waypoints."

He nodded, satisfied.

"You tell Telperion already?"

"Yup."

"What they say? Katz, what did he say?"

"He said, *Way to go, Pearl*."

He grunted and the door closed. Pearl sighed. Perhaps Cal is right, she thought. I could be hanging with my roomie, out of my comfort zone, eating ramen noodles and painting my toenails.

She thought of the smooth, silver drone in her hand, of the difference between the inanimate and the animate, where that line lay.

She went to the window, opened it, and the hot evening air swept in, bringing twists of barbecue smoke, the cicadas an effervescent whine and chirrup in the trees, children's voices from a yard down the street. She stood and listened, trying to envisage other lives, to imagine a life different to her own.

And then her mother was calling her to come and eat.

Her father was already at the table, snuffling and slurping his way through a bowl of noodles fried with mushrooms and snow peas. Some chopped soy chicken and a plate of cabbage sat in the middle of the table. Her mother was folding a dish towel.

"*Chi ba*," she said. Eat.

Her father was giving a terse description of his work day. Problems with the servers, the cooling mechanisms running amok. He'd stepped in and saved the day from the idiots who didn't know what they were doing.

"What are you doing tonight?" he asked her in Mandarin.

She shrugged. "Some problem sets. Integrals. Basic stuff."

"They're not challenging you."

"I can challenge myself."

"Why do they go so slowly?"

"Telperion wants me to do it this way, so I do it, right?"

"Why, though?"

Her mother was watching the two of them, listening.

"We have been over this a thousand times, Dad."

"You did integrals when you were thirteen."

She spooned some noodles into her bowl, some cabbage.

"Okay, so why don't I just go do my Ph.D.? Right? Right now," she said. "Why not? I could. You want a prodigy, I can do that."

"No, no, no." Her father was pointing his chopsticks at her. "You stay with Telperion. Much better that way. The money's good, and it's one of the best tech companies out there." He swallowed. "Defence technology never goes out of fashion."

She shrugged. Her father brooded. She knew what was coming. He just couldn't restrain himself.

"But back in China," her father said, "they would make you go much faster. Qinghua University. Or Jiaotong. They'd make you work."

"Back in China, back in China," she parroted.

"Mitchell," said her mother, "stop it."

"They would challenge you."

"I'm American, Dad."

And as she said it, her father laid his hands on the table, and Pearl caught his glance across at her mother, their eyes meeting for a second.

"Yes," he said, "you are American."

And Pearl, for the thousandth time, sensed an

understanding between her mother and her father that she was not privy to.

Mangan stood in the bathroom, heaving, spattering the sink with blood. He felt his nose, probing the bridge carefully. It was swelling, and a deep stain was spreading beneath his eyes. The pain was lessening a little. He washed his face, went back into the bedroom and sat on the edge of the bed, his head in his hands.

What the hell *was* that?

That, he supposed, was a cease and desist letter from Chinese intelligence. A polite one.

He reached for a cigarette, lit it, his hands shaking.

Since Mangan had begun leading his hidden life, two years earlier, in a cool Beijing autumn, he had come to understand the role of fear in it. Fear seemed to be both the natural condition of the trade and a tool used in advancing its purposes. Fear of discovery, fear of failure, fear of intimacy, fear of betrayal, fear of the future. To cope, he understood his life in espionage as having opened a fissure in him, and it was into that fissure that he crammed his fear, and all the things that had happened. That was where the hidden life was, in the fissure. He sat there and took the memory of the man by the mosquito net, and the pain, and thrust it deep into the fissure, tamped it down.

Mangan looked at his duffel bag, leaned towards it, then stopped himself. He stood and went to the door, pressed his ear against it and listened, before walking slowly round the room, running his hands over the surfaces, under tables, atop the wardrobe. Had they left anything? A camera? Anything? He turned the light off and went to the window, pulled the blind back and looked out to a weed-strewn courtyard, some roofs, a garage, and the first signs of dawn. He took his phone, popped the back off and took out the battery, put the disassembled pieces under the pillow, and sat again, shaky, nauseated.

Now, the duffel bag.

In an inside pocket was a red, plastic ballpoint pen. He unscrewed the barrel, and extracted a tiny coil of paper. On it in minute letters, an address:

Suriname. Paramaribo. 76 Prins Hendrickstraat.
Teng. Lawyer.

What was said.

He took the scrap of paper and put it in his mouth, chewed it and went back to the bathroom and spat the pasty remains into the toilet.

He lay on the bed, touched his face, his nose, trying to ride the pain.

A name, an address, coordinates in space and time. Given to him by a renegade colonel in Chinese military intelligence, some months earlier, by a river in Thailand, moments before officers of China's Ministry of State Security descended. The colonel passed the words to Mangan in the manner of one man handing another a weapon.

Use it, the colonel had said.

Part of Mangan wanted to stop, to walk away. For two years and two operations he had been contracted to British intelligence, probing the China target, acting as handler, courier and cutout, and discovering facets of himself he had never known—some he'd never wanted to. A natural, Hopko had called him, for his powers of observation, his clarity of mind, and his uncertain, cockeyed bravery. *Man's a bloody natural.* The words had sustained him even as the fear curdled inside him, and the fissure grew deeper.

But Mangan, to his own discomfort and surprise,

knew that another part of his divided, doubting nature needed to keep marching. Just over the next hilltop. To face whatever's there. In the knowledge that he held a weapon, and if he used it well he would eviscerate a network of Chinese intelligence. And he would demonstrate his own worth, the value of the path he had taken. And he would matter to those who mattered to him.

Now, as he lay there in the stifling heat and the rustling of night insects, he sensed in himself, beneath the fear and the pain, a quickening of thought and intention. He thought of the angel-faced man, the hard man in the T-shirt, their controlled violence, the system that bred them, lent them agency and licence. He thought of everything that had been taken from him. He felt the hatching of a choice.

I am not finished yet.

Patterson spent the weekend wandering Washington, looking at the monuments in the sodden, buggy heat. And buying rugs. On the Saturday, she ate at a little barbecue place in Shaw where every single person was black, a new experience for her. She sat at the bar and ate ribs in a hot, smoky sauce with a crisp, cold slaw, her fingers sticky and her throat burning. TVs on the walls were showing some baseball game that everyone was riveted to, Nats and Cardinals, and when it ended some young guys, lawyers, chatted her up and tried to place her, her accent, laughing uproariously. *Where the frik is Notting-ham?* One of them was a veteran and they silently acknowledged each other. He bought her a beer and, when she left, saw her decorously to a taxi.

But on the Monday, when she presented herself at the Embassy on Mass. Ave., she was suddenly back in England, in its taut, murmuring contradictions, and she felt the weekend's momentary sense of liberation fall away. She spent an hour and a half getting through a silent admin office and picking up her badge, and then reported to Station—a series of open-plan rooms, their windows tinted, behind secure doors at the back of the building. The Deputy Chief of Station, Tipton, regarded her across a blond-wood table as she sat ramrod straight in her chair.

"The work of Liaison with our American counterparts is among the most important work the Service does," he said. "It is work of great delicacy."

She nodded. He looked at her.

"It is its own kind of diplomacy."

"Yes, sir," she said.

"Call me Anthony, please."

She nodded again.

"You'll need to be across all, and I mean all, the traffic with London. You'll attend Five Eyes briefings at State and CIA. You'll relay requests and questions from London. Considering your background, I'm going to put you into the Counter-Terror Liaison Group as well, so there'll be some work with the FBI."

She nodded. He cocked his head.

"Now I appreciate that this is not an operational assignment, and you may find the change of pace difficult to accept."

"No, I—"

"I do want you to understand that many in our Service would regard this assignment as a most enviable situation."

"I do understand."

"Val Hopko tells me you are an able officer in need of some time to *grow,* was the way she put it, I believe. Though I must say I'm not entirely cognisant of her meaning."

He paused, as if waiting for her to respond. Which she didn't.

"Can you tell me why you need to *grow*?"

She licked her lips.

"I had a very difficult couple of years, operationally. I was engaged in operations that were successful, very successful. But…difficult. So it was agreed I would take some time away from the Far East Controllerate and… broaden my horizons."

Broaden my horizons? Christ. What am I, fifteen?

The Deputy Chief of Station allowed a flicker of bemusement to cross his face. Very deliberate, she thought. A micro-expression, to intimidate.

"Well, I'm very relieved to hear your posting here was *agreed*. And I do hope our horizons are sufficiently wide to facilitate your *growth*."

He was looking right at her now, and she forced herself to meet his eye.

"I'm sure they will be, sir. Anthony."

"Lord, now you've knighted me." He was standing, signalling the meeting was over. She felt a flush of embarrassment, gave him a tight smile and left the room.

They gave her a desk near the heavy steel doors. She had two screens and a monstrous daily load of reading, cross-referencing and annotating. The time difference with London meant that VX was always ahead of her, a pent-up wave of requests crashing onto her desk each morning, many of which she barely understood. Clarification on Ukraine assessments, please, with reference to deployment of Russian surface-to-air missiles. Implications of Kyrgyzstan elections, CIA assessments of, please. FISINT collection, China, overview and implications for customers, please. Patterson had to remind herself what FISINT was. Foreign Instrumentation Signals Intelligence. Stealing the signals from the cockpits of Chinese fighter aircraft, the pilot's helmet display, his computer keystrokes, the sound of his breathing. Why on earth was she dealing with *this*? Surely someone else dealt with fucking FISINT?

There was a café in the Embassy foyer, where she would go and order coffee and sit with her head in her hands. She'd leave the Station by eight or nine at night, jogging down Mass. Ave. in the darkness, stopping to pick up a burrito or some pizza.

Her first Five Eyes briefing was terrifying. She drove out to Langley and sat across a table from a whey-faced CIA analyst who walked her through the agency's assessments of radical Islamist networks in Lebanon and Jordan. The Australians and Canadians present asked knowledgeable questions. She took frantic notes, but understood little, Arab names and aliases and backstories flying past her. She expended blood writing it up, and submitted it. Anthony fired it back at her spattered with red ink.

In the middle of her second week, Markham, who did counter-terror, took her over to the FBI in its brutalist fortress on Pennsylvania Ave. Not a briefing, mercifully, just introductions. They ate sandwiches with three FBI special agents—quiet, burly men in loose-fitting suits—and when Markham mentioned her army background they looked at her and nodded approvingly, as if she had instantly shot up in their estimation. Afterwards, inexplicably, they went to an auditorium and sat in the third row. There was no one else there, just them. Instead of a stage, they faced a huge wall of bulletproof glass. On the other side of the glass, a firing range. For twenty minutes, she and Markham sat and watched the three agents blatting away with their Glocks, their rapid draws from inside their boxy grey jackets, their fires from standing and kneeling positions, popping out from behind cover, all sorts. Patterson found it odd but said nothing. Markham fiddled with his phone.

When it was over, one of the agents, perspiring, gave her a card. Polk, his name. Franklin Polk. Not counter-terror at all, but counter-intelligence. A jowly white guy with the build of a football player, mousy hair and creases around cobalt-blue eyes, one of those big men who'd surprise you with their quickness.

"Anything you need," he said. Patterson wondered if he meant it.

Polk gestured to the range.

"Oh, and how'd I do?"

"Not bad," said Patterson.

"You gonna give me pointers now?"

She smiled.

"Wouldn't want to tax you," she said.

He raised his eyebrows.

"I find it all taxing, all of it. The guns. The spies. This fuckin' place. How long have you been in this game, anyway? Whatever game it is you're in."

"Not long. Few years. I'm a newbie." She glanced at Markham. He was talking to one of the other agents.

Polk shrugged. "Well, like I say. Washington's a bitch. Every fucker thinks he's James Jesus Angleton. So if you need any help finding your way around…"

She leaned in to him a little.

"Careful. I might hold you to that."

"Hold me," he said. "Any time."

In the taxi back to the Embassy, Markham spoke, used a desultory tone.

"So. How did you find them?"

"Interesting. Clever. Street clever."

Markham was looking out of the cab's window.

"Watch yourself around Polk."

"Why?"

"He *is* clever." He paused. "Very, very clever."

"How so?"

Markham shifted in his seat, turned to face her.

"Do you remember the PRIMROSE case? That was Polk."

Patterson didn't know.

"It was a while ago. He was in California then. They had him on counter-intelligence in the LA field office, working the China target. There was an asset, a woman. Chinese immigrant, still very well-connected in Beijing. She worked in venture capital, used to go back and forth a lot. The FBI had her reporting on people, comings and goings. She helped winkle out Chinese front companies, penetrations of the tech sector, that sort of thing. Anyway. Turns out she was a double, working for MSS all along, reporting on the workings of the FBI's LA field office, and feeding the FBI all sorts of garbage. Very neat. Polk finally figured it out. Didn't help that two of PRIMROSE's FBI handlers had affairs with her. Can you believe it? The office was a smoking ruin by the time Polk finished. He put a couple of people behind bars. Destroyed the careers of a whole lot more. Not the FBI's finest moment."

"That's extraordinary."

"You can ask him. He'll tell you all about it. Quite the raconteur, is Polk."

"What happened to the asset? The woman?"

"PRIMROSE? She copped a plea and disappeared. Probably back in Beijing now. Polk was incandescent, still is. He said he was close to unravelling all the support networks and funding and everything else, but it got away from him. Said it was like finding a leech on you, sucking away at a vein, and you rip it off but leave the head buried in your flesh."

8

It was Dubai. Hopko had her arriving late afternoon, and a Service car met her at the airport. Two men in polo shirts and sunglasses gently took her luggage and sat her in the back.

Eileen didn't like it.

"Why, Val?" she said, as they sat by the pool at a safe house in Jumeirah, a villa with high walls, broken glass atop them, overhung with palms. A bottle of Meursault sat on the table, chilling. Hopko wore a beige suit, a necklace of pink coral, and her most indulgent, gratified expression. It was dark, and hot. Eileen couldn't tell how many people were in the compound.

"Oh, Eileen, you deserve a little coddling." Hopko grinned.

"Not necessary."

"Of course it is."

What is this? thought Eileen.

"I make my own way. We agreed. Just us."

Hopko said nothing, leaned forward, poured the wine, green-gold in the glass.

"Something change, Val?"

Hopko picked up her glass, regarded her.

"Do you think you saw him?" she said.

"I don't know."

"But the man on the bench, the smooth-cheeked man. Tell me."

"He's just one man on a bench."

"But you saw something. Something in him."

Eileen was rummaging in her purse, buying time. She pulled out a packet of beedi, wrapped in paper and tied with string. She took one deliberately, lit it from a hotel matchbook, exhaled, and watched the smoke rise in the darkness.

"Fewer people, better," she said. Hopko tilted her head to one side. A younger man was approaching the table. He carried a laptop. Hopko motioned for him to sit.

"This is Brendan," said Hopko. "He's going to be helping us."

The young man held out a slender hand. He was cool to the touch, with dark, wavy hair and a small, pale face—a clever face. A face, Eileen thought, to charm you and judge you at once.

"It's a great pleasure to meet you," said Brendan. "And an honour." Eileen heard Northern Irish in his voice. She turned to Hopko, gave her a questioning look.

"Eileen, listen," said Hopko, "we know roughly where he is, we think."

She said nothing, just listened.

"On the drive you brought out, there's a new letter. No name attached, of course. In it, he toys with us a little. *You don't know who I am, but all China trembles before me* sort of thing. He tells us he's sick to death of the numbskulls he works with, his feeble-minded family, you know the type."

Eileen did. She had watched them, followed them, cleared their dead drops, handled their cash, cleared up their messes, and marvelled at their arrogance, narcissism and neuroses for forty years.

"But he's given us enough to place him. Brendan here

puts him at or around deputy director level, most likely in the front office of Ministry of State Security, don't you, Brendan?" Hopko turned to the pale boy, who spoke softly to Eileen.

"I do, yes. Though which bureau within the MSS is harder to pinpoint. He has—appears to have—access to a variety of operational detail that would place him at senior level, but not too senior, if you take my meaning. He can see across different operational channels, but from a height that is not too elevated. He can see into foreign operations, particularly North American operations. He's definitely close to the Americas desk, may even be in charge of it. So the *detail* is there, but also the breadth of vision." He looked enquiringly at her.

Patronising little prick, thought Eileen. She nodded, drew on her beedi.

A pause. Hopko was watching her, then spoke.

"He offers us his access in return for money and muscle. We beef him up, he vanquishes his rivals."

"Two-way street," said Eileen.

"Two-way street," Hopko repeated.

Eileen pointed at her with her beedi.

"Do it electronic. Go darknet. Safest way."

"He says he won't."

"Why?"

"Why?" said Hopko. "Too hard. Too big a signature. Too many traces. Digital fingerprints everywhere. Evidence. What's he going to do? Lock himself in a bathroom with an encrypted laptop? The answer's no."

Eileen Poon exhaled, shook her head. She thought of the hotel, its murmurings and scufflings, the long, long night. She remembered thinking it might have been the last time. She felt tired, suddenly.

"You want us to courier."

"Are you playing hard to get, Eileen?" said Hopko.

Brendan smiled. Eileen noticed that smile, and stored it away for a moment when she could ponder how to grind it off his face when he was least expecting it. She turned to Hopko.

"I can't do it alone. I need the boys, everyone." She thought of them, Peter and Frederick Poon, their cousin Winston—tough, loving boys—and felt a flush of strength.

"You'll have everything you need," said Hopko.

"This is asking a lot," said Eileen. "Once, twice, even three times, fine. I can clear a drop, scoot in, scoot out. But to make us the primary communication channel? For what, years, maybe? And you want us to find him? Identify him?"

"I didn't say I want you to identify him," said Hopko quickly.

"That's what I hear," said Eileen.

"I think we need to focus on the modalities of the operation for now," said Brendan. Eileen shot him a look that said, *Shut it, sonny.*

Hopko spoke very deliberately. "You are the only person I can rely on in this," she said. "You know that is true."

It was true, of course. Eileen looked at her, this fifty-something woman, her squat, strong frame, her blunt hands, her dark hair and tawny skin—a legacy of her Lebanese mother—the eyes that read you, that shimmered with humour and unspoken understandings. Valentina Hopko, now Controller, Far East and Western Hemisphere. The Poon family's protector, mentor, patron and friend for many, many years. *You're my antennae, Eileen, you and the boys.*

But as Eileen rose to go, the wine undrunk, the Gulf night scorched and dry, aglow from the light of the city beyond the safe-house walls, she sensed that her relationship with Hopko had been overtaken. Some powerful imperative was at work that overrode Hopko's friendship, her loyalty.

So Eileen Poon would be going back to Beijing.

Dry as a bone.

9

They know I am here, thought Mangan. So, move. Keep moving.

In the half-light, duffel bag on his shoulder, he made for the docks at a half run, his flip-flops *thwap-thwapping* on the concrete. He had wrapped a red checkered scarf around his face, put on his shades and a blue sun hat with a brim. The burner he'd left in the room. The streets were quiet but for an early, solitary pedlar of *soto ayam*. Mangan smelled the turmeric broth and chicken as he lumbered past, and his mouth watered. The air was already hot and close, flecked with the whoops and cackles of dawn birdsong.

Twice he doubled back, but there was no one.

At the edge of the port, the wharves and cranes and freighters gave way to a jumble of trash-strewn wooden jetties. Mangan stopped, put the duffel bag down, breathing heavily, sweat stinging his eyes, the bridge of his nose throbbing with pain. The sun was almost up. He looked out across the water, to where the *pinisi* boats rocked at anchor.

Three men squatted on the jetty, smoking. He walked

towards them, and they turned, regarded him, frowning. One, an older man in faded shorts and vest, a face scoured by the sea, pointed at Mangan with his chin, a *what do you want* gesture. Mangan pulled the scarf down and licked his lips, forcing himself into his rudimentary Indonesian.

"*Selamat pagi, pak. Apakah bapak kapten kapal?*" Good morning. Are you a boat captain?

The man looked at him, dragged on his cigarette, nodding stiffly. The other two watched.

"*Bapak ke mana?*" Where are you headed?

The man considered for a moment.

"*Wahai.*"

Mangan had no idea where that was.

"*Pak mengambil ... penumpang?*" Will you take a passenger?

The men laughed, all three of them. The *kapten* broke into English.

"Very 'spensive."

Mangan forced a smile.

"I can pay."

"Why you go Wahai?"

"I'm just a tourist."

The man pointed to his own face, around the eyes.

"Touris have big fight." He made a hitting gesture with his fist. "*Tshaaa!* Big fight." The other two cracked up.

Mangan smiled again, nodded.

"Accident," he said. "When do you leave? *Pak kapan pergi?*"

A car was moving slowly along the road behind the wharves.

"Maybe today."

"How much?"

The *kapten* shrugged. "Two hundred dollar."

"Okay," Mangan said. He took a wad of bills from his pocket, counted them out quickly. "Two hundred."

The *kapten* chortled and glanced at his friends and quickly reached out and took the money.

The car had several people in it. It was black and clean.

"I want to go to the boat now."

"Go boat now?"

"Now. *Sekarang*. Please."

The *kapten* frowned.

"Boat is not…not touris. Not *kemewahan*." He shook his head. "Later."

"Now. Another fifty dollars." Mangan held out the bills.

The *kapten* looked bemused, turned to his friends, who chided him, telling him to take it.

The car was coming towards them.

The *kapten* flicked his cigarette end into the filthy water. He stood and beckoned to Mangan. They picked their way along the jetty. A fibreglass dinghy was tied up, bobbing among the flotsam. The *kapten* lowered himself off the jetty, the muscles in his arms standing out, his skin the colour of teak. Mangan followed, his duffel bag slipping off his shoulder, unbalancing him and almost taking him down into the water. The *kapten* grabbed his arm, steadied him and gave him a look. *Are you sure about this?* Mangan nodded at him, indicating that they should move.

The *kapten* took the oars and pulled away from the jetty. Mangan sat in the bow of the boat, hunched over, putting the *kapten* between himself and the line of sight from the jetty. The car was crawling closer. Mangan sat still, listened to the lap of the water, the *thunk thunk* of the oars.

The boat was anchored close in, stolid and silent on the water. She was about eighty feet, the bow long and flared and standing high in the water, two masts, the superstructure ramshackle and painted an anaemic green.

Mangan thought the car had stopped by the jetty. The sunlight on the water was dazzling, making it difficult to see. The *kapten* rowed to the stern of the boat, putting them out of sight. He tied up the dinghy and pointed to a rusting ladder. Mangan climbed aboard, and the *kapten* followed. Mangan dropped his kitbag and squatted by the rail, squinting back at the jetty. The black car had stopped and a man had got out, and he was standing with his hands on his hips, looking around. Someone in the car seemed to be saying something, because he turned around and spoke back to them, sharply. Mangan could not tell what language they were speaking. The man looked from side to side, scanning the water. Mangan, on hands and knees, withdrew from the rail. The *kapten* was watching him.

"*Ada problem?*" he said.

"*Tidak ada,*" said Mangan. No.

The *kapten* opened a hatch that led into what must have been the crew quarters, and gestured at Mangan to take his flip-flops off. Mangan ducked inside. The cabin had a wooden deck and windows to the sea. It smelled of cigarette smoke and peanut oil and fried fish. A wooden crate held an ashtray and a deck of cards. The *kapten* took Mangan's duffel bag and threw it on a metal-framed bunk.

"See?" he said. "No touris."

"It's fine," said Mangan. "Really."

The *kapten* nodded, then pulled a packet of cigarettes from his shorts, offered one to Mangan, lit it for him. The *kapten* looked at the bruises spreading under Mangan's eyes, gestured to them again, but this time in concern. Mangan gave a shrug. And as the dark, clove-infused smoke curled upwards between the two of them and as they regarded each other, Mangan felt relieved, untethered, the fear in his belly momentarily diffusing.

They got underway at noon, the engine causing the warm deck to pop and vibrate beneath Mangan's bare feet, the boat turning into the wind under a ferocious sun. They had taken on sacks of nutmeg and a little lumber. Mangan watched the *kapten* in the wheelhouse. He seemed to make no use of radio or depth finder or even a chart, just pushed the *pinisi* boat away from the jetties, out into the chop heading west. A Javanese first mate in a bandana named Widodo stood at the bow with binoculars. The rest of the crew, six or seven of them, Mangan thought, hovered around the galley waiting for food.

When it came, he accepted the meal gratefully, the cook's boy grinning at him, gaping at the bruising, and chiding him in some unknown language. A mound of white rice, a tiny dry chicken leg, a few greens and a blistering *sambal*. Mangan ate all of it, but when the boat turned south and started to roll he threw the lot up, hanging over the side. Widodo dug out an ancient pack of meclizine tabs. He took one, lay on the bunk, slept and felt better.

That evening, he sat at the bow, his skin prickling in the spray and the wind, and drank a warm Anker beer and watched the sun set. He had had no contact with Vauxhall Cross in over two weeks, hadn't reported the trouble with the woman in the phone shop, or the visitation in the hotel room. He felt free, unbound. The boat pitched and creaked and the horizon disappeared in a cerulean dusk, and he watched the stars begin to show. And for a moment, once again, he contemplated letting it all go, telling London it was over, telling Hopko to fuck off. He had a little money—enough for a room somewhere, for a while, somewhere he wasn't known. He could teach, maybe write. Maybe even report again, rebuild his reputation.

But there was that hard little bead of possibility, still, present, drawing him back. The boat ploughed on, into the night.

10

Silver Spring, Maryland

Pearl worked at everything, but hardest at sleeping. She would wear an eyeshade, bed socks, clutch a hot-water bottle, drink a vile tea of artemisia and liquorice that her mother ordered from Taiyuan. None of it made any difference. The hours after midnight became hours of pacing and roaming the house, of the silvered glow of the screen. Sometimes she simply lay in the darkness and let the equations unspool in her mind, imagined the physics of the swarm, the tiny silver beings swooping and glinting in sunlight. Sometimes she reread the books of her childhood: *Harry Potter*, *The Hobbit*, *Wimpy Kid*.

And sometimes she would sit on the stairs and listen to her parents, their cryptic late-night whispers—her mother's submissive, her father's urgent and domineering—the soft rasp of the Mandarin. She'd catch some of it, talk of people she didn't know, what seemed to be arrangements, dates, times. Money? Sometimes they'd be tapping away at a laptop, the computer her father kept in his office, in a drawer, the one she never saw him use—only heard him, late at night. Once, years before, her mother had emerged from the living room and caught her there on the stairs, and had hissed at her, furious, to go to bed. But her father was there, too, and held her by the arm, too tight. And he had hit her, wordlessly, a stinging slap to the side of her head. She had been too stunned to cry.

The hours beyond midnight were a place full of betrayal.

Morning would drag her from whatever depth she had sunk to, her mother pulling back the curtains, sitting her up, bringing her warm soy milk in a mug with a lid, brushing her hair. She'd sit on the bed, thick with exhaustion, try to remember what the day was supposed to hold.

And today it was a trip with Dad, who had insisted on taking her, refusing point blank to let her drive herself.

Pearl loathed her father's driving. They were on the Beltway in his Camry, slaloming between lanes at seventy without signalling. He didn't believe in it. He said that if you signalled before changing lanes it was more dangerous because the other cars would just close up to prevent you cutting in. The traffic was heavy and bad-tempered and the sun was blisteringly hot. But he didn't believe in using air conditioning in the car because it wasted gas. So she sat and jammed her feet against the floor, clutching the side of her seat as the car careened along, her father with one hand on the wheel, blathering on about the importance of what was about to happen, how she mustn't mess it up, how she was a good, intelligent girl but she had no experience and no common sense and it was lucky he was there to help her.

"I'm not a girl, Dad."

"When you go in, don't be arrogant. Only speak when they ask a question."

"That's really not the way it works."

"You always ask questions."

"Yes, I do. They want us to ask questions."

"Listen first. Maybe I should come in with you."

"No! God, Dad."

He looked exasperated, pointed at her with his free hand.

"You are not so independent yet. You think you are, but you are too young." He held his hand palm out, moved it side to side, the Chinese gesture for negation, dismissal. She looked at his hands, the bitten nails, and at the perspiration on his forehead, the cheap, ill-fitting shirt darkened by sweat. He was still talking.

"You must listen to us, because you never face any challenge. You are a weak girl."

"I can do this. You don't have to—"

"You can't do anything! You can't even manage live like an adult. Your mother still wash all your clothes, clean your room. Your parents do everything! Everything! Without us you have no chance."

It was the bluntness of his speech that always took her aback. If he said it in his native Mandarin, might it be gentler? More nuanced? She hated this immigrant speak that battered her with its blunt truths.

Probably not, she thought. And she hated herself for hating the way he spoke.

They had turned off the Beltway into northern Virginia, passed the huge intelligence centre at Liberty Crossing, and now moved through a silent, motionless landscape of office parks. No, "campuses," they were called, to suggest academe and rigor and cutting-edge research. Tech was here in force, and the big weapons corporations and telcoms providers in sparkling asymmetric boxes of glass and concrete and steel, corporate logos pinned to them like jewels. The campuses were landscaped with azalea bushes and grass verges. They had vast car parks. Pearl saw no movement, not a living soul.

As they approached the Telperion campus, her father

was muttering to himself in Chinese, something about parking and expense. They stopped at a security gate where a uniformed guard in shades checked their IDs and the car's plates against a list, before waving them through. Mitchell parked, and Pearl got out. She crossed the warm tarmac towards the building, her father watching her from the car.

Carla from Telperion Integrity was waiting in the lobby for her. Carla was tall and auburn and wore a beautifully cut suit in a tan cotton that seemed to allude to travel and adventure, the skirt above the knee and slender. Her nails were carefully manicured, painted in salmon pink. Pearl, short and rumpled in a faded blue Hopkins T-shirt and jeans, thought of her own poor, pale complexion, her crappy glasses, stringy hair.

"Pearl! Welcome. So great to see you. Come right this way," said Carla, handing her a badge on a lanyard.

Pearl followed, through the security gates into an atrium that extended all the way to the roof and skylights. Telperion employees in their lanyards sat at wrought-iron tables among pot plants. They drank coffee, leaned into laptops.

"And Pearl, phone in here, please," Carla held open the door to the strong room. She put her phone in a locker that doubled as a Faraday cage, and Carla closed the door behind them.

They sat in a windowless conference room and Carla pushed piles of paperwork at her.

"And this," she said, "is the big one." The form was labelled "SF86." It had a hundred and twenty-one pages.

"This is the one," said Carla, "where they ask for all, and they mean *all* relatives, living or dead." She paused, waited for Pearl to react, but Pearl said nothing. "So you'll have to check with your folks, okay, Pearl? We need all names, addresses, everything, of everyone in China. Aunts, uncles, cousins, siblings, you name it. The lot. All of them, okay?"

"Okay," she said. She flicked through the pages. Education, employment, citizenship, convictions, every address for the last ten years. *Have you engaged in acts of terrorism? Were you contacted by, or in contact with, foreign intelligence organisations? Counter-intelligence? Persons interested in you or your job? Coerced? Alcohol, cocaine, rock, freebase, weed, ketamine, PCP, mushrooms, juice, the clear, toluene? Mental competence?*

"And because we're looking at a Top Secret clearance, there'll be an interview," said Carla. "We'll help you prepare, of course."

"But if I have all these relatives in China, won't that make them ... well, won't that make it harder?"

"It won't make it easier, but as long as you are completely open and give them everything they ask for, it should be okay. Telperion's on your side, and we know how to do this, trust me." She smiled, and Pearl relaxed a little.

Dr. Katz came by and they went over her coursework and plans for the year. He was tall and jovial, in tan pants and a baggy denim shirt, and he listened to her, took her seriously. He showed her some work he'd been doing on advanced collision avoidance algorithms, and she bent over it and ran a finger down the screen and found workarounds for computational expense right there, pointing them out to him, and he couldn't help but smile.

"So, Pearl, just fill out the form," he said, "and make sure you get everything on there, okay? Let's get that clearance and then we can start inducting you into some of the more, um, let's say, *interesting* work we do here at

Telperion." He was grinning broadly at her, and so was Carla.

"Sure," she said.

Back at the car, her father was waiting.

"What did they say? You apply for the clearance?"

"I have to fill out this form. And it's, like, huge."

"No problem. I'll help you."

"We have to enter the whole family on it. Everyone, all the relatives." She thought of her grandmother and aunt in the concrete apartment in Taiyuan with its filthy windows, running water down to two hours a day, the mealy rice, plates of sodden *baicai* and fatty pork smothered in pickled bean curd.

"Yes, yes. We can do it." He was pulling out of the car park, passing the security gate. "What level of clearance they want for you?"

"Top Secret/SCI."

"Good."

Pearl looked at him, and it occurred to her that he had already considered all these eventualities.

When they got home, her mother was standing in the kitchen holding a plate of *baozi,* the pork mince and chives still warm inside the bread. Pearl took one and wolfed it, noticed the interrogatory look her mother gave her father, who replied with a nod, and went to his office in the basement.

Why all this? Is so much really at stake for them? But then, she thought, I am their only daughter.

The thought burdened her as she lay awake long past midnight, deep in the treacherous hours. *What are my obligations? What are my duties? To them? To me?*

Her parents were still up. She could hear them moving around downstairs. She got out of bed, patted the night table for her glasses, and walked down the stairs barefoot, listening. They were arguing in stressed whispers. Her mother said something she didn't catch, then her father.

"No."

"We should. They said *all* the relatives."

"No. We can't."

"But if they find out, then she won't get the clearance." A pause.

"How will they find out? They can't. Even we really don't know him any more."

"We need to ask."

"They'll say no."

Her mother was silent for a moment.

"This is a mistake."

"Stop being a stupid bitch. We don't put Jiachong on the form. She doesn't even know him. So she wouldn't put him down. So we don't."

Jiachong? Who is Jiachong?

She turned and crept back up the stairs. She reached the landing, heard the living-room door open, a footfall in the hallway, then stillness, as if someone had stopped to listen. She froze.

"Pearl?" It was her father, his voice subdued, quiet.

She didn't answer, just stood, her fists at her mouth.

"Pearl?"

She did not breathe.

Her father murmured something. The door closed. She moved very slowly along the landing into her room, slid silently into her bed and lay in the darkness, wondering at her own fear, then reining it in and forcing herself to think.

Jiachong means "beetle," she thought. A nickname, then. Who is Beetle?

Why will we not enter Beetle's name on the form that demands that all relatives, and I mean *all*, must be entered?

And why are they *so* invested in this?

11

In Wahai, Mangan slipped ashore at dusk. The crew waved him off, the galley boy taking his hand and shaking it solemnly. Widodo, the mate, pressed the remaining seasickness tablets on him and everyone laughed. Mangan felt hollow, regretful. The days on the boat had healed his face and cleared his head and he'd come to look forward to the evenings sitting alone at the bow, and to the raucous card games and lousy food and beer and *kretek*, the incomprehensible banter in multiple languages. He climbed over the stern into the dinghy. The evening was quiet, just the lap of the water and the *thunk* of the oars as the *kapten* pulled. He looked across the water to the lights of the town, wondering what awaited him.

The *kapten* brought the dinghy alongside a slime-covered concrete jetty, rusted metal spokes protruding from it. Mangan stood and threw his duffel bag up, the dinghy wobbling on the water, and the *kapten* held his hand out for Mangan to shake.

"*Beruntung*, Pilip," said the *kapten*. "Luck to you. You need, I think."

Mangan nodded, acknowledged him, then clambered up the concrete, and stood there and watched the *kapten* pull the dinghy away. Then he turned and walked into town.

The night was warm, the town quiet but for the whine of a motorcycle, the barking of a dog. He found a *warung* where a woman was grilling fish over glowing coconut coals. He sat, and she gave him a bowl of rice with three long, slender, white-fleshed fish, all charred and soused in lime juice, covered in scallions, chillies and tomatoes. The woman was young and wore a halter top and jeans, her hair up. He asked for a beer and she wandered off lazily down the street and came back with two tins of Anker. He asked her if there was a *losmen*, a guesthouse, and she gestured vaguely to the west of town.

"Many visitors? Here in Wahai?" he asked her, fumbling in Indonesian. "*Touris?*"

She waggled her hand in the air. *Not so many.*

"Many Chinese coming?" he said.

She shrugged. "Sometimes they come. Groups. But they don't stay."

"Have you seen any Chinese people the last few days? Men? Maybe in big cars?"

She looked amused, made a driving gesture, her hands on an imaginary wheel. Mangan smiled. "Have you seen any?"

She laughed and shook her head.

"*Tidak.* If I see them, Chinese men in a big car, I tell them you are here."

Oh, for Christ's sake.

"No. No, don't do that." He was peeling rupiah notes off a wad, handing them to her. She was startled. "You tell *me* if you see them, okay? Can you do that?"

She shrugged, unsure. He picked up his duffel bag, smiled to reassure her, and left, walking west in the direction of the guesthouse, feeling her eyes on his back.

Philip Mangan, secret agent, attempts to recruit watcher on spur of moment, practises laughable tradecraft.

The Losmen Maluku lay behind a spiked steel gate. Mangan rapped, and a sleepy-eyed boy in a vest let him in. The guesthouse was a squat concrete block painted a horrible bright green, the rooms opening directly onto a courtyard. Mangan paid for three nights, asked if there were other, more private rooms. The boy shrugged and showed him to a smaller room, one of three at the back of the building, the windows looking straight at the rear wall and a rear gate, Mangan noticed. He dropped his duffel bag on the bed, went to the bathroom, stripped and stood under cold water from the plastic shower head, tasting the sea salt as it washed off his skin.

He had, he thought, a couple of days. They'd know, soon. Widodo or the galley boy or the *kapten* or one of his mates would talk about the tall Inggris with the red hair and the bruises, who couldn't keep his supper down. They'd talk in a bar or by a dock and someone would overhear and store it away, pass it on, send a text. He wondered whether to log on, to burrow down into darknet and let London know everything. He even got as far as putting his flip-flops on and taking his laptop, ready to go looking for an internet café, but he thought better of it, lay on the bed, turned the lights off and smoked another cigarette, and began, in his haphazard way, to plan.

The next morning, Mangan woke to a prayer call, put on sunglasses and a cap, found ginger coffee and toast in a little place with a cat, and sat and watched the street for half an hour under a lowering sky. He watched the kids in their maroon shorts and spotless white shirts and little backpacks meandering to school down the potholed, dusty streets, dodging the mopeds and the Toyotas, stopping at the food carts. He paid his bill and made his way to the airline office at the edge of the town. A plane came once a week, on Thursdays. Forty-eight hours away. He paid cash for a seat, the booking clerk tapped his details ponderously into a yellowing computer, and he wondered how far his name would sink into the network.

He wandered back through town, the morning heating up, still, humid. At an internet café he spent an hour browsing the news. He checked his own website, which still stood, in all its earnestness. The tech wallahs in the basement of VX had not been ordered to take it down. So someone—someone meaning Hopko—still regarded him as operational. He checked a bank account online, working through a tangle of passwords and security, and yes, there was his "salary."

So they still had some use for him. For now. Apparently.

He considered, again, trying to duck down into darknet, a flit into the encrypted file-sharing site they used for comms, but decided against it, again. He left the café and wandered back through town.

At an ATM, he took out the maximum, as he did whenever he could, adding to the wad in his money belt.

He passed a little stationery store that seemed to have some books. He went in, looked at the shelves. And there, at knee level, dusty and forgotten, was a set of poorly bound English-language classics. He bought Conrad and some more cigarettes.

As the day wore on he read, slept, paced the room, smoked. He turned on the fan in the early afternoon, and as it hummed and creaked he lay on the bed and tried to map it all out, to work through contingencies. The thought of it brought a flood of adrenalin, made him jittery. *Prins Hendrickstraat. Teng. Lawyer.*

He stood, paced. And as he did so, he thought of Trish, wondered how he would explain it to her, tried to form the words in his mind, mouthed them, whispered as he paced. *Well, you remember the Chinese colonel, right? The one we ran? Who gave us riches, but for all the wrong reasons? The one who died in some tacky casino on the banks of the Mekong River with a needle sticking out of his groin? Him? Well, he gave me a thread, you see. Just after we had thrown him to the dogs, and just before he was dragged off by MSS, he half-whispered, half-spat it at me. A name, an address, nothing more. And that's where I'm off to, right now, with my duffel bag and my laptop and my threadbare cover. To pull this thread of possibility. To see what spills out.*

Why?

Because I need it, of course. I need it all to matter. I need to know that I didn't back away, that I sought a resolution. I need to matter. Me. Does that make sense? Do I convince you?

She had told him once, her arms folded, sitting ramrod straight, in that starchy, brittle, voice of hers, not to expect the stories to resolve. The stories just hang there, she said, without endings.

He watched a column of ants make its way from the window to the pink plastic trash bin in the bathroom, implacable.

He dozed for a while, woke, lit another cigarette, waited for dark.

12

Johns Hopkins University
Baltimore, Maryland

Information can be defined as that which reduces uncertainty.

The more information you have, the less uncertain you are.

Pearl, in the air-conditioned lab, lacing together code in the cold, blue quiet of the afternoon and eating Skittles.

The question she had set herself: how do you reduce uncertainty in the swarm, a swarm of a hundred, a thousand, a million drones? How does a drone know where another drone is, what it is doing? How sure can the drone be? Several questions, in fact. Questions that would ensure her continued presence in freezing-cold labs like this one, that would take her into the chilly, secret depths of the defence industrial complex. She reached for another Skittle.

In nature, swarms have ways of knowing. Ants know. Termites know. Starlings know, in their great murmurations. Pearl had seen a murmuration once, a million birds over a lake in Virginia at evening, the great black billow against the setting sun.

Ants will build a vast colony of underground chambers and tunnels. They will excrete pheromones that indicate what they are doing. Other ants will read the pheromones, and will behave according to what they read, dropping a grain of sand here, picking one up there.

Is each ant consciously building a vast colony? Does each ant say to its ant self: Today we are building such and such a chamber, off such and such a corridor, of these dimensions, and at that depth? Is each ant present at the hatching of its choices? Presumably not, because they are ants, and their brain cells number only a quarter of a million, so self-awareness is unlikely. But if not, how does the colony get built?

Pearl sat back, blinked at the screen.

Is it possible that each ant possesses no consciousness of itself or of its role in the building, but when millions of ants interact, consciousness grows *between* them? The millions of ants, therefore, are one consciousness.

How might we define and measure such consciousness?

How might we create it?

"Spooky," said Cal, who was standing behind her. She jumped.

"Don't do that," she said.

"Sorry," he said. "Are you there yet? Artificial super-consciousness?"

"Not quite," she said. She felt jangled, tense. Cal bent down, looked at her closely.

"You don't look too good."

"Didn't sleep."

"Again?"

She nodded, feeling sudden tears condensing on the surface of her eyes. She thought of her father calling her as she stood frozen at the top of the stairs. She thought of the impact of his thick hands on her.

"Hey," Cal said softly. "What is it?"

"It's just...just everything. The security clearance. Everything."

He looked puzzled for a moment.

"But that shouldn't—" he caught himself. "Well, look, whatever I can do. Support, you know?"

She was wiping her eyes with the back of her hand.

"Thank you."

"I've never seen you cry before."

"I don't, usually. I'm just tired."

"Sure," he said, considering.

"What?" she said.

"You're sure there isn't anything you want to talk about?"

He reached for her hand but she pulled it away and shook her head, miserable.

"Well, I'm here, okay?" he said, and turned away.

"Cal." He stopped, turned back.

"When you did your clearance, you put, like, all your relatives on it, right? I mean, you just list them all. Everybody in Hong Kong and in China?"

He looked surprised.

"I don't have a clearance, Pearl."

"Oh. I thought…"

"You thought what?"

"I don't know. I just assumed."

"You only apply for a clearance if you are going to be in a national security job, or a defence industry job. Most of us don't go that way."

"Right."

"You're… kind of unique like that. I mean, there have been some guys gone from here to NSA, math guys, Ph.D.s. But, you know, most of us don't want to work in secret."

"Right."

"Or on weapons systems."

"Right."

He smiled at her and walked back across the lab to a workbench where dozens of disassembled quadrotors lay strewn about, bringing to Pearl's mind an image of butchered animals, slaughtered birds.

She turned back to her desk, took a deep breath, tapped the space bar to bring her screen back, and forced herself into the code.

Take human cells. Human cells are not, by themselves, conscious. But if you put thirty-seven trillion of them together and make them interact according to certain rules, you have sight, hearing, touch, memory, love, a liking for chocolate, the ability to appreciate MUKBANG videos and cheesy pop songs and the poetry of Bai Juyi.

Drones are not, by themselves, conscious.

How do we build consciousness between them?

Later, Cal made her go with him to a little Korean place they loved, just off campus, and she went willingly, the relief washing over her. *Maybe he likes me after all.* They ordered *bibimbap*, which came in big stone bowls, the rice sticky and laden with radish and bean sprouts and shiitake mushrooms and peppery beef and a glistening fried egg atop it all. They both loaded it up with hot sauce, and were silent for a while as they wolfed it. But then Cal wanted to probe.

"So, maybe you need some time out. A vacay."

"I need time out from my dad."

"Why? What's he done now?"

"Oh, just being him." Careful, she thought.

Cal waited.

"He's just on my case, is all," she said.

"He's just on your case," Cal said. *He's mirroring.*

"You are very lucky, Cal, to have yours eight thousand miles away."

"Am I?" he said. "Am I lucky?"

"Well, they can't interfere."

"Actually, I miss them. I love them a lot; and I am very, very grateful to them for the sacrifices they made so

I can do a Ph.D. at Hopkins and sit here eating *bibimbap* with you."

She frowned.

"I wish they *were* here," he said.

"Okay, so I'm just a really bad person and you're a really good Chinese son. I get it," she said, the tears beginning to come again.

"The point I am trying to make, Pearl, is the relationship you have with your parents is weird. It's not great, from what I can see. Other people have good relationships with their parents. I do, with mine. It's possible. But you are stuck in this weird place and it's not healthy."

"They're my parents."

"There's something going on and you're not telling me what it is."

"Okay, Cal. Thanks. I don't think it's really your business." I sound like a petulant nine-year-old, she thought. He was insistent.

"You say that they nurture your gift. But I don't see that. I see you being stifled by them."

"You only care about how well I code, how useful I can be. My *gift*." She caught herself. I am being ridiculous.

Cal was unhurt, infuriatingly calm.

"That is ridiculous. Your gift, Pearl, is not separate from you. If your parents are constricting your talent, they are constricting you." He leaned forward. "What is it? What's happened?"

"Nothing." She was sullen. "Anyway, we *are* going on a vacation, apparently. Fall break. To the Caribbean."

"Really? The whole family?"

She nodded.

"And how do you feel about that?"

"You sound like a therapist."

"I think a therapist might do you some good. Maybe you'd tell them whatever you're not telling me."

Pearl got the check. She always paid. Cal was horribly broke. He lived in a basement and seemed to subsist on peanut butter sandwiches. They left, and Cal walked her back across campus to her car. He gave her a kiss on the cheek, and she badly wanted that kiss to continue and migrate towards her mouth where it might linger, but it didn't. Why would it, after she had said the things she'd said? He walked away, gave her a wave, and her heart sank. He's an adult, she thought. He has the emotional control and judgement that I lack. And as she got into her car, and pulled away, she realised that she had a secret. She did not know its meaning or its significance, other than that she could not share it, not with Cal, not with anyone. The secret separated her from others, from Cal. The secret was called Beetle, and knowledge of it made her complicit with something, in something.

And she did not know what.

Yet.

A Tao family vacation was a special vision of horror. Pearl's mother making lists, packing boxes of tea, bags of dried cuttlefish, surgical stockings. Her father sitting in the living room, curtains drawn, certain he could game the internet to find the right deal on last-minute plane tickets. The endless discussion of hotels, of medical insurance. Pearl sat on the sofa in her pyjamas, thumbing her phone and listening to them, wondered how on earth they ever managed the process of emigrating from China to America.

For some reason best known to himself, her father had chosen Aruba for their idyll, a tiny fleck of cactus-strewn rock festooned with resorts off the coast of Venezuela. They were booked into a hotel near the airport. Her parents were keen it should have a buffet. Pearl thought of the beach, the sea. She wondered if she'd be able to escape for an hour, go walking on the sand. Or snorkelling, maybe.

Or she could stay in her hotel room and pretend to work. The sudden thought of Cal made her stomach dip with worry. Talking to him like that! *Idiot.* She pictured him in his lab coat, that smile, his holding her hand. She found his astuteness frightening. He would see her, see through her, and that would doom everything, ensure her failure as a friend, as a lover. Soon he would understand that she was an outgrowth of this family, rooted in its strangeness and its unspoken understandings. And when he understood that, well, why on earth would he want her?

Who is Beetle?

She got up from the sofa and went to the kitchen, where her mother had started preparing dinner, mincing garlic and ginger, slicing pork. She walked to the counter and leaned against it, watching her mother chopping, her thin hands, tiny wrists. Two years before, her mother had had breast cancer and most of the weight she'd lost had never returned. Pearl remembered her sitting in the darkened living room during chemo, her cheeks sunken, silent, her father's anger at all of it. Her mother looked at her and frowned.

"Can I ask you something?" Pearl said.

"Depends what."

"It's important."

"Ask then."

"Will you not be mad at me?"

Her mother said nothing, just stared down at the chopping board, the knife through the ginger root. She is so easily threatened, thought Pearl.

"Will you tell me who Jiachong is?"

Her mother replied too quickly.

"I don't know. Who is it?"

"It's a nickname, right? Jiachong? Beetle?"

Her mother had put down the knife, peeling more garlic now, though it seemed to Pearl that there was enough already chopped.

"Can you tell me who he is? Or she? Maybe it's a she," Pearl said.

"I don't know what you're talking about."

Pearl sighed. "I think you do, Ma. Maybe don't tell Dad I asked."

Her mother was still fiddling with the garlic. Pearl saw a little colour appearing in her cheeks. Autonomic nervous response signalling anxiety, she thought.

"Don't tell me what?" Her father was standing in the kitchen doorway.

Pearl felt the world rock a little, her own adrenalin response kick in, her hands gripping the counter.

"Don't tell me what?" He was wearing shorts, black socks and sandals. A white undershirt, turned grey in the wash.

Her mother put her hands flat on the countertop and dropped her head. Then she turned and said brightly, "Oh, nothing, we were just talking about the vacation plans."

Her father was walking slowly across the kitchen towards her, his hands on his hips.

"What was our daughter asking about?"

At these moments, the ones where her father's anger was building, Pearl, since childhood, would find herself retreating inwards, her attention taken by a view from a window or a pattern of sunlight on a wall. She was looking out of the kitchen window now, at the dogwood in the yard, wondering at its gnarled fragility, as her father came and stood very close to the two of them.

"*Mei shi*," her mother said. It's nothing.

He stood there in silence for what seemed a long time. Her mother would not look him in the eye. Then he turned and walked from the room, and Pearl heard him going downstairs to his office in the basement. She found her hands were shaking a little, and her mother put her arm around her and pulled her close, just for an instant, before she too turned away and went back to the garlic.

13

Mangan found the freighter through a little agency online. It was a Panamax container ship of Liberian registry, the *MV Paragon*, leaving from Marseille. Two cabins available, both with shower. Cafeteria and recreation room. Meals included.

He paid cash for the flights to Jakarta, island hopping in little six-seaters to start with, the pilots smoking *kretek* and reading the paper. He paid cash for the flight to Paris, drank himself half-insensible in economy, touched down in an iron rain at Charles de Gaulle and shivered in the taxi queue. At Gare de Lyon, he paid cash for a TGV ticket to Marseille. He booked nothing online, made no calls, minimised his exposure, moved quickly. Jet-lagged, disoriented, he showed up at the shipping line's offices, asked who he could talk to. A harried woman in a head-scarf thrust medical forms at him, telling him to report to the docks in four days' time. He was lucky, she said. The cabins for paying passengers were usually booked, but this one was waiting for him, just so he could pay in cash. He holed up in a hostel, ate kebabs and *mahjouba* stuffed with peppers and harissa in Nouailles after dark.

Eleven days at sea, eleven days of monosyllabic conversations with the Filipino and Ukrainian crew, found him in a boredom so profound he was driven to old sitcoms and jigsaws. He wrote a piece about the economics of the container industry, touching on the security of global sea lanes and piracy, but didn't post it to the website, reasoning it would be insecure, then debating himself about the need to live his cover.

The static, grey Atlantic horizon began to warm, turn to azure. He saw porpoises, fishing skiffs out of the Caribbean islands, and blue-green phosphorescence in the water at night, the bow wave aglow. He stood on deck, the wind in his face, and thought of what he was about to do.

The *MV Paragon* left Mangan—sweating, unsteady, clutching his duffel bag—on the dock at Sao Luis, on the shoulder of Brazil, his passport stamped, details entered cursorily on God knows what computer. He spent a hellish night in a hostel near the port, a club across the street pounding until three, shouting in the street, car horns. The next morning he wandered down to the jetties looking for small boats heading west along the Brazilian coast.

It took him some time, and some arguing, but he found it. A peeling blue scow, laden with cigarettes, soft drinks, cheap clothing, and perhaps other, more profitable, items. A Barca flag dangled from her stern, and she was bound for Cayenne, in French Guyana, seven hundred miles to the north-west, a little sliver of France on the edge of the rainforest. He had an elaborate story ready, a travel feature for a London magazine, very lucrative, but the captain couldn't care less, just stood beneath a jerry-rigged canvas sunshade on the deck and counted out the dollar bills. Mangan brought with him tins of tuna, crackers, tinned pears, cigarettes, water and a half-bottle of rum. He slept on the deck. He was glad of Widodo's motion sickness tabs, and lay silent, his scarf over his face under the blistering sun as the boat clattered along, rolling foully and belching black fumes into the blue.

At Cayenne, he came ashore in darkness, sidling down the jetty and past the harbour master, disappearing into the town. A taxi out of town to the west, and by two in the morning he stood on the beach at Saint Laurent du Maroni, the brown water of the Marowijne River lapping at his feet.

He smoked, dozed for an hour, swatted at the mosquitoes, wondered about dengue and zika. At five, a tall man in shorts walked up to him and jerked his thumb across the river.

"*En face?*" the man said.

"*Oui*," said Mangan.

The man gestured for a cigarette. Mangan gave him one and lit it, peeled off more dollars. The man shouldered Mangan's duffel bag for him and walked him to a slender, yellow craft with an outboard, pulled up on the sand. The man pushed off and turned them into the current.

The sun was coming up, the heat rising and the water beginning to shimmer when they reached the other side.

Exhausted, filthy, his skin red and itching, Mangan clambered onto the riverbank in Suriname.

The last time anyone had asked him for identification was in Brazil, two countries and eight hundred miles away. He congratulated himself, a little.

In Washington, word of a death.

She'd come in early to get a start on the day, pounding up Mass. Ave. in eighty-nine degrees. Cleaners were buffing the floors in the Embassy foyer and the café wasn't open and the Station was empty and still. She sat heavily in her chair, dropped her backpack, put in her key card and started the laborious logon process.

And there, in her classified email, a message from

Hopko. The sight of the name made her stomach swoop and lurch. In the subject line just a question mark, but in the body of the message were two links. One to a public website that claimed to specialise in uncovering intelligence stories, another to an unclassified report on a UK government network.

A suicide.

The man's name was Jonathan Monroe. He had been an analyst at the U.S. State Department's own intelligence shop, INR. Patterson knew the name, having seen it on the coversheets of dense, forbidding China product. Monroe was a heavy hitter, one of those intelligence titans who glide between diplomacy and policy and academia and all the secret compartments of the intelligence machine.

And now he was dead.

A nine millimetre in the back of the mouth, said the website. In a car, parked up under some trees somewhere out by Great Falls. So far, so tragic. Patterson thought of the cold metal against the palate, the taste of gun oil.

Patterson skimmed the government report.

There was a wife, a house in Bethesda. No sign of depression or illness. The FBI was investigating. Of course they were.

Patterson sent a message back to Hopko. *What do you want me to do with this?*

Her phone rang, a secure line from London. *Oh, Christ.*

"My, you're in early." Hopko's deadpan voice, dry as dust. Patterson thought of her lolling behind her desk in her sanctum at VX, the black hair teased up, the chunky, beaten silver jewellery, silk blouse tight across her blocky frame.

Patterson started to reply but her throat caught and she had to swallow.

"They're keeping me busy," she said.

"Quite right. Idle hands and all that. Are you settling in? Is the ghastly Anthony Tipton behaving? Not taking you out for little dinners, is he? Sneaking peeks down your cleavage? He does that, you know."

"I must not be his type."

"Good. Frighten the shit out of him, I would."

"I'll try."

"He says you know nothing outside your subject area and your writing's woeful. So you must be doing something right."

Patterson closed her eyes. Hopko went on.

"Now, look, you'll keep an eye on this Monroe thing. Let me know everything you see, open source or otherwise. I want everything, and I mean everything."

"Do you want to make a formal request to the FBI? Because if you do—"

"I know, I know. I have to go through the luscious Anthony. Not yet. I just want to know if there's anything to it. Did he just get sad and pop himself, or was there motive?"

"I'll send you everything I find."

"And if you can go and work your charms on those lunks at the FBI, well, you never know."

"You want me to go outside channels?"

"Oh, for heaven's sake, Trish, you're a diplomat now. Go and be diplomatic. Show a little leg."

Patterson realised she was digging her nails into her palm.

"I'll try."

"Yes, you will."

"All right."

"And Trish, try not to act as if you're in mourning."

And that was it. She was gone. Patterson collected herself. Was it *meant* unkindly? Did Hopko *mean* to devastate her, every bloody time?

And she was, of course, in mourning. For her own ambition. For a version of herself.

She met Polk at a Starbucks off M Street. She got there early and tried to think of an approach. When he arrived, in rumpled tan chinos, black shoes, a blazer, he ordered some ridiculous concoction with vanilla and whipped cream that he licked from a spoon while he listened to her ask the question. He considered for a moment, then exhaled and made a surprised face.

"My, you're forward, you English."

"You said if I needed anything." She tried a smile.

"Jeez, Patterson, you might take a girl out for dinner before you rip her panties off."

He was toying with her.

"Simple question, Franklin. Is there anything to know? Was he sick? Wife bugging out on him? Was he just fed up?"

"No one calls me Franklin except my Gramma Schatzi in Somerville, Massachusetts, and you're not her."

"What do I call you?"

"Frankie. Or bitch, given the way you're humping me."

"No one wants to hump you, Frankie."

"Ain't that the truth?"

"London just wants to be tipped off as to how nervous they should be."

"Fuck's it got to do with them?"

"I don't know. Something."

Polk sniffed.

"Well, I'll tell you, Patterson." He made a cheap magician's gesture, arcing his hand over the table, fluttering his fingertips. "There's nervousness in the air."

"Because?"

"Because?" He leaned in to her, mock conspiratorial.

"Because as you will no doubt read on the front page of the *Post* tomorrow or the next day, so I don't believe I am giving away too much in the way of professional confidences, they kicked down the door to his very nice house, in a very nice part of Bethesda, decorated in very nice pastel colours and furnished nicely from Crate and fucking Barrel, and they searched the place and found stacks of classified documents in the basement. Big fucking stacks. Very fucking classified."

"Shit."

"Indeed, yes. Shit. Yes. And there were USB drives, too. So, yes. Double shit."

"The wife?"

"All weepy. Nothing to say. Knew nothing." He held up his hands.

"You were there."

"I didn't say that."

"So?"

"So? You do the math."

"There's an investigation."

He snorted. "I think it is safe for you to assume there will be a deluxe, supersized, force-twelve counter-intelligence investigation, and my beloved Bureau will be relaying to its intelligence partners a sparkling damage report, when such a thing becomes available."

"And when does such a thing become available?"

"When? When we've done our thing. Gone hither and thither. Walked back the cat."

"Sounds like months."

"And maybe never. See, Patterson, the FBI is a law enforcement agency. Sure we do counter-intel, but arresting people is what gives us a hard-on. It's what gives our bosses a hard-on. We'll run a spy to catch a spy, but in the end we hate 'em all. So if Mr. Monroe was, in fact, playing footsie with a foreign power, we will want to roll up whatever the fuck network he was a part of. We won't want to let them run, or double them, or otherwise indulge in wet and slippery espio-play with them. We will arrest them, prosecute them and send them to the Supermax in Florence, Colorado, where they can wallow in their own shit for forty years."

"That's beautiful, Frankie."

"Well, fuck you very much. Anyway, Patterson, at least you hump nice."

"Why? Someone not being gentle?"

"Who d'you think? The un-dead of Langley, Virginia."

"Because?"

"Give us all the files! Give us the corpse! Give us the wife! Tell no one!" He was holding his arms out and staring, zombie-like. "It's a human tragedy! Let us feed!"

Patterson was stifling a laugh. Polk licked his spoon, enjoying it.

"So how do you fight them off? Garlic?"

"Crime-scene tape. And bad language. And guns. They don't got guns, and we do."

He made to stand. Patterson tried to stall him.

"But Frankie, what do *you* think? What does your experience tell you?"

"Hump me harder, Patterson."

"Look—"

"No, you look." He pointed off to the left, but looked straight at her. "Channels. Okay? Get your guy, what's his name, your Markham—jeez, that guy, what'd they do to him? It's like they drained his blood and embalmed him at birth. Anyway, get him to put in the paperwork and we'll tell you what there is to tell when the time is right to tell it."

Then he stood up, leaned towards her and spoke quickly, quietly.

"But in the meantime, it's a shit stew. And there's plenty to go around. Enough even for London."

She blinked, realising she'd got something of what she came for.

"Right. Thanks, Frankie."

"Don't mention it."

"I won't."

"Right answer."

She summoned her courage and called Hopko on a secure line. Hopko harried her like a terrier.

"What *exactly* did he say?"

"Just what I told you. The files, it's a shit stew, enough for London."

"And tell me again, you think—"

"He was signalling that there were files in Monroe's basement that compromise material of UK origin."

"But he didn't *say* that."

She had her forehead resting on her palm.

"He did not. But that is my read. Val, honestly, that's what he was saying."

"*Paper* files?"

"He said there were thumb drives, too."

"Well, you know what we have to do now."

"The appropriate thing would be to put in a formal request for the damage report."

"Trish! Get a grip, woman. That could be months, as you yourself so perspicaciously pointed out. You will go back to Polk, and you will endeavour to ascertain what material he is referring to. We need filenames, designations. I will speak to Tipton and Markham. Do you understand?"

Patterson was silent, her stomach churning.

"Do you understand?"

"Yes. Are there any particular designations you are concerned about?"

A pause. She could hear Hopko's breathing on the

line. She's trying to decide whether to tell me, Patterson thought.

"There is one, as it happens. It is a designation that you will not have heard before, and you will keep it entirely to yourself. It is BOTANY. But in the U.S. system, it will have been given a different designation, obviously. You will need to ascertain which U.S. designation matches material originating in BOTANY."

And just how the redacted fuck am I supposed to do that?

"BOTANY. Can you give me any sense at all of what BOTANY is? Or was?"

"No."

"Well, okay, I'll try."

"Yes, you will."

Patterson put the phone down and steadied her breathing. She knew Hopko's tone well enough to read minute variations in it, tiny fluctuations from her wry, ever-so-relaxed norm. There was stress there, she thought, running just underneath, a tiny, brittle edge to her.

Valentina Hopko. Her mentor, turned tormentor. What a difference a syllable makes, she thought.

14

Pearl arrived at Cal's clutching two big bottles of Coke, some brownies, and, as a joke, a bottle of black Shanxi vinegar. She wore a tight-fitting, turquoise, sleeveless top which she hoped might show off her small breasts, or at least might suggest to Cal that she did, in fact, possess breasts.

She pushed the buzzer, and the door opened with a click. Cal's tiny apartment was at the back of the building, in the basement. The corridor smelled of detergent and cigarette smoke. Cal's door was open and Pearl heard raised voices, laughter. She went in tentatively. Five or six people were lounging around on the battered blue sofa and on the floor, talking. Some were Chinese, some white. Pearl recognised faces from the engineering department and from comp sci. They were talking about a movie, a sci-fi blockbuster. A space mission to Mars, a man left behind on the red planet. Could he survive? For *years*? The engineers were taking the movie apart, working over its assumptions, its conceits, mocking it and laughing in loud, hearty bursts. Pearl tried to slip past them with a nervous wave, and they watched as she went to the kitchen.

The kitchen was full of steam, the walls and windows streaming. Cal was wearing oven gloves to take piles of steamers off the stove. He turned and saw her, his upper lip beaded with sweat. He put down the steamers, and held his arms wide.

"You came!" he said. "She came!"

"Yeah, well," she said.

"Dear old dad finally wasn't an impediment?"

"There was, like, negotiations." She held out the bottle of vinegar. "And I stole this."

Cal took it and examined the label as if evaluating a fine vintage.

"Shanxi *Lao Chen* black vinegar. I am intrigued." He took the cap off and sniffed it. "Holy crap," he said. "Smell that." He held the bottle out to another boy, or maybe man, who was leaning against the counter. He was Chinese, thin, had a widow's peak and a sharp, unsmiling face.

"Pearl, this is Charles. He's in astrophysics." Pearl nodded, but Charles ignored her, leaned over the vinegar bottle and inhaled.

"Oh yes," he said. "Very nice." He was mainland China, heavily accented. He looked at Pearl, his eyes flickering over her body. "You are from Shanxi?"

"My father."

Charles looked past her and gestured to someone else.

"Julia! Come!" Julia was bright-eyed, her hair in a messy bun, and she bustled into the kitchen, gave Pearl a big, reassuring smile, and smelled the vinegar bottle.

"*Wah!*" she said, her face lit up. "Mmm! Delicious! For the *baozi*!" She held her hand out to Pearl.

"I am Julia Chen," she said.

"Oh, Hi. I'm—"

"I know who you are! Of course. We all know you. Even over in physics we know who you are!" But it was said kindly, with real admiration. Charles was nodding. Pearl, shrugged, embarrassed. Julia looked earnestly at her.

"So Cal has still not persuaded you to come and live on campus!" Pearl looked at Cal, but he was pretending not to hear, busying himself taking the *baozi* out of the steamers.

"It's, uh, complicated."

"You should come! Come and live in our building. Charles here, he can really cook. Makes everything. Lasagne, cookies, everything."

"I think you can afford it," said Charles. They know everything about me, she thought. Cal has discussed me with them. "Also, maybe you can tutor us in math."

Julia was laughing.

"Yes! You help us with Differential Equations and we cook for you!"

"Like you need my help," she said. But the thought fluttered in her mind: How do I do this? How do I respond so that they like me, but I don't give everything away?

"*Chi baozi! Chi ba!*" Eat the *baozi*, Cal shouted. Pearl took one from a big blue plate. The bread had steamed nicely and was fluffy and light, and inside was salty, juicy pork. It was soft and chewy and comforting. Cal was pouring out the vinegar into little condiment dishes for dipping.

Charles wanted to question her.

"So you have a sponsorship, right? From some big corporation?"

"Kind of a small corporation, actually."

"Oh, a small corporation. Which one?"

"It's called Telperion."

"And they pay your tuition?"

"Uh, yeah."

Charles was nodding. "Huh. That's good. And they make weapons, right? Like cyber weapons."

"Really?" said Julia. "Weapons?"

"Well, they build platforms for different stuff."

Cal was watching her, half-smiling. "But it's national security 'stuff,' right?" He made scare quotes with his fingers in the air around the word "stuff."

"Well, yeah, I guess."

Julia was wide-eyed.

"Wow," she said. "So what sort of weapons? Like, what do they do?"

Cal wiped his hands on a towel. "Classified," he said. "Right, Pearl? We ordinary folk cannot know."

Pearl felt uncomfortable, cornered. And Cal wasn't helping her out, to her alarm.

"Well, I don't work on those things, so I don't really know," she said.

"If you did know, would you tell us?" said Charles. "I mean, I'm from China, right? And you know what? I'm a Communist Party member. So when you have a security clearance you will have to report that you met me and I asked you these questions, won't you? A foreign contact report?"

"I will?" said Pearl.

The other three all smiled.

"Ummm, yup," said Charles.

Pearl was dumbfounded.

"But, not just because of meeting you at a social thing, like this," she said.

Charles just raised his eyebrows.

"I think *especially* at a social thing like this."

"Okay, Charles, I think you've made the point," said Cal.

"I mean, I could be anybody, right? I could be Ministry

of State Security. I could be United Front Work Department. I could be PLA Second Department. You don't know."

"What is that? I don't know what those things are," Pearl said.

Charles stared at her.

"They are very tough people, Pearl, who want your shit. And they will manipulate you to get it."

"But you're a friend of Cal's," said Pearl, hearing her own voice sound whiny, weak.

Charles looked at Cal, and snorted.

"He's from Hong Kong. He doesn't know anything about who I am." Cal looked taken aback.

"Okay, Charles," said Julia. She came over to Pearl and put an arm around her. "Don't pay him any attention, Pearl. He's a bully."

"I'm not a bully," Charles said, his tone veering into exasperation. "I just want to know why a scientist—a real scientist—would go and jump into this world of… of weapons and violence and nation states at each other's throats just to win some stupid capitalist competition."

Pearl struggled to find a response, but none came.

"I mean, you are working on drones, right?" Charles continued. "Drone swarms? Cal said so. You know what that means, right? It means weaponised drones, in their millions. That's our future. Some small as insects. Some big as houses. Everywhere. Killing, maiming. I mean, why do you want to build that?"

"All right, Charles. That's *enough*." Cal put his arm around her.

Charles smiled, held up his hands.

"Okay. Sorry. *Duibuqi*."

Pearl stood in silence, holding her half-eaten *baozi*. She felt ridiculous and young, much younger than anyone else present. There was an awkward silence between the four of them.

"Well, I'll just see if anyone else wants *baozi*," said Cal, and he went to the next room.

Charles was still watching her, chewing. "How much is the stipend?" he asked.

"Stop it now, Charles, I mean it," said Julia. "Hey, Pearl, look, we are going to go for a hike tomorrow. Up in Patapsco. There's a lake, we can swim. Will you come with us? Charles will stop being so obnoxious, I promise."

"I don't think I can, but thanks," Pearl said.

"Really, go on. It'll be fun."

"I just don't think so," said Pearl. She put down her *baozi*, gave them a brief smile and slipped out of the kitchen, out of the front door, and away.

Later, she sat in her bedroom under her blanket, listening to K-pop—something else Cal had turned her on to, the music so corny, shiny, carefree. She felt hollow, as if the brief time she'd spent at Cal's had sucked her sense of self out of her. She'd never been challenged like that before, never had her achievements questioned. She must be weak. How quickly she'd been wrong-footed, even come close to tears. And Cal hadn't sided with her. Why not? He wasn't loyal. She didn't deserve his loyalty.

It was nearly ten before he texted her.

P, You left so quickly. I'm sorry. I guess Charles made you feel uncomfortable. You okay? C xx

She texted back.

Kind of upset.
I'm sorry. He can be kind of a douche.
He really hates me.

No he doesn't. He admires you. He hates
weapons manufacturers.
What about you?
I think you could come live on campus and get
exposed to different PoV.

A pause. Then Cal again.

What ya doin?
Lisning to Fab Boy Five.
Ooooh gonna build a tower o'power oooh ooh.
You just like their abs
You think I should leave Telperion?

Another pause, longer this time. She stared at the
screen, willing him to respond.

It's what you think that matters Pdawg. Xx

15

Patterson gave it twenty-four hours, then called Polk again. He was on his cell phone, breathless, traffic and a siren in the background.

"I need to buy you another coffee. Or maybe lunch this time. Or tell you what, how about a drink after work? Let's go and get a beer or five." She was gabbling.

"Why? Nothing's changed since you ravished me in Starbucks."

"It's changed for me."

"And that, my dear, is your affair."

"Come on, Frankie. You know you want to."

"I want to? Yeah, no."

"I've got a name. A designator."

"And I've got chlamydia. Go away."

"I will be at Vapiano's on 19th at six o'clock."

"Enjoy yourself."

He hung up.

Vapiano's was full of a youngish after-work crowd, journalists from the bureaux on M, Peace Corps types from around the corner, some K Street suits, loud, smart and gossipy. Not a good choice, she thought. She sat at one of the tables outside, drank a beer, watched the minutes tick by. No Polk. At 6:23 p.m., she was pondering a second beer when a text came in.

BLACK ROOSTER. NOW.

Clueless, she searched on her phone. A "pub," two blocks away. She grabbed her bag and ran, clattering down the pavement.

It was dim and half-empty and smelled of disinfectant and stale beer. Polk was right at the back, in a corner, with a bottle of pale ale and a plate of fries.

"Don't ever, ever invite me to Vapiano's, ever again," he said.

"It's not that bad."

"I would sooner stay home and chew off my extremities."

"You're a right charmer, Frankie." She signalled to the waiter for two more beers. "Nice you changed your mind."

He gave her a direct look, the humour gone.

"Yeah. Well."

She waited, but nothing more came.

"So," she said. "London is—" She stopped as the waiter came over and put two more bottles on the table. The place was filling up a little, and someone had put music on, eighties songs, little shards of her childhood. "London is saying they are concerned, particularly concerned over this one designation. I don't know why, but they are."

Polk looked at her, shrugged. It occurred to her that he really didn't want to be there. Someone had told him to come, perhaps. Something had, in fact, changed.

"Frankie, can you help me with this? I'll return the favour."

"Oh, really? And how will you do that?"

"Well, I don't know, but there'll come a time…"

"No, there won't. There never comes a time." He took a long pull at the bottle, but his eyes stayed on her.

"The designator…"

"Are we in a SCIF?" he said.

"What? Are we what?"

"Are we in a SCIF? A Secure Compartmented Information Facility? You know, those shitty rooms that are the only places you're allowed to discuss this stuff? You've heard of those places? Forgive me, I thought we were in a shitty bar downtown."

She looked down at the table, pursed her lips.

"How do I get it to you?" she said.

"Why would I want it?"

"Because you're not an asshole, and it's important and you know it. Otherwise you wouldn't be here."

He took a notebook and pen from his pocket. He wrote something, tore the page out and pushed it across the table to her. It was a classified email address—no name, just a number.

"Does this go to you?" she said.

Polk shrugged.

"Who sees this?" she said.

He picked up his beer and pulled on it, saying nothing.

"I have to send it here?"

He nodded.

She sighed and put the piece of paper in her wallet.

"What's the problem, Frankie?"

"You. You're the problem."

"Why?"

"Who else are you talking to about this?"

"Just London."

"Who in London?"

"Who? I can't tell you that."

"Who?"

"Really, I can't tell you that."

"You talking to your bosses here in DC? In Liaison? Markham? Tipton? They know you're here?"

"Well..."

He turned his head part way, looked at her out of the corner of his eye.

"Why this particular designator?"

"I don't know."

He shrugged again, stood up, dropped a twenty on the table, and left without a word. She watched his back, his weightlifter's gait, the arms hanging outward at his sides. He'd been lulling her, hadn't he? Feeling her out, then wrong-footing her, then opening the door, hinting she could come in.

When, back at Station, she reported to Hopko by secure email, the response was immediate, even though it was one in the morning in London. "You will send Polk the designator at the address he gave you. Insist on an immediate response."

They're frantic, she thought. Why?

She imagined some operation somewhere betrayed and failing, agents drifting into the dark, Hopko trying to reel it all in.

Who was Monroe? What had he betrayed? To whom?

There was the piece in the *Washington Post*. It had taken a few days, but there it was.

(Washington) The FBI is rushing to assess the damage to national security after a senior intelligence official was found dead and a search of his house revealed boxes of highly classified files and computer drives loaded with secret material.

The body of Jonathan Monroe, 61, of Bethesda, Maryland, was found in a car near Great Falls earlier this week following what police called "an apparent suicide." Mr. Monroe was a highly regarded specialist in Chinese affairs at the State Department's Bureau of Intelligence and Research.

The FBI confirmed it is investigating the circumstances surrounding Mr. Monroe's death. An official, speaking on condition of anonymity because he was not authorised to comment on the case, said it was "far too early to conclude whether or not Mr. Monroe had been involved in espionage," but he said the files found at his house contained "extremely sensitive" material, and were "concerning."

And what about his wife? Who had her? Molly, her name was. The paper had a picture of the house, a dignified faux Victorian with a porch, a garden of azalea bushes and a cherry tree.

"Probably worth well over a million." Anthony Tipton was looking over Patterson's shoulder. "Lucky fellow. Must have had his own money. Or his wife's. You don't buy a place like that on a State Department salary, do you? Not these days."

She turned.

"I'm sure there'll be an explanation," she said. She thought of Monroe in the car, the gunmetal in his mouth. Tipton stood over her, hands in his pockets.

"Oh, I'm sure there will. Now, Trish. Indulge me. Apparently, you've been having cosy chats with the FBI. Or so I'm told. And not by you, incidentally. And I was rather hoping you might illuminate me as to why. You see, I've just spoken to Val Hopko, and I distinctly get the feeling I've been *handled*. Honestly. You have to count the spoons after talking to that woman."

She couldn't tell if he was angry, or what he was.

"Well, I'm sure she told you."

"Well, no, that's the thing, really. She didn't tell me. So I'm all ears."

"She just asked me to make some informal inquiries with the FBI."

"About Monroe."

"About Monroe."

"Hmm. Well, I think that's all a bit fucking bizarre, frankly."

She swallowed. He was looking down at her.

"Well, I didn't mean to—"

"You tell me. All of it. This afternoon. Three. My office. Clear?"

"Clear."

"Hope so."

He stalked away, jingling the keys in his pocket. She turned back to her screen, and there was an email from Polk. *Oh, for Christ's sake.* It just read:

STARBUCKS 19th. 9:30 OR BE SQUARE.

It was 9:17. She put her jacket on and picked up two empty cups, as if she were going to the kitchen, and walked slowly from the Station.

Polk was in shirtsleeves, chewing doggedly, muffin crumbs down his front.

"What?" he said.

"You know there's six hundred calories in those things."

"Don't be cute, Patterson." He gestured to a chair.

"Hi, Frankie."

"And don't get comfortable. We're moving."

"What? Where?"

"Come with me." And in one rapid movement, he'd gathered up his jacket and briefcase and then he was out of the coffee shop, wordlessly striding down 19th, turning onto K. She kept pace with him, said nothing. The sun was blinding, bouncing off the plate-glass office buildings, the heat magnified and pulsing over the traffic. She was sweating, her shirt sticking to her back. Polk abruptly turned right, cutting her off, thrusting his way into a lobby of glass and reclaimed wood. A chiselled young man at the front desk looked up enquiringly. Polk flashed his ID. Patterson had to fill out a form and was issued a printed sticker with a bar code for her jacket. They took an elevator lined with copper to the ninth floor. Polk shouldered his way through more plate-glass doors etched with the words Bouverie & Higgs.

"Frankie, what is this place?"

"Friends," he said.

He waved to a platinum-blonde woman at the reception desk who, without a word, gestured down a corridor. Patterson followed him, stopping as he punched a keypad, which opened a heavy door that swung shut with a *clunk* behind them. Polk made a sweeping gesture.

"Now, we can talk," he said.

A SCIF, then: insulated walls and floor beneath an electrically conductive shell to prevent leakage. Baffled air ducts, hidden speakers broadcasting pink noise, motion detectors, and cameras in each corner—God only knows where or what they'll be hooked up to.

Careful now.

"Are we being recorded, Frankie?"

"I shouldn't think so," he said. He gave a broad, fake grin.

"You got the email."

"Yes. Yes, I did." He nodded.

"And?"

"And? Well, I am authorised to tell you the following. So listen the fuck up because I'll only say it once."

One of those moments, she thought. A moment when my professional life, my aspirations, my sense of self all shiver and wobble like a plate spinning atop a pole.

She reached for the notebook that was in her bag, but caught herself. *You can't take notes out of a SCIF, you idiot. You amateur.* Polk was watching her.

"Are you listening?" he said.

"Fire away."

He waited a beat, as if to emphasise the infantile nature of her answer.

"An initial trawl of the files found in Monroe's house—initial, mind you—found four designators that correspond to material of UK origin. Among them, our designation DTCREEKSIDE was found to correspond to UK designator BOTANY. DTCREEKSIDE designators were found on three files, all of them digital. The—"

"Three files?"

He ignored her, carried on.

"The files contained finished intelligence products. All of these intelligence products were related to Chinese targeting of private corporations here in good old God save America. Spying, Patterson, you get me? Spying, for the purposes of purloining proprietary information and stealing from our hard-working corporations all their most valued and profitable secrets, everything from jet engines to genetically modified rice to computer-related stuff that I do not and will never understand. And then they are reverse engineering it, and building it cheaper. This is not good, Patterson. And the Brits, God bless you and all who sail in you, were able to tell us which of our noble corporations the Chinese are targeting, what they're stealing, and, perhaps, how, through this BOTANY."

There's an agent, she thought. BOTANY is an operation with an agent at its heart, an agent in China. And BOTANY product was shared with the Americans, who called it DTCREEKSIDE. And it's corporations, commercial secrets. So there's money and investors and shareholders and fund managers, all the people governments are terrified of, all baying for blood. It's China's future—its renaissance—that is at stake.

And Monroe saw the BOTANY product. And stole it.

Polk was reading her mind.

"Don't get spun up, Patterson. DTCREEKSIDE product was all scrubbed. No names, no pack drill. So if there *is* an agent, and I know that's what you're thinking 'cause it's written all over your scary little face, he ain't blown by Monroe."

Patterson imagined the operation collapsing, the black Audis in Beijing pulling up outside an apartment block or a courtyard or some faux-Tudor house in a distant grey suburb, and everything that would follow. And just for a moment, Patterson's self-loathing gave way to a surge of anger.

"So is that what I tell London, Frankie? Don't worry, it's all fine. Monroe looked right up our skirt, at one of our most precious operations, but he didn't see anything, and even if he did all the private parts were covered. And we don't even know if he was a spy anyway. Oh, and by the way, he shot himself in his car, so we'll never know what he saw or what he said or who he said it to. Are you bloody serious?"

She thought she saw a flicker of surprise on Polk's face.

"Don't get your panties in a bunch. You'll tell your people the files were there but they were scrubbed."

But she was angry now, and picked up her bag and stalked from the room, wrenching the door open.

The day after, a Saturday, Patterson found an invite pushed under her door. Emily and Esteban from downstairs were grilling burgers—that very evening! Everyone in the building to come! She thought about it for a moment, then looked out a nice pair of jeans—capris that showed off her legs—and a green silk blouse.

She sat in her living room, looking out at the fire escape, drinking instant coffee, and thought about the previous day: the strange exchange with Polk in the SCIF, and then the monstering from Tipton in the afternoon. He'd wanted every detail. She gave him the bare essentials, unsure why she was protecting Hopko. Perhaps she was just less frightened by him than by her.

In the early afternoon, she went for a run, a long one, up to Rock Creek Park, deep into the woods on a muddy trail that wound and rose and dipped, waving away the clouds of gnats that swarmed in shafts of sunlight. Then back, by the river, the warm, wet air pawing at her. She pushed hard, opened up a little on the flat, let her mind wander. She was back in Iraq, pounding around the base perimeter with Joanie Linklater in ninety-five degrees and the reek of fuel and plastic from the burn pits, sweat pouring off the two of them.

She slowed a little, made way for another runner, a tall guy with muscled calves who wanted to show off to her. Then she was off again, the track skirting the river and its tumble of rock. And she was standing by a river in Thailand, waiting for her agent. An interminable wait, that one, sitting in the reeds while mosquitoes ate her alive and she worried about the malaria. And when

Mangan had come, after hours in a fetid, stinking compartment in the bottom of the boat, he was soaked and befouled and shattered and angry and close to tears, and he stood there shaking and dripping on the jetty, yet he was still keen as a tack, still had about him the acuity of mind that she so admired. He had leaned on the car as the MSS dragged the other guy, the Chinese colonel, away for interrogation and slaughter.

China makes exiles of us.

The memory came barrelling up in her like a huge sea creature breaching the surface. Her breath caught and she had to stop. She bent over double by the river, her shoulders heaving.

Another runner, an older woman in a headband, slowed and called to her.

"Hey, you okay, hon?"

Patterson couldn't speak, just held up a hand. The woman jogged over to her, leaned down, touched her shoulder.

"You okay, girlfriend?"

Patterson nodded, steadying now, grateful for that touch.

"Yeah. Thanks."

"Hey, no problem." The woman nodded, gave her a last look and jogged away. Patterson knelt on the grass, stayed there for some minutes, her sense of dissociation overwhelming her, dissociation from home and family, from work, from others, from herself. From her agent. *We are exiles.*

By the time she got back to 18th Street, it had clouded over and heavy, thick raindrops were spattering the pavement. Emily and Esteban cancelled.

16

Albina, Suriname

Mangan walked away from the boat, up the muddy beach. The town was only starting to wake, so he sat outside a Chinese supermarket and waited. It was a Saturday, market day, and the stalls were going up: hair-braiding stands, sellers of fish and bush meat, women with spices and arrays of twigs and leaves for use in medicine and *winti*, balls of white clay for adornment. He caught the smell of cannabis in the air. A man was setting up bottles on a stall. They were filled with rum, but also with wood chips and leaves. One had an armadillo's tail in it. The man saw Mangan watching and pointed at the bottles.

"*Wilt u proberen?*" he said in Dutch.

"Bit early for me, thanks," said Mangan.

The man waved him over. "Good for man things," he said. He made a gesture with his forearm, fist clenched—an erection. "Good for this."

"Not much need for that just now, but thanks."

The man looked Mangan up and down, evaluating him. He was lean, dark, eyes bloodshot from the smoking. He wore a black T-shirt, and a ring in the shape of a skull.

"America?" he said.

"Something like that," said Mangan.

"Where you go now?"

"I need to go to Paramaribo."

"Paramaribo, okay. You get taxi, my brother he has."

"Well, all right then," said Mangan.

The taxi was a white Toyota station wagon, with six passengers and their bags all crammed into it. Mangan had made a bid for the front seat but had been shouldered out of the way by an elderly woman in a headdress. He sat in the very back now, leaning against the window, rigid with fright. The driver had them at seventy or eighty miles an hour on the wrong side of the road, slowing and pulling in only in the face of oncoming traffic, his reluctant concession to physics. The suspension had been replaced with something much harder and every ripple in the road surface sent shock waves up Mangan's back. *Secret agent plans complex operation, dies of fright brought on by inexplicably dangerous driving.* The car careened past an immense eighteen-wheeler carrying an earth mover and it was all he could do not to cry out. *Jesus Christ, no.*

They stopped at a place called Moiwana and the men got out to piss. Mangan took his duffel bag and went to the driver's window.

"You know what? I think I'll just stay here for a bit. Thanks, though," he said.

"Where you stay Paramaribo?"

"I don't know yet."

The driver looked him up and down, then shrugged. The car pulled away.

Moiwana was a few newly built houses set back off the highway and beyond them, deep, thick forest. Mangan picked up his bag and began to walk in the direction of Paramaribo, then stopped.

To his right, in a roadside clearing, stood a monument of some sort. A central pillar, concrete at the base, then iron as it tapered upward. Atop it, in iron, there were symbols—pictographs?—that Mangan couldn't identify. More strangely, around the pillar were littered small plinths in concrete and rusting iron, on each a nameplate—Sonny Ajintoena, Difienjo Misidjan—the incomprehensible symbols curling underneath. People had laid tokens on each plinth: flowers, shells and rocks. They looked like altars scattered through the clearing, reminding Mangan of Holocaust memorials.

He found an explanation on a panel. There had been a massacre here. In 1986, during Suriname's vicious civil war, troops loyal to the government had descended on the village, shot everyone they could find—women and children included—and burned the houses. The villagers, the soldiers believed, were supporters of the rebel Ronnie Brunswijk and his Jungle Commando. And they were black, descendants of slaves who had fled the plantations and their Dutch overseers. *Maroons*, they were called, from the Spanish *cimarron*, "runaway." Thirty-five had died, maybe more.

Mangan lingered, drinking from a water bottle. Who built the memorial? What other massacres? He lit a cigarette and leaned against the pillar, smoking. The air was hot and still, and birdsong echoed around the trees.

Around the houses, he saw movement. He walked across the road towards them. Two boys were kicking a ball on cracked, weedy concrete. An old woman sat in a hammock, low to the ground, very still. Scattered around her were empty plastic containers and some grimy blankets. She wore nothing but a sheet wrapped about her middle. As Mangan approached, he took off his sunglasses, and she crossed her arms to cover her breasts.

"Hello," he said.

She didn't respond, just swayed slightly in the hammock. The boys stopped kicking the ball.

"Do you live here?" said Mangan, gesturing to her and to the houses.

The woman frowned. One of the boys walked over.

"She here," he said.

"She lives here?" said Mangan.

The boy nodded, not comprehending. Then he pointed to her, and to the monument.

"She," he said, and made a gun gesture, shooting, a *pah pah* sound with his lips.

"She was here? When there was the killing?"

"Yes, yes," said the boy. "She...children." And he waved something away in the air, so as to say, *all gone.*

The woman, understanding now, looked to Mangan. The boys stood, waiting.

Mangan didn't know what to do, what was expected. He'd been here often, as a reporter, at the edge of someone else's abyss, peering in. He just gave a nod, to show he'd heard. The woman's eyes were still on him.

He took a twenty-dollar bill from his wallet, leaned down and tucked it beneath one of the grimy plastic containers, gave an awkward smile. The woman was expressionless, just gazing at the money as Mangan walked away.

About half a mile down the road, dense forest on both sides, the temperature into the nineties, he got a ride. An older, dapper man in a polo shirt and spectacles pulled over. He was of Javanese descent, Mangan guessed. He offered the man fifty dollars for the rest of the way to Paramaribo. The man smiled and opened the car door.

The man was a teacher. And yes, of course he could drop Mangan near Prins Hendrickstraat, in the old centre of the city. He chatted amiably about Paramaribo, its famous stately houses of weathered wood in white and green, the beauty of their ornamented doorways, the lively Waterkaant—the waterfront. But the politics. Well! Such a *dyugu-dyugu*.

"A what?" said Mangan.

The man smiled.

"A *dyugu-dyugu*. It's a word we use in Sranan, our Creole. It means, a big…" He held up a finger. "Wait, there's an English word. Yes, yes, I have it. *A kerfuffle*. Yes." He was pleased, then began to slow the car down.

"Are we stopping?" said Mangan.

"Yes, yes, for the checkpoint. You need your passport." *Oh, shit.*

"A checkpoint? For what?"

"Yes, yes. Check for drug smugglers coming in from French Guyana without going through border checkpoints."

The man looked at him.

"You have stamp in your passport, yes?" he said, worried.

Mangan just smiled at him.

The car came to an abrupt halt. The checkpoint was just in sight, perhaps 200 metres away.

"Out," said the man.

Mangan got out, took his duffel bag from the back seat and ducked into bushes at the side of the road. The car drove off. He stood there, midges swarming him, the whistles and whoops of the forest birds rising in his ears. With a sinking heart, he realised that if he was to avoid the checkpoint, he'd have to go round it, through the forest. He began to walk, or rather to push his way into the undergrowth, his duffel bag on his shoulder. Within a minute he was drenched in sweat. He had no water, he realised. *British operative bravely skirts rural police checkpoint, fearing immigration irregularities. Dies of dehydration.* Jesus Christ.

It took him the better part of two hours, and at one point he was calf deep in swampy water. He saw parrots in the trees, and an extraordinary lizard, two feet long, a streak of luminous green as it shot past him. But there was the road. He emerged onto it exhausted, dripping, his arms and shins bleeding from thorns, his feet sopping. The checkpoint was a half-mile behind. The first car to pass him tooted its horn and the driver made a finger-wagging gesture. Mangan started to walk.

It cost him another fifty dollars in the end to get a truck to stop and the driver to ignore his mud-spattered clothing and leaking shoes. What a *dyugu-dyugu*, he thought. They drove in silence to Paramaribo. Mangan watched the towns flit past, saw the grey dogs lying in the road in the afternoon heat, felt inside himself for the hard bead of possibility—and there it was, warm and ready.

17

Washington, DC

Polk picked her up in a car this time, a giant American thing, a Buick or something. It was black and idling 200 metres up the road from the Embassy. She got in. Polk said nothing, put the car in gear and drove to a backstreet next to a playground in Tenleytown, and parked.

"You look grim, Frankie. Why the cloak and dagger?"

"Whatever I tell you, Patterson, it's going straight back to the right people, isn't it? The operations people, the case people."

"Yes, it is."

"It's not going to sit in some bullshit report on Tipton's hard drive while he cleans it up for style, right?"

"No. I am talking direct to London."

"Well, things just got a little more complicated." He sniffed, looked straight ahead out of the car windscreen.

"Oh?"

"And I'm telling you because it turns out your guys may need to act after all, okay?"

"Okay." She spoke quietly, waited for him.

"I am authorised to tell you this, but this is all you're getting for now. That's it, you understand me?"

"Okay."

"They've been checking Monroe's shit. Tracking back his movements. Bank accounts, credit cards, phone use, whatever."

"And?"

"And stuff is coming up."

"Stuff."

Polk was all but writhing in his seat, hating to articulate what was coming next. Patterson could feel the fury in him. He exhaled.

"It's the normal fucking stuff. He thinks he's the smartest guy in the room. No one will suspect him. No one will ever find out. Counter-intel is just jumped-up beat cops with bad shoes and facial hair. We won't notice shit, 'cause he's *way* smarter."

Again, she just waited.

"There's credit card bills for pricey meals he didn't have with his wife and he didn't expense. There's jewellery. There's a thousand bucks dropped in Tiffany's in Taipei, for Christ's sake. Last year. He wasn't even supposed to be in Taipei. He never declared a trip to Taipei. Who the fuck was he buying jewellery for in Taipei?"

Patterson made to speak but he cut her off.

"No, no, we searched the house, there's no Tiffany jewellery. Wife says he never bought her Tiffany jewellery, didn't know he'd gone to Taipei."

She decided to play devil's advocate.

"Well, that says affair to me, Frankie. Doesn't say spy."

The look he gave her, the cold anger in those chemical-blue eyes—to be interrogated by him would be terrifying.

"Oh, really? It says liar to me. No. It screams pants on fuckin' fire. And it whispers, ever so quietly, honey trap."

"That's a lot of assump—"

"There's more."

He took another deep breath.

"So he's in Baltimore, like, five months ago. We got credit card stubs from some fancy restaurant, two people, sea bass, crab cakes, whatever. And then he's at some sorry-ass motel off the interstate. Double room. So we go up there, and praise be to St. Joshua, they still got the surveillance tapes. It's evening. He checks in, he's got an unidentified female with him, of Asian appearance. They go to the room, they do what they do. But after an hour or so, a big group, like six people, all check in. All in baseball caps, shades, usual shit. Five of Asian appearance, one Caucasian. One of them is a woman. These guys are in a big hurry, not much luggage. They go to their rooms. And then, like, fifty minutes later, an interior camera catches the woman from the big group, and she's hustling Monroe's love interest down a corridor, between rooms. Love interest is in a bathrobe. Just three seconds of footage but it's there."

"I'm not following. What are you saying?"

He shrugged. "No clue. No fuckin' idea. Something went down, is all."

"IDs on the people who checked in?"

"Not a one. Paid cash, showed driver's licences, no record of them. Names, addresses lead nowhere."

"And when they all left, what then?"

"Yes. Indeed. What then? Well, Monroe's love interest leaves by herself, dressed and with luggage. The six leave in pairs over the next forty minutes. And Monroe, he's out of there like a scalded cat, running through the car park, fumbling with his keys. The guy's in a panic."

Patterson just held her hands out, shook her head.

"Something happened," said Polk. "Between Monroe and his gal, and the six others. Was it a burn? Were they putting the muscle on him? What?" He handed a folded piece of paper to her. It was a terse timeline of Monroe's final months. *Journey to Taipei. Return from Taipei. Check into motel. Exit motel. Body found in car. Declared dead at scene.*

"That's the tick-tock. Your guys should check, see what they see."

Patterson thought of the Security Branch people at VX, crowding Hopko, slicing open the case, timing every twitch and twist of it, hunting the correlations. The thought nauseated her.

Polk drove her back to the Embassy. As he pulled up to the driveway, Patterson reached for the question that had been scratching at the walls.

"Frankie, the woman at the motel. Monroe's love interest."

"No idea who she is."

"What did your people say about her?"

"Probably Asian, in her thirties. Five eight, slim. Elegantly dressed, scarves, fancy coat. *Bourgeois demeanour,* whatever the fuck that means. Confident. Physically fit, but not military. Probably not a trained operative. Diplomat, intellectual type. Body language said resolve, tension. Like she was planning."

"Presumably the jewellery was for her. So she was in Taipei with Monroe."

"Fair assumption, but not proven." He looked at her, snorted. "Why? You got someone in mind? Hmm?"

Patterson was thinking of a room in an Oxford college—its creaking floorboards, the smell of unwashed clothes, furniture polish. And in the middle of the room, a nameless woman with the eyes of a raptor and the clip of the China coast in her speech. The two of them, Patterson and this nameless being, had stood there, scenting, each knowing the other for exactly what she was.

Patterson despised intuition, and like any good intelligence officer, hated coincidence, too.

"No," she said. "Of course not."

"Shame," he said.

At Monroe's house, there wasn't any crime-scene tape. There was just the wife, Molly Monroe, standing behind a mesh screen door, her fingers to her chin. A show of concern, even fright. She had manicured nails, an oversize engagement ring alongside her marriage band.

Patterson stood on the porch holding a bouquet of white lilies, working her depleted reserves of charm.

"The British Embassy wanted to share our condolences, Mrs. Monroe. We are so very sorry for your loss."

Molly Monroe said nothing, just looked at her, unsure.

"We knew your husband very well, and we were very great admirers of his work."

Molly's hand went tentatively towards the screen-door handle.

"Here's my identification, of course," Patterson said, holding up her Embassy ID. The screen door opened a crack, and she grabbed it and pulled it open, pushing the bouquet at Molly.

"Thank you so much. I'll only come in for a moment," she said, stepping inside.

Molly walked them through to the living room. It was painted in salmon pink, and had uncomfortable, low-backed leather sofas, Asian art on the walls—some old Mao-era revolutionary posters, framed.

"Please. Sit," she said. Her hair was straight and grey, cut strangely in a pudding bowl. She wore a white cashmere jumper and slacks. Her face was collapsed, exhausted, eyes blank.

"This must be a very difficult time for you," Patterson said.

Molly looked away, held her hands in her lap.

"If there is anything we at the Embassy can do, you will let us know, won't you?"

Molly looked back at her.

"Do?" she said.

"Well, yes."

"Can you get the FBI out of my house?"

Patterson blinked.

"I…"

"No, of course you can't."

Patterson, calculating now, wondered whether to probe.

"Have they been here a great deal? That must be exhausting."

"Oh, it is. They've taken everything. All our papers. Our computers. Our phones. They searched the entire place, dividing each room up into little grid squares. Going around on hands and knees. They even pulled out drywall." She had started to knot and twist her fingers.

Had they placed surveillance devices too? wondered Patterson.

"Well, I'm sure you have absolutely nothing to worry about."

Molly turned and looked straight at her.

"Oh, really?"

Patterson affected surprise.

"Why? Are you concerned?"

"Did you know my husband?"

"By reputation only."

"Well, he…" Her face was puckering, lip trembling. "He was not, *not* the kind to…to shoot himself."

Patterson knew to say nothing.

"He was *not*."

Patterson wondered when she'd last eaten or slept. Or talked to anyone.

"Mrs. Monroe, do you have relatives? Someone who can come and be with you?"

And at that, the woman crumpled, the tears coming. Patterson went and sat next to her, put an arm round her. She was thin as a bird.

"Is there anyone?"

"There's our son. But he's not here."

Patterson sat for a moment, just holding her. Then took the initiative.

"Mrs. Monroe, I'm going to go to your kitchen and make you something to eat. Would you do that? Eat something?"

The woman wiped her nose and shrugged.

"When I eat, I throw up," she said. Patterson went to the kitchen and opened cupboards. There was a tin of tomato soup, some crackers. Patterson microwaved two bowls and brought it all back on a tray. The woman hobbled over to the dining table and sat. She took a mouthful of soup.

"Molly, sorry, may I call you Molly?"

She gave a fractional nod.

"Molly, you say he wasn't the kind, but what are you suggesting? I'm sorry to ask, I'm just a bit startled by that."

She shook her head. "Oh, talk to the FBI."

"But did something happen? Was there something—perhaps a few months ago, that made some sort of difference to him?"

Molly looked up, her eyes red.

"Do you know something?" she said. "Anything? About what happened? They don't tell me what they've found out, the FBI. It's infuriating."

Careful, Patterson thought.

"I'm so sorry. I don't mean to be intrusive. Is there anything I can do for you? Anything at all? Can I come and see you again?"

The woman was sagging again, now, looking down at her soup. She seemed to give a small retch, put her spoon down and placed a hand on her stomach.

"Look, I can talk to the FBI," Patterson said. Now dangle it, she thought. Seal the deal. "And perhaps I can let you know what I find out. Quietly. Just us. What about that?"

"Would you do that?"

"Yes. Yes, of course."

Molly's eyes searched her.

"Are you involved in the case? In some way?"

"Molly, a great many people are very concerned. Really. And we at the Embassy just want to ensure that we're doing everything we can."

"You'll contact me? If there's anything you can tell me?"

"I promise."

And having recruited Molly Monroe as an unconscious source, Patterson slipped out of the house, her own stomach lurching at the idea that the FBI would find out, and at what Polk would say.

18

Paramaribo, Suriname

Mangan chose a small hotel called the Buena Vista as
his base of operations. It was quiet, retaining at present only three guests besides himself, as far as Mangan
could tell. It had tiled floors, air conditioning that filled
his room with a sodden, chemical cold and, importantly,
three exits. The desk staff were over friendly, demanding to know his plans, his needs, his touristic desires. He
smiled, deflected their enquiries and pressed them on the
question of a good restaurant. Mangan should, they said,
ensure that he sampled the fine cuisine at Spice Island,
richly influenced by Suriname's South Asian heritage.
Nor should he miss the novel and eye-catching fusion
cuisine at De Magazijn. Its locally produced beef was as
fine as any on the continent. The many *warungs* around
the city also offered pleasing light meals with their roots
in Indonesia. Would he be requiring driver and guide to
accompany him on his forays into the city? Regretfully,
Mangan informed them, he would not. They took his
passport, but Mangan did not see them make a copy.
He paid cash in advance for the room, and left cash as a
security deposit, apologetically informing the staff that

his credit card had expired. From overuse, he joked, and the staff laughed appreciatively.

In his room, he closed the curtains, sat on the bed in the gloom and felt his heart race.

76, Prins Hendrickstraat. Teng. Lawyer.

Mangan thought of the moment he had been gifted this information, this nugget of possibility. The words, hissed at him in fury and despair, were a weapon crafted to injure and to eviscerate, Mangan's to wield.

The sense of flatness and dislocation he had experienced in the past weeks was leaving him, he realised. The place and the task were taking on texture and immediacy, bringing with them the hyper-awareness he'd come to know, even to crave, and rekindling the fear in his gut that he'd learned to live with. The thought that he was working without London's knowledge, let alone its authorisation or support, quietly terrified him and thrilled him. I am a journalist, he said to himself in moments of self-justification. I follow the story, and screw the rest.

But you are a spy, too. And the rest, well, they may have something to say about it.

With good footwork, he thought, he had a week— maybe two. Borrowed time, after that.

He worked on his silhouette as far as he could, trying to lose the ragged backpacker look. He showered, shaved, ran a comb through the wet, red hair. He pulled out a crumpled white shirt from the depths of his duffel bag, smoothing it out ineffectually. He put on knee-length shorts and a pair of exhausted topsiders, which gave him the look of a visitor, but fell short of idiot tourist. He put on sunglasses, and left the hotel.

Picking his way through old Paramaribo, Mangan was surprised by its stateliness, the white mansions of wood, their sidings embalmed in centuries of paint, their balconies and heavy door-knockers and shining name-plates. He took some photographs, made some notes. He made his way down to the Waterkaant, stopped at an open-air café, bought a coke and watched the Suriname River, its brown, sluggish undulation to the sea.

He watched the street, its steady pulse, people Mangan did not know, could not read or understand. He was absurdly conspicuous.

And yet. The city felt manageable. Few cameras, fewer policemen. A slow-moving, somnolent place of sodden heat and palm trees where people seemed uninterested in him for the most part. He had no sense that he was under surveillance. He had come from the other side of the world, and now the address lay only a short walk away. His stomach turned over at the thought of it.

It was perhaps at this point that Mangan's choices crystallised. Hopko would say, much later, that this was his point of no return, and all that was to follow grew from this moment at the café in the late afternoon, the breeze coming off the water laden with river-smell: mud, weeds, petroleum, sewage. Mangan drank his drink and rose, dropped the bottle in the trash, heard its glass *clink*, wiped the sweat from his forehead with the back of his hand and walked north towards the fort. Then he turned west towards Prins Hendrickstraat to conduct what was, in his mind, a first pass.

19

Aruba

Pearl had the window seat. As the plane banked, she saw rocky coastline give way to sand, hemmed in by shallow water of crystalline blue. She could see sunloungers and umbrellas on the beaches. The plane came in low over the water.

Her parents, a row in front, were out of their seats and fussing with the baggage as soon as the seat belt sign was off. Pearl gathered up her phone, her tablet, her notepad and waited.

They emerged from the terminal in sharp sunlight and a warm wind. They took a short taxi ride towards Oranjestad, her father complaining at the cost, her mother silent. The hotel was on the edge of the town, on a highway. The traffic was heavy with trucks, tourists in jeeps, and a stream of overweight men on motorbikes, the ones with the big handlebars. The bikers wore black helmets and gunned their engines for the deep-throated roar, and they seemed to ride up and down the highway, up and down. In the hotel, the rooms opened onto a pool and withered succulents in pots. That evening they ate burgers and fries in the hotel coffee shop, the only people there. The solitary waitress sat at the bar, thumbing her phone, and when her parents went to bed Pearl sat outside on a lounger in the dark, watching the pool lights shimmer. She read for a while, drank a coke.

When she went back to the room, her parents were already asleep. But she saw that they hadn't unpacked, and Pearl wondered why.

The next morning, at breakfast, they were silent, tense. She looked at her mother.

"Are we having a good time?" she said.

"Don't be rude," her mother replied.

"The two of you look like you're about to go to the dentist. What's wrong?"

"*Mei shi*. Nothing wrong."

Pearl leaned forward.

"You haven't unpacked."

Her father looked up from his phone.

"We might have a change of plan," he said.

Pearl frowned. "What change of plan?"

"We are going somewhere else," he said.

"What? Why? I mean, this hotel is pretty gross, it's true, but you won't get a refund. Not now."

Her father made a dismissive gesture.

"You go pack your things. We leave in one hours and a half."

"Excuse me?"

"Just get ready. Please."

"Well, where are we going?"

"We are taking another flight."

"I'm sorry. I'm confused. Are we going home?"

Her father stared at her, and Pearl felt her stomach turn over; she drew back a little.

"I mean, can't you just, like, tell me where we're going?"

"Shut up. Go get ready."

They left the hotel without checking out, her father holding Pearl by the arm and guiding her to the taxi. Her mother said nothing.

At the airport, her father checked them onto a flight to Paramaribo.

Where the heck is Paramaribo? She took out her phone. Suriname.

PART TWO

The Approach

20

Prins Hendrickstraat
Paramaribo, Suriname

Number 76 was a pretty, white, three-storey house. The second-floor frontage was a lovely, shaded wooden balcony. The drainpipes and shutters were dark green. The front door was flanked by plant pots, and to its right hung a nameplate, its brass recently polished.

The nameplate read:

SOEHARDJO, N. T. – NOTARIS
TENG, T. Y. – ADVOCATEN
WINTER, F. – NOTARIS

The door was closed, an intercom next to it. For a moment he toyed with the idea of just pushing the button, winging it, bellowing that he needed a lawyer as a matter of grave urgency, and only Mr. Teng, T. Y. would do, but the thought was crass and he pushed it away. He walked past. A driveway ran down one side of the house, bordered by a long, carefully tended flowerbed. One side door, with screen. At the rear, as far as he could see, was a concreted yard with some bins and what appeared to be a storage shed.

The rest of the street was a mixture of small businesses and residences, overhung with palm trees. Some thirty or forty paces down the block was a café. It had three small tables outside, under an awning. Mangan went in, sat, ordered coffee, a sandwich—anything to give him time. He put his tourist map of Paramaribo on the table in front of him, and watched.

At six minutes past four, a woman parked a white Toyota outside the house, approached the front door and used a key to gain access.

At four thirty-two, an elderly man emerged, carrying a briefcase. He wore a short-sleeved shirt and a tie. He appeared to be Creole, a black man. He jogged across the street, and walked away.

Mangan ordered more coffee and some plantain chips. The afternoon was blindingly hot. He moved his chair further into the shade.

At eleven minutes to five, the front door opened and two men left, both carrying briefcases. One appeared to be white, the other of East Asian appearance. The two were deep in conversation, the Asian man gesticulating, explaining something. The white man locked the door behind them on a key that was attached to a chain, which was, in turn, attached to his belt, Mangan noted. The keys went in his right pocket. The two walked away from the house, towards the restaurant where Mangan sat conducting his rudimentary static surveillance. The man of East Asian appearance wore a pale shirt and a grey tie, with grey slacks. He was of late middle age, the hair thinning, combed optimistically towards the pate. His posture—a rigidity to the spine, a forward lean— betrayed long hours at a desk. He walked like an old man, Mangan thought, yet there was a cast to his face that was serious, ill-tempered, relentless, even. The two men seemed to be disagreeing, thrashing something out. They were speaking Dutch. Their path would take them right past the café. Mangan looked down at his tourist map.

They were coming up on the entrance to the café.

Mangan pored over his map.

The two men, still speaking animatedly, entered the café and selected a table directly opposite Mangan's.

Oh, for Christ's sake.

Mangan stood with his back to them, put on his sunglasses—as if that might in some way render his rangy six-foot frame, red hair and pale legs less noticeable. He dropped money on the table, too much, and attempted to sidle from the café. As he passed the two men, he allowed himself a glance. They were still in conversation, paying him no attention, sipping lager from chilled, dewy glasses. The Asian man's briefcase was at his feet. And on it, in large gold letters, in the manner of men who stamp their belongings to personalise them, his initials: TYT.

Patterson had just got home to the flat, dropped her bag, stripped and walked to the shower when her phone went. She answered it, standing naked in the living room. For a moment there was nothing at the other end, just squelch and crackle. But then a broken voice—distant, hesitant.

"Hello? Hello?"

"This is Patterson."

"Hello? Oh. Yes. This is Molly Monroe. I'm…"

"Hello, Molly. Hi. Goodness. How are you?"

"I'm in the hospital. Sibley."

"You are? Oh, no. What's happened? Are you all right?"

"My doctor, he was worried, so they brought me in three days ago. They say it's stress. But, well, tests, and everything."

"Molly, I'm so sorry. What can I do for you?"

"I want to see you."

"Of course. I'll come tomorrow."

"Come."

"I will."

She put on a bathrobe and looked up the Sibley visiting hours. Eleven till eight. She had a Five Eyes briefing at three. She might make it out of the office by seven. She sat heavily on the sofa, then stood and went to the kitchen and poured a glass of red wine—and then added a little more.

Molly will know, Hopko had said. *But she won't know she knows. So find it in her.*

She thought of the woman, shivering next to her, blowing on her soup.

I wonder what I won't do, thought Patterson, holding her glass. Is there anything?

Molly Monroe had been put in a private room on the fourth floor. There was no one on the door, no cop, no diplomatic security. Patterson tapped and opened the door.

The room had a view of treetops, a park, a lake. Molly lay, partially reclined, her mouth open. She had a nasal catheter and a drip. Patterson went to the bedside. She'd brought chocolates, which she put on the nightstand. Molly's eyes followed her.

"Molly! Good heavens! Look at you, you poor thing. What on earth has happened?"

It seemed to take a moment for the woman to focus and recognise her.

"Oh. You came."

"Yes. Of course. What did the doctors say?"

"They can't seem to find anything wrong. They think it's just stress, maybe depression. The whole thing. I'm seeing a psych tomorrow. They might do medication."

Her face was a dreadful yellowish grey.

"I just have these cramps in my stomach and I keep throwing up, and I feel exhausted."

"Well, you've been through such a lot."

Molly's hands fluttered on the blanket.

"Thank you for coming."

"Not at all, Molly; it's good to see you."

"I just wanted to ask you if you had talked to the FBI."

"Yes, I did."

"And did they tell you anything? About Jonathan?"

Patterson calculated silently for a moment.

"Well, I'll tell you. I don't think they've reached any conclusions, Molly. But they are interested in some things that happened."

"What things?"

Patterson frowned, spoke as gently as she could.

"A few months ago, there was, there was something that caught their attention. Your husband was in Baltimore."

Molly was silent, just listened.

"And he was in a motel. Have the FBI asked you about this?"

Molly shook her head.

"No."

"Well, there were people with him."

"Who? Who were they?"

"That's what the FBI is trying to figure out. Do *you* know who they were?"

"Was one of them a woman? An Asian woman?"

The question caught Patterson cold. She blinked.

"There may well have..."

But Molly had closed her eyes. In resignation?

"Do you know who that was, Molly?"

Molly sighed.

"Do you know?"

"I met her once. If it's her."

Patterson waited.

"Jonathan was...having an affair with her. I'm fairly certain. I mean, he never admitted it, but he was. He'd go off on these trips, and I'm sure she was along, or they met."

"How are you so sure?"

"Oh, come on. Married people know. He'd come home and he'd be different. Smiling to himself. He'd lean on me less, share with me less. There was some part of his life that was happening without me. You can tell."

Patterson made to ask another question but Molly held up a quivering hand.

"What happened at the motel? Tell me. Please."

"They're not sure. But an Asian woman was there. And there were other people too." Patterson realised she was wading out a long way, too far, perhaps. "And something happened. The FBI looked at the camera tapes. Something happened that seems to have frightened your husband. He was seen running from the motel, shocked, scared."

"And this was when?"

"Five months ago."

"So that was the moment," she raised a hand feebly, "when everything went so strange. Our marriage just... was like it didn't exist. I asked him what was wrong but he'd go and hide in his office. He was so anxious. All the time."

"What did you think it was?"

"I didn't know! But I thought...I guessed it was to do with *her.*"

"And, wait, you said you met her?"

"I'm fairly sure. That was earlier, a year ago maybe. It was at some reception, some diplomatic thing, I forget what. And we were there and there were a lot of

Taiwanese there, Singaporeans. Taiwan National Day, or something. I forget. Anyway, Jonathan was mingling, soaking up the limelight, and I caught sight of him across the room and he was talking to this girl. Very striking girl, really something. Chinese-looking, tall and leggy. She was wearing this sort of halter top with a Chinese collar in red silk, and her shoulders were bare, and this long silk skirt and she was just, just…"

She paused, exhaled, as if trying to regain control.

"Anyway, I saw Jonathan approach her and she just lit up, and she reached out and touched his arm and gave him a look. Such a look. Really perfectly done. And he just glowed. It was obvious they were…obvious to me they were intimate. And then he said something to her, and she sort of scanned the room and clocked me. It was all so obvious. Jesus. Anyway, later I approached her, and she really worked me. Told me what a genius my husband was, how he'd given her all this help in her academic life—she was Taiwanese, she said, some sort of academic, a post doc or something."

Her breathing was accelerating, coming fast and shallow.

"Molly, what was her name?"

"Nicole."

"Surname?"

"I don't know."

She was struggling to sit up.

"Do you know where she was an academic?"

But Molly was starting to retch and Patterson reached for a plastic basin on the nightstand and thrust it under her and she retched again and heaved a hot spume into the basin.

When she'd finished and spat, Patterson wiped her mouth with a tissue and gave her water to rinse with. She lay back and closed her eyes, exhausted. Patterson waited. Molly seemed to be dozing. A nurse came in and Patterson gestured to the vomit-filled basin and the nurse made a face and took it away. Patterson walked to the window and looked out. She began formulating her report to Hopko. A woman. A name. A betrayal. All the human frailties on parade.

She wondered again why Hopko was using her this way—having her creep about, going behind the backs of the senior Station officers. Hopko was, she was coming to understand, manipulative to a monumental degree. And she just allowed herself to be manipulated. Hopko pointed, she marched. Why this pathological need to please her? Even as she didn't trust her. She screwed her eyes shut and swore through her teeth.

Molly stirred. Patterson went back to sit by the bed.

"How do you feel?" she said.

Molly blinked slowly, then spoke.

"I'm...I don't know. They don't know what's wrong with me."

She looked as if she might cry, the lines in her face deepening, lips working. Then she just took up where she'd left off.

"He had been seeing her for a year, maybe," she said.

"And did you know, all that time?"

"No. I wondered. It took time to know. I think he even took her to Wachapreague."

Patterson leaned in to her.

"I'm sorry. Where?"

"We have a little cottage on the coast. At Wachapreague. We used to go, often, when Blake was little. It was our place. So beautiful. Very simple, just a clapboard cottage, a deck, a little jetty. But then Jonathan didn't want to go any more. Too busy. Too...done up. Too self-important."

"But you think he went there with this Nicole?"

"I don't know. I think so."

"What makes you think that?"

"I used to go down by myself occasionally, when he was away. And things would be, you know, moved around. And I found—and I know this sounds ridiculous—I found hair in the shower. Black hair."

Safe house, thought Patterson.

"Just a few strands. But there it was."

"Did you tell the FBI this?"

"No. No, I didn't."

"Really? Why not?"

"Because it's ridiculous. What am I, some sleuth? Anyway, they've been so callous. I wonder why I talk to them at all."

"The house, Molly. Where is it? Tell me again."

There was an address, and Molly described the place. Somewhere down on Virginia's Atlantic coast, hours of driving from Washington. She was getting tired, and visiting hours were almost over. She asked for a drink. Patterson poured water into a paper cup and helped her sit up, her hand at the top of Molly's back. When Molly lay down again, Patterson noticed on her own hand loose strands of Molly's grey hair. Just a few, but there they were.

21

On the Friday night, Patterson hired a car at a rental place on M, parked it in the street and left in a clear half-light the next morning. She wore hiking pants and a T-shirt and took a backpack with a torch, phone charger, mask and gloves, and an ASP baton that sprung open to two feet in length to wield a lethal weighted tip. The District was quiet and she took 50 the whole way out of town, through Washington's slatternly eastern edges, its weed-strewn strip malls and battered overpasses, towards the Chesapeake Bay.

At seven, the city far behind her, she reached the Bay Bridge in cool, clear sunlight. She'd never seen it before, and had had no idea of its scale, its sheer bravado, its vast arc across the water. She couldn't even see the other side, and experienced a momentary pleasing thrill as she accelerated up its curvature. She came down on the eastern shore amid marinas and mansions half glimpsed along the water's edge. She stayed with the highway for a while, then pulled off, meandering south along silent wooded roads, checking her back.

Just past eight, she stopped. A sign said COUNTRY STORE. She got out and stretched. The morning was still bright, but cooler here than in the city. She climbed wooden steps and pushed open a squeaking screen door. The place was almost empty. Two old white men in plaid shirts and trucker caps sat eating pancakes amid shelves of tinned goods, cans of motor oil, boxes of ammunition and humming refrigerators. She went to the counter, where a teenage girl shovelled eggs and sausage onto a styrofoam tray and poured her a cup of weak black coffee. The city fell away so quickly, she thought, and silent, rural America was always waiting, its vast blankets of trees, its creeks and craggy waters, its endless highways.

She spattered her eggs with hot sauce and ate, watching the door.

She came to Wachapreague a little before ten and drove once through the town, past the Volunteer Fire Department, a white clapboard church, down still streets lined with weather-beaten cottages. It had the feel of an old fishing village, a lost, salty place, generations of its men heading out to trawl on the grey water. Its harbour was surrounded by sandbars and barrier islands. A marina held stubby fishing boats, a few yachts. *Welcome to Wachapreague—Flounder Capital of America!* She circled back, looking for familiar vehicles. Nothing.

The house was just beyond the town. Patterson ground down a gravel track, through trees and scrubby undergrowth, towards the water. She parked, meaning to approach the house on foot, took her pack, and as she stepped out of the car into the warm air, she was swarmed by mosquitoes, hordes of the things. She swatted and slapped at them. *Dear God.* Flapping her arms, she knelt, looking at the track, searching for tyre indentations, but could make out nothing recent.

She walked on, then started to jog, the mosquitoes coming at her relentlessly. They were on her neck, her eyelids. The house came into view. It was two storeys, pretty, built of blue clapboard. It stood in a rocky inlet, looking out over the sandbars and winding channels, but mostly shielded from view. She wondered how she'd get in, but even as she approached the steps, she saw the broken window pane, smelled the chemical reek of fire.

Someone had tried to burn the place. The interiors of the kitchen and living room were blackened. The burn pattern in one corner looked like accelerant had been used, the floors charred. But the thing hadn't caught. The windows were sooty. They must have dropped the match and run. No one called the fire department, so no one saw it. Perhaps it was at night, and they botched it. Their search had been quick and dirty. Every kitchen drawer had been yanked out and dropped, smashed crockery all over the place. A sofa was ripped open, a desk overturned. They'd worked on the fireplace, ripped out the mantle, though God knows why you'd hide anything there.

She knelt, took the surgical gloves and mask from the backpack, slipped them on and climbed the stairs. The bedrooms were a wreck: mattresses slit open, drywall torn out, the bathroom trashed. Fewer mosquitoes in the house, at least. The smell was very strong.

Was there a basement?

She went back down the stairs, stopping halfway to peer from a round window up towards the gravel track. What was that? Something skittering across the corner of her eye. She stood still, watching and listening for a good minute. Just the breeze, and the chatter of the cicadas. More bloody mosquitoes.

The door to the basement was just behind the kitchen, in a musty, empty pantry, the shelves speckled with dead insects. The door wouldn't shift at first, its bottom rail jamming against the sill. Patterson wondered if they'd got down there, whoever they were. She put her shoulder to the door. It opened abruptly and she had to catch herself. The stairs were dark. She tried a light switch, but nothing happened. She stopped, listened again, took the torch from the pack, paused and thought, then took the baton, too, hefting it in her hand.

She stood at the top of the dark stairway.

She thought of other dark places she'd gone into: a bunker in Afghanistan, near Khost, carved into a mountain, crammed with enough artillery rounds to keep an insurgency in IEDs for a decade. And there'd been a basement in Iraq filled with makeshift concrete cells, the walls stained with God knows what. No one there, just the smell of it, of horror. The squad had stood there, sweating in the echoing dark, trying to make sense of it. Both times she'd gone in first. She hadn't been afraid. She hadn't been alone. There'd been soldiers either side of her, hard, driven men and women, people who could handle themselves.

She stood, alone, at the top of the stairway.

My memories undermine my present, she thought. *We are exiles*.

She turned, looked from the kitchen window, searched the treeline, took a deep breath. Her stomach hummed with adrenalin, her mouth was pasty. Why? What's here? she thought.

Something.

She started down the stairs, slowly, one at a time, the torch held high, by her shoulder. The steps were of wood, and creaked. She could feel mosquitoes weaving around her again. One step at a time. When her shoe touched concrete, she stopped, ran the torch around. The basement was only roughly finished, the walls whitewashed, pipes criss-crossing the ceiling. There were five wooden chairs in a circle, and at the far side of the space a desk, with drawers. She stayed very still, listened again.

She began to work her way around the wall, slowly,

towards the desk, all her senses heightened now. She had been bitten on her face, and her lower lip was swelling. Something was underfoot, a granular crunch with each footstep. Broken glass? She ran a finger along the wall and felt cables. She turned the torch on them. They were fairly new, and someone had tacked them hastily to the plaster; they ran up towards the ceiling and disappeared, while their other ends lay loose on the concrete floor, attached to phone jacks.

She moved to the desk and bent over, studying it. Dust here, too. No one had touched the desktop in weeks. But there in the dust was a rectangular outline, a shadow. Something had lain there—a box, or a book, or a stack of paper—and had been removed. The desk drawers were empty, but for a paperclip and a small yellow notepad, nothing written on it but several sheets torn off. Patterson put it in her pack.

She ran her torch around the rest of the basement, along the whitewashed walls. Definitely a safe house.

From above, the creak of a floorboard. The footfall tentative, stealthy in a manner that seeks to avoid attention, yet immediately attracts it. The trainers taught that; nothing awakens the ear like the sound of stealth.

Patterson stood stock still, held her own breath, every sense open, alert.

There, again. The old wood shifting and groaning.

The moment fear takes hold is an anti-evolution—a falling away of knowledge and reason, a loss of control, the limbic surge that drags us down to our true, preconscious selves. She was rigid against the wall, up on her toes, her knees quivering, her breathing coming shallow and fast now, the torch flashing pointlessly around her. Then she was lurching towards the stairs, taking them two at a time. She burst out into the kitchen and snapped the baton open and whirled around. No one—but a flicker of movement in her peripheral vision, something black, and she swung the baton hard, clipping a china lamp which fell and shattered on the floor, the broken pieces skidding across the room and the dust rising, and any effort at self-control was gone and she crashed through the house and out of the door and the mosquitoes were immediately on her and she was breathing through clenched teeth. A hundred and fifty metres to the car. She leaped down the front steps and just let the flight response take her, opened up, the baton in her hand, elbows and thighs pumping, and tore away up the track. *The keys, where are the fucking keys?* And then she had them and her thumb was on the unlock button and she was in, cranking the ignition, ramming the thing into reverse, and she looked back at the house and on the front deck stood a slender, hooded figure, very still, and her foot was on the floor and the car was roaring backwards in a shower of gravel and grit and she was wrenching the wheel around and tearing back up to the main road, the rear wheels fishtailing and tears on her cheeks.

She had driven at breakneck speed back to the highway, knuckles white on the wheel, then forced herself to slow, check her mirrors. She looked for a gas station, and when she found one, pulled over and sat for few minutes, breathing, watching. No one was behind her—unless it was a team.

I've never panicked like that, she thought. Never.

There had been a time, Patterson knew, when she would have fronted up to that slender figure, dared him to get physical, and, if he'd dared, she'd have put him down hard and gone through his pockets.

That time had passed, it seemed. Something in her, some tension, had slackened, left her vulnerable. Panic attacks when out on a run. Quivering with fright whenever Hopko rings. Wetting myself at the sight of some prick in a hoodie.

What the living fuck has happened to me?

Is it a team? *Oh, Jesus Christ.*

She started the car and pulled out fast, ducking and diving up the eastern shore, as thorough a vehicle surveillance detection run as she'd ever done. Once, she saw a grey Mazda circling around and coming back at her and her heart was thumping again as she squinted at the plate and accelerated away. And there was a blue Audi with a bumper sticker that said "My Karma Ran Over Your Dogma" that floated a little too close to her for eight miles as she came up on the Bay Bridge, but then disappeared.

She was back in the District by the late afternoon, returned the car to the rental place and walked back to the flat, stopping in a shoe shop, sitting on a bench at Dupont Circle pretending to read in the muggy heat, watching.

Emily and Esteban were sitting on the fire escape again. They called down to her, but she just waved and went inside.

In the flat, Patterson searched every room methodically. She took a handheld device from a box in her wardrobe, held it to her eye and moved slowly about each room as it emitted bursts of red light. She booted up her laptop and searched for wireless signals she couldn't identify.

She poured a glass of red and sat at the kitchen table, trying to calm herself, picking at the skin around her fingernails. She was covered in mosquito bites. From the backpack, she took the notepad she'd found in the basement, and held it to the fading light.

22

So it was him.

The respectable man of East Asian appearance who spoke forcefully in Dutch—who sat in cafés sipping his cool lager, who was a little stooped, a little stiff, whose demeanour and fine office spoke of professional rectitude—was *Teng, lawyer,* and was somehow of pivotal concern to Chinese military intelligence. He was the weapon pressed into Mangan's hands in the closing moments of an agent's life. To be wielded how, exactly?

Look for linkages, his trainers had once told him. If you have nothing else, look for associations, the place where one thing meets another. That's where the cracks in the cover are. Look there, and you will find what we call intelligence. The hidden, real shape of things.

So, to what—or whom—is Teng, lawyer, linked?

He ate at a raucous Chinese hole in the wall near the waterfront, a styrofoam plate of rice and chopped crispy pork with a few strands of green. The woman behind the counter spoke to her customers in *sranan tongo,* yelled at the chef in a language that might be Hakka. He said nothing, just pointed to what he wanted, sat at a greasy table by himself and watched the *telenovela* on the wall-mounted screen. A woman in a tight scarlet top was learning to play golf. Behind her, an older man, venal, manipulative, reached naughtily around her to assist her putt, pressing himself against her. But look! In the bushes, a spy with a camera—and even worse intentions.

Mangan left half the food, walked out into the darkness, the traffic, the night smells of cigarettes and cooling asphalt and twists of perfume, the river beneath it all. He let his mind wander back to Teng, let the thoughts shape themselves into narrative.

Teng, lawyer, points somewhere. He is indicative, or predictive. He leads to an agent, or a network. The network of which he is a part unfurls from the Chinese state, and through it run currents of Chinese power, pulsing through nations, across borders, through the markets and banks and offshore, humming in the fibre, breeding in the server farms.

He walked north, past the Torarica Hotel, glowing with light amid the palm trees, past a vast outdoor café where Dutch tourists, sunburned, drunk, lounged and stared at their phones, past a casino whose frontage boasted a twenty-foot screen that showed a grinning chef preparing *teppenyaki*. He felt the sweat start again.

Where might Teng, lawyer, take me? he thought. If I watch him, what will I see? Will I know it for what it is?

He needed a drink.

Across the street was a café, bright with cold, blue-white light, open to the street, candles on the tables. He jogged over to it, took a seat at the bar, and ordered Black Cat rum with ice. The bartender was a doughy boy with slicked-back hair, in an apron. He ran his fingers along the bottles, poured without a measure and placed the glass in front of Mangan with a napkin and a flourish.

"Haven't seen you in here before," he said. "Welcome."

"Haven't been in here before," Mangan said, forcing a cheeriness he did not feel. "Tell you what, I'll have a cold beer with that, too."

The boy poured him a lager, pushed it across to him.

"You know all your customers?"

"Sure, man. This place is a village. Every place, they know you."

"Really? Paramaribo's not that small."

The boy snorted. "Only half a million people in the whole country, man. And nothing to do. So we all watch each other, nose in each other's business."

He leaned back, folding his arms.

"So. Visiting? Taking a jungle trip? River boat? Monkeys? Birds? Creepy-crawlies?"

"Don't tell me. You know a guy."

The boy feigned surprise.

"You know what? I do."

Mangan laughed.

"No, just taking a look around. Thinking about some business."

"Oh, yeah? What kind of business?"

"I don't know. That's what I'm here to find out. There's a little capital looking for places to go, things to do," Mangan said conspiratorially.

The boy's eyes widened.

"No shit. Like, an investor? Here? But our economy's in the toilet, man. Fuck you gonna invest in?"

"My old dad taught me that's the time to buy. When things are cheap."

"We got casinos. You want one of them? We got a boatload of fuckin' casinos."

"I'd noticed that. Do they make money?"

"I don't know, man. They're all run by Turks. Guys from Turkey. They come here, set up a casino on every street corner." The boy had picked up a toothpick and was chewing on it.

"Who's gambling?" said Mangan.

"Every stupid fucker. Surinamers, Dutch, Chinese. Lot of Chinese."

Mangan nodded. The boy suddenly pointed at him with his toothpick.

"You thinking about that, the casinos, business and shit, there's a guy you should talk to."

"Oh yeah? Who's that?"

The boy jerked his head towards the back of the bar.

"Him."

Mangan turned to look. At a table, alone, sat a man in a tan suit, an open-necked shirt, shiny loafers. He sat with his legs crossed languidly, a pair of glasses low on his nose. Perhaps sixty, tanned, iron-grey hair. He held a document of some sort. But he was looking straight at Mangan.

"So who's that and what's he got?" Mangan said to the boy, who smirked.

"*That*, my friend, is a man who knows his way around. Everybody, he knows them. He got houses here, Martinique, Bahamas, every place."

"No kidding. You going to introduce me?"

But there was no need, because the man in the tan suit was standing next to Mangan, holding out his glass to the bartender, jiggling it from side to side in a *fill it up* motion. The doughy boy reached for an expensive, gold-coloured bottle and as he poured, he tilted his head towards Mangan.

"An investor! Looking for opportunity."

The man turned to Mangan with a warm, easy smile.

"That so? You told him there isn't any, right?" He spoke with a slight Dutch accent, a fleck of American.

He had grey eyes, a wry humour that Mangan liked immediately.

"I told him casinos," said the bartender.

"Casinos? Really? You think? I tried casinos once, a while back. I lost about a quarter of a million and some-one left a dead sloth on my doorstep."

Mangan laughed.

"A sloth? Really?"

"It's true. A sloth. At first, I didn't realise it was dead. I thought it was just not moving. You know, being a sloth. It took me a while to realise it was a threat."

Mangan and the bartender were both laughing now. The man looked wistful.

"It was a very Surinamese threat. Sort of slow-acting."

"What did you do?" said Mangan.

"Do? I got out of casinos and went to Martinique for three months."

He held out his hand.

"My name is Posthumus. Peter Posthumus."

"Philip Mangan."

"And you're here ... what, looking to invest?"

"Well, to be completely honest, I'm a journalist by trade. But I'm having a look around on behalf of a few people."

Posthumus raised his eyebrows.

"My, your people are looking far afield."

Mangan tried to turn it round.

"What's your business, if you don't mind me asking?"

"Oh, not at all. I consult, mining mainly. Gold, down in the interior, and minerals. You know this place used to do bauxite. Well, there's Chinese interest in what else is here. So I'm trying to channel that and a few other things."

"Big Chinese interest?"

Posthumus shrugged. "Is there any other kind? Maybe that's why your people are looking here, no?"

Mangan felt the ground move a little, felt his cover flex and wobble, said nothing, just gave a knowing nod.

Posthumus put his glass down on the bar and pulled out a name card from an inside pocket.

"So, if you want any help getting stuff set up—meetings, that sort of thing—I know a few people. Give us a call if there's anything I can do." He gave an apologetic smile, as if to say, *For what it's worth,* the sentiment at odds with the cool confidence, the good suit, the understated, expensive watch. And Mangan, feeling his look, read something else there, something a little too interested.

"Okay, thanks, I will," he said.

And Posthumus grinned at him and gave his upper arm a squeeze, and left. The bartender was nodding.

What the fuck was that?

23

Capital Forensics occupied a suite of offices in Silver Spring, Maryland, close to the Beltway, in a blank building of dark brick and mirrored glass. The receptionist waved Patterson through to a conference room. The document examiner—elderly, moustachioed, fussy—introduced himself as Dr. Pillsbury. He put on a pair of rubber gloves and took the notepad from Patterson with a pair of forceps, and dropped it into a plastic bag. He looked at her.

"Can I ask what sort of investigation we're talking about here? Civil? Estate? What?"

Patterson smiled. "I'd rather not say."

Dr. Pillsbury shifted in his seat.

"It helps enormously if we know what we are looking *for*," he said.

"I just need whatever you can find on that notepad."

He sighed and scratched his head.

"I mean, I need to know what *standard* you expect me to work to. Will this be evidence in a court of law?"

"I need to know everything you find. To any standard."

"You want DNA? Prints?"

She hadn't thought of that.

"Start with indented writing."

"All right." He shrugged. "May I ask who you represent?"

"No, you may not."

He raised his eyebrows, picked up the plastic bag containing the notepad and left without a word.

Dr. Pillsbury called the following afternoon, was about to tell Patterson what he'd found on the phone when she stopped him, saying she'd be there within the hour. She ran from the Embassy without telling Tipton or Markham, hailed a cab, and looked from the rear window as it drove away.

Pillsbury was waiting for her in the same conference room, a plastic transparency in front of him on the table. He held it up to the light for her.

997488673364
VCCSVGV1
Raafveugel YF Trusts Inc. PO Box 3364.
Paramaribo. Suriname

"It was written quickly, but deliberately, by hand," said Pillsbury. "The pressure is firm, the intent is to pass on important information. The writer was writing for clarity. You can see the indentations, very clear, very distinct."

He pointed at the transparency, the revealed writing.

"You know what it is?"

"Yes," said Patterson. It was an account number, followed by a BIC identifier. So, a bank, but where?

"The bank is in the British Virgin Islands," Pillsbury said. He had allowed a little smirk to form at the corners of his mouth, pleased with himself. "I looked it up. It's a small outfit called Berhasil Clearing Ltd."

Patterson turned to him.

"And what else did you look up?"

He blinked.

"Well, I just wanted to see—"

"It might be best if you didn't investigate any further."

"I thought you might not—"

"I might not what?"

"I wanted to make sure you knew what we had found. That's all."

"Thank you. I'm well aware. And I expect you will not retain any record of what you found."

He was looking at her, alarmed now, his mouth working.

"No," he said. "No, I won't."

"Don't," she said.

She ended up paying in cash, peeling off hundred-dollar bills beneath the eyes of the bemused cashier, wondering how the hell she'd expense it. She stood outside in the warm breeze, watching the traffic rocket by, waiting for a taxi, staying aware. She wondered if Polk would pay, and found the thought of meeting him, talking to him, strangely comforting.

The thought of Hopko, less so.

Patterson waited until Markham and Tipton had gone for lunch, then called on a secure line from the Station to tell her about Wachapreague and the notepad.

There was silence on the line.

"Val, are you there?"

"Well, that was very enterprising of you."

Patterson swallowed. Hopko spoke slowly, in a tone of preternatural calm.

"You'll send the details, and the notepad, to me."

What am I not understanding here? wondered Patterson.

"And what about the FBI? I'll have to tell them."

"Really? Why?"

"Well, it's evidence."

"It's evidence you've tampered with, my girl. Your Mr. Polk will be frightfully upset."

Christ.

"Trish, you will keep the channel open with Polk, do you understand? Tell him where you've been. Let him fulminate. But do not give him the bank account."

There's something here.

"Can I ask why?"

That pause again, the Hopko pause. The silent sound of calculation.

"No, you may not."

24

Lawyer Teng, it appeared, lived within walking distance of his office. Mangan, on day three, summoned up the nerve to follow him, at a distance, when he left Prins Hendrickstraat. He carried his briefcase, walked alone, and for twelve minutes wound his way west and then north to a low, gated, single-storey house painted in cerise and festooned with flowering plants. Lawyer Teng unlocked the gate with a key from his pocket and, as far as Mangan could tell, passed an evening of domesticity.

Mangan returned to the Buena Vista hotel, spiralling through dark, empty streets. At the hotel, some new guests had checked in. Mangan heard them in the stairwell, speaking loud, accented Mandarin. A trade delegation, said the woman at the front desk. From China.

"Really?" said Mangan. "What are they trading in, do you know?"

The woman made a wry face.

"Everything. Buildings, casinos, gold, supermarkets. They buy the whole country, then they sell it back to us," she said, becoming animated. "We cannot compete

with them. And if you complain, then, well, just a big
dyugu-dyugu."

Mangan nodded, extricated himself from the conversation, and stood in the stairwell, listening.

On day four, he hired a car from a rental place near the
waterfront, paying cash in advance. He parked on Prins
Hendrickstraat, watched lawyer Teng leave his office
for lunch, which he took alone at Toothsome Chinese,
emerging wiping his mouth with a napkin. The target
then attended a meeting at a suite of offices near the
presidential palace, subject unknown. Mangan then
completely lost him, the entire afternoon a blank, only
picking him up again later, on his way home. After dark
he drove to the lawyer's home, parked near the house,
watched an elderly woman come out with a watering
can, stopping laboriously at each pot, her hand quivering
with the weight of the can. The windows flickered silver
blue with the television screen.

The utter futility of what he was doing was starting
to become apparent to him. He sat in the car, wound the
window down and lit a cigarette. What should he do?
Burgle the offices? How? How would he know when
he had found what he was looking for? Confront Teng?
And say what, exactly? He began to think about how he
would explain all this to Hopko, her searing response.
He pulled away, ate fried noodles and chicken and *sambal* at a little Javanese place, before passing a restless
night in the hotel.

On day five, he sat in the restaurant in the morning, watching lawyer Teng arrive for work by car. Mangan had not
seen the car before, a blue SUV. The car had a driver, who
lingered outside. Lawyer Teng entered his office, only to
emerge moments later and climb back into the SUV.

Mangan walked quickly to his hire car. By the time he'd turned around and pulled out, the blue SUV was nowhere to be seen. He sped up the street, checking each way at every intersection.

There it was, stuck half a block ahead, trying to nose out onto a busier thoroughfare. Mangan slipped in two cars behind. Any attempt at discretion abandoned, he struggled simply to keep the blue SUV in sight. At a tricky right turn, he narrowly missed a kid on a moped, jammed on the brakes, and the whole street seemed to be shouting and honking at him. The SUV was picking up speed, heading away from the centre of the city, onto quieter roads lined with scrub and new-growth forest. Mangan fell back, his knuckles white on the wheel, and checked his mirrors. He had no idea where he was. The SUV was turning into a dusty car park.

Paramaribo Zoo.

Mangan parked, watching in his mirror. Lawyer Teng got out of his car and put on a white floppy sun hat. He stood for a moment, looked around, as if searching for someone, then went to buy a ticket and walked purposefully into the zoo. Mangan waited a moment, then stepped from the car, feeling the heat like a walk-in oven. He felt feverish, his mouth dry. He leaned for a moment against the car, then made for the ticket booth and through the front gate. He could smell the reek of the animal cages on the air, heard the yowl of peacocks. He followed a sandy path past the ostrich enclosure, a tree draped in howler monkeys. The zoo was mostly empty of people, a few schoolchildren, the odd tourist. He paused to watch a jaguar, its maddened pacing along the bars, back and forth, back and forth. There was no one behind him, but even so he jogged off the path into the forest, then doubled back. Nothing.

Teng was sitting at a concrete picnic table, his white

sun hat visible from a distance. He was alone, but Mangan saw vigilance in him, in his looking about, checking his watch. Mangan cut a slow, wide arc around him, keeping him in sight, absorbing himself in a dusty iguana, otters, owls. He was sweating profusely, his heart pounding.

When Mangan looked back, a man in a pale green polo shirt and shorts had come out of nowhere and was approaching Teng. Teng clearly recognised him, half stood to greet him, then sat again, indicating that Polo Shirt should sit too. Polo Shirt was also of East Asian appearance, middle-aged, with a paunch; ungainly, pre-occupied. He sat, then signalled to someone just out of Mangan's vision to say he would be only a couple of minutes. The two men talked. Lawyer Teng seemed to be asking questions, the other man giving short replies.

Mangan moved carefully on, taking himself out of vision for a few moments, behind a reptile enclosure. He leaned against its plywood wall, breathed deeply, then emerged the other side. The two men were still there, and perhaps thirty or forty feet away from them, at another picnic table, sat two women, also Asian. One older, one younger.

Mangan eased himself closer.

The younger one was very pale and wore spectacles, her hair shoulder length, dressed carelessly. She seemed flushed with the heat, bothered, recalcitrant. The older woman sat very still, unmoving, as if she wished to be anywhere but where she was. The two men were still talking. But then they both stood abruptly, Polo Shirt looking around himself intently. Mangan turned away, too quickly, he knew, busied himself with an enclosure that was, he discovered, empty. He wandered off, his back still to them, shaky now.

What had he just seen?

When he turned back, lawyer Teng was gone, and Polo Shirt was leading the two women back towards the car park, chivvying them along. They looked like a family, the three of them, a dispirited family, amid a dull and incomprehensible holiday, waiting around in the heat while Father conducts brief, intense meetings with lawyers who are linked to Chinese intelligence.

As they walked away, the younger one—the daughter?—turned and looked straight at Mangan.

He abandoned any hope of following either Teng or the family. He drove back to the Buena Vista, crashed and slept for four hours, waking less feverish but weak and listless in the freezing air conditioning. He lay on the bed for a while and turned on the television, a news channel, a meat-faced British anchor rumbling earnestly on, the lack of comprehension in his eyes. He drank a litre of water, forced himself to sit up. He seemed ridiculous to himself.

That evening, Mangan sat in the Mazda down the street from Teng's house as the sun turned the palm trees to black shadows. He saw the woman come out and water the flowers, and wondered if he was reading far too much significance into the meeting at the zoo. He still felt ill, his limbs heavy and aching, a featheriness in his head. He was appalled by his own clumsiness, and was feeling his incompetence like a welt when he remembered the younger woman's eyes on him. Surely, she had made him? Sitting in the car now, hour after hour, felt like penance for his own ineptitude, his own vanity. *Surveillance? How hard can it be?*

But at nine, as he was admitting defeat and hunger and was allowing himself to contemplate a cold beer and a burger and bed, a yellow taxi pulled up, leaving its engine running and its lights on. The front door opened, and a figure emerged, moving quickly. Mangan saw the stiffness, the slight stoop. He started the car, let the taxi pull away before turning on his lights, and pulled out after it.

It turned out to be a short journey, terminating in a car park outside Club Ruby, a vile-looking place, decked out like a hacienda and lit up like a steamboat. But lawyer Teng was positively scampering up its steps, clearly anticipating something. Mangan paid protection on his car to a boy in a baseball cap and went in.

It was the usual thing, he saw, with sinking heart: the would-be hard men on the door and behind the bar with their shaved heads and the stupid tattoos, shatteringly loud music, ultraviolet light that made everyone's teeth float around in the darkness, the smell of dry ice, cigarettes, cleaning fluid, perfume and body odour. And there were the strung-out girls pumped full of silicon draped on the banquettes, sad simulacra of the women in magazines and on porn sites, while their eyes said closure, attenuation. The über brothel of the world—same in Bangkok, Addis, Santiago, same in Cape Town, Moscow, Jakarta, the same sticky tables, the same pointlessness.

Lawyer Teng had taken a booth and one of the bartenders was there with a bottle of Chivas, ice, tumblers, ducking his head deferentially. So, lawyer Teng is a regular, and a tipper. Mangan eased back into shadow and ordered a Coke, considering how long he should stay. Long enough to see a squad of girls forming a perimeter around Teng's table, one now sashaying over to him, bending over, running a finger down his lapel, asking him something. Teng shook his head, and the girl, rebuffed, walked away, smiling.

There is a moment, recognisable to an experienced operative, when, after weeks of preparation and cultivation, months of effort, years even, an operation flickers into life, when the hard little bead of possibility breaks open to reveal the actual. A journalist knows the moment, too, that second when the shape of the story starts to show itself, its scope, its layers of meaning. The moment may come with the acquisition of a specific piece of information, or the making of a connection, or an event. Or it may be something far smaller, an inconsistency, a gesture, a look on someone's face that tells of a lie.

Mangan, over his many years as a reporter, knew such moments and could sense their presence.

And as he watched, Teng looked up and greeted a man in a green polo shirt—the same man who he had met at the zoo. The two of them sat and leaned in, talking intently, Teng tapping the table as if describing his dispositions. And as the music clanged and blared, and the girls' eyes flickered and lingered in the gloom, and as Teng took something from his pocket, clamped it in his fist and then pushed it across the table to Polo Shirt, who palmed it quickly and stuffed it in his trouser pocket, Mangan knew that he was in such a moment.

The two men looked at each other with a sense of finality and accomplishment and understanding, picked up their whisky glasses and drained them. Polo Shirt reclined, relaxing now, his eyes moving to the girls, and Teng leaned over and gave him a tap on the chest with the back of his hand and pointed to a languorous, wide-hipped girl in a white clingy dress and bronze eyeshadow. Polo Shirt's eyed moved up and down her, then skated away to the others, comparing.

And Mangan knew he had to move very carefully and very fast.

25

To Mangan's right sat a girl in jeans and a leopard-print top which fell from one bronzed shoulder. Her hair was long and loose, and her gold jewellery cheap and thin. Venezuelan, perhaps? She sensed him looking and turned to him with a high-wattage smile, a full, deep smile, the ultraviolet light rendering her skeletal. She walked over, and Mangan gave her an encouraging nod. She slid onto a chair next to him and touched his arm.

"Hey, baby," she said.

"Hi there," said Mangan. "Do you speak English?"

"Yes, baby. I speak whatever you want. My name Eva." She held out a hand. Mangan shook it, feeling cool, dry skin.

"Well, Eva, let me buy you a drink, and then I want to ask you something."

She ordered vodka, which she drank through a little straw, her big eyes on him.

"Eva, you see that man over there, in the green shirt?"

"Yes, baby."

"Well, I need to know who he is."

"You ask him."

"No. I don't want to talk to him."

She was losing interest fast, her eyes skating around the room.

"Well, I don't know, baby."

"Eva, I'll pay you a hundred dollars if you go over to him and talk to him, and find out what his name is, or where he's staying or anything at all."

"Hundred dollars? U.S.?"

"Two hundred."

Her eyes widened. Then she frowned.

"Why you want to know?"

"There's no problem. I just need to know."

"You are police?"

"No. No, nothing like that."

"Oh baby, you are police."

"Really, I promise. Not police."

"So why?"

Mangan leaned into her.

"I am a journalist."

She looked at him, wondering.

"Journalist? Like, newspaper."

"Yes! That's right. It's a big story. And I need you to help me."

She looked back at Polo Shirt, considering.

"He is bad man?"

"No. He's okay. Just…some business. We need to be quick, Eva, or he might go with another girl."

"Maybe he don't want talk to me."

"You're beautiful, he'll talk to you."

She rolled her eyes, made a face at him.

"Three hundred, Eva." He took a one-hundred-dollar bill and gave it to her. She put it in her purse with a sigh.

"After you've spoken to him, you come outside. I'll be waiting in my car. I'll wait for you."

"You want to know—"

"Anything. Who he is. Where he's staying, his name, where he's from. Try for me, okay?"

She looked back at him, tilting her head slightly to one side, as if to ask him, *What are you making me do?* Then she stood up—tall, slender—and walked across the dance floor towards lawyer Teng and Polo Shirt.

Mangan sat in the car in the dark, watching. Just after eleven, Teng came out, by himself. He was very drunk and he looked around, bewildered. A taxi driver went to him, took him by the arm and guided him to a cab.

No sign of Polo Shirt or Eva. Mangan smoked while he waited, jabbed his fingernails in his wrist to stay awake.

At eleven thirty-three, there she was. She walked out of the front doors quickly, her face down. The doorman said something to her but she ignored him. When she got to the bottom of the steps she looked up, searching the car park. Mangan was up and out of the car. She saw him. When she got into the car, he smelled cigarette smoke and sweat on her. He started the car and drove in what he thought was the direction of the city centre. She was silent, looked straight ahead. When he saw a quiet side street, he turned down it and pulled over.

"So? Eva?"

She turned to him and her face was set, hard.

"Eva?"

"You have my money?"

"Are you okay?"

A car passed behind them, its headlights sliding over her face and he saw that her mascara was smudged and her face was older, the lines around the eyes showing. We call them girls, he thought, though they're women. And her lip, he saw, was fattened and split.

"What happened?" he said.

"So I go talk to him, and he want to go to the room, so we go upstairs." She stopped, looking straight ahead.

Mangan waited.

"And then..." Her voice tailed off.

"What happened?"

She just shook her head.

"You say three hundred."

"Yes."

She took a deep breath.

"I ask him, but he don't say nothing."

"Nothing at all?"

She just shook her head.

"He don't want to talk. I say, where you from, baby? You from China? Where? He just tell me shut up."

"What about—"

"I try. I say, 'Where you stay? You stay in Paramaribo? You very wealthy guy, baby, I can tell, you stay at Torarica?' He just say no, shut up." She had started to cry a little, the tears welling, on the edge of spilling onto her cheeks.

"Eva, I—"

"Don't give me bullshit. You are bullshit. You say he's not bad guy."

"I didn't know."

"Fuck you. Bullshit."

Mangan swallowed.

"What happened?"

"He tell me shut up. Then he hit me. Then he fuck me."

She wiped her eyes with the back of her hand. Mangan looked away.

"You see?" she said. He turned back to her and she was examining the front of her flimsy little leopard-skin top, smoothing it out, picking at it, and Mangan saw that it was stained, and understood that the stains were blood. *You see?*

"Three hundred, you say you will give me."

Mangan reached in his pocket, pulled out a wad of bills. He counted them out and added another hundred and she took them without a glance.

"I'm so sorry," he said.

She was making to open the door, readying to get out, when she stopped, pursed her lips, wiped her eyes again.

"He is from America, USA."

Mangan sat very still.

"His name, Tao. T-A-O. Mitchell Tao."

"I thought you said—"

"He went in the bathroom. His pants on the bed. I look in his wallet. Driver's licence from Maryland, USA."

"Eva—"

She got out of the car but then turned, leaned back in and tossed something in his lap.

"And this."

A matchbook. The Regal Hotel, Paramaribo.

"You never talk to me again. Never."

She slammed the door hard, and walked off into the night.

26

It was the ghastly Black Rooster again. Patterson got there first, after an hour-long surveillance detection run, cutting over towards Georgetown and along the river for a bit, then cabbing it to Dupont and spiralling her way back down to M Street in the soft evening light, through the college kids and the commuter crowd and a group of bowler-hatted black guys busking on trombones. Not much, but preferable to nothing at all.

Is that what this is? Playing at being operational?

But then she remembered the charred house by the bay, Molly Monroe's hair stuck to her hand. Washington. Just beneath the surface it was foul with secrets.

She took a seat and ordered a glass of red. And then Polk was standing over her in his awful suit, breathing hard, trying not to show it. She looked up at him. He held his hands out.

"Patterson," he said.

"It's Trish," she said.

"Gesundheit."

He turned to look for a waiter.

"In England," she said, "we don't have waiters in pubs."

"Really? You amaze me."

"Detracts from the authentic pub experience, in my view."

"Jeez, you detract much more from this place, there'll be nothing left but the smell."

"You said it."

"That's why it suits me." He ordered a pale ale in a bottle and sat with his hands on the table, as if to show he wasn't about to reach for his Glock.

"So, Patterson. Why the urgency? Is there a flap? That's what you guys call it, isn't it? A *flap*?"

All right, she thought. Go carefully. Don't explain, just tell.

"So. I went to see the wife. Molly. In hospital."

"Excuse me?"

"I went—"

"I heard what you said, Patterson, I'm wondering why the fuck you would do that."

Oh, shit. Push on.

"Did you know they had a cottage? Like a vacation home?"

He said nothing, but those blue eyes were locked on her.

"I went and took a look," she said.

He allowed his head to fall forward and his eyebrows to shoot up. Still, she pushed on.

"It's in a place called Wachapreague. That's down in Virginia, on the coast."

"I know where it is, Patterson."

"Yes. Well. Someone had searched it. And then tried to burn it. The house."

He started to rub his chin.

"And there was someone there, keeping watch. Gave me a bit of a fright, I don't mind telling you."

He was starting to do his writhing thing.

"Okay. I see. A bit of a fright," he said. He was staring at her now, wide-eyed. "What else d'you find?"

She paused, took a sip of her wine, working the moment.

"Might need your SCIF at this point, Franklin."

He brought his fist down with a crash on the table. She managed not to jump, just watched him. At other tables, customers were looking over at them.

"What else?" he hissed.

"Best get some of your chaps down there with the crime-scene tape."

"What. Else."

She shifted register, dropped the facetiousness.

"Nothing. I took a quick look in. It's a wreck. There had been a search."

"You touch anything?"

"No."

"Nothing at all?"

"Nothing."

Polk had narrowed his eyes, breathing heavily.

"You sure about that, Patterson?"

She stared him down, heart accelerating. But she had the sense that his anger was directed less at her and more towards some predicament of his own that she couldn't fathom. She wasn't unnerved by him, for all the bluster.

"And this guy? Keeping watch?" he said.

"I just glimpsed him as I was pulling away. Slim guy, in a hoodie, just crept out of nowhere."

"Age? Ethnicity?"

"No idea."

"You touch any fucking thing in that house?"

She didn't reply, just picked up her wine glass, sipped.

"Jesus *fucking* Christ."

"Frankie?"

"Don't you dare ask me shit."

"Share, Frankie. What else have you got on the woman? Monroe's love interest?"

Polk sat back, pulled on the beer again.

"Tell me, Frankie."

"Nothing. We don't know who she is. Was. Whatever."

"You must be able—"

"There's no case."

"No case?" She was incredulous.

"What do you want us to do? Monroe's dead. His wife isn't implicated. The Asian lady's mystery meat. We don't have a suspect. What am I talking about? We don't even have an allegation. No case."

"You're dropping it?"

"What's to drop?" he said. "Don't look at me like that, sweetheart. I'm law enforcement, remember. You bring me evidence of an operation and I'll be on it like fleas on a beagle. Until then, fuck you."

She didn't know what to say. He finished his beer, the mouth of the bottle making a *plock* sound as he pulled it from his lips. He was readying to leave.

"You saw the wife, in the hospital," he said.

"Yes."

"How'd she look?"

"Not good."

"That is not a well woman."

"Do they know what's wrong with her?" she asked.

"No. They were talking about stress, and then about a virus, and Guillain-Barré. You know what that is?" He had calmed down a bit, and Patterson thought she glimpsed empathy in him, kindness even, behind those crystalline eyes.

"No. What is it?"

He shook his head. "It's like a post-viral thing. You get neuropathy, pain in your hands and feet." He wiggled his fingers. "Then it spreads. She's complaining of pain

Someone, probably Jonathan Monroe, deceased intelligence doyen and adulterer and liar, had a secret bank account in one of the least accessible offshore secrecy jurisdictions in the world. And it was linked to a PO Box in Suriname.

She liked Polk.

And now she'd lied to him. The lie, light and pretty as a petal.

She left the pub, turned onto 19th and walked north. It was almost dark, still warm. The traffic had thinned and the sidewalks were empty. She walked past a restaurant—*Oysters! Steak!*—and glimpsed candlelight, tulips of red wine in the fists of grey-haired men who leaned and murmured. Polk's kind of place, she thought. Big, meaty, white. A Washington restaurant, where the dishes are accompanied in her legs and arms. So they think maybe that, but they don't know."

He was watching her closely now.

"What do you want me to say, Frankie? I'm not a doctor."

He nodded as if he'd confirmed something.

"You always such a hardass, Patterson?"

The question surprised her.

"Only around other hardasses."

He snorted. "Jesus. What's that, an offer of friendship?"

"In your dreams. Don't stop talking to me, Frankie."

"Don't tamper. I mean it."

"Nothing to tamper with. You've dropped—"

But he was up and gone. She sat a while longer, ordered another glass of red and let the noise of the pub wash over her, its sticky tables and air-conditioned reek, the haggard after-work drinkers, eyes bright with exhaustion, reaching for the bottle.

PART THREE

The Tell

29

At Sibley Memorial Hospital, Trish Patterson waited in a corridor. She had to be accompanied into the Intensive Care Unit, where Molly Monroe now resided. This time, there was a cop on the door. A male nurse in green scrubs took her in. Molly was connected to a welter of tubes and monitors. She was barely conscious, her eyes open but glassy. She was entirely bald, all her hair had gone, and she had wasted away. Patterson felt a jolt of shock.

"What happened to her hair?" she asked the nurse.

"It fell out," he said.

Patterson gave him a direct look.

"Thank you," she said. "I can see that. Can you tell me why?"

"I'm not at liberty to discuss her case with you. You are not family."

Patterson sat by the bed, laid her hand on Molly's.

"She's paralysed, isn't she?"

There was a pause while the nurse wrestled with the question.

"Yes. She has lost the use of her arms and legs over the last few days."

"And soon it'll be her breathing, won't it?"

"I can't—"

"Her diaphragm will become paralysed too, won't it? And she won't be able to breathe."

"I—"

"What have they tested for?"

"Everything."

"And?"

"I think you know."

"It's a heavy metal, isn't it? Thallium?"

The nurse sighed.

"Is she still able to speak?"

The nurse just shook his head.

"The cops have been?" said Patterson.

"They were called in three days ago."

"What did they say?"

The nurse shrugged. "They tried to ask her questions, but she couldn't really reply. So they took photographs and left."

Patterson bent over Molly, searching for any sign of recognition in the woman's eyes. But as she did so, Molly stiffened and let out a long, keening wail. Patterson took a step back. For a moment she thought she saw fear on the woman's face, but the look guttered and vanished and Molly convulsed violently, her torso arching off the bed and quivering, the cry turning to a choking, attenuated rattle.

The nurse said "Oh, God," and hit a button on the wall, and in a moment two more nurses appeared, but there seemed to be little for them to do, other than to ensure that Molly didn't propel herself off the bed. She was struggling for air now, her breath coming in snorting, animal gasps. Patterson slipped out of the room, took the stairs down and ran out into the night.

It had rained and the trees were wet and filled with the soughing of the cicadas. She walked quickly away from the hospital and wondered at her own disgust, the deep roiling of her anger.

Polk was angry, too, though Patterson was coming to understand that anger was a part of his state of being, a sort of incredulous fury at the state of things. They were at a kebab place on N and Polk was inhaling charred cubes of lamb and rice and peppers.

"Now we've got a case," he said. He framed a headline with his fingers. "We've got a doozy of a case. And it's a homicide. A *homicide*, Patterson. A suspected fucking poisoning, using methods from fucking Torquemada, or Saddam. Just fucking baroque. Who knew?" He tore off a piece of bread, rammed it in his mouth, chewed. "So who the fuck is a suspect? What do you say, Patterson? Who did it?" He wasn't looking at her, instead concentrating on his food.

Patterson nursed a plastic bowl of spinach and lentil soup.

"They've done tests on the house, by now, surely? Did they find the source?"

"Nope. There are traces where she threw up, but all the foodstuffs are clean."

"So someone fed it to her in a restaurant. Or a delivery? Takeout, maybe?"

Polk just chewed, saying nothing.

"The Chinese don't do this, Frankie."

"Don't do what?"

"Poison the wives of their own agents. It's not like them."

"Thing is, Patterson, why'd they do it? Whoever did it. Why?"

"Well, she knew something."

"What'd she know?"

"I don't know, Frankie. She knew his friends. She knew his history. She knew his movements, his bank balance. She knew stuff that would correlate when you walked back the cat. When he was here. When he was away. When he got funny phone calls late at night. Sudden unexpected trips out of town, purpose not entirely clear. She knew Nicole."

Polk looked up.

"She knew who, now?"

"Oh. Nothing."

"What did you just say?"

Idiot.

"Frankie, have you put a tail on me?" she said quickly.

"Why would we do that?"

"Have you?"

He looked right at her.

"No. We have not. And you can take that to the bank. You being tailed?"

She nodded. Polk thought about it, chewing.

"Huh," he said. "Who the fuck is Nicole?"

"It's nothing, Frankie, it's not relevant."

"Well, it sure sounded like you thought it was relevant."

"It's not."

He dropped his fork on his plate and wiped his mouth.

"Something about me, Patterson," he said, "I bear grudges. Just so's you know." And with that he rose and walked out of the restaurant.

30

Pearl's father had not spoken to her in four days. Not a word as they left the hotel in Paramaribo, not a word on the plane, not a word as they landed at Dulles, not a word on the interminable taxi ride home, the Beltway jammed, a sea of red brake lights blurred by rain, and not a word since.

Now he ignored her across the dinner table as he shovelled *jiaozi* into his mouth, leaning over his bowl, the tablecloth spattered with vinegar. Her mother sat in silence, too. She was pale, emotionally drained. Pearl felt the atmosphere as explosive, fraught with potential energy, requiring only the tiniest catalyst to turn kinetic.

She pushed a *jiaozi* around her bowl, watching the dark vinegar pool, the flabby dough break apart and the pork and chives and fat spill out.

She put her chopsticks down and pushed her chair away from the table. Her mother looked up at her, the worry soaking her gaze.

"I think I'll go do some work," Pearl said. She walked across the room to the stairs, looked back towards her father.

"I don't know what I did," she said. "All I did was talk to some random guy in a hotel coffee shop. I don't know why this has caused you to freak out. I genuinely don't—leaving aside the whole question of the bizarre nature of our so-called vacation, and your weird behaviour, which is hard, trust me. But if we are going to fix this, you are going to have to communicate." It sounded like a little speech.

Her father didn't look at her, just continued eating.

"Should I say it in Mandarin?" she said. Her mother was shaking her head, fear in her eyes. *Don't*. Her father didn't respond.

She went to her room, undressed, got into bed with her laptop and put Bach on her headphones—the E major Partita. She had no email and no messages, apart from one from Cal, which was just a question mark and a smiley emoji, and an abrupt acknowledgement from Telperion that they had received her security clearance forms and submitted them.

With someone named Beetle absent from the relatives' column.

She leaned over to turn off her bedside light. But then the door crashed open, and her father stood there, in hiking boots and a waterproof.

"You get up," he said.

Pearl pulled the blanket up to her chin.

"What? Really, Dad? What are you doing?"

Without a word he walked across the room, ripping the blanket from her grip and off the bed, grabbing hold of her arm, pulling her upright, hard.

"Get up. Get dressed."

"Dad, what are you *doing*?" She was shaking, on the edge of tears.

"*Now!*"

She put on her glasses, pulled on jeans, her Hopkins T-shirt, pink sneakers, her hands trembling as she fumbled with the laces. He was standing by the door, waiting. They went down the stairs and to the garage. Her mother was nowhere to be seen.

"We take your car," he said. "You drive." She got into the red Honda, and her father was putting a shovel on the back seat.

"Dad?" she said quietly.

"Shut up," he said. They took 29 north, past the Beltway, the suburbs thinning. They had almost reached the Patuxent River when he told her to turn off. They wound through some darkened subdivisions, neat places with lawns and playsets and mailboxes and minivans in the driveways, places that spoke to Pearl of normality, of comfort. He made her pull into a parking lot adjoining a neighbourhood sports field.

Her father shoved her out of the car and they walked past the silent baseball diamond and a little skate park towards a stand of trees. He carried the shovel and a flashlight and a handheld, the screen silvering his face in the darkness. At the treeline he stopped and looked around.

"What are we doing here, Dad?"

"You look for a little blue tag. On a tree, or bush, something," he said.

"What? What is it?"

"Just look."

There it was, on a scrubby sapling, eight inches or so above the ground, a piece of blue duct tape. She saw it first, in the beam of the flashlight. Her father went to it, scratched aside leaf litter and twigs, started to dig. A few inches down, he knelt, feeling around with his fingers, starting to work something free. He couldn't get it out at first, so he took the shovel again and loosened the earth around it.

Pearl just stood and watched. She was cold. The thing in the hole was in a black plastic bin liner, heavy, perhaps half a cubic foot in size. Her father wrenched it free from the soil and filled the hole in, then spent some time covering the surface with leaf litter, trying to mask the depression in the soil. He took the blue duct tape off the sapling, picking at it with his fingers. The park was quiet, but he was watchful, scanning the approach to the treeline. He picked up the thing, whatever it was, and they made their way quickly back to the car.

He said nothing at all as she drove, just worked at his fingernails, trying to get the dirt out.

Back in the garage, he took the thing to his workbench. He handed her a box cutter.

"Cut the wrapping off. Take it out," he said.

She swallowed.

"Dad, I don't want to do this, whatever it is."

"You do it. Now."

She sliced open the bin liner.

The money was all in old twenties, in wads of maybe a thousand held together with elastic bands. There must have been a hundred thousand or more. She didn't know what to do. Her father stood behind her. She could hear his breathing. And she felt a sensation almost like falling, this new knowledge propelling her into new understandings of who she was—what she was.

"What's this for?" was all she said.

He didn't answer, but stepped around her, his shoulder brushing against hers. He picked up a wad of bills and turned to her. He leaned down, held the bills in front of her face.

"We do this for us," he said, "For me, for you, for our family."

He stared at her, and she sensed his fury, his fissile nature.

"It is for all of us. Family. You will understand this."

Ask, and risk his anger? Or stay silent and comply?

Choose silence. Choose safety, no matter how temporary.

"Go to bed," he said.

She looked down, walked to the door.

"Pearl," he said.

She stopped, waited.

"You tell anyone, you put your family in danger. Mama, me, Auntie, Nai-nai, everyone. You put them in danger."

And as she stood there, under the neon lights of the garage, shock and tears in her eyes, her throat, she understood that until now she had thought her world was one way, when in fact it was another. And now her father was revealing the real world to her, little piece by little piece, so her view of it was always incomplete, rendering her unable to give an account of it, even if she tried. And only at some point in the future would its true, awful shape be apparent.

31

As the plane banked, turning into its approach, Mangan saw a vast, brown, angular building surrounded by an ocean of cars, and realised he was looking at the Pentagon. He sat back, closed his eyes. By the time he was at passport control, he'd be exhibiting every indicator of anxiety and deception: perspiration, hyper-vigilance, fidgeting. They'd read him like a bloody book.

The queue at immigration was long. He stood beneath the surveillance cameras, amid the families chattering in Spanish, the tourists, the students. He took out his book, read while the queue inched forward, yearning to lose himself for a minute or two.

The officer's name badge said Alvarez. She was petite in her blue uniform, dark-haired, glasses. She didn't look at him as she fingerprinted him and made him stare into a camera.

"What brings you to the United States, sir?"

"Just a visit. Holiday," he said.

A pause. She looked from his passport to him to the computer screen.

"And how long are you planning on staying?"

"Two weeks."

"Mm-hmm. And are you going to do any work while you're here?"

"No. Just holiday."

She looked at the passport.

"What do you do, sir? What's your job?"

"I'm a journalist."

"Cool. Who you write for?"

"I'm freelance. I have my own website."

"You going to do any writing while you're here?"

"No. No work at all."

"C'mon. You guys are always working."

"Not me."

"And you're coming from Suriname. Was that work?"

"No. Just travel."

She paused, studying the screen. Looked at his passport again.

"Where are you staying while you're here?"

"Oh. I have an address. I booked it online. It's a room."

"Like, in a hotel?"

"No. In a house." He made a show of searching in his pockets, pulled out a scrap of paper. "It's in ... Brookland."

"Brookland. Sure."

She nodded, as if he finally made sense. The *slunk* sound of the stamp on the passport, and he was headed, shakily, to baggage claim. Outside, on the pavement, he lit a cigarette, feeling the fear rising like vapour in him.

Her phone rang.

"Patterson."

"I have your husband on the line."

Patterson opened her mouth to tell the operator that she did not, in fact, have a husband, but stopped herself.

"Thank you," she said. There was a click on the line, then a voice.

"Hello? Trish?"

"Who is this?"

"Trish, it's Philip."

She sat forward in her chair, put her hand over the receiver but said nothing.

"I'm outside," came the voice.

What?

"Trish, you there?"

She swallowed.

"Yes."

"Will you come down? I'm outside."

Jesus moustachioed Christ.

"Stay there."

She left the Station, ran down to the foyer and walked out onto Mass. Ave.

And there he was, tall, angular, a little stooped, hands jammed in pockets. He was standing some distance away on the sidewalk, off to the left, too far to see his expression with any clarity. He wore jeans and some sort of grubby jacket. She turned right, walked briskly towards downtown. It was a beautiful, crisp, early fall day, the leaves turning, little flecks of gold. After a couple of hundred yards, she glanced back, and he was following her. Improvising frantically, she jogged across the street, and walked into the park that faced the Embassy, past the monument to Khalil Gibran. It would, she thought, be difficult to imagine a less appropriate location for a crash meeting between agent and handler. The park was thickly wooded, little paths winding between the trees. She slowed, letting Mangan catch up.

Where the hell was he?

She stopped and turned. No sign of him. Dear God, she'd lost him. Should she go back and look?

And then, ambling round a bend in the path, he appeared, walked unhurriedly towards her—he even gave her a wave. And then he was standing in front of her. He was tanned, and he looked older, the cheeks and mouth a little harder. A little more lined. He looked unkempt, the red hair long, a mess. For a moment she was speechless.

Patterson had had a physics teacher once, at her comprehensive in Nottingham, who had pushed her, trying to get her to believe in herself. A great, craggy man in a cardigan, face like a serving dish; thick, hairy arms. Mr. Cranley. He'd kept her after class, looked right into her with eyes that said he'd seen thousands upon thousands of scrappy, sullen teenagers but that the one he was looking at right now mattered. He'd been the one who'd told her to buck her ideas up and go to college. The way Mangan looked at her now reminded her of Mr. Cranley. Not brittle, not domineering or defensive, like the men she'd dealt with in the army and in the Service; just intent, searching, affirming.

"Hello, Trish," he said. He was wearing his grin, but there was strain in it.

"Philip, are you under surveillance now?"

"I don't think so. No."

"If we are interrupted, you will be at the bar, at the E Street cinema, at 21:30 hours tomorrow. Do you understand?"

He nodded.

She suddenly wanted to hug him, the urge taking her powerfully, but she didn't. Neither of them said anything for a moment. Then she spoke quickly.

"Philip, what the gilded fuck are you doing here?"

"I can explain all this."

"I hope so. But not here, not now."

"Okay, not here, but Trish, you need to listen."

"Don't tell me what I need to do, please."

He closed his eyes and nodded in self-reproach.

"Where can we talk?" he said.

"Why have you not communicated with London?"

"I had...visitors. They told me the comms were compromised."

"So you just stopped using them."

"Well...yes."

"What were you doing in Suriname?"

He opened his mouth, closed it again. He looked genuinely shocked.

"How did you know?"

"I work for an intelligence agency, Philip."

He looked so deflated, she almost wanted to laugh.

"Look," she said, "there's a motel on Route One in College Park. It's a Motel 6. Come tonight—9:10 p.m. exactly. I'll meet you outside, and we'll go in separately."

He frowned.

"Is that secure?"

"Is that *secure*?" she said, disbelieving. "Is your being here secure? Is your calling me in the Embassy secure? *Hello, it's Philip, I'm outside.* For Christ's sake. Not exactly Moscow bloody rules, is it? And your bimble around South America? Was that secure?"

She made to walk away, but turned back to him.

"Just...just don't get your hopes up," she said.

He sagged slightly, ran his fingers through his hair. And she let her gaze linger on him for a moment, felt the pull of him. She didn't want to leave, to her surprise.

"It's important, Trish," he said.

"Good. It better be," she said. She walked away.

They sat on the bed, traffic rattling the windows. The room smelled of toilet cleaner and old cigarettes. They left the lights off, sat in darkness. Mangan had been late—there were two Motel 6s on Route One, it turned out—and she'd stood on the sidewalk in a fall drizzle, fuming. She'd spent two hours on a counter-surveillance run, convinced herself more than once that they were there, and then convinced herself they weren't. She was damp and tired and snappish. He was subdued, focused. He'd brought vodka, and she'd given in and had a shot. He'd talked, she'd felt the memory stir and waken. She found herself back on that riverbank in Thailand, in the heat and the clouds of insects, the Chinese colonel, code-name HYPNOTIST, standing there pleading with her as the MSS men waited by their car.

"It was then, just before they took him away, and we let them," said Mangan. "He just said it. The address in Paramaribo, the name. And then, in Mandarin, he said, 'Use it. Use it to hurt them.'"

"Hurt who?"

"The people who were about to kill him. MSS."

"Why didn't you tell me?"

"I told you there was a lead. I told you. You weren't listening. You were furious and disgusted and you wanted to get away, back to London. You were so angry. I was exhausted; I didn't know what I was going to do."

Patterson saw HYPNOTIST going down on his knees in the dust, the MSS men dragging him away.

"And the lawyer, Teng, in Paramaribo, tell me again," she said.

He walked her through it once more: the zoo, the meetings with Posthumus, the vile club. The man, Mitchell Tao, as he reached across the table, palmed something, pocketed it, the violence in him. His terrified wife.

And the small, bespectacled, bewildered, luminously intelligent girl. The daughter.

Patterson walked to the sink and ran cold water, letting it pool in her hands, holding it to her face.

"What is it?" he said.

What is it? she thought. It's a network. And Paramaribo is a node, for logistics, money, housekeeping. Teng keeps the books, moves the funds, strokes, cajoles. He's executor, matron and accountant. And, perhaps, executioner.

This network touched Monroe, before he ate a nine-millimetre round under the trees at Great Falls. It touched Monroe's wife, leaving her insane and convulsing in a hospital bed. HYPNOTIST knew of it, before he overdosed in a flyblown casino on the banks of the Mekong.

And my brilliant, hopeless, blown agent insists that this network extends to a dysfunctional immigrant family in a Washington suburb.

What assets does this network possess that make it so lethal?

She shivered and poured herself another vodka.

"What?" said Mangan.

But she just shook her head and wondered how much time they had.

If any.

32

Hopko was incandescent, spewing rage. Patterson had never seen her like this.

"You bloody well tell him, and tell him *today*, that he is to stop what he's doing immediately. *Immediately.*" She was back in London, coming in on secure video link, looking down from a wall-mounted screen. Tipton and Markham were both there, but they were silent, and Patterson was sat out front, an offering to be devoured.

"He cuts off communication, swans halfway round the world, and starts tailing a target in an environment he knows nothing, *nothing*, about. What the hell is the meaning of this? Answer me."

Patterson sat, rigid, trying to compose some sort of rational response, to convey it despite her own fear, despite the sense of failure that Hopko induced in her.

"He believed communications were compromised. The operatives who assaulted him in Sorong clearly indicated that they knew his communication protocols."

"Oh, really? And there weren't contingencies? Like, heaven forbid, coming back to London and making a quick phone call to you, or me? Or going and knocking on the door of an Embassy somewhere? Dropping off a letter? Jesus *Christ*."

"I'm not defending him."

"Don't you dare. And you keep him there, in Washington, until I decide what is to be done with him. And he *will* stop everything he's doing. Everything. Do I make myself clear?"

"Very clear."

Hopko had taken off her glasses and was looking at a document in front of her, the screen glitching now, little blizzards of pixels sweeping across it.

"So he went from Indonesia to South America, and got into Suriname without anybody stamping his passport or knowing he was there. And then he launches a one-man surveillance op that turns up the corner of a Chinese network in the U.S."

Suddenly calm, she was wearing her hangman's grin now.

"That's what he says."

Hopko shook her head.

"I tell you, Trish, the man's an absolute bloody natural."

Her mother had made meatballs, Pearl's favourite. *Shizi tou*—lion's heads, they were called—and they sat atop cabbage braised in broth, and Pearl had loved them as a child. Now they looked like some craven token, Mom's pathetic attempt to win back some good will. *Thanks, Mom, you love me really, even though you appear to be involving me in something so secret, dangerous and illegal that you won't even tell me what it is.* Both her parents were at the table, their attitude to Pearl's hypersensitive eye a weird mix of expectancy and threat.

She sat, and her mother spooned a *shizi tou* onto her plate and it sat there in a puddle of broth.

"I hope you've calmed down since yesterday," said her father.

Pearl didn't answer.

"Well, we have some news," he said. "We're taking another short vacation."

Pearl stared at him.

"Another vacation?"

"Another vacation."

"Can I ask why?" The alarm was rising in her.

"Because it's important. And it will be fun and interesting." Mitchell pushed a meatball around the serving dish, trying to get it onto a spoon, but it wouldn't cooperate.

"I can't," she said. "I have class."

"Yes, you can. It's just a short trip."

"To where?"

"Hong Kong."

"Hong Kong? Dad, are you serious?"

"Very serious. We can do some shopping, spend some time together."

"This is insane."

Her father brought his fist down on the table and the impact rattled all the crockery and the knives and forks and the sound clattered around the kitchen and Pearl recoiled with the shock, the adrenalin flooding her stomach and heart. She saw the pattern on the vinyl tablecloth, bouquets of flowers and herbs, birds. She sat, rigid.

"We leave on Thursday night," he said quietly. "We will be back on Tuesday night."

She glanced up, saw her mother sitting, face down, hands in her lap.

"And Pearl," he said, "you will tell nobody. Nobody."

In the treacherous hours, her room darkened, Pearl sat on her bed with her laptop, and examined her situation anew—and found chaos. Blinding, stultifying, thought-stopping chaos.

As was her habit, she sought to disaggregate the chaos,

break it down into its constituent parts, contemplate their interrelationships and contradictions, and ascertain which were constant and which were variable.

Constituent part number one: her father's behaviour, now verging on mania. His project—as yet not fully articulated—to induct Pearl into a set of undefined, certainly illegal, activities, which included digging up cash at night in parks, holding clandestine meetings in small South American countries, and short, secretive trips to Hong Kong without explanation. The threat of physical violence. Variable.

Constituent part number two: her mother's psychological and emotional freeze, rendering her unable to affect events in the Tao household to any noticeable degree, other than to deepen Pearl's sense of powerlessness and dread. Constant.

Constituent part number three: Telperion's Ltd.'s assumption that Pearl Tao is an honest, fit, uncompromised individual who can be trusted with priceless and highly classified intellectual property, and who would never commit a felony by lying on her security clearance forms. Variable.

Constituent part number four: Cal, friend, potential lover and object of Pearl's betrayal through her own withholding and deceit. Constant.

And finally, constituent part number five: the existence of a tall, dishevelled guy with red hair, rather striking green eyes and what Pearl takes to be an English accent, who shambled over to her only once and briefly in a hotel coffee shop, yet who manged to convey, without saying a thing, knowledge of her predicament, and who left an invitation to discuss said predicament in the form of an email address on a scrap of paper and one cryptic phrase. *When you need to talk…* Variable or constant? Unknown.

Think, now, she said to herself. Think hard about how to survive this.

Think about what to do, when the right moment will be to do it, to move, to act. Get ready, if you can. No one will help you. So grow up, fast.

And there, just at the very edge of thought, a possibility was crystallising. And the Englishman's cool gaze, his green eyes, were visible in it.

An online search: How do you disappear?

33

Guangzhou, China

The first meeting—for that was what it was, no matter how assiduously it characterised itself as a dinner—took place in a private room at the Shanxi Grand Hotel. The room, in a basement, was windowless and chill. The wallpaper was grubby, its bamboo pattern fading, the blond-wood fittings battered and streaked with grime. Pearl was cotton-wool-headed with exhaustion.

The three of them—Pearl and her parents—had flown in to Hong Kong. They'd passed through immigration to be greeted by three tall, silent men in suits, who had already picked up their luggage. Nobody told Pearl anything. The men walked them to an anonymous door. One of them punched a keypad and waved a card, and they were suddenly airside again, the door slamming behind them. One of the men took out a black bag, and spoke quietly and very politely.

"Please place all your electronics—your phones, laptops, tablets, anything you have with you—in the bag."

Pearl wanted to object. She turned to her father, gave him a *WTF* look, but his glare in response was enough to shut down her desire to object. She took her phone and tablet and put them in the proffered black bag.

"Thank you," the man said, in English. "And the chargers as well, please." Pearl had to root around in her luggage, found them, dropped them in the bag.

Nothing was said. They walked a long, sterile corridor to a doorway and out into the night to a waiting car that drove them off across the tarmac, flitting past airliners that glowed beneath the lights. They drove for fifteen minutes, to a quieter part of the airport. The aircraft got smaller: private jets, Pearl assumed, some helicopters. The car pulled up next to an anonymous white plane, no insignia save its tail number. They climbed rattling aluminium steps to board, and an attendant waved them to their seats. The interior was a little shabby, with a utilitarian, military feel, the seats cloth-covered and uncomfortable. The safety belts were unfamiliar, reaching over the shoulders and fastening four ways over the stomach. Pearl couldn't figure it out and asked the attendant for help, and she came over and fastened the belt without once looking at Pearl's face. She averted her eyes the whole time.

They took off, and were in the air for no more than half an hour. When they landed, another car was waiting, right there on the tarmac. It drove them off the airport onto an expressway, the driver silent.

Pearl looked at the road signs.

Guangzhou. They were in China.

Think, Pearl.

The food was superb. Pearl watched as the waitresses in shiny red *qipao* with split skirts brought plates of paper-thin pork, braised with garlic bolts and scallions and translucent mushrooms; bowls of *daoxiaomian*, the noodles shaved into long ribbons in broth with beef and coriander; steamed fish in peppers and sesame and the earthy black vinegar. A special Shanxi meal, for a family whose roots lay there.

Pearl focused on the details of each intricate dish, because the whole was too difficult to take in. She was in China. But why? No one was going to enlighten her. There was only this room, the steam curling off the fish, and an assemblage of people also unknown to her, but all of whom seemed to know her father—and to know all about her.

There were six at the table: Pearl and her father and mother, and three others who remained a mystery. One was Lao Xiong—no full name, just the respectful *Lao* and a surname. He was clearly in charge, a wiry man with a face like a beaver, sleek and sharp-toothed. He made the conversation, flattering her father, asked him questions about life in America: the politics, the wars, the popular disaffection with Washington, declining power. Questions from a Party man, thought Pearl, questions that require predictable answers. Her father was expansive, emphatic in his answers, which were, Pearl felt, mostly baloney.

Next to her mother sat an older woman of minute stature, gold-framed spectacles and elegant grey hair kept short and parted to one side in a style suggestive of earlier, more utilitarian days. She said little, but listened, keenly, her eyes flickering about the table.

And the last man at the table ate little, but smoked, to Pearl's quiet disgust. Lao something-or-other, she'd missed it. He was battle-scarred, with a face like leather stretched on a rack, dark and lined with the crevasses of some unnamed, unimaginable combat. In his sixties, perhaps, losing his hair. He had about him the air of a discarded, tough, unkillable thing. He held his cigarette peasant-style, between the second and third fingers, his hand in a claw. And he watched Pearl.

Who were they? Beyond being her father's "associates," the only one on whom she heard any background was Lao Xiong—apparently an old classmate from Taiyuan University of Technology, where they lived eight to a room in the eighties and studied outside under the street lamps late at night, surviving on noodles and peanuts and weak beer. Such days! What a time! Lao Xiong leaned across the table, his face a little flushed from the wine, and spoke straight to her.

"Those were the days when China was coming back to life! When Deng Xiaoping was prising the country open and telling us anything was possible. *Anything*."

Her father was nodding. "And, by God, we knew what we had, didn't we? The moment we were living in. We *knew*."

Pearl realised they were all looking at her, and now the battle-scarred one spoke, an illusionless rasp in an accent Pearl had never heard, something from deep in the red-earthed heartlands of central China.

"You live in an important moment, too," he said. "Do you understand how important this moment is?"

She said nothing.

"This moment is important because of technology. Don't you think?" he said. He didn't speak unkindly, despite his fearsome looks. In fact, he was quite gentle, twinkling a little like a proud uncle.

"I suppose," she said.

"Oh, yes. Technology is strategic capital, isn't it?"

She nodded.

"So, it follows, doesn't it, that those who possess the technology will be those who have the greatest strategic advantage. What do you think?"

She considered for a moment.

"I think that innovation is more important than technology."

He looked interested.

"Is it? Is it really? Now why do you say that?"

Think, Pearl. Get through this.

"Ideas," she said. "You can have all the technology in the world, but unless you have ideas, you'll never be able to use technology in new ways. It's innovation that brings advantage."

The table had gone very quiet. The older woman spoke.

"And, if I may ask you, Pearl, how do you find yourself thinking about and using innovation in the work you are doing now? I find this fascinating. Could you give us an example?"

She calculated for a second. I'm not telling them anything they don't already know, she thought.

"Well, one of the projects I'm working on at Hopkins uses drones. The drones themselves are pretty basic. They're elegant, but simple. But what we're trying to do is find ways of making them work together on a task. So we put sensors on each drone. That means the drone can see and hear and maybe even digitally sniff other drones. Then we give each drone algorithms that allow it to figure out what its own role should be, depending on what the other drones are doing. So the drones, like, look around and make decisions. So there's nothing particularly technologically advanced about this, but what we're doing is very difficult and very innovative. It'll change everything, actually."

"So the drones will function as a sort of single entity."

"Uh, yeah, if you like. A single large consciousness, made out of many small processors of information." She swallowed, waited.

The woman acted astonished. Pearl glanced over at her father. He was looking down, concentrating on his food, sucking on a bone.

"Well, that is amazing. And may I say also, that you speak Mandarin extremely well. *Extremely* well," the older woman said. She looked around herself, as if an idea had occurred to her. "We should make sure Pearl is invited to conferences and workshops here, Beijing, and Shanghai, wherever they are doing similar work. We should make sure she meets our scientists so they can exchange ideas. Shouldn't we?"

Murmurs of assent around the table.

"Would you do that, Pearl?" asked Battle Scar. "Would you do that for us?" He turned to the older woman with concern. "She's so busy! She's still doing her undergraduate degree. Don't put pressure on her!"

"Oh, I didn't mean to. But Pearl is embarking upon a remarkable career. I hope that in the coming years..."

Her father was staring at Pearl now with a look that said, *You know what you must do now.* And she felt herself shrinking inward, her focus narrowing: to the table-cloth, to the film of oil atop a bowl of soup and the smell of the cigarette smoke.

"I'd be happy to," Pearl said.

"Well, that's excellent. Just excellent," said Lao Xiong, the beaver face. "We can talk more about it at the meetings tomorrow."

What meetings tomorrow?

Pearl and her parents were taken to rooms at the top of the hotel, on the sixteenth floor. Her room was silent, and the air came through a special purification system to keep out particulate pollution. The room adjoined that of her parents, but she locked the door between them. She pushed the curtains to one side and peered outside.

Guangzhou was a luminous, glistening, night city. So alien to her. Every street a promise.

She put on her shoes, grabbed her backpack, took her key and eased the door shut behind her. But at the elevators, there was a man in a suit who gave her a regretful smile and politely walked her back to the room.

They were picked up the next morning by two black Audis. Her parents were ushered into one, she into the other. There, in the back, sat Battle Scar, looking like he'd been stitched together out of sinew, reeking of tobacco, in a black golf jacket and an absurd pair of sunglasses. He gave her a big smile, seemed genuinely pleased to see her, taking off the sunglasses to address her.

"Now, Pearl, we're going to visit some more associates of your father's. They're very keen to see him, and to meet you."

"Who are they?"

"They're smart people. Thoughtful people. Some are in business, some are in government, some are scientists and are thinking about technology and innovation, same as you."

"What do they want?"

He looked surprised.

"Want? Oh, they don't want anything. I mean, they'll probably get overexcited and start making all sorts of proposals and promises." He smiled fondly with a shake of his head. "But don't worry, I'll protect you." He gave a deep chuckle.

The car nosed its way through backstreets. She didn't know where they were going. Battle Scar sat silent.

They pulled in before a grey iron gate on a tree-lined avenue. Battle Scar got out and gestured to her to follow. He walked to a keypad beneath a surveillance camera, punched in numbers and leaned in to a screen, and the gate slid open to reveal a scrubby lawn, some moth-eaten trees, and a house that looked to date from colonial times. It had a veranda, a portico, shutters on the windows.

Battle Scar walked her up some steps and they entered what seemed to be a reception room. They sat on sofas of pale green, antimacassars atop them, and waited. Battle Scar lit a cigarette, holding it in his claw, and nodded at her encouragingly.

After a while, a young woman in a grey suit came in and made a wordless gesture, and they walked down a corridor to a meeting room, the same green armchairs around the walls, facing inward, a low table next to each, a red carpet, the shutters closed. Her parents were already there; so was beaver-faced Lao Xiong, and several others.

Pearl's eye was caught by a younger woman, sitting alone. She wore soft, brown calf-length boots over jeans and a cashmere shawl in a shade of pinkish beige that in and of itself spoke of money, of boutiques and hotels and Paris or Geneva or London, of how Pearl imagined these places. She was perfectly made up, her hair in an elegant, layered bob. She sat with her ankles crossed, like a fifties movie actress. Pearl felt again her own shapelessness, her thick glasses, the stringy hair in its ponytail.

Her father was deep in conversation with a short, sprightly man she did not recognise. They seemed to be quite familiar with each other. Her mother sat next to him, not speaking. The sprightly man nodded at Pearl and smiled, as if in recognition. Battle Scar showed her to a chair, and gradually the room quietened, awaiting something. She had no idea what.

A door opened. Some of the people half rose from their chairs, anticipatory expressions on their faces. An elderly man walked in. He was very trim, wore an open-necked shirt, a blue sleeveless sweater and well-ironed slacks, and moved with assurance. He did not look at Pearl as he passed her, and in his wake she smelled soap, perhaps a hint of cologne. He sat in one of the green armchairs at the far side of the room, opposite her. He sat with his knees together, his hands folded in his lap, the posture striking Pearl as slightly effeminate. Everybody else in the room deferred to him, clearly. Pearl noticed his soft, smooth skin, its even tone, as if he had lavished care upon it. She thought of him as pure, spotless. He had eyes that shone like little dark gems.

Lao Xiong was sitting next to him, speaking quietly to him while gesturing to Pearl. He nodded, regarding her. Then he spoke, in a high, reedy voice.

"It's very good to meet you."

"And you," she said.

"How are you finding China?"

"Fine, thank you."

"Is it good to be back in your homeland?"

"Well, I guess I don't really consider China..." She felt her father's eyes on her. "It's fine, thank you," she said. The elegant woman was writing something in a notepad.

"Of course, you have spent most of your life in America," Spotless Man said gently. "That probably feels more like home, doesn't it?"

"Well..."

"But you still have many relatives and friends here. So, a foot in both countries, perhaps."

"Perhaps," she said.

"Of course! Your aunt, your grandmother, in Taiyuan. And your cousin." He was gesturing across the room to the sprightly man, the one who had been talking to her father.

My cousin? she thought. What cousin?

"Your cousin. Whom everyone calls Jiachong." *Beetle.*

The sprightly man whom everybody called Beetle raised his hand in greeting. The elderly, clean man carried on.

"Your cousin is a very able man, and I am very fortunate to have worked with him for a long time. We are old comrades." Polite laughter rippled round the room. "So, whenever you and your father would like to come back to China to visit, or perhaps for a conference or a study tour, your cousin will handle all the arrangements. Everything! You just let him know. Your father knows how to be in touch with him."

Pearl had no idea what to say.

"Thank you," she managed.

Spotless Man had raised a finger as if thinking of an important question.

"And tell me, Pearl, when do you graduate again? How embarrassing! I should know this but I seem to have forgotten."

"I graduate in eighteen months' time."

"Of course, and then you go to work for . . . ?"

Lao Xiong leaned into him, whispered.

"That's right. Telperion. That's right. And you'll do your Ph.D. while you're working there. Such ambition! Really, we should all be so ambitious. And your Ph.D., it will continue your work on artificial consciousness?"

She swallowed.

"That's my plan."

"Your plan, yes. And that's what Telperion will want you to work on."

Pearl looked around. The whole room's eyes were on her. *What* is happening here?

Battle Scar saved her.

"I'm sure she doesn't know what Telperion will have her working on. How can she know what her future bosses will want? None of us know that, do we?" There was more polite laughter, and Spotless Man looked a little rueful, as if there were some backstory there, something the room knew that she did not. He flapped a hand in resignation, smiled.

"Of course. I apologise. But perhaps Pearl can tell us what *she* thinks she will be working on. What the most important challenges will be."

The thought came out of nowhere. *Are they recording this? Filming it?* She felt a flash of adrenalin, the colour rising in her cheeks. Her father sat very erect in his chair, mouth clamped shut, jaw tight. Her mother was looking at the floor.

"I'm...not sure," she said. She laughed nervously.

Battle Scar cleared his throat.

"Perhaps you could speculate a little for us. What do you think the most important challenges in technology will be in the coming, say, twenty years? Just for interest's sake."

Should I pass this test? Or fail it? Which will get me out of here?

"Well...I...uh...well, the quantification of consciousness. Artificial Intelligence. The transition to Artificial General Intelligence. And then Super Intelligence. Deep learning. These are certainly things that will be so, so important. Uh, nanotechnology, of course. Quantum computing, evolutionary computation. That stuff matters." She exhaled. "Um, photonics?"

Spotless Man held up a hand.

"Well, your understanding is way beyond mine. I am just a foolish old man who has trouble with his mobile phone. I have to ask my grandson to help!" Cue more sycophantic laughter. He held his hands out to Pearl.

"But, let me ask you a question. Probably it will sound very naïve. You talk about Artificial Intelligence. Is this...real? Do you think it will happen soon?"

Pearl blinked.

"It's already happening."

"But, I mean, what you call Super Intelligence. When you talk with your peers, young, smart people, do they think that it will happen?"

"Of course. It's only a matter of when."

"And when do you think?"

She shrugged. "I don't know. Sooner than you think. Someone will do it."

"Who?" said Battle Scar. "Who will do it? Will it be a government? Or military?"

"Uh, I doubt it," she said. "You won't need the resources of the state. It will just be someone in a lab or a company or a start-up somewhere, some unregulated space maybe, who makes the right tweak to the right deep-learning algorithm. And, boom."

Spotless Man nodded, as if a troubling question had been made clear to him.

"And when you say 'boom,' what do you mean?"

"I mean that a computer that can teach itself will learn exponentially. Its rate of learning will accelerate. It'll just get faster and faster, until it surpasses the human brain. And then it will keep going, faster and faster."

"And do you anticipate, Pearl, that your work will be relevant to this moment? This 'boom'?"

She felt a flush of annoyance.

"Well, maybe. I don't know. I mean, consciousness and intelligence are aligned, but I don't know." What did they want of her, these old men, fumbling around in the dark? Did they have *any* idea?

She thought suddenly of Charles, at the awful *baozi* gathering at Cal's. *They want your shit, Pearl. And they will manipulate you to get it.*

There was a silence in the room. Then Spotless Man spoke.

"Well, Pearl, it has been a great pleasure meeting you and I hope we'll meet again soon, and I hope we can talk about all these big questions much more." And with that he stood and made his way out of the room, this clean, dapper little man. But as he went Pearl saw how her father caught his eye and the two of them exchanged a look. And then her father turned to her "cousin," Beetle, who gave a small nod.

And then the whole room was moving, and Battle Scar was at her side, and her mother was taking her arm and they were being walked out.

There followed a short tour of the compound, with a smart young man giving potted explanations of the architecture, the elegant stonework, the notable eaves, the European influence. Pearl suffered through it. Her father was impatient, hands in pockets, pacing. The elegant woman was there. She approached Pearl and stood beside her as they all gazed out over the garden. She gave Pearl a quizzical smile. Pearl felt a flush of self-consciousness.

"That was really impressive, back there. I thought you handled it really well," she said. "I just wanted to say that."

"Okay, well, thanks," said Pearl.

"Honestly, some of them barely understand what the internet is. It's like talking to a peasant." She used the word, *nongmin*, dismissively, Pearl noted.

"Maybe we could carve out some time to meet, get to know each other a little better. I'd really like that," the woman was saying, and Pearl realised at once how vulnerable she was to charm, and how much she mistrusted it.

"Maybe we can do that. Thanks," said Pearl, and walked away, leaving the woman standing there alone.

And at the edges of Pearl's mind, the realisation was growing and taking shape, gaining weight and power, and it was like ashes in her mouth.

34

Washington, DC

Mangan's basement room was wood-panelled, with lino-
leum on the floor, a single bed, a rectangular window at
head height—barred—a desk and a chair.

It was two in the morning. He sat, now, his chin in his
hand, a cigarette in his fingers, staring at his laptop—
staring at the email that lay like a silent digital scream in
front of him.

> Dear Michael Barclay,
>
> I don't know if that's your name.
>
> If it isn't then maybe you could tell me your real
> name? Because I'm having issues with trust right now
> and I feel like I need to trust someone. And I'm thinking
> that maybe I can trust you.
>
> Which is stupid because I only met you once in a
> coffee shop in Suriname and I think you were probably
> lying to me when you told me you were a travel
> journalist or whatever it was you said you were. So why
> should I trust you, right?
>
> Because you seemed to know that something was

going on with me, and you seemed to know something about what it was.

And if you could share I'd be super grateful, because some seriously weird stuff is happening to me right now and I literally don't have a clue what it is or why.

Pearl Tao

Mangan sat back.

Patterson's instructions were ringing in his head. She'd delivered them in her starchiest voice, with her flintiest expression on, quite the hardass. *You're to do nothing, Philip. You're to stand down. Nothing, do you understand? There are other operational contingencies in play.* She hadn't even sat down, had just stood there, in this foul little room, with its smell of mouldering wood, and said what she'd been told to say.

Other operational contingencies.

He stubbed out the cigarette.

Dear Pearl,

Can I suggest we go encrypted? I think it might be wise. Open an account, and email me here.

He included a link to an encrypted email server, and an address. And waited.

The reply came an hour later, just past three.

OK. Here I am. So?

Pearl

Mangan sat and thought, then typed.

Pearl,

    My real name is Philip. You are quite right, I wasn't being wholly truthful with you. I am a journalist, but I'm not really interested in your vacation.

    The truth is I'm concerned that you may be in some sort of difficulty.

    The man you met in the zoo that day—I've been looking into who he is as part of a story I'm working on. And I'm concerned by what I've found. I think he might be dangerous and involved in illicit activity. And I wondered why you and your parents—they are your parents, right?—were meeting him. In a zoo, of all places.

    Can you tell me anything about him? Or about your father's connection to him?

    I promise not to publish or write about anything you tell me—I'm just very concerned, and would like some reassurance you're okay.

    You say in your message that some "weird stuff" is happening to you. Can you tell me what sort of weird stuff? Perhaps I can help figure it out a little.

    Philip

He lit another cigarette and waited. It was nearly four, and nothing. He lay on the bed, still clothed, pulled the duvet over himself, tried to sleep.

He awoke at nine, traffic noise coming through the window, the room stifling. He stood in the shower for twenty minutes until the water ran cold, and only once clean and dried did he check his laptop.

Dear Philip,

    You seem very concerned and I am very touched by that, but now you've made me even more worried.

Please tell me who is the man my father met at the zoo,
and what "illicit activities" is he doing.

Are you maybe doing some illicit activities yourself?

I am a scientist. Did you know that? I try to
imagine the world in new ways. Nothing else matters
to me. That is where I live my life, in the world of
mathematical language. All this other stuff, this weird
stuff, is nothing to do with me. But I am starting to think
that my life is not what I thought it was, and that I am in
real trouble.

And I am now super-tired and am going to sleep.

Pearl

He boiled the little electric kettle and spooned instant
coffee into a mug with sugar and powdered creamer.

Pearl,

I understand that you are worried. And I fear that
you are right to be.

I can help you—but only if you tell me what your
situation is.

Let me ask you this: does your father keep strong
connections to China? Does he talk about his work with
people there a lot?

Philip

A reply straight away this time.

Well, we make little trips to China via other cities, and
we meet people in weird offices in Guangzhou who
won't tell me their names. Does that count?

Pearl

Mangan felt his stomach lurch, saw the future unfurling.

Pearl,
    Does your father have a security clearance? Does he work on classified material?

    P

He waited, sipped the coffee.

No, but I will have a clearance soon.

    Pearl

It's her, he thought. They want the daughter.

35

Beijing, China

Yip Lo Exports Ltd., supplier of plastic novelties to the European and American markets, found itself tumultuously busy. A children's animated movie, meeting with box office success, had generated sudden and unanticipated global demand for a species of tiny, clockwork space creatures blessed with goggle eyes and Technicolor fur. China's factories had geared up. Yip Lo's astute purchasing staff, sensing an opportunity, readied for a foray into the vast manufacturing complexes of south-east China.

They touched down in Wenzhou, on the coast; Eileen Poon and two of her boys, Peter and Winston. They'd call their contacts and drive out into the cluster of plastics factories, take some chances, see what was what, sniff around for a deal.

And then, when business was done, it was a quick hop to Beijing, by train this time, a sleek, high-speed affair, direct. Only a brief visit, so they hadn't checked out of their hotel in Wenzhou, where, coincidentally, they had left their phones and other devices. Eileen sat in first class, knitting, while her boys sat quietly in second, reading, planning, as the train rocketed towards the capital.

The three of them arrived at Beijing South Railway Station just after six on a cool evening. Eileen left the station first, the two boys behind, arcing and weaving in her wake. She shoved her way through the crowd. They stayed out of the subway, wary of the cameras. Eileen walked north, crossed the moat and headed for Taoranting Park. The boys circled.

The evening was chilly, hinting at the winter to come, the air thick and dry, touched with grit and something sulphurous. Eileen put on her old-lady hobble, a hat and a scarf, and walked on into the gathering dark, the lights from the tide of traffic rendered soft by the haze.

Taoranting Park at dusk. Eileen, dry as a bone, stopped for a moment, listened, watched. Some 200 metres ahead of her, silhouetted against the sky, was a little pavilion of red pillars and a tiled roof. It stood at the lakeside, a place to sit on a hot summer day, to take out your *erhu* and play for your friends, sing a little opera, an aria or two. Su San as she's led away for execution, perhaps. Or Yang Guifei, inebriated and dancing as she contemplates her fate.

It was colder now, the sky taking on the orange-blue wash of the city at night. She gritted her teeth and walked towards the pavilion. Peter was off to her right, hands in pockets, waiting; Winston was close by, in the trees, watching.

She walked stiffly up the steps and sat herself on a concrete bench with an old woman's grunt and exhalation. She let a moment pass, looked out of the pavilion to Peter. She could just see his nod in the gloom. She leaned forward, and ran her hand beneath the bench. Honestly, it was like the old days, the feel of the little packet, the envelope, the film canister against your fingers, behind some brick in a wall or taped to a pipe down some sodden, filthy alley. And the bracing for whatever was to come, because that was when they took you, in the act.

Her fingers fluttered against the concrete. She leaned over further, reaching under. Where the hell was it?

Peter was there now, coming up the steps, a questioning expression on his face. She just nodded and continued to search.

"Hurry, Ma."

She shot him a look. She was running her fingers into corners, contemplating getting down on her hands and knees. Peter was looking out from the pavilion, for Winston, perhaps. And then, there it was, three feet away from where it should have been, a pellet wrapped in plastic, no bigger than a bean, or a piece of White Rabbit milk candy. With her fingernail Eileen picked at the tape holding it to the underside of the bench; she swore softly.

And then it was done and in her pocket, and Peter was away, down the steps and disappearing into the almost dark to clear her way. She waited a beat, letting him get a little distance, then moved. Down the steps, back along the path, her heart pounding, and something like fear touching the underside of her mind with ink-black fingers. *Why?* Was Winston behind her? Wiry, hard Winston, with his easy smile, and his solidity, his presence? She almost turned to look, but forced herself to face forward, to walk slowly.

Ahead, Peter had almost reached the park's front gate, readying to move out onto the street.

But then she saw he'd stopped, saw the tension in him as he sped up and moved right, cutting off his planned path.

What was there? She looked into the darkness and saw nothing. But Peter had.

And so had Winston. Because out of nowhere he was suddenly beside her, taking her arm, his grip gentle but his fingers like steel bars, and he was steering her off the path towards the trees. She shed her old woman's gait, moving fast. They followed a walkway into a grove of cypress, pushed through and emerged on the other side. The park's western gate was ahead of them, and beyond it on the street, a cab.

They came out of the park, Eileen breathing heavily, Winston tense. They hailed the taxi, gave the address, and the driver nosed out into the traffic. No sign of Peter.

It was a difficult night. The basement in Fangzhuang was their own safe house, off the books—not even London knew about it. It lay beneath a mouldering brick apartment block and was dark and dank and the pipes rattled, and the family who held the lease on it were long gone and asked no questions of their renters. Eileen sat on the couch, lit a beedi, blew smoke into the stale air. Winston put the kettle on, then fished in a closet for a quilt to wrap her in, because she was shaking, something he'd never seen before. They left the lights off.

"What was it?" she asked.

Winston took off his cap and put it on the table. Her sister's boy, this one, loyal—and far more ruthless than he looked.

"I'm not sure. I just saw Peter move, and there was... I'm not sure, just a shape, a figure, moving along the edge of the park. I'm not sure."

"Could be nothing."

He shook his head.

"Peter doesn't move like that for nothing." He went to the window. "Where is he?"

"He'll come," she said.

"I'm worried."

"You're never worried."

"I'm worried because you're worried. What is it? This operation?"

Eileen took a long drag on the beedi.

"This operation is...different. I know," she said.

"Why?" he said. "What's different?"

She sighed, wondering what she could tell him.

"We're inside," she said. "We're deep inside. And it's different."

"Different to what?"

Different, she thought, to the know-nothing Party cadres who tried to organise in Hong Kong, sitting bewildered in the old walled city years ago while she penetrated their underground cells and wrecked them one after another. Different to the mid-ranking officials in Chongqing and Wuhan who'd sell their own mothers, let alone the contents of their safes, for hookers and gambling money. Different to the military officers, the angry, under-promoted men who realised they'd done it all for nothing, the Air Force colonel who brought out condom-wrapped USB drives, popping them out of his arse in the Wan Chai Holiday Inn. Different to the fat, homicidal aerospace engineer she'd trailed around Beijing a couple of years back.

Different, because they were inside now, deep in the guts of the adversary. And these little packages contained treasure. Real treasure. Not rumour or speculation or hearsay, not data points to be injected into some turgid briefing in Whitehall or Washington months from now and then forgotten.

Eileen took out tonight's little package and put it in a sterile bag. She thought of the rest of the night, of what might come, of searches. She walked to the darkened bedroom, knelt and, using her nails, prised from the wall a loose electrical outlet. She placed the plastic bag into the dark cavity behind and jammed the outlet back into the wall.

She went and sat on the couch, wrapped herself in the quilt again and lit another beedi. Winston sat stock still, listening.

And here she was again, the night unravelling into terror, second by leaden second, the sound of a footstep outside the window, every hiss and shudder in the pipes causing her to tense, her jaw to lock, her fragile old hands to clutch the quilt. Perhaps, she thought, we have a finite reserve of courage, a pool we draw on over a lifetime. And with each act of nerve and self-control, we deplete it. And perhaps mine, deep as it was, is now running dry.

At three they heard the squeak of a door from above. A footfall, hesitant and soft, of the sort the ear is immediately drawn to.

Winston was on his feet, flexing his fingers, moving to cover the entranceway.

Feet on the stairway now, moving slowly. Eileen swallowed, but stayed put on the couch.

A tapping at the front door.

"Anyone there?"

Silence. Winston, tense as a cat.

"Anyone there? It's me."

Winston was calculating, his mouth working, and then he slipped the latch and opened the door a crack and stepped back, ready to move if he had to, and the door opened slowly, to reveal Peter Poon, bug-eyed, hair awry, breathing heavily. Eileen got up and went to him and touched his arm. Winston closed the door.

"It's okay. I'm okay," Peter said.

"Anyone behind you?" Winston said.

"No. No, I'm sure. I've been going round and round for hours."

He sat heavily on the couch, leaning his head back.

"God, I'm hungry."

"What was it?" she said.

He shook his head.

"I don't even know. Maybe nothing."

"Was there someone there? In the park?"

"I thought . . . I don't know. I'm just . . . jumpy."

He raised his hands and let them fall in despair and resignation.

"This city . . ." he said. "It's not the same. The whole place."

She nodded, and they were all silent for a moment, and then Winston said, "Let's go home."

She took the plastic bag containing the tiny packet from the wall. Winston would carry, it was agreed, and they left the safe flat separately in the pre-dawn dark, Winston flitting away first, Peter and Eileen following on. There had been an early, sudden rain, and the streets were shining and Eileen smelled rainwater and fuel, and dough frying in bubbling oil from a food cart, and she wondered if she would ever be back here.

TOP SECRET STRAP 2 BOTANY—UK EYES ONLY
ANNEXE DCOPY 2/5
//REPORT
1/ (TS) Source FULCRUM addressed a further letter to C/FE. This is his fourth. It is printed below in full.

Beijing
To: Controller, Far East and Western Hemisphere,
United Kingdom Secret Intelligence Service,
Vauxhall Cross, London

Dear Friends,
    Thank you for you most recent communication. I hope you will find the material I am supply to you in

this device of interest. It is most valuable material, and should deliver great insight for you, if you are able fully to understand and analyse. I do not know how are your analysts, but it is worth cultivating deep understanding of Chinese affairs for they are complicated and hard for foreigners to understand. Your analysts must work hard and be diligent before they can make use of this valuable material. Otherwise, my work and its attendant dangers must be wasted.

1/ I must say it again that I will NOT identify myself for you. You say it will help if I tell you my name and my position but I tell you again NO. This is for security. The anti-corruption campaign here is still fierce, and many are under suspicion, though not me.

2/ I will confirm what you say you have surmised. Some foreign operations, including some in North America, fall under my responsibility. There can be room for great cooperation here between our two organisations. Remember that the success of these North American operations make me stronger in my position, and will bring me more authority and even access, which can be helpful to you. Perhaps you can help me by informing me what you know of U.S. counter-intelligence efforts against our networks in America.

3/ I require that you continue to limit distribution and pay attention to my security. Courier work remains very good. This old lady is most impressive.

4/ You have not responded to my request for diamonds. Please give me a response.

Next communication will be in six weeks, according CASTLE protocol.

Thank you, my friends, and until next time.

Z

END REPORT

Her father's voice was rising, and Pearl could feel the twisting in her stomach, the prickling behind her eyes. He thumped the steering wheel, then prodded her arm.

"It's easy. For God's sake, why do you make such a fuss? Go. Do it."

"What am I doing?"

"You are doing what I tell you. Now go."

She unbuckled her seat belt, took the laptop bag from where it rested by her feet, opened the door. Her father was checking his watch.

"Eighteen minutes," he said. "Go."

She got out of the car. They'd been back in Washington only five days. She was on Wisconsin Ave, in Tenleytown. Her father gave her one more look through the car window, then pulled away. The traffic was light—it was early Sunday morning, bright and cool. She saw starlings on telephone wires, noticed the first flecks of orange in the leaves.

The coffee shop was half a block away. They'd only just opened up, and one of the baristas was cleaning the plate-glass windows with newspaper. She went in, ordered a cappuccino and sat on a tall stool by the window, as her father had told her to.

She opened the laptop and turned it on—again, as her father had told her to. He had kept her up, late into the night going over it again and again, all through the betrayal hours. He let her sleep for a stretch, then woke her up before dawn to make her do it again. He had sat on her bed, jabbing his finger at the screen. He never sat on her bed.

She thought about her childhood, its long, tense silences, its absences. Years passed as she sat in her bedroom, in the nook by the window, reading, looking out on other people's summers, the fireflies in the trees. She wondered at how her father's anger had shaped her, grinding through her emotional landscape like a glacier, relentless and inescapable. And now, all it took was his silence, the movement of a hand or an eyebrow for fear to erupt in her.

She remembered a family trip to the beach at Lewes, Delaware, on the Atlantic coast. She must have been eleven or twelve. He'd got into an argument with the hotel clerk, some stupid misunderstanding—the wrong room, the wrong key. He'd become convinced it was because he was an immigrant, because he was Chinese, because his English was awkward. He'd exploded, screaming over the counter, spittle flying, then swept his arm along the counter top, knocking the register and a vase of flowers to the floor. The clerk was black, and her father was yelling epithets, foul words at her. Everyone was appalled. Only when a bystander threatened to call the police did he suddenly calm down. Just like that. His equilibrium restored in a split second. It was astonishing. When she remembered it, a wave of despair came over her, as if *his* actions were hers, as if *she* were at fault, her character permanently impaired by being there, witnessing it.

She sipped the coffee and waited.

At exactly twelve minutes past nine, as ordered, she activated a local wireless network and entered the password.

Someone was waiting for her.

At fourteen minutes past, she uploaded twelve files, large ones.

Who were they? They were close. Were they in the coffee shop? Outside? In a car?

She closed the laptop, wiping her eyes. She could see her

father's car, circling. He was looking at her from the driver's side window. She left the coffee shop, walked down the block and then he was pulling in beside her. She got in.

"Did you do it?" he said.

She nodded. They drove home without speaking, and he had a self-satisfied look the whole way.

Mangan left the basement, in the early-morning sunlight. He walked beside railway tracks, stopped and looked at a lugubrious basilica, wandered into a café and ate pancakes and bacon.

He was running low on cash. At some point he'd have to make a withdrawal. He was logging on now regularly from his own laptop. So he was visible. Patterson hadn't contacted him in three days. And the last time was simply to repeat the order to do nothing. Was he being cut loose? Was this it?

The whole affair felt as if it were drawing to a close.

He had no idea what he would do. Where would he go? Back to London? What would he do there? Look for some newsroom job or some editing gig, rent a tiny flat and take the bus and hit forty, on his own, without friends, possessions or purpose. Should he go back to Asia, become an expat in Thailand or Indonesia, watching himself become one of those wizened white men perched like old crows in the bars and strip joints.

He bought more cigarettes, went back to the basement, and logged on.

Dear Pearl,

I think we should meet. I am in Washington. Just name a place and a time, and I'll be there. We can just talk. I think I can help you.

Philip

This is it, he thought. There won't be anything after this.

Pearl had shut herself in her room when they got back, lying under the duvet for a long while.

"Pearl?"

Her mother tapped feebly at the door. Pearl said nothing.

"Can I come in?"

The door opened. Her mother came into the room. She was still in her dressing gown. She looked like a little, frightened bird.

"Pearl?" She sat on the bed. "Pearl, you must understand."

"Must I?"

Her mother sighed. "This is who we are."

"What? What does that mean?"

Her mother looked meaningfully at her.

"And it is who you are, too."

"Why? Why is it who I am?"

"A lot of people are depending on us, Pearl."

"Who's depending on us?"

"Our relatives. My mother, and your aunt. Beetle. Your cousins. Many people."

She pulled herself up onto her elbows.

"I don't get it, Ma. Why are our relatives depending on me going out and digging up—"

Her mother put her finger to her lips anxiously.

"We don't talk like that, Pearl."

"But—"

"Not ever."

Pearl lay back down heavily.

"If we do not do our work, they are vulnerable. You have to understand that."

"Vulnerable?"

Her mother rubbed her eyes and switched to Mandarin.

"When you start, you know, at the beginning, you do it because it's so exciting. It all feels so important. And the officials of the State Security organs are there and they look at you, and their look has such respect in it. And you know that you have found your place, your life's work. And there's the training and ... and everything."

She paused, and Pearl looked at her little frail back, her thin shoulders in the cheap robe.

"But over the years, well, we change, don't we? Things that once seemed important maybe don't seem so important any more. So they must keep us focused, keep our minds on the work."

Pearl was incredulous. Her mother went on.

"So they just hint, you know, 'Oh, your mother's not so well. But the hospitals in Taiyuan are very crowded. She's not sure she can find a bed.' Or, 'Your cousin's little boy, he's taking the university entrance exams, isn't he? Let's hope he does well.'"

"*What?* And you just accept this?"

Her mother turned to her.

"And you will accept it too."

"Will I?"

"You already have."

"What do you mean?"

"You are already doing the work. You are part of it now."

Pearl felt the thought hit home, a hot metallic flush in her cheeks, her chest. She was part of it now.

"Is it just us? Or are there others?"

"Oh, there are others. A lot of people. Not just us. So you are responsible to them as well. You have to accept it."

"No. We do not have to accept this, Ma. We can just—"

"Just what?"

"We can go to the authorities, to the police, FBI."

"*What?* Are you quite mad?"

"We can, Ma."

"Pearl you *never* say that. To even think that is to betray me, and your father, and your family, and your country."

"*My* country?"

"You put many, many people in danger."

"But Ma—"

"Have you any idea what would happen? Do you know what they *do* to people like us? Have you heard about the Supermax prisons? Where you are in solitary confinement for years? Just a concrete cell, concrete floor, concrete bed. Years. They would separate us. We would never see each other again." She was becoming animated, her eyes shining, her features twisting in frustration. "You stupid, selfish girl. You *never* say that. *Never*." And she leaned over and tried to slap Pearl, batting at her face. Pearl started to cry as well, suddenly, hot tears dripping onto her hands, and she was yelling at her mother.

"But this is all lies! It's lies. You have lied to me all my life. *All my life!*"

"No. We *always* love you. You're our daughter, for God's sake!"

Pearl brought her arms up and held her head, drawing up her knees, sobbing.

"My whole life and it's one big fucking *lie*!"

Her mother bent double as if struck in the stomach, her hands shaking.

"Pearl, no! No, no, no. *Stop*." She was close to hysterical.

Neither of them spoke for a moment, and Pearl just heard her own shuddering breaths. She was lying on her side, curled up.

"*You* did this," she said. "*You* gave me to them."

And her mother reached out and swatted at Pearl again.

"No!" And then she put both her hands to her mouth, her face contorted. "I'm going to tell your father," she said, and ran from the room.

Silence.

Pearl lay beneath the duvet, rigid. Minutes passed.

Then his footsteps on the stairs. She felt sick.

He had stopped outside her door. Then his soft knock.

She found herself gazing at the tiny flowers on the cover of the duvet—orange and green print on white cotton, the little leaves curling around the petals—and her nails, bitten and ragged, the whorls and friction ridges of her fingerprints.

He was in his jeans, a pair of slippers and the same green polo shirt he'd worn when he came back staggering and reeking from that club. He walked to the bed, standing over her.

"What did you say to Ma?"

"Nothing."

He folded his arms.

"What did you say to her?"

"Why can't you talk to me?"

"I am talking to you."

"Everything you say is a threat."

"I'm not making any threats."

"Ma made threats. And now she's sent you and you'll make threats."

"Pearl, you have to understand some things."

Pearl made herself look at him.

"You didn't even want me, as a child. Not *me*. You just wanted me for this."

He responded quite matter-of-factly.

"No. That's wrong. We wanted you very much, even though you were a girl. No matter you are our only daughter. We had no intention of involving you, but when it became clear that you were ... gifted, it was inevitable. It wasn't even our idea."

"Whose idea was it? Those people we met. Was it theirs? They decided?"

"Those people think a lot of you. They were impressed."

"Why don't I have a choice?"

He ran his hand through his hair. A warning sign.

"Because we don't have choices. Now tell me what you said to Ma."

"I said, we could go to the police." She mumbled it.

He nodded.

"I see. And why? Why would we do that?"

"To...get free of it."

She could hear his breathing.

"To get free." He leaned over her, his hands on his knees. "Child, if you go to the police, you destroy everything. Everything."

His face was close to hers. She stared at the little petals.

"I won't allow that," he said.

She shrank at his words, the finality. He leaned close and placed a thick hand on her face, cupping her cheek—it hinted at love, but promised violence.

After he left, she lay still for a long time, cried a little. She was adrift. All links—to her family, to her previous self—were compromised, stretched to breaking point.

She sat up, and the thought rose unbidden and terrible in her, and took a moment to settle and form.

What would happen if she severed those links? What would be out there?

She reached for her phone on the nightstand and opened her email.

Philip,

    Since nothing makes any sense any more, and you will just be one more thing that is new and unfamiliar and dangerous, I will meet you. You better have something to tell me.

    Pearl

36

Mangan lay awake at four in the morning, dry-mouthed, nauseated. He had left the basement flat the previous night, gone to a pub that served "craft" beer and steaks and had drunk far too much thick hoppy beer followed by red wine, a bottle, nearly. He'd ended up leaning against the bar, talking rubbish to a girl, no, a woman, an almond-eyed grad student with long black hair and beautiful teeth. He'd reeled back to the flat after one and gone to sleep fully clothed, waking with a scabrous mouth and loneliness flooding him. He stood up in the darkness, went to the sink, groped for a glass and drank tap water.

He thought of the woman in the pub, her light, easy laughter. She'd told him about her family. They came from El Salvador, she'd said. So, an immigrant story, an American story, the mother and father working three jobs, the little girl the first in her family to go to college, her *abuela* weeping at graduation. She'd told him all these things in such a gentle, engaging way, marvelling at all the things that had happened to this kid from a shack in San Miguel.

And then, when he'd talked to her, he had lied, all the time. Even the alcohol couldn't shut down the little lie machine in his head. After a while, she'd looked at him quizzically, as if she could tell something was amiss. Or maybe she just saw how drunk he was. He thought about her skin, the glossy hair draped on her shoulders, disgusted with himself. The loneliness was like a tide in him, surges of need lapping in his chest. He picked up his laptop from the floor, opened it, saw the email.

I will meet you. You better have something to tell me.

He closed the laptop, lay down, curled his knees up and sought sleep.

And then, at nine, a banging at the door. He struggled up and leaned against the wall in his underwear, hair awry.

"Who is it?" he said.

"Who do you bloody well think it is?" said Patterson.

He opened the door. She stood erect, feet slightly parted, hands clasped in front of her, in jeans, trainers, a waterproof. She might as well have been in uniform. She looked primed and hard and fit, but her eyes gave away something: a reservation? Doubt?

"Expecting someone else?" she said.

He just shook his head and walked back to the bed. She came in and wrinkled her nose as if she smelled putrefaction.

"Jesus Christ, Philip."

"Yeah, all right." He was pulling a pair of jeans over his long, pale thighs.

"You look like death warmed up."

"What do you want, Trish?"

"I want you to get up. You have a meeting."

"No. I don't," he said. "Not with you, anyway."

"Yes, you do. You really do." She was serious now. "You need to get yourself ready. And bring your laptop."

Then she frowned.

"What do you mean, not with me?" she said.

"I mean the girl. She's been in contact. She wants to meet."

At which point she walked over to him, grabbed him by the arm and forced him towards the bathroom.

"Get in the fucking shower and sort yourself out. We leave in ten minutes."

She was half shouting now, and he was startled, staggering through the bathroom door. She slammed it behind him. His feet tingled on the cold, tiled floor.

"Where are we going?"

Her voice came back through the door.

"Shower. Get dressed. Now!"

She drove fast and expertly, easing them up 16th and onto the Beltway, then Interstate 270, headed north. He tried to ask again where they were going, but she just shook her head. When they came off the interstate, he implored her to stop, and they pulled over at a Dunkin' Donuts. She watched the parking lot while he got coffee and a Big N' Toasted. They did a U-turn, headed south, ducked into smaller suburban streets, parked up in strip malls, waiting, Patterson staring at a secure handheld. The morning was grey and threatened rain. Mangan finished his coffee and closed his eyes. They headed south, over the river, into Virginia.

At Tyson's Corner, the rain started, coming down hard, and the traffic slowed. Patterson swore and pushed on, until, with no signal and a last-minute flick of the wheel that had Mangan straining against his seat belt, they were off the highway and into an underground car park at speed, circling down into the concrete gloom.

They parked three floors below ground, and Mangan found his door opened from the outside by a thick, sandy-haired man in a fleece, who didn't meet his eye, but scanned the rows of cars.

"This way, Philip," he said, and they walked towards the elevators, Patterson behind him. The air was cool and smelled of exhaust fumes, and their footsteps echoed on the concrete; Mangan realised he had become hyper-attentive. Fear again, he thought. As they waited for the elevator, he turned to Patterson.

"Tell me something, anything," he said.

She just shook her head, looking away.

They went up six floors, to an apartment that looked out over eight lanes of traffic, a long blurred streak of brake lights in the rain. The sandy-haired man drew heavy curtains, turned a lamp on and motioned to a couch for Mangan to sit. The room was blank, wallpapered in pale green, with an empty bookcase. It smelled of emptiness, disuse, old coffee, cardboard. These rooms, Mangan thought. These arid, empty rooms, where we sit and wait for it all to start. Patterson stood by the door.

"What is this, Trish?"

"You'll know soon enough."

"Oh, for God's sake. Drop the bloody mystery. What's going on?"

But as he spoke, the sandy-haired man was opening a door, and Hopko was walking into the room, and over to him, holding her arms out as if for an embrace. He stood up, towering over her, then bent and hugged her, feeling her blocky frame, her thick, strong shoulders under his hands. Over her shoulder, he glimpsed the interior of the room from which she had come. It was brightly lit, several laptops sitting on a table, a tangle of wires cascading to the floor, open flight cases, blinking LEDs. Hopko stood back and looked at him, as if at a successful young relative.

"Philip!" she said.

"Val."

He could smell her perfume. She wore a mannish white shirt, the collar turned up, and brown leather jeans over flat shoes, and jewellery of hammered silver, a great glistening bracelet, ingots in a necklace. Her hair, a deep rich black, was big, teased up.

"Sit, sit," she said. "Good heavens, you look frightful. Was it a *very* heavy night?"

"I wasn't expecting—"

"Of course you weren't. I do apologise. We're terribly

sorry, aren't we, Trish?" Patterson stood in shadow by the door, silent.

This is it, he thought. It's all over. The last two years. Everything I've done. This is the end of it. He was, he realised, angry at Hopko, and full of regret at the same time—regret at having failed in her eyes, regret at being unable to master the world she had pulled him into. He felt himself tipping into petulance, but pulled himself back. That's her trick, he thought, she dangles her approval at you—and knows how to make you seek it.

"This is Brendan," she said, indicating vaguely to her right. A younger man had entered the room. He wore a suit that was a little too large for his slight frame, had clever, mobile eyes, thin lips.

"Now, we've lots to talk about. Don't worry, we're very secure. This is our little Washington hideaway, one of them, anyway. We come here on the rare occasions when we don't want our esteemed American partners to know exactly what it is we're dreaming up." She had sat in an armchair opposite him, crossing her legs and leaning back. "Now, you'll forgive me for expressing mild surprise, Philip."

"You're forgiven," he said, but she wasn't listening.

"I mean, your wandering South America, your communications with this little girl. What on earth are you hoping to achieve?"

"She's desperate. She wants our help."

"We're not bloody therapists," said Hopko, laughing— a harsh laugh. He thought he glimpsed contempt there, or her own anger.

"She's a line in."

"A line in? To what, though? That's my question, Philip, what sort of ghastly places are you leading us, unasked, unbidden? Where on earth might we all end up?"

"That's what we'll find out. I thought that's what you chaps did. Find things out."

Hopko's eyes glittered a little.

"Indulge me," she said.

He waited for a moment.

"Are you sacking me?" he said.

She cocked her head.

"I think that rather depends on what you say next."

"Oh, stop the fucking fan dance. You know what I've said to Pearl Tao. You know what she's said to me. We have a line to her, and, I am certain, into a Chinese network. She is ready to talk to me. I can...I may be able to bring her over."

Hopko exhaled. Brendan, who hadn't said a word, had opened a laptop and was squinting at it.

"Do you enjoy this, Philip? This...life you have?" Hopko said. "Grubbing around, living your cover. Spying for us. Getting the living daylights beaten out of you. You seem very invested in it, if I may say."

Patterson was very still, leaning against the wall, watching him. And he understood that Hopko was feeling him out, was readying herself to take a decision.

"Do you not think you might have done enough?" she said. Her tone had softened a little. "China was rough on you. Ethiopia and Thailand were rougher. You've done a lot. More than most."

"You are being very patronising," he said.

"Am I?" She seemed genuinely startled.

"Do you want me to meet the Tao girl or not? Do you want to penetrate this network or not?"

Hopko took off her glasses.

"Tell him," she said.

Patterson came over from where she was standing and leaned against the back of the sofa. Brendan looked up at her.

"There's another side to this whole thing, Philip," Patterson said. "There was a man, an American intelligence analyst at State. Bigwig. It seems he was the target of an operation. He was coerced, blackmailed by a woman he was having an affair with."

Mangan saw her stiffen at the mention of the affair, as if she could barely contain her disgust at the idea, and he almost smiled. God, she's a prude, he thought. She went on.

"He shot himself. They found evidence in his house— very incriminating evidence—of clandestine activity."

Mangan wasn't sure where this was going and shrugged.

"His wife was murdered, Philip. With poison."

He shifted in his seat.

"Well, that's very John Buchan," he said.

"Not really," she said. "Her hair fell out, she went into convulsions and took two weeks to suffocate in an intensive care unit."

"Oh."

"The FBI are treating it as a murder. They say they don't know who did it. But our assumption is that it was the opposition."

"I thought they didn't do that kind of thing, the Chinese."

Hopko leaned forward.

"They gave *you* quite a kicking, I hear," she said.

Patterson tried to keep control.

"The point here, Philip, is that Monroe—that was his name—is linked to a bank account in the British Virgin Islands—administered from Suriname."

Mangan swallowed.

"So, point one," said Patterson, "is that this network— if it is one and the same network, or at least administered by the same structure—is big, and it is powerful. Point two: someone is willing to defend it. In ways we haven't seen before. Very aggressive, unpleasant ways."

"Point three," said Hopko, "the Americans don't know."

"And we'd rather like to keep it that way," said Brendan.

Mangan tried to piece it together.

"Why don't you want the Americans to know? Surely

they have to know, don't they? Frightened they'll muscle in or something?"

There was a stony silence in the room. He pushed on.

"In fact, why not just hand it all over to them? It's their country. Their stuff that's being stolen. Their agencies that are being compromised. Their people being murdered. In fact, should you be operating here at all?"

But Mangan noticed Patterson looking to Hopko for an answer, too. She didn't understand either.

Hopko was wearing her patient smile.

"There are other operational contingencies in play," she said.

"Fuck does that mean?" Mangan retorted.

"Are you trying to get something off your chest, Philip?"

"I'm trying to gauge what this thing is, what it's about."

"Do you know, for a business that revolves around betrayal, ours is awfully dependent on trust, isn't it?"

Mangan didn't answer. Hopko put her glasses back on.

"If we are to continue, I require that you demonstrate trust. No more freelancing. No more pootling off on your own. And please, for God's sake, spare us the theorising. You will do what we need you to do, when we need you to do it. Can you live with that?"

"How did you know I was in Suriname?"

Hopko gave a little barking laugh.

"Oh Philip, honestly. Sometimes you're such a wily operator, and sometimes you're innocent as the day you were born. Posthumus is one of ours, for heaven's sake. Has been for years. At least on weekdays. Weekends and high holidays, well, I have no idea who he works for. He can spot people like you a mile off. We got a rather amusing note from him. In it, he described a tall, red-headed, odiferous Englishman with cover skimpier than a whore's knickers. Did it ring any bells? To which we said, Ah, it's Philip Mangan, last heard of fleeing a flap in Thailand with a bad case of the sulks. What's he doing? To which Posthumus replied, He's sniffing around T. Y. Teng, lawyer to the global kleptocracy and suspected channeller of covert funds to Chinese intelligence networks."

Patterson had shrunk back, and Mangan could see, beyond Hopko's glassy glibness, her capacity for contempt.

"I got this far," he said.

"Oh, you did. We're just wondering what you might have broken in the process. Those goons in Paramaribo were chasing you for a reason. You exposed yourself by talking to the girl, Philip. You showed too much leg. Teng got a peek of you. That means everyone else associated with this network now has wind of you. Might I ask how you feel about that, knowing what the same people have done here in Washington? With poison, for heaven's sake. Poison! Bloody ludicrous."

"Are you asking me if I'm too concerned for my own safety to go on?"

"Well, believe me you'll be signing something that limits our liability if you do, dear."

And Mangan saw, in her look, that she knew exactly how much he wanted it.

There was the usual business about communications. Brendan took his laptop, installed encryption software on it, walked him through new protocols, took him down into darknet and made him work them, for practice. Hopko sat very still, listened. Mangan forced himself to concentrate. The sandy-haired man brought ham and cheese sandwiches and a bag of pretzels, and coffee, which Hopko sampled and declared unpalatable. "Honestly, Micky, can't we do a tiny bit better?" Patterson ingested hers rapidly and without complaint, caught Mangan smiling at her stolid, soldierly chomping, and made a *what are you looking at?* face. Sheets of rain thrashed the window.

The timing and location of the meeting with Pearl would be up to him. He'd be reserved, diffident, even, letting her come to him. Get her talking, Philip. Do what you do, be the reporter. Listen. Listen with every strand of your being. Listen for every word, every inflection, every little current of anxiety running through her speech. Don't look for answers; she won't have any. Look for possibility. Look for where she might take us, what she might offer. Don't rush her; walk her slowly, slowly towards the summit.

They came close to an argument over Patterson's role. Hopko deemed her non-operational, that she would have a communications and liaison role only, but he insisted she be available for him, that she walk through it with him. They went back and forth on it, and then Hopko suddenly relented, as if she'd meant to all along, and Patterson gave him a look that said, *Thank you, and I'm slightly surprised.*

"Do I tell her who I am, who we are?" he'd asked.

"You tell her that you are exactly who she needs you to be," said Hopko.

Patterson drove him back into DC, winding around the Beltway and cutting up through town, along Independence, across the mall and north, watching the mirrors. It was afternoon, and he was drained. The rain stopped and the sky cleared to a metallic blue, and as they drove, Mangan looked out at the vast, grey federal buildings, saw them as monuments, eulogies to a senile state, to a kind of power that was leaking away into a digital abyss.

At Brookland, near the flat, she pulled over.

"What's the backstory, Trish?" he said.

"What do you mean? What backstory?"

"What's Hopko not saying? Will you tell me?"

"Is she not saying something?"

"Yes, of course, for God's sake. She's holding back. You know perfectly well she is. What the fuck is *other operational contingencies*?"

He saw her sigh. "I don't know."

"Do you remember what I said to you, in Addis?"

She was looking straight ahead, watchful.

"I told you that you were the only person with whom I had an honest relationship," he said.

She didn't answer.

"It's still true," he said. "I lie to everyone else."

"Yet you choose the life. Here you are, again."

"I know, I know." He shrugged. "Isn't that just the strangest fucking thing? Why is that?"

She turned to look at him, and he found those dark eyes locked on him, full of wariness.

"Why?" she said. "Because you're looking for your own story, full of sound and fury. All tragic and manly and full of meaning. And you think you get redeemed at the end."

He couldn't think of any response.

"But you don't," she said. "There aren't any endings. There never were. And there's no audience, Philip. It's just you and me."

Pearl,

I would like to meet you on Saturday, three days from now. Do you like frozen yogurt? Perhaps you could be at the Sweet Frog frozen yogurt store, off New Hampshire Avenue in Silver Spring, at 3:40 p.m. I'd like you to take a seat and wait for me, even if I am late. If I haven't come by 4 p.m., you should leave, and I will contact you again to make a different arrangement. Is that okay?

I hope everything is all right with you, and I'm looking forward to seeing you again, and hearing about everything that's been going on.

All the best,

Philip

37

Patterson had been on the road since ten in the morning, checking her own back. She was in a swept Service car. She'd had her flat swept. She'd changed her secure handheld for a new one. She'd sat in a rattling metro car for an hour, far out into Maryland, bobbed and weaved, taken cabs. Where was the surveillance now? In the days since she'd encountered the fatuous watchers downtown, she'd not seen them again.

Perhaps they were no longer there.

Perhaps that's an assumption that gets operations blown, that invites a dusting of thallium on your pancakes, a spoonful in your tea. She felt a clenching in her chest, the surge of heat on her skin, her breaths coming faster. *For God's sake, stop it.* She put her hands on the wheel, controlled her breathing. *Am I really losing it?*

She'd taken up this static post at two. She'd shopped in a drug store and a grocery, buying a paper cup of thin, bitter coffee, and then sitting in her car, watching the weekend hours play out in a suburban strip mall: the SUVs disgorging bright-eyed children in soccer strips, ballet costumes, martial arts kits, herded by mothers in sunglasses and yoga pants, laden with tote bags. A Latino family headed for the bowling alley, the kids capering and jumping. A woman on a mobility scooter argued with a man on a motorbike. A homeless man sat on a milk crate holding a saucepan.

For a moment she thought she'd seen something, a young couple, dishevelled, tattooed, who'd lingered in a way that wasn't right—too much movement to them, too much awareness, anxiety. But in the end, having watched them pace and slouch and shiver for twenty minutes, she'd realised their demeanour was chemically induced, and they were waiting for a deal, or a mark, maybe. They walked to a black camper van and drove away.

She exhaled and signalled, *Clear*. They'd brought in two other watchers, but she couldn't see them, only hear the clicks in her earpiece as they signalled back. *Clear*. She'd asked for more, planned a full three-sixty, but Hopko had said no. A light footprint, as light as possible, she'd said. And if that made them vulnerable, so be it. The locals must not notice a thing, and if they did, the consequences were too awful to contemplate, apparently, though Hopko was not disposed to explain why.

At 3:17 p.m., a woman of Asian appearance entered the frozen yogurt store, but she did not resemble Mangan's description of the girl, and she emerged immediately with her purchase in a paper cup, and Patterson signalled, *Not her*, then took another walk around the parking lot. She moved the car, parking it in a space some sixty feet from the entrance to Sweet Frog Frozen Yogurt. The store was an odd, unpractised choice on Mangan's part—too small, not sufficiently anonymous for her taste. But, well, here they were, the operation small, full of holes, her stomach a churning pit.

At 3:38 p.m. precisely, a young woman of Asian appearance emerged from a red Honda Civic, looked both ways and crossed to the sidewalk, heading for Sweet Frog. Patterson sat up, eyeing her. She was dressed in a light blue fleece and faded jeans and a pair of pink sneakers. Her hair was shoulder length, tied in a ponytail. She wore thick, silver-framed glasses. To Patterson's austere, over-observant eye, she appeared unfit—not overweight but untoned, soft, a little ungainly, round shouldered; a pale complexion, suggestive of an indoor life, artificial light. A woman who did not care greatly for appearances, or who perhaps had never mastered the art of creating them. She was walking towards the store now, and towards Patterson's car. Patterson got a good look at her face, and saw there mobility, a quickness of expression, and apprehension, too.

She stopped outside the store, peering through its plate-glass window, then turned and looked around. Patterson signalled, *Eyes on target.*

The girl was still outside the store, looking through the window. She had raised one hand to her shoulder, and was clenching and unclenching her fist in a clear gesture of anxiety. Get a grip, woman, Patterson thought. She was pulling the glass door open now, stepping hesitantly inside.

Clear.

At 3:48 p.m., Mangan walked across the parking lot, hands in pockets, his lazy amble, a breeze catching the copper hair, blowing it about. He was his usual rumpled self, a pair of green cotton slacks, that linen jacket, abysmal scuffed leather shoes. He stopped just short of the store, looked at his watch, shot a look in her direction that sent another shock of adrenalin through her, and went in.

Pearl was sitting in the far corner, looking like a frightened fawn, eyes wide behind her glasses. Mangan gave a smile, went to the counter, bought two Creamy Mint Cookie frozen yogurts and went to her table. The store was empty except for one other group of teens at a distant table.

"Pearl," he said.

"Oh, hi," she said. "You came. I wasn't sure you'd come."

He grinned at her.

"Of course I came. It's good to see you. Really." He

pushed the cup of frozen yogurt across to her, and she looked at it, wide-eyed, as if it might explode. He spoke very gently. "Does anyone know you're here?"

She shook her head, still fixed on the yogurt as if some truth lay encased in its crystalline surface, its nubs of chocolate.

"Where do your parents think you are?"

She shrugged.

"Okay, Pearl, listen just for a moment. If we are interrupted for any reason, any reason at all, I want you to walk down that little corridor there, past the rest rooms, and go out of the emergency exit. Don't go to your car, okay? There will be people outside there who will make sure you're okay and will get you home."

She just looked at him.

"Pearl?"

She nodded, though she looked like she might cry.

"What people?" she said.

"Friends of mine. Good people. Look, it's just in case. Everything's going to be fine. It's really great you're here."

She picked up her spoon, returning her attention to the frozen yogurt. Mangan saw that her hand was trembling.

"So you've had a rough few weeks," he said.

Another nod.

"Can you tell me anything about it?"

She looked straight at him, a searching look, and he saw again, behind those thick, smudged lenses, the deep, warm intelligence of her.

"Am I allowed to ask you something?" she said.

"Yes. Anything."

"Well, I guess, who are you, really, and why are you so, like, concerned?"

"I'm—"

"I mean, are you American?"

"No. No, I'm British."

"Well, who do you, like, represent?"

Mangan rested his elbows on the table, leaned in, spoke very quietly and quickly.

"Pearl, I'm supposed to give you all sorts of rubbish in response to that question. But I'm not going to. I'm with British intelligence. There. Said it."

Her eyes went wide.

"You're *what*? What does that even *mean*?"

"It means that…It means you're in a very tricky situation, to be honest." He held his hands out. "The man your father met in Paramaribo, he's…we think he's an agent of Chinese intelligence."

He waited a moment.

"So, what we don't know is why your father—"

"My father is a spy, isn't he?" She was almost whispering.

"Pearl, we don't know anything for certain. That's why we need to talk to you."

She looked at him.

"I just don't know what I'm supposed to do," she said.

"Well, a start might be just taking me through everything that's happened."

"I—"

"We can't do it here. We'd have to go somewhere we could talk more openly."

She frowned. "I'm not going anywhere with you."

"Really? I think it would—"

She just shook her head, and Mangan could see the resolve, that he was wasting time trying to persuade her. He looked around. The teens had gone. There were two other couples in the store, one girl behind the counter, looking at her phone. Thin, sibilant Christian rock music came from speakers mounted in the ceiling. Where the hell to start?

"All right. All right. Look, you mentioned a trip to China. Can you tell me about that?"

She thought for a moment.

"My dad, he just announced we were going. He'd got tickets and everything. We flew to Hong Kong, and we were, like, spirited into Guangzhou, and just met all these people in a weird house and they wanted to know about my work, and my plans."

Mangan probed, looking for names, descriptions, places, tried to draw the picture. The "cousin" she hadn't known about. Her future at Telperion. The veiled threats, delivered so elegantly. The woman in the cashmere shawl. The little smooth-skinned man. It all came tumbling out of her, to Mangan's astonishment.

"Why you, Pearl, do you think?"

She shrugged. "I'm going to be at the top of my field. I already am, pretty much. And they're interested."

He almost smiled at her forthrightness.

"And your field is...?"

"Artificial consciousness. Artificial Super Intelligence. At the moment I'm trying to make drone swarms act autonomously."

"Oh. Right. And that's something the Chinese would be, uh, interested in?"

"Interested in?" she said.

"I mean," he said, flailing, "these are things that might have military applications? Strategic value?"

He felt her looking at him as if he were from another century, some ridiculous throwback mired in curly telephone cords, floppy disks and the hiss and burble of dial-up connection.

"I think we can safely assume that," she said.

And then there was more. The midnight excursion to the park, the money. Uploading the files to God-knows-what network in a Washington coffee shop. Mangan felt his chest tighten. *I found it. I fucking found it.*

But Pearl was looking up, beyond Mangan, with fright staining her features.

38

The car came into the lot too fast, a blue Lexus, bouncing over the speed bumps and pulling into the parking space crooked. Patterson saw it immediately and signalled. *Seen. Wait out*, came the replies. The driver's door opened and a middle-aged man of Asian appearance got out. He was looking around, searching the lot. He began walking up and down the rows of cars, his posture exuding anger and urgency.

Christ, is that the father?

He spotted the red Honda and strode across the lot towards it. When he reached it, he peered in, tried the door, then straightened up, hands on hips, surveying the stores, looking for her.

Patterson was out of the car and into the Sweet Frog store. She moved to the table where the two of them sat, the girl looking at her in what seemed to be abject terror, Mangan turning, exasperation all over his face. She kept her voice very level.

"Pearl, your father is here. He's seen your car, he'll be in this store in sixty seconds. Stay calm. We'll be in touch soon. Philip, with me."

He started to speak, but she just said, *"Now!"* and he

was out of his chair and they moved quickly down the corridor to the rear exit.

Mangan looked over his shoulder, to see Pearl staring at them, deep distress on her face. Patterson was leaning into the crash bar on the door, when Mangan stopped.

"What, for God's sake?" she said.

"Two bowls. On the table." He turned to go back.

"No." She grabbed his arm, pulled him back. "I'll go."

She ran back down the corridor. Pearl's father was at the window, looking in, shielding his eyes. Patterson walked past Pearl's table, and in a single motion reached out and snatched Mangan's half-eaten frozen yogurt and kept moving.

Pearl's father pushed through the front door. He saw Pearl now, and strode across the store towards her. He brushed past Patterson, and she smelled sweat on him, his fury.

She walked to the trash can, took a napkin, wiped her hands, and lingered. He stood over his daughter, berating her in a rushed whisper, one hand on hip, the other jabbing at the air. Patterson couldn't hear what he was saying, but Pearl was cowering, and Patterson saw him reach out and in a strange, pinching movement, grab the flesh of her upper arm and twist. It was so quick, you'd hardly see it, but her face was crumpling, and the tears were starting, and she had brought her elbows in as if to protect her torso. Patterson felt a surge of anger, and the thought crossed her mind to walk up behind him and kick him hard in the knee, just to watch him go down. He had hold of Pearl's wrist now and was saying, "*Zou, zou.*" We're going.

The other couples in the store were paying attention, and the woman behind the counter had her hand to her cheek, dithering about what to do. Mitchell Tao pulled Pearl towards the door, and she shuffled beside him, strands of hair loose around her face. As she passed, Pearl glanced at Patterson, then looked quickly away, but her father didn't notice, and then they were out of the door and across the parking lot to her car.

Dear Pearl,

I am so sorry about today. We decided it would be disastrous if your father saw you with me, and that is why we ended the meeting in such an abrupt fashion. Again, I am so sorry. My colleague saw the way your father treated you. But can you tell us the reason for his anger at you? Did he realise you were meeting someone? Or was it just that he didn't know where you were?

Also, I think your father has planted a tracking device of some sort on your car, and can tell where you are from that. You should check your phone and see if he is tracking that, too.

It seems to me that we must now find a way to keep you safe, extricate you from your father's scheme, and allow you to get on with your extraordinary life. Does that sound right to you? I am certain that I can help, and I wish to do so.

Let's please meet again soon. How about this Friday, 8.15 a.m. at the Starbucks on Hopkins campus?

Philip

Hopko stood by the window in the Tyson's Corner safe flat, her venal, anticipatory expression on. Mangan was slumped on the couch, cigarette in hand. Patterson wondered why Hopko looked so pleased.

"Extraordinary!" Hopko was saying. "Absolutely bloody extraordinary! Whipping her off to China, job interview at an MSS safe house. Hoping no one would notice. By all the pestilential saints! And right after she's applied for her security clearance, cheeky sods! I confess, Philip, I am floored. Utterly floored." She started pacing about the room, gesticulating.

Mangan was tiring of the theatrics, Patterson could see. He studied the end of his cigarette and ran a hand through his hair. It was strange. Patterson had always attributed to Hopko a preternatural understanding of her agents, had always seen hers as the dominant understanding in the room, any room. She was startled to realise that Hopko didn't always get Mangan, didn't always read him right.

"Astounding, isn't it?" said Mangan levelly.

"It bloody is," said Hopko. She paused, collecting herself. "Now, from here, we will be constructing the operation as we go. All players have been assigned P numbers. Cryptonyms are coming. There will be a subvention for operational funds and a small team will be on permanent standby to provide surveillance, liaison and communications. We're bringing in from London and from Canada, and utilising local assets. We will have mission objectives and modalities defined and circulated in the next thirty-six hours."

"And what actually is the objective, Val?" said Mangan.

She turned to him and gave him her best, nuclear-powered smile.

"You do what you do best, Philip Mangan: build trust with her, and find things out. You're a bloody marvel. And the objectives will come clear, soon."

The treacherous hours, the house silent, the street outside still; a few late cicadas rustling in the trees, the air damp, a fine moisture in the light of the street lamps. Pearl, at the window of her childhood bedroom, looked out, trying to make sense of her life, of herself, trying to recast the narrative.

How do you remake memory? she thought. How do you rewrite the neural map? How do you take years of life and, in the light of new data, understand it differently?

She pictured her schooldays, her huge high school, the bus in the cool, fall mornings, the anticipation of the new school year, the dreadlocked bus driver playing his crazy music as they bumped along; the corridors, the lockers, the smell of floor polish and gym clothes; her tribe of smart kids, eating their peanut-butter sandwiches together in the clatter of the lunch room. She thought of how she was never allowed to go to their sleepovers, or to hang at the pool. Of how, on the rare occasions her father met her friends or their parents, he became almost manic—the terrible back-slapping, the strained attempts at fellowship, at faked intimacies, the singing of songs that left them startled and confused. Once, at a neighbour's backyard barbecue, she had told him to stop interrupting, to be quiet—she must have been thirteen or so—and later, when they had gone home, he had hit her. She touched her temple, the imprint of his thick hand still burning there.

On the bed behind her lay a backpack, her tablet and an envelope containing nine thousand dollars she'd withdrawn from the bank. And there was a letter for Cal.

She listened for a moment, shouldered the pack, picked up the money, tablet and the envelope, and walked silently out onto the landing in the darkness. They were asleep, she was certain. She crept down the stairs, down to the basement, to his office. It smelled of him—not of his body, but of his life, of who he was; there in the basement dankness, the dust and paper, the airlessness, the hint of mothballs, the stench of emotional confinement.

The smell of the lie.

His laptop was in its drawer. She took it out, wrestling

the charger from the extension cord. She moved, very slowly now, back up the stairs.

Opening the back door took her several minutes, easing the latch over in tiny incremental movements, closing and locking it the same way, tiny step by tiny step.

Her car was parked nose out. She'd made sure. She dropped the pack and the other things on the back seat, put it in neutral, and pushed it into the street, one hand on the wheel, one on the driver's side door. The car lumbered forward, her sneakers scrabbling on the asphalt, her breathing coming in gasps.

She stopped for a moment and looked back. The house was still, dark. It was 2:17 a.m. She leaned into the car again. She was two blocks away before she jumped in and started it, easing out onto 29, heading for the interstate.

Philip,
I'm so outta here.

Pearl

PART FOUR

The Break

39

I-95 South

Pearl estimated she had about four hours, so she drove like a bat out of hell, south into Virginia in the dark with the eighteen-wheelers, their cabins glowing, their grilles filling the rear-view mirror. She was skirting Richmond in an hour forty-five, pushing on towards the south, passed Suffolk before six as the dawn was beginning to show.

On a quiet back road, east of Suffolk, she pulled over and got out. The land here was forested and wet, ribbons of still, murky water and marsh between the trees glinting in the early light. The Great Dismal Swamp, a reeking expanse that stretched way into North Carolina. She'd always liked the name, and felt that, at this moment, it fitted her predicament. She had prised the tracker from where it had been attached with duct tape, inside and above the glove compartment, and held it now, ready to pitch it into the gloom. She almost did. But if it landed in water, well, perhaps it wouldn't work. So she laid it by the side of the road, and covered it with moss and leaves, a kind of burial.

She went back to the car, picked up her phone, turned

off its location features, put it to airplane mode, and shut it down, before popping out the SIM card. Then she wrapped it in a sheet of silver foil that she took from a pocket of the backpack. She checked her tablet, made sure it wasn't signalling either and wrapped it in foil, too.

She drove on, making Norfolk, the big Navy town on the Atlantic coast, fifteen minutes later. Her lovely red Honda she left parked in a filthy, graffitied underpass, the sidewalk strewn with blankets, boxes and bottles. She left the car door open, the keys in the ignition, hefted the backpack, and walked away.

The bus was heading west now, away from the coast, into the interior. She slept, only waking as they pulled over at Roanoke in the early afternoon. She got out, went to the bathroom, then stood in a line for coffee and a burger. Against the surveillance cameras she had a hoodie and sunglasses, but that was all. It didn't matter, yet.

She bought a ticket for Knoxville, Tennessee, sat on the sidewalk in the warm afternoon, eating the burger draped in its lank pillow of cheese.

The next bus was half empty. She wanted to listen to music to soften the edges of her feelings, some K-pop, some blow-dried boy band, something normal, but she dared not turn on either of her devices. She curled up in her seat, trying to think, to fend off the clawing in her chest. The bus hummed and shivered and rattled down a road that was forested on either side. It was late in the afternoon now. She spoke to no one.

They'd be after her already. She knew it.

The blank email and the childish declaration contained within it stopped them all in their tracks. Mangan hadn't even checked his account until mid-morning, so it had been there for hours. Patterson had hauled over to the house at eleven, making two passes. She saw the father's SUV in the driveway, and another vehicle, a silver Camry. She photographed it, noted the plates. No sign of Pearl's car, but there was her father's face at the window, a phone clamped to his ear, watching.

When she got back to the Tyson's Corner flat, Hopko was livid.

"So just what the hell does this mean? Has she run away? Where the hell is she?"

The extra team members were touching down at Dulles airport, on their way to the flat. Hopko was going to have to explain, and she didn't like it, at all.

Mangan, dark circles under his eyes, hollow-cheeked, said nothing. He typed slowly and carefully on a laptop.

"Philip? Well?"

"We have no means of knowing what she means, or where she's gone, if she's gone. The only way we are going to find out is if she tells us."

Patterson took a deep breath.

"What about the FBI? I can call Polk."

Hopko rounded on her.

"You will do no such bloody thing. Do I make myself quite clear?"

There was a silence, and then Mangan spoke, even as he stared at his screen.

"Perhaps it's time you told us the rest of the story."

"You are not cleared for the rest of the story," Hopko muttered.

Pearl, my friend,
   Can you tell us where you have gone? And why?
We are very concerned. The people you are running
from—if they are who we think they are—are not

forgiving, and they will be searching for you. Please, let us help.

And please be in touch with me as soon as you can.

Philip

That first evening, they ate take-out sushi around the table. The extra help had arrived, and two of them sat on the sofa, silent, listening to Hopko plan—though it was more like improvisation. There was Harker, in from Ottawa, a fortyish contractor, with thick arms and a greying beard, ex-army, something secret, wearing a leather jacket; and next to him, O'Riley, an Irish woman with brown eyes, a soft smile and a watcher's eye and sensible shoes, on loan from Five in London. Sitting there, they looked like a married couple whose plane had been delayed.

Hopko was in triage mode, sorting through the elements of her crippled operation, searching for what was still live. And while Pearl's disappearance was problematic, Patterson couldn't help but feel Hopko was freaking out a little too much. Something was at stake, one of the "other operational contingencies," presumably, that neither she nor Mangan—nor anyone else in the room except Brendan—was privy to.

If we talked to the FBI, thought Patterson, we could easily get the car from number-plate recognition on the freeway. But Hopko was adamant, so no FBI.

"We are operating," she said, "on the soil of an ally without their agreement or knowledge. We are operating under a set of authorisations that are very rarely—read never—invoked. We are on thin, thin ice. If we give so much as a hint to the FBI that we have an operation underway, they will eviscerate us." She smiled a raptor's smile. "Are we all clear? I want us to be really, really clear." She looked at Patterson questioningly.

"We're clear," she said.

"No nuzzling up to Polk."

Patterson nodded.

"No night-time chats, flirty texts."

"I understand."

"Do you?"

She's protecting something, Patterson thought. She can't let the Americans know what it is.

Hopko had started the wheels turning, passing everything to Cheltenham, requests graded PRIORITY. Pearl's details, email addresses, her car licence plates, images—everything they had on her was seeded in the servers, waiting for something, anything.

Mangan was fingering a cigarette packet: its plastic crackle, the *snick* of the lighter, his long exhale. O'Riley looked disapproving.

"They'll find her," said Mangan. "Whoever is running her father and mother. MSS. They'll find her and they'll take her."

"Not if you find her first," said Hopko brightly.

Pearl,

Are you receiving my messages? Just answer. So we know you're okay.

Philip

In Knoxville, Pearl stayed in the bus station all night. The waiting area's metal seats were bolted to the floor, the air full of disinfectant. She didn't sleep or eat. She would have gone out for food, but through the doors she saw the indigent and the ill, some begging, others collapsed, wrapped in blankets, and she wondered who else was out there. She ate chips from a vending machine, held on to her backpack, shivering. At two or so, a man approached her. A white guy, in chinos and a black golfing jacket. He was thick around the middle, with slicked-back hair and pale, delicate hands. She couldn't tell how old he was.

"Hey, sweetheart," he said, standing over her. "What you still doing here?"

She didn't meet his eye.

"It's a bus station. Waiting for a bus."

"Well, where're you headed?"

"Away from here."

"Well, okay then. I guess we all are. Mind if I sit down?"

He lowered himself into the seat next to her, and she smelled alcohol on him.

"It just seems pretty late for you to be here all on your lonesome. What time's your bus?"

"It's soon," she said.

"Well, I was thinking of going to get something to eat. You can come along if you want. We could go to the all-night place on Ransome. It has burgers, steaks, all that stuff. We could get a beer."

"I'm okay, thanks."

"Oh, c'mon. It'll be fun, and I'll get you back here for your bus, I promise."

"I think I'm going to try and sleep."

He paused, his eyes flicking over her.

"Well, I don't think it's safe for you to sleep here."

"I'm fine, thanks. Really."

"Well, I'm just trying to help."

"Okay, thanks."

"You don't have to be rude."

"I'm not being rude. I said thanks."

"Fuckin' rude bitch." He stood up. "Fuckin' bitch."

She looked away, held her backpack tight and focused on its straps—the black buckles, their orange nylon weave. He leaned forward and allowed a gobbet of saliva to fall from his mouth and land with a *splat* sound by her feet. Then he walked some distance away, sat, and watched her. She got up, picked up her pack, went to the women's lavatory and sat in a filthy stall with the door locked, trying not to cry.

Her bus left at five. North now, on Interstate 75, up into Kentucky, the traffic moving freely in a grey-blue dawn. She wondered if they'd found the tracker and the car yet.

And who were "they"? She imagined sleek, sculpted Chinese men, wearing black, moving silently out into America, hunting her, breaking into her bank account, her credit card account, her phone; hacking the surveillance cameras; watching her sobbing in a bus station toilet. She wondered if the tall, dishevelled English guy was looking for her, thinking about her. Whether he cared.

She dozed for a while and woke up fiendishly hungry. To take her mind off it she busied herself with a cohomology problem—*Let F be a functor between the following abelian categories*—and lost herself for a while as Lexington went by and the bus crossed into Ohio and the Cincinnati skyline came over the horizon.

In Columbus, Ohio, Pearl got off the bus in the cool afternoon. She was stiff and her blood sugar was low and she felt weak as a kitten. The bus station sat amid a forest of office buildings and she had to walk for blocks before she found a restaurant. When she did, it was a Korean place, and she was the only person in it. She sat away from the window and ordered *bibimbap,* and thought of Cal and nearly started crying again.

The food came and the smell of it nearly made her faint. She wolfed it, the egg yolk breaking and running into the rice, a tiny dish of *kimchi* speckled red with chilli making her nose burn and her eyes water.

That first night, Pearl checked into a motel near the airport, the Gala Motor Lodge, paying in cash, the morose woman behind the counter only glancing at her driver's licence. The room was overheated, the walls stained beige and paper thin; there was hair on the pillow.

She walked to a fast-food place, bought chicken and biscuits and took it back to the motel, eating it while she sat on the bed and watched television. She badly needed to sleep, but before she did, she took her father's laptop from the backpack and used a small screwdriver to take the back off. She extracted the hard drive and laid it on the bedside table.

Her tablet was still in its jacket of silver foil. Unable to resist, she unwrapped it and booted it up. She had hardened the machine: built a virtual private network, disabled anything that could leak. She was, she thought, well hidden. Now she logged on to the Wi-Fi connection, just for a moment, downloaded her messages and logged off. Three messages from Cal.

Pearly, you okay? Didn't see you today. You sick?
What's up? Dr. Halberman was asking about you, some paper due? C xx

P, where you at? Texting you but no answer. You said you'd go with me to the grad seminar, but NO SIGN OF YOU. 'Sup? C xx

Hey P, I called your home, and yr dad was really weird. Wouldn't let me talk to you. Why'd he do that? Three days now I didn't see you. Talk to me. Did I do something that upset you? I'm so sorry if I did, just tell me what it is, cause I have no clue. Miss you Pdog. C xxxxxxx

There are many different species of betrayal, she thought, and here was one of them. She pushed the pain of it to the margins and scrolled through the messages.

And there he was, her English guy. So polite, so measured, so economical of speech. *The people you are running from are not forgiving, and they will be searching for you.* No shit, Sherlock.

Four messages from him, imploring her to be in touch.

She turned off the lights, stripped, showered and lay on the bed in the darkness listening to the sounds of exile, the mutterings and shouts from the next room, the slamming of a car door, the percussive hiss of the trucks braking on the freeway, and beneath it all, the deep vibration of the city's subconscious, its barely audible hum.

So this is to be alone, she thought. This is to be utterly adrift, with no audience, no soundtrack, no ending in sight. No promise of redemption.

They did this to me, and now I must find a way out of it, alone. Think, Pearl.

Are they coming? When?

40

Columbus, Ohio

In the morning, Pearl began.

First, breakfast at a pancake house. Eggs, bacon, fruit, toasted bagel.

Then, a phone. In a shabby mall not far from the motel, she bought a prepaid SIM card and an unlocked, second-hand smart phone from a store with barred windows that offered to buy your gold for cash. The Latino man behind the counter regarded her curiously as he handed her the phone.

Next, she walked to a big box store more than a mile away and paid, in cash, for three hundred dollars' worth of prepaid gift cards issued by a big credit card company. She repeated the exercise four times at different tills. She had researched these purchases—which stores, where—on the big laptop she had left at home, the internet histories untouched, there for a capable investigator to find.

At times, during the morning, the panic that roiled just below the surface began to rise and engulf her in a storm of fear and self-recrimination, but she forced herself to breathe, to think, forced it back down.

The letter to Cal went in a blue post box.

Dearest Cal,

I am so, so sorry to be writing to you like this. As you may have guessed, I've skipped town. I needed to get away for a while, not from you, you're my only real friend, the only person I can trust right now.

Everything has just become too much. I feel like I'm under pressure from every direction, and I'm not able to live up to all the expectations that are being put on me. All I want to do is try to lead a normal life, and to work at the things I'm good at. I'm going to hang out here for a while, where I am now, and I'll be in touch soon.

All my love,
P

Betrayal takes many forms.

Now, the hard part.

Back in the motel room, she logged on—as herself this time, no VPN. She went to the Columbus, Ohio, listings on a big classified ads site.

Three-month let, move in immediately, 2BR, 1 bath. Students welcome. $235 per week.

The apartment was close to the university, the top floor of a shabby clapboard house, the floors sloping and creaking, the carpet thin, dark brown, a single air-conditioning unit jammed in a window. A good, strong wireless signal.

"It's perfect," she said.

The woman was short and obese, in a flowered dress that hung to her knees. She smelled of tobacco.

"I'll need to see your driver's licence," she said.

And Pearl gave it to her. The woman photocopied it, dropping the copy in the folder with the lease.

"Thank you so much," said Pearl.

"It's my pleasure, hon," said the woman, folding the

bills, handing her the keys and the Wi-Fi password. "I ran the credit check, and it's just as I expected, so it's all yours. You be good now. No parties, no pets, you hear me? I know you do. You Asian girls. You are my best tenants." She gave Pearl's hand a squeeze. "Just the best."

Later, Pearl walked across the campus at Ohio State University. She put up flyers on three noticeboards. The flyers were in Chinese and read:

Three-month sublet, available immediately. 2BR 1 bath. Wi-Fi. Close to campus. Very good price $120 per week only! Call.

That evening, drained, she ate at a Chinese restaurant that looked promising, but it was a disappointment, the *mapo doufu* shorn of its acrid heat, a mystery fish dish sickly sweet. But just as a sullen waiter cleared it all away, the burner phone rang. An excited voice, speaking Mandarin.

"The apartment! So cheap! May we come and see it?"

Of course. Tomorrow evening. See you there.

41

The help had been staking out the Tao house in Silver Spring for two days. The street was way too quiet for a static post, so they'd made passes as often as they dared, in cars, on foot. Apart from curtain-twitching, and Mitchell Tao's face at the window, nothing.

Until the evening of the second day.

It was O'Riley that got it, though she insisted it was more down to luck than judgement. But there they were, sixteen digital snaps of the car in the driveway, and, emerging from the house, three unidentified individuals, Mitchell Tao standing in the entrance hall, half in darkness, closing the door behind them. One Caucasian male, six foot three in his socks, two hundred pounds or so, forties but fit, muscle in a good suit, likely armed given the cut of the jacket and the way he looked about. One male of Asian appearance, thirties, in a black thigh-length leather jacket, five ten, hundred and fifty pounds, slender, and—O'Riley was quite clear on this—the body of a dancer and the looks of a reality TV angel, a face to launch a thousand memes. And the third? Female, of Asian appearance, elegant, hair in a bob, sunglasses atop it, in a belted mackintosh, collar up, jeans, boots. Pricey, this one. The look of the executive suite, the superior table, the fundraiser.

And O'Riley, who had an ear for such things, fancied that all of them, including the Caucasian muscle, were speaking Mandarin.

As Patterson said herself, what on earth could explain such atrocious tradecraft? Parading around in broad daylight, trooping in and out of the Tao house. Was it arrogance? Panic? Though all present were agreed that the intelligence gods—so capricious, so brutal in their ironies—had smiled on them for a fleeting moment.

Patterson leaned into the laptop and zoomed in on the woman. That look, somewhere between the sculpted and the gamine, spoke to her.

"I'm damn sure it's her," she said to Hopko. "I'm absolutely sure it's 'Nicole.' It's the woman who was screwing Jonathan Monroe. The woman Pearl saw in Beijing. It's the woman I encountered, before..."

"Yes, Trish, I know. And with the facial recognition, we'll all know soon enough."

And they did.

Nicole Yang was Taiwanese, of aristocratic parentage, the father something big in the KMT. She'd been a Ph.D. candidate at Harvard, no less, and post-doc at Oxford. The subject of her research was *New Ontologies for the Modelling of Evolving Security Metrics in the Asia Pacific Region.*

"Fuck's that mean?" said Mangan, to Patterson's relief.

"It means she has good, natural cover," said Hopko absently.

The Caucasian was one Krause, ex-German special forces, contractor to a variety of fly-by-nights in Iraq, now apparently joining the exodus of talent to China's espionage-industrial complex.

Of the beautiful man, nothing.

"But with only three of them..." said Patterson. "I

mean, I don't know how you start a nationwide manhunt with that."

"Oh, there'll be more," said Hopko. "They'll be working the servers, firing up whatever they already have planted on U.S. networks. We should assume they'll be able to make use of law enforcement systems if they want to. Cameras, recognition. We must assume—we *will* assume—that they are ready for something like this." She was tired, Patterson could see, her voice flattening into a monotone. "Pearl doesn't have long."

The three of them were christened HAMPER 1, 2 and 3. Harker was told to stay on them, and he silently picked up his bag and jangled his keys. It was left unspoken that surveilling three trained hoods with a single watcher was an impossibility. In fact, it actively imperilled the entire operation; a single exhausted watcher, getting sloppy, giving himself away. They'd know, and soon.

Why would Hopko take that risk? Needs must, Patterson supposed. But still.

Mangan went to the balcony to smoke. Hopko planted herself at the dining table, wrestling with deployments, signalled London demanding—no, begging for—more resources.

But it was unclear to Patterson where the objectives of the operation lay. Were they to hunt Pearl? If so, what for? Were they in the business of saving runaways? Or were they to stake out the father and mother in order to flesh out the size and shape of the network, with a view to wrecking it, bringing the Americans heads on a plate? Hopko seemed utterly unwilling to commit to an operational direction. Patterson considered confronting her, but knew she would bridle, snatching away any hope Patterson had of redemption. The soldier in her chafed at the uncertainty. What was commander's *intent*? She didn't know.

Mangan had come back in, reeking of tobacco smoke. She wanted to talk to him, alone, away from Hopko. And that, she understood, was a dangerous impulse.

The next morning, and the next item on Pearl's list: a gun show. It was in a hotel in South Columbus. She took a bus down there in a light fall drizzle, arriving early. The men on the door looked her up and down, but took her money anyway. She walked in as some of the vendors were still setting up. She looked around, hardly knowing where to start. At the first stall she went to, the guns all looked big and heavy. Some looked battered and old.

"Do you have any...new guns?" she said. "Or are they all, like, used?"

The seller wore a veteran's cap, a camouflage jacket. He was grizzled, ponytailed.

"Well, I guess they're all pretty old, 'cause this here's World War Two weapons, hon. Some Korea." He pointed to a sign above his head: *Vintage Militaria*. He grinned, but not unkindly. "They all work, though. What exactly you looking for? Maybe I can help you find it."

"I...I just want something for protection," she said. "Something small."

He rubbed his chin, then stood.

"Hey, Gordie," he called. The man at a stall behind her looked up. "You help this lady? She's looking for some protection." He drew out the o, *proooootection*.

"That's all I got here," said Gordie, overweight, sweat patches on his tie-dye T-shirt. "I'll protect you all the live-long day. C'mon over here, miss." He made a big, theatrical *come here* gesture. They act kind, but they just patronise and unsettle me, she thought. She walked over to his stall.

"So, let me guess, you're looking for something small, discreet, but credible, something you can keep by the bedside, in the glove compartment, something like that? Am I right?"

She nodded.

"What is it, you got an admirer gone a little crazy? You get robbed? Something like that?"

"No, I just feel a bit... I just want to protect myself."

"Course you do. Everybody should." He thought for a moment, then reached for a handgun from the dozen or so on the table in front of him. To her eye, they all looked the same: small, black, full of tension.

"Now, this here's a Sig. Nice little weapon. Good size for those small hands of yours. It's .380 cal, so not the most powerful. But she's a beauty. Here's the baby Glock. Most reliable weapon on the market, for my money. And here's the Ruger 9mm. Belle of the ball. Got some stopping power. Take her, give her a feel."

She took the Ruger, wrapped her hand around it, felt a surge of adrenalin that surprised her.

"Oh, yeah," said Gordie, as if he felt it too.

"Okay, I'll buy this one. And some bullets," she said.

"You'll be needing the bullets," he said. Then he looked at her. "You should get some practice, you know. Get to a range. Get the feel of her. Also, clean her, okay? Keep her clean and she won't let you down."

Is there no ID check? No paperwork? she wondered. Apparently not. Gordie was putting the weapon in a box, rummaging for a box of 9mm ammunition, which he found and put on the table.

"Now, I used to be law enforcement. And I would say you need to make sure you stay within the rules in the state of Ohio. You clear on that?"

She nodded. He frowned, something bothering him.

"You sure you're okay? Somebody threatening you?"

I'm giving off a signal, she thought. My fear is visible. And he sees it and wants to play saviour.

"I'm okay, but thanks for the advice, and the...protection. I feel better now," she said, appeasing him. He seemed pleased. She had put nearly five hundred dollars on the table.

"Well, if you're frightened of something you should tell law enforcement. That's what we're here for," he said.

"Oh, I will," she said, moving away.

He'll remember me. He'll talk about me at the bar, at the football game. *There was this tiny Asian girl, wrists like sparrow's ankles, short-sighted as hell, looked like a baby owl, but real scared, you know? Shoulda seen her gripping that little Ruger like she's about to blow some guy's balls off.*

What did he see that gave me away? Do others see it?

42

Cal had been assisting at Mechanical Engineering Freshman Lab when the text came in.

> Hi Cal. Im a friend of Pearl's. Can we talk. Its important. Im here on campus.

He had wrapped up and quietly slipped out of the lab, heading for the coffee shop on Pond Road. A woman in her thirties was waiting for him. She was very good-looking. Classy, Cal thought. She wore a blue quilted jacket and a grey scarf of some expensive-looking material. Her legs were long and slender, and she sat with her ankles crossed and tucked to one side, like an actress in a black-and-white movie. She spoke Mandarin to him.

"Cal, thank you so much for meeting me. I apologise for not making an appointment. Very rude of me."

Cal couldn't quite place her accent, something coastal, or Taiwan maybe, which confused him.

"Can we speak English?" he said.

"Well, okay," she said. She was looking around herself, scanning the room.

"You said you're a friend of Pearl's?"

"Yes. I'm a friend of the family. And we're all very

concerned about her. And I'm sure you are too. I just wanted to check in with you, see if we can...figure this out." She spoke really good English.

Cal regarded her. She was laying it on, giving him a wide-eyed, earnest look.

"Figure what out?"

"Well, what's going on with her. Her parents haven't heard from her in days. They're very, very worried. She's a very special girl. You know that, right?"

"Of course I know that. I think I know that better than you."

"Why do you say that?"

"Do you even understand who she is? What she's capable of? The things she's going to do?"

"Oh, we understand that very well. And that's why we're so concerned that she's not responding to messages or email. She's not answering her phone."

Cal heard that *we*.

"Well, maybe she doesn't want to be found right now," he said.

And just there, he saw her expression change fractionally.

"How do you know that, Cal?"

He shrugged.

"Has she been in touch with you?" she said.

He opened his mouth to speak but she was there first.

"She has, hasn't she? How did she contact you, Cal?"

"There was a letter, okay? But she gave no details as to where she was."

"Show me the letter, please."

He bridled.

"I don't take orders from you."

She smiled, a warm, wide, startling smile, the smile of a performer, one who wins hearts for a living. It felt like a lamp being turned on him.

"Of course you don't. But Cal, you can tell me where the letter was posted, right? We need to know what's happening with her."

"The letter is private."

She cleared her throat, putting her finger to her lips, as if in thought.

"Cal, you're from Hong Kong, right?"

"What does that have to do with anything?"

She nodded, bit her lip.

"Your parents are there, aren't they? In Hong Kong? And you have two sisters?"

He felt his stomach turn over, a little flash of alarm.

"Why is that relevant?"

"Think about how you would feel if one of *them* were to disappear. Wouldn't you want their friends to cooperate in the effort to find them? To get them back? Surely you would."

She can't be serious, he thought.

"What are you saying?"

"I'm saying that you really need to tell us where that letter came from, Cal. And what was in it. So we can find Pearl. Just the way you would want it if *your* sister disappeared."

"Who are you? Who do you work for?"

"Like I said, I am just a friend of Pearl's family. I worked with her cousin. In Beijing."

Beijing? Oh, crap.

"She never talked about a cousin in Beijing."

"No? Well, her cousin cares about her, a lot. Now, Cal, the letter. Please."

"I don't have it with me."

She leaned forward, and her eyes resembled blades.

"Where was it posted? And really, you need to respond now. Otherwise, things are going to get difficult." She pursed her lips—a *there'll be nothing I can do* expression.

He swallowed, and notions of betrayal, its myriad shapes, flitted across his mind. And he knew that what he was about to do would mark him forever, a lifetime of erosion.

"Columbus, Ohio," he said.

She was reaching for her phone.

The first girl who wanted to sublet the apartment wasn't right—too tall, too glamorous—and Pearl had to turn her away, which led to an ugly scene and some insults, but Pearl, having read the instruction manual and figured out how to load the clip and work the slide, had the little Ruger tucked in her waistband, and felt weirdly empowered.

The second girl came with a friend, and they were quieter, more amenable, in T-shirts and jeans. They were both from Qingdao, studying dentistry. Sweet girls. She would have liked to get to know them, she realised.

"You pay in advance," said Pearl. "In cash." The girls nodded.

"I'm ordering some new furniture for you. Some kitchen stuff. You can move in the day after tomorrow. When the stuff arrives, you can sign for it. Just say you're me, okay? Pearl Tao. Just sign Pearl Tao. And then you can use all the stuff." The girls nodded again.

"Why are you moving?" one of the girls asked.

"Oh, my boyfriend," said Pearl. "He lives over the other side of campus. I'm moving in with him. We've got an apartment together," she said, sounding proud.

"Ooh, lucky. Is he an American?"

"Yes. Yes, he is."

"Very lucky," said the girl. "Better hope your parents don't find out." And they all giggled.

She bought a cheap laptop in cash from a pawn shop, under a low sky that warned of winter. She spent an hour configuring it to pick up her messages, and then to drop them off in a secure file-sharing site, deep down in dark-net. She configured it, also, to allow a remote login. Pearl found a place for it atop one of the kitchen cupboards, just below the ceiling, out of sight. She wired a power sup-ply from an outlet above the counter, ran it up inside the cupboards, so only a few inches of unremarkable wiring remained visible. There the laptop would stay. The apart-ment was cold, bleak. She'd be glad to be out of it.

She went to the bank and made another large with-drawal.

Then, a trip to the big box store, where she spent a considerable amount of time in the make-up and hair aisles, and made a quick stop in the toy aisle, buying an inflatable plastic ball, like a beach ball, but smaller.

Nothing you can do will be definitive, she told herself. She had read the line in some hard-boiled private inves-tigator's memoir she found online, and it appealed to her. You'll never be certain of the outcome. Real action is never definitive. What counts is what you do with the time and resources allotted you.

Pray it's enough.

On a swampy roadside in southern Virginia, HAMPER 1 knelt, pawing through the grass and scrubby weeds in soft, afternoon light, the traffic roaring past, swearing in German. HAMPER 2 stood over him. Then HAMPER 1 got to his feet, holding something up, a black plastic disc the size of a hockey puck. HAMPER 2 shook his head and tapped at his phone.

43

In as much as Pearl had consciously forged a strategy, she knew it was time now.

That evening she stayed in the apartment until late. At nine, she went out for pizza at a nearby place which, she had discovered, she really liked. It had exposed brick walls covered in posters and was full of students from Ohio State; it was cheerful and a bit ramshackle and a little boozy and she thought that she could enjoy coming to a place like this, if she lived here and had friends who would go with her, someone like Cal who would sit with her and talk earnestly and make her feel like she had something to offer, something feminine and maybe even a little sexy, something beyond her coding and her facility with Partial Differential Equations. She sat alone at the bar and ordered a thin crust with artichokes and prosciutto and a Coke, watching the groups at the tables, talking, touching each other.

Later, back at the apartment, online and in the open, Pearl ordered, from three different retailers, a cheap television, plates, cutlery and glasses for four, tablemats, a blender, a rug, a duvet, two beanbags, some Shanxi black vinegar, a man's hoodie, three T-shirts in men's sizes, some men's pyjamas and an expensive man's watch. She charged all of it to her credit card.

She took her own phone from the backpack, unwrapped the silver foil, put the SIM card back in and turned it on. She called a number she'd taken from the classified ads site, enquiring about buying a second-hand car, left a message on voicemail giving the number of the burner phone. Next, a restaurant, where she made a reservation for a week's time. *Pearl Tao, for two*. Last, she called the twenty-four-hour number on the back of her credit card, checked her balance.

Then she slept.

In Norfolk, Virginia, a strange incident caught the attention of the desk sergeants, and even a crime reporter for the local TV franchise.

The man had showed up at the emergency room, his arm broken in two places, face bloodied up, his scalp opened by what looked like the edge of something hard. He was ranting about a carjacking, and the cops were called. He was well known to police, with a multicoloured record—some pilfering, some drug stuff, basically a harmless white kid, not a bad guy. Ticky, they called him, for the pacing and scratching and endless twitching that the meth set off in him. The resident had stitched his scalp, and now Ticky sat on the gurney in a robe, waiting to have his arm set, fulminating for whoever would listen.

"'Sup, Ticky," said the barrel-chested cop. "Who did this to you, man?"

Well, there'd been this car, and when the cop asked whose car, Ticky said he "found it." A red Honda Civic. Just sitting there, keys in ignition. Like it was being given away. And so he'd, well, he'd taken it. The cop sighed.

And, well, Ticky was just, like, driving it around, wondering if he should keep it or sell it, pull in some cash. And he was just parking up outside the apartment block in Portsmouth where he was hanging when this guy pulls in next to him, and, like, starts pounding on the window. And Ticky was, like, *what the fuck, man*, and this guy had the door open, and had Ticky by the arm and this guy was *hench*, like, made of rebar, and Ticky was thinking this was prolly an instance of mistaken identity, 'cause he'd never seen this dude even one time, but anyway Ticky found himself on the pavement and this guy was busting his balls and saying, like, real quiet, like in this calm voice, *Where's the girl, where's the girl?* And Ticky be all like, *Dude, what girl? There ain't no girl.* Ticky didn't see no girl. And this guy, he didn't say nothing, he just took Ticky's arm, and, like, positioned it, and then, crack! And Ticky's screaming on the pavement 'cause his arm's hanging all funny and shit and there's two of them and they're all over the car, like searching it, ripping shit out of it. Ticky didn't get a real good look at them, 'cause he was trying to get up and get the fuck out of there, but he'd swear the other one was Asian. But then Mr. Fuckin' Nuts-of-Rebar was standing in front of him pointing a 9 right between Ticky's eyes, and he had this look on like a total psycho, like he'll just do it and give zero fucks, and when Ticky started pleading with him, the guy just brought the piece down on Ticky's head and that was the last thing Ticky remembered.

And the cop was watching Ticky now, because he'd never seen the kid like this. The kid was terrified, fragile, close to tears, like he'd seen something from way outside his experience, and Ticky's experience covered a good deal on the spectrum of human behaviour.

And the cop wondered what the hell this was.

44

Harker, exhausted, glimpsed it all from the end of the street, and signalled. *Car found. HAMPER 1 assaults driver. Car searched by HAMPER 1, 2. No sign of CYPRESS. CYPRESS NOT PRESENT.*

In the Tyson's Corner flat, there was silence for a moment, as they worked the implications. Mangan wondered who CYPRESS was, then realised it was Pearl.

"They found her car? But how?" said Patterson.

Hopko shook her head.

"Resources. Commitment," she said.

Mangan shifted on the sofa.

"They're dangerous, aren't they? And they're on to her. And they'll find her."

Patterson took Hopko's silence for assent.

"Does mean one thing, though, doesn't it?" Mangan said.

"What? What does it mean?" said Patterson.

"Means we just have to stick to HAMPER," he said. "To find her."

Hopko was standing by the window, her glasses in her hand, looking at Patterson.

"I mean," Mangan said, "rather than launching our own half-arsed search, we just stick to them, and they'll take us to her." He sounded uncertain, was looking at the two of them questioningly. Patterson spoke.

"Philip, that is the most stupid, irresponsible—"

"He's right," said Hopko.

More help had arrived, a twofer, a married couple in from California, tanned and slim and bright-eyed and utterly out of place in this grey East Coast fall: the Paulsons, regular contractors, competent.

"Who we chasin'?" said the husband. Hopko had them pore over the photographs, gave them a spare briefing. She sent them out to buy new clothes and to hire a car. The Paulson woman sat Patterson down and produced a small black plastic case.

"I'm to give this to you, apparently," she said. She opened the case, and there it was, the little black tile. Patterson was no stranger to the use of vehicle trackers. She'd used them in Iraq. And she knew that the consequences of detection were operationally catastrophic.

"They'll sweep for trackers, surely," she said, incredulous.

"Not sure they will, actually." Hopko was standing behind her. "Given their tradecraft thus far."

"Val, we risk total compromise," she said.

"Total compromise? Sounds like a movie," Hopko said. "*Total Compromise*. Starring the entire leadership of British intelligence."

Patterson sat in stunned silence.

"I have weighed the risk against the benefits accruing," Hopko went on. "And I've decided we will go ahead."

And Patterson once again detected in Hopko's calculation some set of variables to which she was not privy.

Patterson left shortly afterwards, in a rental car, driving south towards Richmond, muttering imprecations that the HAMPERs would stay put, at least for now. The Paulsons hovered behind her, watching her back. It was getting dark and the traffic on I-95 was sluggish as the suburbs fell away and the highway was lined with scrubby forest swathed in vines. As she left Washington behind, she wondered if she'd ever get to the life that, just for a second, had beckoned her: barbecue in Shaw, glasses of wine with Emily and Esteban on the fire escape, runs along Rock Creek. People to talk to, know—befriend, even.

The tracker lay on the seat next to her, in its case. And her every glimpse of it brought back the Iraqi boy on the moped, *put-put*-puttering across her mind in the gathering dark. She'd put a tracker under his rear mudguard. A small one, state-of-the-art, with a powerful battery. He was a courier for the insurgents, local Sunni nasties, but she'd turned him, promising him the moon. And over a few weeks—or was it days? She couldn't really remember—the tracker had given them the location of every insurgent safe house in the area, as he *put-put*-puttered between them in his flip-flops and his *dishdasha*, dropping off messages and money.

And then the tracker disappeared from the screen, and so did the boy.

She forced herself to concentrate on the road, changed lanes, sped up, gave the Paulsons something to do.

She made Richmond in two hours and ten minutes, where, it transpired, HAMPERs 1 and 2, the German and Beautiful Man, were holed up in quite a nice hotel just outside town—no shitty safe flats and takeout for them, Patterson noted—presumably awaiting instructions, or perhaps awaiting metadata gleaned from the grid that would point them towards the girl.

Harker, yawning, rambling, exhausted, met them in a coffee shop, briefed them on the position of the car, then staggered away to sleep. It was a blue Acura, nose out, close to the exit of the hotel parking lot. The Paulsons took a stroll in the Virginia evening, hand in hand, and confirmed it was there. They confirmed, also, the existence of two surveillance cameras covering that area of the lot where the Acura now resided, but Patterson knew there was nothing she could do about that.

She opted for a tracksuit and running shoes, and jogged from half a mile away towards the hotel. The adrenalin was running far too strong in her; her heart rate was up and her mouth dry, her thoughts skittish. Get a grip, she thought, furious with herself. She was approaching the parking lot. The blue Acura was still where it should be, HAMPER 2's vehicle, Beautiful Man's. She thought again of the Iraqi boy, his eyes, the dust in his hair, the horror of what happened.

Focus, for Christ's sake.

She was coming up on the corner of the parking lot. The Acura was perhaps five spaces in, and to its rear lay a grass verge. She slowed a little, veering off the sidewalk onto the grass. Walking now, she came up on the car. She stopped, looked at her watch as if checking her time, and then went into a stretch, bending double, coming back up. She let her gaze flicker across the parking lot, looking for movement under the street lamps. Nothing.

She moved towards the rear of the Acura, felt in her pocket for the black tile, turned it on. She knelt, her face level with the tail lights, to tie her shoe. *Nothing to see here.* She reached under the rear bumper, feeling for the chassis, the steel to which the tracker's magnet would adhere. *Was that it?* She leaned in with the tracker, but the thing wouldn't stick and clattered to the ground. *Jesus Christ, now where is it?* She couldn't see where it had fallen and ran her hands over the asphalt under the car, hunting for it.

And that was when the rear lights flashed, half-blinding

her, and the car emitted an electronic *yip* and she heard it unlock. Frantic, she felt for the tracker.

Footsteps, and a voice.

He was at the front of the car, and she could hear the jangle of his keys. He was talking on a cell phone in quiet Mandarin. She couldn't hear what he was saying, but his speech was fast, his tone urgent. Where the hell was the bloody tracker?

He opened the driver's door, and she heard the *thunk* of a piece of luggage landing on the passenger seat. She felt the car lurch as he got in.

Desperate, Patterson reached for her own phone, fumbling it out of her pants pocket. The screen lit, and she flung herself down on her stomach, pressing her face to the asphalt. She reached under the car with the phone and the screen glow cast a feeble light. She moved the phone around. *Where in Jesus' name is it?*

A deafening bark as the car started.

And there it was, the tracker, lying flat next to the rear right wheel, a tiny glint in the glow. She lunged, rescued it, but where the hell to put it? *Dear God.* Hopelessly, she rammed the tracker up towards the underside of the car, searching for anything it might stick to, running it along what she thought was the cross member. The car's engine shifted register as it went into gear. And, in a sensation that would live in her fingers for minutes afterwards, the tracker was sucked out of her grasp. She thought she heard a *snick* sound as its magnet snapped onto steel, but she couldn't be sure.

And then the car was pulling out fast, leaving her lying rigid on the asphalt, her arms extended, one hand clutching the phone. The Acura bolted for the exit, pulled out on to the street and took off at speed, while Patterson lay stock-still, praying that he wouldn't look back.

And then there was just stillness.

She hauled herself to her feet, looked around.

The Paulsons were on the opposite side of the street, watching. The woman had her hand to her mouth, and they seemed to be laughing.

But on her phone, when she opened the app, the little red orb was bright as a button on the screen, making its way west.

By the time she raised Hopko, the tracker showed that HAMPER 2's vehicle was heading west out of Richmond on I-64 at a blistering pace. To Charleston? Into Kentucky? Or up into Ohio? Cincinnati? Columbus?

Something had got the HAMPERs' attention.

Hopko was bleary. Patterson pictured her sitting up in bed, in a hairnet, scrabbling for her glasses on the night table.

"What? What is it?" she said.

"HAMPER 2's vehicle is moving."

"Moving where? How?"

"Moving very fast, out of Richmond, west on the interstate. They've got a sniff of something."

"Have you told Harker and the others?"

"They're on standby."

"Well, for God's sake get them moving."

"I was waiting for—"

"I don't care. Get them moving in pursuit. Now."

"So, I'll head off with them."

"You'll do no such thing. Get back here immediately."

The line went dead.

45

HAMPER 3, Nicole Yang, got to Columbus first. She pulled in at midnight in the silver Camry and parked outside a clapboard house on a gritty side street near Ohio State. The boy at the lab in Baltimore had given her the city, Beijing had confirmed it with an address and a phone number gleaned from an online purchase made by the target three days previously. Home furnishings, a beanbag or something. And some vinegar.

The house was dark, but for one window.

She sat in the car for a while, smoking a cigarette. The others wouldn't be there for hours, that psychotic German and the other boy, the one with the looks, the fair skin and sweet eyes. Bambi, she called him, to herself.

She debated whether to wait and watch, whether to go in. The girl would be incapable of serious resistance. She'd watched her in Beijing, this frog-like creature, sitting there offering up her earnest answers.

And yet. The girl had shown enough wit and fortitude to up and leave. And to take her father's laptop with her, the little shit, with God knows what on it, enough to roll up a network twenty years in the making. Enough to force all of them to abort and run or face a lifetime of concrete toilets in Colorado, probably. All of which left

Nicole sitting out here in the middle of a cold, fall night, contemplating her next step.

Fuck it. Let's go and get this over with.

She stepped from the car, closing its door quietly, and crossed the street. She stopped outside the front door and listened. Nothing but the night insects' rustle in the scrubby bushes, distant traffic, a siren somewhere drifting through the still air. She climbed onto a peeling porch, opened the screen door, pushed the buzzer and waited.

Silence for a moment, then the thumping of feet on the stairs. The door opened and she smelled damp, and burned food. A girl stood there: short, Asian, a little overweight. She wore a T-shirt and plaid pyjama bottoms and slippers, her hair in a ponytail.

"Uh, yeah, hi?" said the girl.

Wait, was that her? Pearl?

"Hi," said Nicole.

"Yeah, hi," said the girl.

"Pearl, it's me," Nicole said. "You remember? We met, a little while back."

The girl looked at her with an expression of total incomprehension for a moment, then a smile spread over her face.

"Oh, right, you're looking for Pearl."

"That's right."

"Uh, yeah, I'm not Pearl."

"Of course not, I'm sorry. Is Pearl here?"

"Oh. Right. Uh, no, she moved out."

"She moved out? When?"

"Uh, like, yesterday?"

"Really."

"Yeah, really. Sorry. So. Goodnight." The girl moved to close the door. Nicole put a hand out, kept it open.

"Look, I'm really sorry. But do you know where she moved to? It's kind of important."

"Um, no. Sorry. Goodnight."

Nicole was still holding the door open.

"Can I come in, just for a minute?"

The girl was starting to look alarmed.

"It's kinda late, so—"

"Yeah, I really won't be long." And with that she gave the door a hard shove and it caught the girl on the cheek, quite hard, and she shrieked and sprang back. Nicole stepped inside and closed the door behind her.

"Wait, why did you do that?" The girl was close to tears.

"Let's go up to the apartment."

"Don't hurt me, okay? Please. We don't have anything."

"Just take me up to the apartment, and this will be over soon."

"What... what do you want?"

Nicole didn't answer, just grabbed the girl by the shoulder and pushed her towards the stairs. The girl gave a little wail, stumbling up.

"Is there anyone else here?"

"My roommate. She's in bed. Don't hurt us."

"Wake her up. Go and sit in the kitchen." But the other girl was awake, peeking with terrified eyes from behind her door. Nicole reached for her and she gave a shocked screech, dodged around her and ran into the kitchen.

Nicole stood over them.

"Where did Pearl go?"

"To her boyfriend."

"What boyfriend? Where?"

The two girls looked at each other, petrified.

"We don't know. She just said she was moving..."

"...somewhere near campus."

"How do you contact her? Come on, think."

The girls looked at each other again, silent.

Nicole walked over, looked from one to the other, calculating which of the two was the stronger. The first girl, the one in plaid pyjamas, marginally. Nicole reached over to her, and grabbed her ear, pressing her thumb-nail hard into the ridge of cartilage. The girl breathed in sharply, grimaced with the pain, then began to moan, the moan rising towards a scream. Her hands began to flail and she knocked a cup from the table. It shattered on the floor. The other girl had her hands at her mouth, tears on her cheeks. Nicole jammed her nail into the car-tilage, increased the pressure, and the girl was twisting her torso towards Nicole, her face contorted, her breath coming in gasps and sobs.

"How do you contact her?"

"She left a number. There's a number."

"Get it for me."

The second girl stood and ran to the fridge, unfas-tened a magnet, took a piece of paper and held it out, her hand shaking. Nicole snatched it away, releasing her hold on the ear.

"Give me your phone," she said.

Both girls were in tears now, one holding her ear with both hands, her body heaving, while the second walked abjectly to her room, coming back with a phone. Nicole dialled the number. It went to voicemail—Pearl, sound-ing chirpy. *Leave a message, peeps.*

"Stay there," Nicole said.

She walked around the flat, taking in what she could. She opened drawers, pulled clothes out, threw them on the floor. She opened the medicine cabinet in the bath-room, but it was empty. She went to the trash in the kitchen, pulled out the white plastic trash bag and emp-tied it onto the floor: tea bags, a half-eaten slice of pizza, apple cores, a used sanitary towel.

A receipt. Itemised. From a big box store.

She picked it up.

"Is this yours?"

The girls shook their heads.

She'd bought a bra. A camisole. Hair dye. Make-up.

"What's the name of the boyfriend?" she said.

"We don't know."

Nicole switched to Mandarin now, barking at them.

"Nimen bu yao ti zhei jian shiqing." Don't talk about this.

The girls blinked.

"Don't talk about it; don't raise it with anyone, not your teachers, not your friends, not the police. This is a matter of state. Do you understand?"

The girls sat, silent, unmoving.

Nicole walked over to the second, smaller girl. She stood there for a moment looking at her, while the girl shrank under her gaze. Nicole made her right hand into a claw, leaned down and took the girl by the throat, her fingers probing, searching for the trachea. The girl's face was a mask of shock and terror and her hands came up, pawing at the air. Nicole held her there, let the seconds tick by as the girl jerked and thrashed. Eventually she released her, and the girl fell to the floor, a weird animal noise coming from her.

"If you speak to anyone, I will know, and I will be back, and your families in China will receive a similar visit. Do you want that?" she said.

The girls just sobbed.

Nicole left them, went to the car and pulled away fast. She drove to a motel off 270, where she sat in the parking lot for a while, thinking. She lit another cigarette. They'd have to use the number, track the phone, search for the boyfriend. It could take days. And the little bitch had changed her appearance. Still, at least she was here.

Pearl woke at 6 a.m., the morning chill and dark. She wrapped the tablet and phone up in their foil sleeves, packed the backpack.

In the bathroom, she used a pair of clippers purchased at the drug store to cut off nearly all her hair. She left about an inch. It made her look a bit punk, a bit rough, she thought. She rubbed in a thick mousse-like dye that she'd hoped would turn her blonde. But after an hour, she was a dirty brown, with patches of orange. Whatever.

She took thin adhesive strips and applied them to her eyelids for a second fold, and her eyes immediately changed shape. She put in green contact lenses, thinking of the English guy—his look, his eyes, her own urge to trust him.

The make-up was difficult. She was trying to contour her cheeks and nose, but she wasn't sure how well it worked, if at all.

Last, she blew up the beach ball to about half its capacity, and taped it to her pale belly. She put on a padded bra which made her small breasts appear larger, heavier. Over it she put a tight camisole, and then a loose, shapeless cotton shirt and a black wool beret.

She hadn't lost all her girlishness, but the face that looked back at her from the mirror was that of an older, less predictable soul, one of indeterminate ethnicity. The silhouette was that of a pregnant woman. And there was no sign of the stubby Ruger in her waistband.

It just might be enough for the cameras, enough to deflect the gaze of a bored spook scrolling through hours and hours of surveillance footage. But enough to fool an algorithm? Unclear.

Before she left the apartment, she took the burner phone and called a doctor's office, asking what insurance they took. She called a random number with a local area code, and left a voicemail message. *Hi hon, see you later, what can I bring?* She called a handyman and made an appointment for him to come to the apartment in four days' time.

By nine, Pearl was gone. She bought a sausage muffin and a coffee from a convenience store, and walked as she ate.

As she approached the bus station, she crossed the street to where a homeless woman sheltered in a doorway. She was in her fifties, perhaps, draped in a checked blanket stained with age, her face collapsed, skin like sandpaper, a shopping cart next to her.

"Do you need a phone?" said Pearl.

"A what now, sweetheart?" said the woman.

"A phone. I have this phone that I don't need any more. It has, like sixty dollars on it. You can have it if you want."

The woman looked at her, a half-smile on her face.

"Is it a smart phone?" she said.

"It is," said Pearl. "Here." She handed the burner phone and the charger to the woman, who took them and examined them.

"I can call my daughter," she said.

"Sure," said Pearl.

"Thank you, sweetheart."

"Okay."

"You're a kind girl. And you look after that little one now, you hear?"

"I will," she said, touching the beach ball.

And Pearl walked away, wondering what she had done.

46

Pearl moved slowly across the ticket hall, toting the back-pack, one hand on her belly. She bought a ticket on the first bus to leave, heading north. It was for Toledo, up there by the Great Lakes, but she decided to get off some forty miles short, in Findlay, Ohio.

There, she walked to the edge of town, and, behind a chain-link fence, amid towers of scrap and the stench of oil, prevailed upon an elderly man to sell her a car.

It was an ancient black thing, its sporty wedge shape mocked by the scabrous, dull paint, the moss growing at the base of the windscreen. The man was attached to an oxygen bottle which he walked around with him on a little trolley, the clear plastic tubing hooked into his nose. He coughed and haggled with her, and she paid him three hundred dollars.

"Well, I sure hope it gets you where you're goin,' young lady," he wheezed. "And I hope God grants you a safe journey, and a beautiful and healthy child. In His wisdom." He gave her a pamphlet. It was called *Prayers of Love and Deliverance, Parenting in the Name of Jesus.*

The car shuddered and started, and the old man raised his hands as if in his own prayer, and Pearl pulled out onto the street as it began to rain, her only company the muffled *clack* of the wipers, the headlights coming on, the endless miles of highway.

She drove for hours, long blank hours on the interstate, hugging the slow lane, hanging on the lights of the eighteen-wheelers, skirting Chicago, heading west and north. Every now and again she'd pull off, drive down some dark back road, stop, piss in the bushes. Once she took a catnap, but woke after an hour, cold and deeply frightened. She opened the window, listened, heard voices somewhere off in the trees, saw lights and just panicked, starting the car and roaring off down the road. She merged back on the interstate and didn't stop for another hundred and twenty miles, her hands clamped to the wheel.

She finally stopped for gas—it must have been two or three in the morning—somewhere up in Wisconsin. She paid cash in advance and bought a chocolate bar and some water. The forecourt was empty, neon lit, and she stood there, the gas hissing from the pump, and she shivered. There were cameras, she realised, counted at least five.

A pick-up pulled in, coming too fast onto the forecourt, and lurched to a stop, music pounding. A guy got out, in a camouflage T-shirt and a trucker's cap. As he reached for the pump he saw her, did a mock double-take, and then just stood there, chewing on something, looking right at her. She looked away, but she could feel his aggression, his desire to toy with her like some fanged animal toys with prey. She got back in the car, locked the doors, felt for the Ruger under the seat, and drove away into the night.

Outside Madison, she pulled over at a rest stop as it was getting light, ate some chocolate, put the seat back, and closed her eyes. Sleep wouldn't come. The car was too cold, and trucks were constantly rumbling through. Her mind raced. Where would this end? Where would be far enough? How would she know?

She reached into her backpack, bought out her tablet, opened it, and again made sure it wasn't signalling. She opened a blank document and started writing.

So, Philip.

I just wrote someone I love a letter. I told him he was the only person I could trust right now.

I didn't tell him about you.

Can I trust you? What does British intelligence want with me? Won't you just hand me over to the CIA or FBI or whoever deals with people like me, with people like my parents? I mean, you are allies, right? And I'm a criminal now.

So what do we do? You and me?

They're coming for me, aren't they? Those people. The ones who control my parents. The man they say is my cousin, Beetle. That disgusting lawyer in Suriname. The expensive woman. And the neat and clean little old man. I'm going to hide from them, but I think they're going to find me.

Yours in despair,

Pearl

PS I stole my father's laptop.

Finally, she dozed.

Later, eighty miles on, she stopped at roadside services. In the food court she bought a hot chocolate and found a Wi-Fi signal. She submerged herself into darknet, deep into the encryption. Invisible, she navigated back to the laptop that she'd left in the apartment in Columbus. There it was, up there on top of the kitchen cupboards, still working, still online. She used it to send the email to Mangan.

TOP SECRET STRAP 2 BOTANY—UK EYES ONLY
COPY 2/5
//REPORT
1/ (TS) Source FULCRUM addressed a further letter to C/FE. This is his seventh communication. It is printed below in full.

Beijing
To: Controller, Far East and Western Hemisphere,
United Kingdom Secret Intelligence Service,
Vauxhall Cross, London

Dear Friends,

I am very troubled by recent events in our relations. Even though I have adopted a reasonable and generous attitude in our professional intercourse, yet you are making unreasonable demands. This is most arrogant and unacceptable. I feel I must again repeat the principles upon which our arrangement is based, and which can lead to mutual respect and cooperation.

1/ I will NOT tell you my identity. Your demand is unacceptable.

2/ The information I provide will be at my decision. I will not accept tasking from you. I will provide information only that I think you need to know.

3/ It is a big insult to question the importance or veracity of materials I am provide to you. I will not respond to follow-up questions.

4/ I now suspect you are finding ways to pressure me. Do you think you can do this? I remind you that my position is secure and my work is respected. Pressure or threats will have no effect. If this is true then I am most disappointed. Pressure or threats to me are like a whining mosquito, of no consequence. Perhaps I will look for other partners who have a better understanding of my value.

5/ You have still not respond to my request for diamonds. Please give this your urgent consideration.

I hope we can proceed on the basis of seeking common ground and avoiding disagreement.

Your friend,

Z

ENDS //

The HAMPERS had torn up the interstate to Columbus, Ohio. Harker and O'Riley were close behind them, the Paulsons on their way. In Columbus, the tracker on HAMPER 2's vehicle showed him darting around the city like an agitated rodent.

In the safe flat in Tyson's Corner they sat, the four of them, around Mangan's laptop. Brendan had been on a conference call with VX. Po-faced, self-important, he relayed something of the hysteria building at VX.

"I *would* say, without wanting to sound overly dramatic, that the top floor is demonstrating a measure of concern." He paused for thought, looked down. "I think that, while there *is* appetite for a continued presence in this operational arena, it's fair to say that there is concern, too, over the operational modalities, and, of course, over the degree to which we risk infringing upon or destabilising the norms of inter-agency liaison and cooperation."

He looked directly at Hopko, who was wearing her iron face.

"And I say all this even as the top floor is fully cognisant of the operational rationales in play."

"And what are those exactly?" said Mangan abruptly.

Hopko smiled at him, but he wasn't looking at her.

"I rather thought we were clear on that," she said. "The knowledge that she is in possession of her father's laptop makes finding her an imperative."

Mangan turned to her, and Patterson saw it, the side of him she sometimes sensed. What would she call it? Principled? Empathic? Not really—more clear-eyed, illusionless, hard to impress. The side of him, she realised, she waited for, that she respected.

"If these people get to Pearl first, if they find her before we do," said Mangan, "what will they do to her, do you think?"

Hopko sighed. "We've seen it before. They'll get her out to a third country. On a gurney, probably. There'll be an interrogation."

"And then what?"

"They won't kill her, if that's what you mean. She'll end up locked in a house somewhere on the outskirts of Beijing, probably. Out of sight. Somewhere with minders, high walls. And that will be that for her. For a very long time."

Mangan was sitting very still.

"And us, if we find her first, what will we do?"

"Philip, we will behave like decent human beings. Is that what you need to hear, my love?" She smiled, a hard smile, shot through with intention. "And in order for that to happen, you need to be persuasive, don't you?"

Mangan regarded her for a long second

And it was then, in that evaluating look of his, that, much later, Patterson would recognise the beginning of his dissent.

Pearl,

    Time is running very short now. You have been tracked to Columbus, Ohio. Is that where you are? Can you tell me? I will come and meet you. You do not have to be alone in this, I will come and help you decide your next steps. We can get you out of this situation. We can get you to safety.

I realise that you must be going through enormous personal pain and loss. Please talk to me about what you are thinking and feeling.

I give you my word that I will help you.

Philip

Mangan's first draft had included a commitment to her security and well-being, but Brendan had asked him to take it out.

"I'd rather we kept it general, at this stage," he'd said. "Clearly, it would be inadvisable to make any commitment that could be construed as a financial guarantee."

Pearl was in North Dakota when she stopped.

She pulled over by the side of the road fifty miles out of Bismarck, rolling farmland to the horizon, cold, clear air, the chatter of insects and strange, fluttering birdsong. She stood there for a while in the long grass by the side of the road, feeling the breeze on her face.

Time to catch her breath.

She checked into a motel in a place called Watford City. A tattooed girl with a toddler glanced at her driver's licence and gave her a key—a real, old-fashioned metal key, attached to a wooden fob. The place was full of oil men, burly, silent guys in trucker caps and pick-ups, scouring the state for work on the fracking rigs. They ignored her.

The room was hot and smelled of drains, air freshener. She sat on the bed, took off her shoes and tried to keep the despair at bay. On the bedside table was a paperback entitled *God's Word for the Oil Patch*: Bible stories interspersed with inspirational tales from the oil rigs. It seemed to have been dropped in the shower, its pages puffy and crinkled.

She slept for a while, and when she woke it was nearly dark. She opened the window, and the temperature had dropped. And off in the gloom, beyond the town, she could see the gas flares on the rigs speckling the prairie, flecks of flame in the gathering dark.

She went out for food at about eight, the Ruger in her waistband, bought a burger and fries and went back to the hotel room. A car had pulled up on the forecourt, next to her door, a white sedan. It hadn't been there before.

She stepped back around the corner, out of sight, waited for a moment. There was no movement, and she walked quickly to her door and went in.

Dear Philip,

It's so strange. I used to have a family. A pretty whacked-out one. My dad was always so angry. Or else trying to persuade everyone he was such a nice guy, like a real assimilated immigrant. He was so embarrassing. My mom, not so much. She would come to the school gate to meet me and she never talked to any of the other moms. And I never got to go to anyone's houses or anything. And summer vacations were like these long empty periods when either I would stay home by myself or I would have to go away to math camp. Actually, I quite enjoyed math camp. At least there were other geeks there.

But it was my life, at least. And I thought I understood it. And it had a feel, a texture, of its own. Like when I would sit out on the deck in summer and eat watermelon, and feel the juice run down my chin, and watch the fireflies. Do you have fireflies where you are from? They're my favorite thing. They come out in

June for about a month on the east coast, and in the evening there they are, sparking and winking in the trees, these beautiful little green flickering lights. And when it gets dark, and you go outside and let your eyes adjust, whole trees are flickering green. And they fly so slowly, you can just reach up and grab them with your hand and they'll sit on your fingers and their bellies will light up fluorescent green.

I think of them as a metaphor for us, for our consciousness. Consciousness as a tiny flicker in the dark. It's there, then it's gone.

I had planned to spend my whole life studying that tiny moment of light. Trying to figure out what it's made of, where to find it.

And now I'm sitting in a crappy motel by myself, far from that life, watching fire on the horizon.

I don't know what to do.

Help me.

Pearl

The white sedan worried her though she couldn't say why, and she left before dawn. She headed west again, then south, over mile after mile of prairie, watching the storms sweep across it in great pillars of cloud, dragging ribbons of grey rain. The fracking rigs squatted on the landscape, their flares billowing flame up into the rain. Once she saw a herd of spotted ponies thundering through the grassland, their manes long and wild, kicking up great clods of earth as they went.

Pearl found herself utterly alone on a back road, stopped the car, got out and stretched. The bleached skull of a steer sat atop a fence post, a rainbow in the far distance. She felt a spatter of cold rain on her face and wondered when it would turn to snow. Soon.

She looked back down the road a mile or more. The only other vehicle she could see was coming slowly towards her. It was white.

She tried to control herself, tried to manage the rising panic, but it had hold of her. She ran back to her car, jumped in, pulled away and put her foot right down, leaning forward, hunched over the wheel. In her mirror, nothing, just open road behind her. She pushed west, and crossed into Montana.

At Lame Deer, there was no sign of a white sedan. She stopped to fill the car. The place was Cheyenne, a reservation town in rolling hills with a water tower and a casino. At the trading post she bought Coke and a big bag of Cheetos and toothpaste, and the girl behind the till smiled at her, asked her if she was doing okay today, and she nearly cried again. The tattooed men outside leaning against their pick-ups watched her go, this dumpy little green-eyed kid with dirty hair in her skanky car who clearly had no clue where she was or where she was going.

Philip,

There's a poem I love. It's by this ancient Chinese poet called Bai Juyi, and it's from the Tang Dynasty, like twelve hundred years ago. One of his slave girls ran away, and he was really cut up about it and he wrote this poem.

"Losing a Slave Girl" by Bai Juyi
Around my courtyard house the wall is low, and on
   the door they rarely check the names.
To think we were not always kind brings shame, the
   knowledge of your unpaid work, regret.
But a bird won't long remain inside a cage, and in
   the breeze a flower leaves the branch.

As for news of where you are tonight, there's none,
and only the moonlight knows.

Isn't that lovely? I just wonder if that little slave girl felt the way I do right now. Were they hunting her? Was she alone?

I don't know where I'm going or how I'll know when I get there.

Am I going to you?

There's a white car, and I think it's following me.

Pearl

On, into Crow, the towns little more than hamlets of prefabricated homes and beaten-up pick-ups adrift in the huge landscape, the skies strewn with vast, strange striations of cloud. A man flagged her down some way out of Busby by just standing in the middle of the road, refusing to let her pass. He wore a filthy padded jacket and a woollen beanie. He came over to her window and she opened it a crack.

"You going to Billings?" he said.

"No," she replied.

"You gotta take me to Billings," he said. He smelled of something, of piss maybe, and his pupils were constricted, almost to pinpoints.

"I'm not going to Billings," she said.

"But I gotta file for my account there. My Treasury account," he said. He was holding a wad of paper, the sheets covered in handwriting. He pushed them against the window. Pearl read: REGISTERED WARRANT CLAIM FOR TRUST SPECIAL DEPOSIT.

"You gotta take me there." His voice was rising.

"Look, I'm sorry, I don't know what any of that is—"

He thumped the window.

"I'm a free citizen under common law and I gotta get to Billings!" he shouted. He began to kick the side of the car. "Open the door."

Pearl checked her mirrors and began to pull away, but she was too slow and he saw and tried to run round to the front of the car to prevent her leaving, his arms out, clutching the paper. Pearl yanked the wheel around and she could hear him screaming obscenities at her. He tried to jump on the hood but she was putting her foot down now and the car threw him off and she saw his hand flutter by the window as he went to the ground and she accelerated away, shaking, shocked, frightened to her very core.

She skirted Billings, that evening finding herself driving towards mountains that were not there one moment, and then they were, their snowcaps rising out of the horizon. Minutes later she was in them, the air suddenly alpine, full of spruce and ice. She took a winding back road for three miles that rose through forest, the surface slowly deteriorating to a hard shale, the mountains' flanks soaring on either side, leaving her in deep shadow.

There was a campsite somewhere up here. She slowed, peered into the trees, driving another mile before she found it. She headed down the track towards it, ignored the signs telling her to register, and parked under the trees. Two camper vans, a few tents; some kids in fleeces and hiking boots running around. She sat in the car as the dark came on, drank some Coke, ate trail mix and Cheetos. She took the Ruger out, checked the clip and rested it in her lap.

Sometime after seven, someone approached the car, leaned down, tapped on the window.

Pearl was speechless with fright, and found herself jamming her feet into the floor of the car, forcing herself back in the seat. The person tapped at the window again. It was a man with a ponytail and a grizzled beard.

"Hey, are you okay in there?" He spoke insistently, as if affronted. "I want to know if you are okay." Pearl looked straight ahead, hyperventilating, the breath coming in small juddering gasps. There was a woman there now too, peering in.

"Would you like something to eat?" she was saying slowly, as if Pearl were deaf or mentally deficient.

"Go away," she shouted, the words coming out thick and choked.

The man shrugged and walked off. The woman stood there a moment longer, looking concerned, then turned and left too.

It got dark and a lot colder, and she cried for a while, then put on a fleece and a woollen hat and tried to sleep, thinking of fireflies in the warm Maryland summer night.

In Columbus, Ohio, there were reports of an odd and vicious mugging.

More than a mugging—an assault. A homeless woman, pushing a shopping cart laden with plastic shopping bags along Van Buren Drive, was set upon by a white male, forty years old, two hundred pounds, demanding her phone. And when the woman—who had a history of mental health issues—refused, he struck her repeatedly with a closed fist and ransacked her belongings, leaving them strewn across the street. He took the phone, and left the scene in a silver car. The woman was unable to give a full description of her attacker, except that he had short brown hair and spoke English with a foreign accent and appeared exceedingly angry.

At dawn, Pearl opened the car door and the cold air flooded in. She stood and stretched, walking a few steps under the fir trees, the ground soft underfoot with their needles. The camper vans and tents were still quiet. She felt weak and slightly sick, her body reacting poorly to the stress. Her heart seemed to be skipping a beat about once every twenty seconds, its rhythm fluttery and irregular. She needed food.

She started the car, pulled out, and immediately the door of one of the camper vans came open and the man with the ponytail was looking out at her, frowning. She accelerated up the track to the road, then wound her way back down towards the interstate. At a Denny's, she stopped, went in, almost the only customer there. She took a table where she could see the road and the parking lot, and ordered pancakes and eggs and bacon and coffee. The waitress brought a pot of coffee and poured her a mug, the steam rising, the smell hitting her. Pearl cradled it in her hands, feeling the warmth, gazing out of the window towards the mountains.

At the edge of the parking lot, a white sedan was just sitting there, idling.

The fear rose up through Pearl's spine. Her hand began to shake, spilling coffee on the table. The waitress came with a cloth.

"You okay, miss?"

Pearl managed to stand, drop some bills on the table and walk to the door, her knees on the verge of giving out, her throat closing into a gag. The white sedan was still there.

She walked to her car, got in, and pulled away as slowly as she could manage, making for the interstate, past Fishtail and Absorokee. On I-90, heading west again, Pearl put her foot to the floor. She passed Big Timber doing ninety, more. She couldn't see the white car in her mirror.

What she could see was the flashing red and blue of the Highway Patrol.

47

Pearl slowed, changed lanes. The Patrol vehicle was right behind her now. She pulled over into the emergency lane, coming to a halt. She put her hands on the wheel and the tears came again. And then a deep, soul-crushing resignation.

This? After everything, this would be how they'd find her?

The trooper was approaching her car from behind. It was a woman, in green, with a wide-brimmed hat and a weapon at her hip. In the mirror, Pearl saw her reach over and touch the tail light as she passed it. Why did she do that? Now she stood by the driver's door and tapped on the window. Pearl opened it.

"Good morning, ma'am. Do you know why I pulled you over?"

Pearl, crying now, mumbled something incomprehensible even to herself.

"Ma'am? Are you okay? I pulled you over because I clocked you at ninety-two miles per hour. Do you understand?"

Pearl nodded.

"May I see your licence, registration and proof of insurance, please?"

Pearl pulled out her wallet, gave her the licence and the insurance card, pulled the registration from the glove compartment.

"Ma'am, there's no need to be so upset. Just wait right here."

She walked back to her vehicle to run the licence. Pearl tried to get hold of herself. In a matter of minutes the trooper was back, peering into the car.

Something not right. Pearl saw her eyes moving over the seats, the dashboard.

"Well, your licence is clean, so congratulations on that. Can you tell me why you were driving so fast?" As she spoke she was looking at the back seat, the empty Cheetos bag, plastic water bottles, the half-inflated beach ball, with duct tape trailing from it.

The Ruger was under the front seat, loaded.

"No reason," she said. "I didn't realise. I'm sorry." She wiped her eyes.

"Mm-hmm. Well, your licence is Maryland, and your plates are Ohio. So what brings you up here?"

"Just a road trip."

"A road trip, huh?"

Pearl nodded.

"All alone?"

She nodded again.

"Ma'am, I'm sorry, but are you in some sorta trouble?"

Pearl felt herself stiffen, and the trooper saw it, she could tell.

"It's not anything," she said. "Not serious. I just needed to get away for a few days. I'm sorry."

"Mm-hmm. How long have you owned this car?"

"Just a few days."

"It's not registered to you."

"Uh, no. Not yet. When I get back to Ohio."

"Mm-hmm. Okay. You got the title and bill of sale, right?"

"Yes." She reached for the glove compartment.

"No, it's okay, I don't want to see them."

The trooper stood there for a moment, contemplating. She wants to search the car, Pearl thought.

"You sure you don't want to tell me what's going on?"

Pearl forced a smile.

"Really. It's just…just a family thing. I just need to get away."

"Okay. Well, I guess I can understand that. But I am going to have to write you a citation for speeding today. You'll have twenty-eight days to pay it. Sign here."

Pearl signed—and knew that was it.

"Now you bring your speed down and be safe, and you're free to go." The trooper was walking away.

How long would it take?

The heating and air conditioning system in the Tyson's Corner building was faulty and had been turned off for repair. The air in the safe flat was thick with the smell of microwaved food, coffee, stress, exhaustion. The smell of an operation. Mangan had been told firmly he had to go to the balcony to smoke. Hopko had tied her hair back and wore a pink track suit and sandals. She would sit in silence for long periods, punctuated by murmured consultations with Brendan, the contents of which remained private. Patterson, in jeans and sweatshirt, had turned silent, hard, and Mangan thought he was seeing the soldier in her for the first time. But then she argued with Hopko over the need to deploy to Columbus, and Hopko had slapped her down, telling her that her place on the operation was "not secure," and she should prepare to return to Station. Mangan had watched her, seen her turn in on herself, the disappointment and hurt.

Mangan's own role seemed to have been reduced to writer of emails, his value to the operation residing solely in his personal connection to Pearl.

And then Harker signalled.

HAMPER 2's vehicle, the tracker still in place, had barrelled out to Columbus airport at speed and had been returned to the rental agency. He, or they, were flying, but impossible to know where.

Hopko bristled at Mangan.

"So Columbus *was* just a feint. All of it. Clever girl. And now they've realised it was all just a feint. You do understand, Philip—and it pains me to say it—but we are now entirely dependent on you."

Pearl,

I loved the poem. I studied Chinese, did you know that? I lived in China for a long time. I loved to read the Tang poets.

In your last note to me, I sensed despair.

There is so much out there for you, Pearl. You must envisage a future for yourself, a realised life, one free of the terrible choices that have been forced on you. That future is attainable for you. Will you let me help you attain it? Tell me where to meet you, and I'll be there, with help and food and money and warm clothes and protection and a future.

The people who are after you have left Columbus. What you did was extremely clever, but it only held them up for a few days. They are flying, but we don't know where to, yet. It seems likely they've got some hint as

to where you are. Has something happened? They may
be coming to intercept you.

The time has come now to let us help. Please.

Philip

Brendan leaned in.

"I think I'd like some assurance that she still has her
father's laptop," he said. "Do you think you could put
that in? I mean, word it carefully, but I do think we need
to know."

"Don't be fucking ridiculous," said Mangan.

Harker and O'Riley had bought tickets to get airside,
and were scouring Columbus airport, looking for the
HAMPERs, but no sign. Cheltenham was working the
passenger lists, but that would take time.

From Pearl, silence.

TOP SECRET STRAP 2 BOTANY—UK EYES ONLY
COPY 2/3
//REPORT
1/ (TS) Source FULCRUM addressed a further letter
to C/FE. It is printed below in full.

Beijing
To: Controller, Far East and Western Hemisphere,
United Kingdom Secret Intelligence Service,
Vauxhall Cross, London

Dear Friends,

Events are moving quickly. Please see summary
of urgent points for your consideration.

1/ A counter-intelligence investigation has
started. It is very aggressive. Investigators from
Ministry of State Security 9th Bureau are making

interviews with many senior officers associated with North American operations. I will face such interview soon. This is a very serious development.

2/ It seem probable that material passed by Monroe before his death have alerted Ministry of State Security. Rumour here that Monroe material allowed MSS to deduce it has a leak. Rumour is that source inside MSS was American operation codenamed DTCREEKSIDE. Also rumour that death of Monroe's wife was not MSS operation. Much confusion.

3/ While I currently feel quite secure, I must take precautions in face of investigation. I am confident of my position, but I must say I will take a pause in my business dealings with you, and will be out of contact for foreseeable future.

4/ The matter of the diamonds remains unresolved, and I wish for conclusion at future point.

Best regards, and be alert for my contact in future under HOPSCOTCH protocol. I will be back in touch when all clear.

Your friend,

Z

ENDS///

Pearl turned south, into Idaho, driving in darkness as much as she could in the faint hope she'd be less visible to the cameras. During the day she lay up in car parks, on the backstreets of tiny mountain towns, then in a manicured suburban street in Idaho Falls; she would start out as the sun went down. She ate microwaved pizza slices on gas station forecourts, drank bottled water and coffee. She felt her concentration fraying, her thinking becoming cloudy.

Then west again, into Oregon in a cold rain that gave

way to a sunset so beautiful she began to wonder if she was hallucinating. She'd entered the high desert. She stopped for a moment by the side of the road, got out, and the air was redolent with sage and wet stone, the chirrup of some small animal. She stood and watched the light fade.

Her situation seemed impossible, right here, right now. The notion that they were out there, that they were closing in on her, ridiculous. And she felt again a sense of inevitability, of how it would probably end. It came on as a flood of regret, breaking on her as sadness.

The light went, leaving the horizon a deep indigo. The stars began to show. She got back in the car, pushing on towards Bend in darkness.

At two in the morning she could keep going no longer, so another motel. The place was called The Pines Suites 24/7, and it sat back from the road behind a gas station, a single-storey block, the rooms opening directly to the parking lot, the musty reception area of dun carpet and wood veneer. A man was asleep behind the counter, his head on a desk. Pearl, reeling from tiredness, cleared her throat.

"Uh, hi."

The man stirred, sat up, looked around, his eyes slits, a frown. He turned, saw her, yawned and slouched towards the table. He hitched up his jeans.

"Can I get a room?"

"Sure can. Need some ID. Pay cash or card?"

"Cash." She held out her driver's licence for a moment, took it back.

"Sorry, can I see that again?" he said. She held it out to him, and this time he took it from her.

He was looking at the driver's licence. Looking hard. Then he looked up at her.

She had the green contacts in, but wore no make-up.

"Uh, okay," he said. He looked down, tapping out her name on the keyboard.

"And your vehicle tag number?" he said.

Pearl told him.

He keyed it in and printed a registration form.

"Just sign please, and that'll be sixty-seven dollars."

He wasn't meeting her eye. He stood straighter than before and his movements had become stiff and directed. She saw how he gripped the edge of the counter as he waited for her to count out the money. He leaned slightly away from her.

She felt her own autonomic response kick in, heart rate rising, adrenalin spewing into her chest. *Get out, now.*

She tried to speak, but her mouth was so dry she had to catch herself, lick her lips, start again.

"Has anyone been asking for me?" she said.

He was looking at the computer screen.

"I don't know anything about that," he said.

"I thought, maybe, someone had been in. Asked."

"Like I say, I don't know."

"What did they say?"

He looked at her now, mustering some aggression.

"Look, you want the room or not?"

"Can you tell me who they were?"

The man looked behind him, as if looking for someone, wondering if he should go and get them, that they could provide an answer.

"Look, I don't know anything, okay?"

"Did they offer money?"

"I don't know anything."

"I can offer more money."

He stopped speaking.

"I can give you five hundred dollars. Right now. You just tell me what happened. Who they were. When."

He was calculating, glancing over his shoulder again, then back at her. He gestured with his chin, and she noticed a tattoo on his upper arm. Something military, a dagger, some stars. The word IRAQ underneath.

"You got five hundred dollars?"

She nodded.

"You show me first."

She opened her purse, showing him the corner of a hundred-dollar bill. He leaned over the counter, his eyes hungry. She'd left the Ruger in the car. He looked over his shoulder one more time.

"Okay. There was a guy come in. This morning. Big guy. Foreign. He was asking for Pearl Tao. Said he was a PI. That's it."

"What kind of foreign?"

"How the fuck am I supposed to know what kind of foreign?"

"Was he Asian? Chinese?"

"Uh, no. No. He was, like, European maybe. But my dad said he saw the car outside, and there was a woman in it and she was, like, Asian. Okay? That's all I got."

"What did this man say? Did he leave a number to call? Anything?"

"Jeezus. Yeah, okay, he left a number. You show up, we're supposed to call him. Now just give me the fuckin' money, okay? Why's he looking for you anyways?"

Pearl counted out five one-hundred-dollar bills.

"Please don't call him," she said.

"Ain't up to me," he said, smirking.

Pearl thought of the Ruger, the gunmetal cold against her skin, the weight of it in her hand.

"What car were they in?" she said.

"Shit, I don't know. It was red. An SUV. Now you taking the room or not?"

Pearl said nothing and turned to leave. As she reached

the door, she looked back, and saw he wore a self-satisfied grin.

"Don't call. Please."

He made a *get lost* gesture. She walked out into the parking lot, into the darkness, back to the car. It was cold, no moon, but bright starlight. She got in, reached under the seat for the Ruger, held it in her hand, laid her finger along the trigger guard and worked the slide. She looked back at the door to the reception area, the light coming from it.

She raised the weapon and placed the barrel in her mouth, her teeth against the gunmetal. She tasted the oil, closed her eyes. A car passed on the highway; night insects chirruped; her breathing was ragged.

She took the barrel from her mouth, laid the gun in her lap. She started to cry again, great heaving sobs, started the car and headed out onto the freeway, going west.

Dear Philip,
   I'll be in San Francisco.

   Pearl

48

Mangan was on the balcony, alone. Patterson opened the screen door and joined him, shutting it behind her. Mangan leaned against the balustrade, looking out over the parking lot, the highway, a sea of orange neon in the pre-dawn dark.

"You're up early," she said.

He was lighting a cigarette, shaking the lighter, then cupping it.

"Heard anything?" she said.

He just looked at her, saying nothing.

"Share," she said.

"We should go," he said. "We should go and meet her."

"They're on their way, Philip. They'll find her, Harker and the others. They know what they're doing."

"That's what I'm afraid of."

"What do you mean?"

He spoke very quietly. "What do they intend to do with her, when they find her?"

"She's given us assurances."

He drew on the cigarette.

"And how much weight do we attach to Val Hopko's assurances?" he said.

She swallowed, thinking of the Chinese colonel,

Mangan's agent, her agent, kneeling in the dust by a river in Thailand, the two MSS men hauling him to their car as she watched—following orders, Hopko's orders.

"What are you saying?"

"I'm saying, Trish, that Pearl is—"

"Pearl is an extremely valuable asset, is what she is. Her father's laptop is probably even more valuable than she is. They'll find her. We'll get to her."

"The lady doth protest too much." He was very calm.

"Fuck's that supposed to mean?"

"Just think it through for a minute," he said. "Hopko's been all over me since this thing started. I thought I was being all clever, bold, seizing the initiative, following the lead. To Suriname, here. But she knew, didn't she? All of it. For Christ's sake, Posthumus was reporting directly to her. She's working me, Trish. She's…she's…" He shrugged. "Why?"

"You feeling used?"

"I think I don't understand my position." He looked straight at her. "I think perhaps I never did."

"What's this? A galloping epiphany?"

"I think you know what I mean."

"I think you have delusions of grandeur."

"What?"

"So you're the centre of the story now, are you?"

"That's fucking nonsense." They were talking over each other now. "She is using me, and you, too."

"All about you."

"You're being puerile."

"You may believe that your contribution is central, but believe me, Philip, it isn't."

"She is being fundamentally dishonest with us."

"Oh, grow up."

"Don't talk to me like that," he said slowly.

"I'll talk to you any bloody way I like."

"Trish. *Stop!*"

She caught herself. He was looking at her, astonished.

"What the actual fuck?" he said.

She shook her head, jabbed a finger at him, but could think of nothing to say.

He leaned away from her, regarding her with that straight, unmoving look, and took another drag on his cigarette.

"What?" she said finally.

"I'm leaving."

She felt her stomach turn over.

"Where to?"

"To where Pearl is." He stepped past her, opened the screen door, went inside and walked quietly to his room. She followed him, seeing that he'd already packed the ridiculous duffel bag. He picked it up.

"Has she told you? Where she is?"

He didn't reply, just made for the front door of the flat. But the hallway light came on, and Brendan was standing there in a T-shirt and shorts. He stood between Mangan and the door.

"What the hell is going on?" he said. He spoke very quietly.

"Get out the way," said Mangan.

"You just stay right the fuck where you are," Brendan said, pointing at the floor. "What has she said?"

"Out the way. Now."

"You tell me immediately what Pearl has said to you."

Mangan stepped towards him, making to shoulder past him, but Brendan stepped in his way again. Mangan was a head taller.

"Fuck off," he said.

And then Brendan moved quickly, a ducking movement, and did something that Patterson couldn't quite see, but Mangan doubled over, his arm out, his face contorted in shock and pain. Brendan took a step back, clinical.

Patterson stepped between them and Mangan lurched for the door, flung it open, and was off down the corridor towards the elevators, one hand on the wall to steady himself, the other dragging the duffel bag.

Brendan stared after him, then looked at Patterson, gauging how he would get round her.

"Don't try it with me, sweetheart. The result won't be the same," she said.

Brendan backed away, his expression stone.

And Patterson knew she'd just taken a step off the path, out into treacherous ground, like the ground in Iraq, where you didn't know what lay buried just below the surface, where a scratching in the earth presaged catastrophe, the rending of limb and artery. And she had a sudden vision of the little boy barefoot on the moped, her agent, those warm, dark eyes laughing at her the last time she'd seen him alive. *My habashi*, he'd said. She thought of the morning they found him, just after dawn, eyeless, splayed across a garbage pile on the outskirts of town, smoke rising in the air, buzzards wheeling overhead.

Not this time, she thought. Not this time.

At around five in the morning, Pearl passed a turning onto a dirt track that appeared to lead away into low hills. She took it, bouncing along for a half-mile or so, and pulled the car into a narrow ravine, out of sight. She got out, pissed, then got back in and closed the door.

To her surprise, she woke in early, cool sunlight. She scrambled up to the high ground and lay down, looking over at the highway. The traffic was sparse. No red SUVs.

She turned over and lay on her back, looking up at

the sky, adhering to the rock beneath her as the void spread out before her. She thought of the physics of one human being's violence upon another, the transmission of kinetic energy used to snuff out conciousness.

She lay there most of the morning, in the sun, watching buzzards soaring on the thermals above the road. Once, her father had taken her birdwatching. She'd have been ten, eleven, maybe. They had driven to a state park near Baltimore and sat in the bushes; he had a big pair of binoculars, and they used them to watch a blue heron flap lazily along a creek. It was the one and only time they went birdwatching, and the pursuit of ornithology left the family as abruptly as it had arrived. Other enthusiasms—barbecue, Civil War history, guitar—had come and gone too. She had sat in her room, waiting for math camp and wondering where this frenzied search for distraction came from. What he was displacing.

Now she knew.

Her parents had been coerced. That much was clear to her. And the elusive cousin Beetle was the man behind it, she guessed. And now she was coerced as well. The threats disgusted her, and when she thought of her mother, sitting there on the bed, giving her pathetic explanation of their entrapment—*At the beginning, you do it because it's so exciting*—she felt her heart break a little. A whole life lost, she thought, stolen by these manipulative, lying men, with their threats and their petty, pointless ambitions.

And now a whole life was being taken from Pearl.

In the early afternoon, she got back in the car, feeling for the Ruger under the seat, then pushed on.

At least she knew where she was going now. She felt hungry, a little stronger, the feeling of inevitability having receded an inch or two.

Would he be there?

Could he give her a life back?

At Eugene, she turned onto I-5 heading south, watching her mirrors.

Five hundred and thirty miles to San Francisco, down through the Cascades, the country rolling out towards the mountains, the cold air thick with pine resin. If she didn't stop, she could do it by midnight.

She was almost at the California line when they found her.

49

Hopko's rage was silent, deep.

"And why didn't you stop him?" she said.

Brendan ignored Patterson, speaking across her.

"I had him stopped, until Typhoid Mary here stepped in." He jerked his head towards Patterson.

Hopko took off her glasses, put a finger to her temple.

"Tell me, Trish."

She shrugged, opened her mouth to speak, but Hopko had changed course, starting to shout.

"Don't shrug at me. Don't you *dare* shrug your shoulders at me. You will take a good look at yourself and attempt to regain some professionalism. You will tell me, immediately, what you know of why Mangan has left, despite his explicit orders. Tell me, now, and then get out. Get out and return to the Station, and prepare to re-examine your career and your reasons for being here."

Patterson felt herself falling. Going to a place where she hadn't been for a long time. She felt like a child facing some incomprehensible wrath for some unfathomable wrong, the futility of resisting the parent, the teacher. She felt the tension go out of her, felt her shoulders fall, her knees start to shake. She wondered if she might be sick.

"I think he'd had enough," she said quietly.

"Had enough? Had enough what?"

She shook her head. "Of what? Of this. Of *you*. Of being used. Of being told he's a natural, when in fact he's realised he's entirely fucking disposable. As we all are."

Hopko looked—there was no other word for it—disgusted.

"What in God's name do you mean?"

Patterson could feel a sort of fatalism setting in.

"Do *any* of us have any value to you?"

Brendan snorted with contemptuous laughter.

"Trish, I think you are becoming a little overheated," said Hopko.

"You won't even tell us what this operation is about, what it's for."

"You are not cleared—"

"How are you going to use Pearl, when you get her?"

And for a moment Hopko paused, and Patterson saw it, saw that she'd hit home, though she didn't know why. She could feel that the answer was just on the edge of her consciousness, almost in reach. She saw Brendan's eyes flicker over to Hopko, too. Hopko spoke slowly.

"That is none of your concern."

Patterson thought, I'm throwing it all away, right here, right now.

"She's linked in some way to BOTANY, isn't she?"

"Stop it. Now," said Hopko.

"Monroe threatened to blow BOTANY. And now you need Pearl."

Brendan had a hand to his forehead.

"You need Pearl," said Patterson, "to save BOTANY, or to use as leverage, or something. You need her, and you're going to get her, and then you are going to use her."

Hopko was silent. She's calculating, thought Patterson. And it was then, as the three of them faced each other in the stale air of the safe flat, in the pre-dawn, that she sensed the enormity of it. Perhaps it showed on her face, because Hopko had a pacifying hand up. Brendan was reaching for a phone.

"Trish," said Hopko quietly, "Please sit down. I need to talk this through with you."

"Stay the *fuck* away from me," said Patterson. She turned to where her overnight bag lay next to the camp bed. She kept it packed, like she did her daysack in the army, ready to move. Now she picked it up, reached for her jacket and checked her handheld was in her pocket. Brendan stood between her and the door. The movement made her feel stronger and the adrenalin was kicking in.

Let it come, she thought. It'll come. The speed, the clarity. It'll be there, for the soldier in me.

Brendan had his phone to his ear, and was signalling she should stay where she was. Hopko was shouting something, but she didn't listen. She moved towards Brendan. He looked absurd, this wiry little white man in his T-shirt. She felt the surge of aggression taking hold. Brendan took the phone from his ear, tossed it onto the camp bed. He had raised both his hands now so they were either side of his face—*I don't want any trouble*—but Patterson could read it, the way his elbows were tight to his torso, the way he was on the balls of his feet, ready to move hard, fast.

And he was fast.

She was equal to it, but only just, the heel of his right hand coming at her face, at her upper lip or her nose, his whole torso behind it, hips turning into the thrust. She fell away from the waist, felt the strike miss her by a whisker, his left coming straight after but wide, this time. And she had a split-second wordless memory of a sergeant who'd taught unarmed combat on a close observation course, some godforsaken training area somewhere, the grey rain dripping from the trees. The sergeant, SRR, sandy-haired, moustached, had yelled at them, *Go for the fucking legs. Smash the knees, the fucking ankles.* And the sergeant had watched Patterson, watched her drive the stamp kick into the inside of her opponent's knee, watched her aggression, and he'd yelled at the others, *Watch her, watch ma'am here, and do it like that, you fucking mincers.*

She pivoted on the ball of her left foot, drove the heel of her right straight into Brendan's knee, felt it give and heard his intake of breath, and then she was turning back into the strike, the heel of her right fist making contact with his right ear, and he was going down, inert even before he hit the floor.

She turned. Hopko was watching her, standing very still, hands at her sides, her eyes alight.

"He came at me," Patterson said.

"Oh, he did," said Hopko. Her tone was terribly calm. "And what are you going to do now?"

Patterson licked her lips. She went to reply, but caught herself and turned away to leave.

Hopko spoke to her back.

"If you stay, I can probably rescue you, repair the damage," she said. "If you go, it's over."

Patterson stopped, looked at the floor.

"If you go, you lose everything. Your career. Your rank. Your reputation."

Patterson felt her own heart beating.

"Your *honour*, even."

Hopko took a step forwards, her footfall soft on the carpet.

"Matters to you, doesn't it? That word. So archaic, yet it's all bound up in who you are."

Hopko was right behind her now, speaking so quietly, her words incisions.

"Do we disappoint you, Trish? Do *I* disappoint you? You poor thing, you. Desperate to serve. Desperate to find the master you can believe in, the objective you can march towards. But we always disappoint, don't we? The moment we accept you, *you*, we disappoint you."

Brendan was stirring on the floor. Patterson was very aware of her own breathing, her fingernails digging into her palms. "You will give Pearl to the opposition, won't you?" she said.

Hopko said nothing. Patterson still had her back to her.

"Why?"

Nothing.

"Did you kill Monroe? His wife?" said Patterson. She heard Hopko's sigh, and turned to look at her.

"You are being utterly ridiculous," said Hopko.

Patterson shook her head and made for the door.

TOP SECRET STRAP 2 BOTANY—UK EYES ONLY
COPY 3/5
//REPORT
1/ (TS) Source FULCRUM sent a brief message to C/
FE. It was marked Most Urgent. It is printed below
in full.

Beijing
To: Controller, Far East and Western Hemisphere,
United Kingdom Secret Intelligence Service,
Vauxhall Cross, London

MOST URGENT/RESPOND IMMEDIATELY

My friends,
    WHY do you threaten me? I have been most
cooperative and our business together has much

potential. Still you are make UNACCEPTABLE
THREATS. You may not pressure me in this way.

I am now beginning to understand that YOU are
making direct troubles for me, for my operations, to
threaten and pressure on me. I understand that YOU
are threaten to destroy my work and my position
unless I reveal my identity and following your
tasking. This is UNACCEPTABLE.

Respond immediately with assurance that such
threats will cease, and we can return to business as
normal, or YOU will shoulder full responsibility for
all consequences.

ENDS///

Pearl pulled off the interstate for gas at a place called
Talent, a little tangle of tree-lined streets and clapboard
houses and a brick strip mall. It was evening, overcast,
and the place was silent. She stood on the forecourt listening to the *tick tick* of the pump. She bought coffee and a
pupusa from a convenience store and got back in the car.
The car smelled bad now, the engine was running hot
and San Francisco was still three hundred miles away.

Would he be there? The Englishman. Philip. She had
only a hazy recollection of what he looked like now, but
remembered his rumpled calm, his easy way of moving.
He was like Cal that way. He cared and didn't care at the
same time.

What would he do? What did he want from her,
apart from her father's hard drive, apart from everything? What could he give? A life?

She started the ignition and put the car in drive. It
shuddered into motion and she headed back towards
the interstate. She was sipping coffee with one hand
on the wheel when she missed a turn that would have
taken her to the on-ramp, and found herself first in an

underpass, the interstate thundering above her, and then on a two-lane road, wandering off towards the mountains. She looked for a place to turn around.

In her mirror, close, a red SUV.

She thrust the coffee in the cup holder, put both hands on the wheel, and tried to hold down the panic. She looked in the rear-view mirror again. She could make out two figures in the car: one, a woman, in shades; the driver was male. She was half a mile away from the interstate now, no other traffic on the road. She sped up. The SUV kept pace. The road was taking her through farmland, then orchards on both sides, mountains coming closer, grey, speckled with scrub. She thought of throwing the car into a turn, speeding back to the interstate, but had no idea how. And then she heard the urgent, rising moan of an engine accelerating very rapidly, and out of nowhere a second car was overtaking her, fast, roaring off ahead—a blue van this time, no windows in the back. It braked, skidded into a turn, came to a halt side-on, blocking the road, rocking on its suspension. She braked hard, thought of pulling off and bumping along the verge, but the way was blocked by scaly black trees.

She stopped some twenty yards from the blue van, leaving the engine running. The red SUV stopped behind her. In her mirrors, she saw the two of them get out, the man, the woman in shades. Ahead of her, the blue van's door was opening, and another man was getting out. So, three of them that she could see. They just stood by their vehicles, waiting.

Pearl felt her chest heaving, her breath coming in great juddering gasps, and a flash of heat through her body that brought a prickle of sweat. She wondered if she might faint.

They were just standing, waiting.

Did it end here? How could she tell Philip?

She leaned forward and grasped under the seat for the Ruger. There it was, the cool gunmetal amid the candy wrappers and plastic bottles. She picked it up, still breathing hard, worked the slide, clicked the safety off, its bright little *snick*.

The man from the blue van was now walking very slowly towards her, his hands out, palms turned upwards. He was Chinese, she guessed, slender, all in black. As he drew closer she focused on his face, his eyes, his hopeful little smile, and registered his features, their extraordinary symmetry. A face to reach out and touch, to wonder at.

She got out of the car and stood in the open door, the Ruger out of sight at her side. She looked over her shoulder. The other two—the woman in shades and the large, white man with thinning hair—were standing still, watching her. Handsome Man was calling out, in English.

"Hey, Pearl." He was smiling. She didn't respond.

"Pearl, can we just talk? I'm sorry for all…*this*."

She went to speak, but her throat was closed, and she had to swallow and try again. The words fell out of her and the effort of just speaking was torture.

"What do you want?"

He took a few more paces towards her.

"Really, just to talk. Can we do that?"

"Go on, then. Talk."

"Look, everyone is really worried about you, okay? Your mom, your dad. Cal. They just want you home. Are you ready to go home?"

Somewhere, behind the fear, a little flame of anger began to flicker.

"Do I look like I'm ready to go home?"

He looked away for a moment, towards the mountains, as if considering.

"Well, I guess you don't. You got me."

"I want you to leave me alone." Her voice sounded thin, whiny almost. She took a breath, trying to bring herself under control. She felt very small, as if her fear reduced her physically.

"I suppose we all want to be left alone sometimes. *I* sure do. But, Pearl, this is some important stuff right here, and we just need you to come home and not freak everybody out."

"What stuff? What are you talking about?"

"Well, your mom and dad, your family in China, your friends, your work. I guess I don't know why you'd throw all that away. I mean, why, right?"

He raised his arms and let them fall as if confounded. God, he was beautiful.

"See, the thing is, Pearl, we've found you now." He was holding his hands out again, appealing to her. "So we're going to be with you, okay? I don't want to sound like this is a threat or anything, really I don't, but, you know, we can't just let you go, because that will make a lot of trouble for a lot of people."

"I won't be trouble," she said. "You can't make me do this... this thing. I just want to be left alone."

He held up a hand, a resigned expression on his face.

"Pearl, you are way, *way* too important for that." He smiled and beckoned. A bird was singing somewhere high above them, and for a minute she felt her attention shift to seek it out against the grey sky. Anything to take her away from this beautiful, terrifying man in front of her. She thought of the fragile beauty of the prairie birdsong, the pulsing and sighing of the cicadas in the hot Maryland night, the tiny, gorgeous signalling of the fireflies in the dark. The thought of everything she was to lose welled up in her and she had to hold herself, her hands on the car door.

Footsteps behind her. She turned. The large white

guy had taken several steps towards her, but the woman had her hand on his arm restraining him. He looked angry. He looked like he was going to take her physically. When she turned back, Handsome Man had come closer, too. She felt the panic rising again, a great billow of it, tears coming behind her eyes.

"Stay *away*!" she screamed.

Handsome Man was still saying something about just coming with them, and it would all be okay, but she turned around again and the big guy was moving, perhaps only twenty feet from her now.

Pearl raised the Ruger. It was slippery with sweat in her palm, and she brought her other hand up to cup the first one, steadying herself.

The man stopped mid-stride, shaking his head, and the Asian woman had her mouth open...and Pearl squeezed the trigger.

The little weapon bucked in her hand and she heard the *chenk* of the moving parts and the report clattering off the cars, the metallic tinkle of the empty case on the asphalt.

And then everyone was moving. The big man and Asian woman scurried—no other word for it—behind the red SUV, ducking. Pearl whipped around and Handsome Man was backing quickly away from her, but with a calm to the way he moved, a half-smile on his face, his head cocked to one side in a *Really?* expression.

She raised the weapon again and his hands came up and the look on his beautiful face changed, and she fired, the report clanging down the road, and suddenly the man was running, bent double, back to his car, hiding behind the engine block, peering out at her. She fired again, and he disappeared, and Pearl just stood there, hearing the echoes of the gunshot rolling away through the trees.

Behind her, no movement, but a voice. The woman.

"Pearl, sweetheart, really you have to stop this. It's me, Nicole. I know you don't want to hurt us—"

Pearl fired again, low towards the red SUV and she saw the round go through the door, a perfect little black void in the paintwork, a silvery splash around it. She heard furious swearing from the other side. She took four or five steps towards the vehicle, and fired again, this time at the front tyre.

Nothing happened for a moment, and she wondered if she'd missed, but then she heard the hiss and whine of air escaping, and the vehicle began to sink to one side. She did the same with the rear tyre. How many rounds left in the clip? she wondered. I should have counted. They tell you to count.

Pearl walked towards the blue van, fired once more at its front tyre, and that was it, she was out. She ran back to her black car and got in, slammed and locked the door, and in her mirror she saw the big white guy coming at her. He was holding something, a metal bar of some sort. She turned the key in the ignition and the car juddered to life and she threw it into reverse, spinning the wheel, and then the big white guy was in front of her, blocking her way, one hand on the hood as if he could hold the car back with his own strength. He shouted something at her and waved the tyre iron or whatever it was, ready to strike. She caught his eye and he raised his eyebrows, as if to say, *Do you get my full meaning?*

She put the car in drive and tapped the accelerator and the car lurched forward four or five feet and he half-jumped, half-skidded backwards, working to keep his balance, shouted something furious at her. Then he brought the iron bar down hard on the hood with a terrible crash and stared at her through the windscreen. His hair was awry and he looked ready to murder her. She wanted to tell him to get out of the way, and she shouted it but her voice sounded tiny; he just shook his head and leaned on the hood, and then she saw Handsome Man was right there, just the other side of the driver's side window, and he was trying the door and banging on the glass. She hit the accelerator again and this time kept her foot down and the car took a huge leap forward and kept going.

The big white guy sort of rolled off to one side, his arms flailing, and then he was gone—she couldn't see what had happened to him. She swerved to avoid the red SUV. The Asian woman ran down the road in front of her, away from her.

Then an ear-splitting bang, and the nearside window was gone, and the air full of glass. She heard herself screaming and shut her eyes and the car was pulling to the right and she hit the brakes but then thought *no no* and forced her eyes open and hit the accelerator again, shooting past the Asian woman, who was running off into the trees.

Pearl felt the car come back under her control. Straight ahead of her was the interstate. And she could just see the two men in her rear-view mirror, watching her go.

50

San Francisco International Airport

Mangan stood outside, on the pavement, his duffel bag at his feet, smoking.

Patterson had taken a different flight, and it had been delayed, so he'd spent an hour in an airport restaurant, eaten while he could, kept it to two glasses of wine, then went to hire a car. Like the idiot he was, he'd neglected to withdraw cash before he left Washington, so he had to use his card at the car hire place, and therefore it wouldn't be long, he assumed, before all and sundry knew he was there.

And there she was now, striding out from the double doors, in jeans and trainers and a navy blue waterproof, a backpack on one shoulder. Patterson stopped, back straight as a ramrod, looking around for him. He watched her for a moment, this lithe, powerful woman. He had seen her at work, operational, in Thailand, in Ethiopia, and had marvelled at her discipline, her formidable ability to focus, attending to details that would bore and frustrate him—the agent. Now her face betrayed her anxiety.

What had she done?

Mangan stubbed the cigarette out on a reeking steel

ashtray and walked towards her. She saw him and he nodded in greeting, but the expression on her face didn't change. He wanted to embrace her, but her stance said, *Stay away*.

"You didn't have to do this," he said.

"Bit late for that now," Patterson said.

"What did you tell Hopko? Before you left. What did you say to her?"

"What did I say? I said, in effect, I'm blowing off my chain of command, disobeying orders, and running off with my agent to save a blameless girl from evisceration by China's secret services, or Britain's, or America's, or all of them. Cheers. Bye."

Mangan didn't smile.

"Quite the exit. How did she take it?"

"How the hell do you think she took it?"

"The way you put it, it sounds quite romantic."

"Oh, *fuck* off, Philip."

"Sorry. Sorry. But look, why?"

"I—"

"You sounded as if you believed her. Hopko, I mean. All that *other operational contingencies* bullshit. Oh, there's something going on that I just can't tell you because it's super secret and, by the way, Pearl's just the price we all pay. All that crap. I thought you bought it."

Patterson shook her head.

"I mean, you've just—"

"I've just blown it. My career. Such as it was. Yes, I'm aware. Thanks."

It wasn't just your career, he thought. The decision has uprooted your certainties. Some portion of yourself, the soldier-spy, has abdicated and made way for doubt, for something new.

"Doubters, you and me," he said. "Someone said that to us once."

She looked down, hating it.

"We do have to get to her. Right? To Pearl," he said.

"And when we do? You think we can protect her?"

"Do you think we can't?"

"What'll you do? Hit them with your notebook? Maybe you could write about it and bore them into submission."

He smiled.

"I'm glad you're here," he said. "In fact, you've got no bloody idea how glad I am."

"Why?" she said. "Don't you have a plan?"

"Nope."

"Didn't think so." She said it with a half-smile but he could see real pain, coursing just below her skin.

This is where I am. Please get here. Please.

Pearl's final message had given them an address. It was a women's shelter in the Tenderloin. Patterson got them there fast, expertly, in the hire car, into the city in the chill, fading light. It had been, by Mangan's reckoning, about eighteen hours since Pearl had arrived in San Francisco. The women's shelter was a clever idea—no men allowed. She'd be safe there, for a little while.

They parked two blocks away. The Tenderloin was dirty, tense, febrile, the panhandlers persistent, talking trash. A woman lay on a piece of black plastic on the sidewalk; she caught Mangan's eye and shouted at him *fuck you lookin' at* and made a masturbating gesture with a bottle, rubbing it against her crotch. They passed a corner store, bars on the windows, *Liquor Cigarettes Money Orders*, skittish men loitering outside, hands deep in their pockets, eyes glassy.

And there was a girl, whose image imprinted itself on Mangan's mind, something to be thought about, written about later. She was crossing a street. Her jeans were stained and torn. She wore a black hoodie, her hair a filthy blonde, her face grimy. She couldn't have been older than seventeen, and she walked with a terrible limp, her right leg next to useless, and every step an agony for her. Elbows out, grimacing, she inched across the street, her leg dragging. Had she been shot? Hit by a car? Or was it an infection, a sketchy needle? The men outside the store watched her through filmy, yellowed eyes.

"Concentrate," said Patterson, her tone sharp. She fell back, and he looped around, up O'Farrell Street and down to Turk as she hovered behind, watching. After twenty minutes she was suddenly at his side again.

"Nothing," she said. "Best we can do."

He just nodded and took out a cigarette, noticing the tremor in his right hand. He was very tired, but fear was beginning to work on him the way it did, shutting down his words, crimping his vision.

"Come on," she said. She looked watchful, tense.

At the shelter, he stayed outside, standing in a doorway from where he could see the entrance and the street. It was dark now, and the traffic was thinning, but the street seemed to get busier, figures flitting in and out of the headlamps, rows of kids with dreads and hoodies and dogs sitting on the sidewalk. The air smelled of piss and cannabis and was filled with shouts and sirens. A man approached him and offered him something in a little baggie. He just shook his head and the man walked away, muttering. A police prowler moved slowly down the street, the kids watching it go.

After thirteen minutes, Patterson emerged from the shelter's front door, looked over at him. He nodded, and she walked carefully across.

"She's there," she said.

"You spoke to her?"

"Yes."

"How is she?"

"She's...all right, considering."

"Will she come with us?"

"She wants to see you." Patterson wasn't looking at him. She was scanning the street incessantly. "I don't think we have long."

"Okay, so how—"

"At the back of the building, there's an alleyway. She can see out of a bathroom window. She's waiting."

They walked quickly around the block. The alley was filthy with garbage and pooling water. It was dark, too, and he hesitated, but Patterson shoved him on the shoulder. Halfway down, they stopped next to a forest of garbage cans, which made Mangan think of the memorial to the dead by the side of the road in Suriname. Behind a five-foot brick wall was the shelter, a window, a figure looking out at them. He raised a hand, and the figure, hesitantly, did the same. There was a moment's pause. Mangan wondered what would happen next, but then the window was thrown open and a leg emerged, then another, and Pearl dropped three feet to the ground and ran flat-footed towards them. They had to help her over the wall, and then there she was, a little, pale, rumpled figure with short, mottled hair, breathing heavily and peering up at them through her glasses. She wore a T-shirt and leggings and a backpack. She looks as if she's going on a school trip, he thought.

"Hello, Pearl," he said.

"Um, hi," she said.

"It's good to see you. Are you okay?"

She blinked.

"No. Not really."

"No. You're probably not. Well—"

Patterson interrupted.

"Time to go," she said quietly.

They moved quickly, Patterson in the lead, back down the alley, towards the car. Mangan stayed behind Pearl as she ran, splay-footed, through the puddles.

When they reached the street, Patterson held up a hand and they stopped. Mangan watched her step out into the light of the street lamps, look both ways and linger for a moment, searching for the anomaly, the tiny disconnect, that ripple on the street's surface. Pearl looked as if she were about to cry, and Mangan made to put a hand on her shoulder, but she pulled away. Patterson turned back to them and nodded, and they moved towards the car. Pearl started to run, but Patterson held her back.

The hire car was small, a white VW Golf. Patterson waited, scanning the street, while the others got in the back seats.

"Where are we going?" said Pearl.

"We're going to get out of town," said Mangan. "There's a motel, over the bridge and up into Marin a way. We'll stop there for the night, and talk. Make a plan. Is that okay?"

"They found me. You know that, right? They will find us."

"No. No, they won't," said Mangan.

Pearl looked at him. She seemed weirdly calm. Resigned? Mangan pointed at Patterson.

"She's really good at this stuff," he said. "She'll keep us safe."

"She looks kind of tough," said Pearl.

"None tougher," said Mangan. But Patterson, buckling her seat belt, gave a dismissive little snort and shook her head.

She got them out of the Tenderloin and took them west, down through Haight and Sunset, towards the ocean, watching her mirrors all the way. Pearl was silent, withdrawn. Mangan tried to watch, craning his neck, but could see nothing. She turned north, up through the park. Mangan opened the window for a moment, and the air was cool and smelled of eucalyptus. Patterson took them onto 101, and as they crossed the Golden Gate Bridge, Mangan looked across the Bay, the lights of the freighters flickering far out to sea. The horizon still held a last wash of pale blue, and the ships were tiny, dark insects beating out into the Pacific. No one spoke. Patterson held the wheel with both hands, tense, ready to react, her jaw clenched. Pearl seemed diminutive, blinking at the oncoming headlamps. Mangan wondered if she were in shock.

Sausalito, Marin City, Strawberry.

Patterson pulled off the highway and parked up in a side street for a while, a beautiful street full of mission-style houses in pastel colours, great profusions of flowers and lights twinkling through the vegetation, and ribbons of smell on the air—perfume, herbs. As they all sat in silence, waiting, watching, Mangan wondered how it would be to live in a place like this. He thought of the lives he hadn't lived. Wouldn't live.

The motel was beyond San Rafael, next to the highway so they could get out quickly. Patterson paid for a room with cash, and Mangan realised he had ceded control to her almost completely.

The room was decrepit, stained, smelling of mould. The door was flimsy and rattled in the jamb. Patterson left the lights off and drew the curtains. Pearl lay down on one of the beds, clutching her backpack as if it were a stuffed animal. Mangan went outside, lit a cigarette and inhaled, tried to stop shaking. Patterson came out.

"Philip, you need to stay inside."

"Okay," he managed.

"I'm going out for some food."

Twenty minutes later, she came back with pizza, already cold, a layer of orange grease atop it. The three of them sat at the table and ate. Pearl only picked at it.

"Pearl, do you have your father's laptop with you?" said Mangan.

She bridled. "I was wondering how long it would take to get to that."

"Do you know what's on it?" said Patterson.

"Everything, I think."

Mangan leaned forward.

"Listen. I don't give a shit about the contents of the laptop. But the people who are after you *do*."

"We can use it to bargain," said Patterson.

"They bargain? These people?" said Pearl.

"Sometimes," said Patterson. She stood up, went to the window, looked out. "Sometimes they do."

Mangan made them all tea from little sachets, and then they tried to sleep for a couple of hours. He lay in the darkness, listened to the girl's laboured breathing, her muttering. Patterson lay like a statue.

Mangan woke abruptly, disturbed not by noise but by some change in atmosphere, in emotional pressure. He sat up and blinked in the darkness. Patterson was by the window, her hand out for quiet. Pearl knelt on the bed, holding her backpack, rocking back and forth.

"What is it?" he whispered.

"Maybe nothing," said Patterson.

Pearl was shaking her head and started fumbling inside her backpack.

He got up from the bed, walking in his socks over to where Patterson stood. She was absolutely rigid.

"Pearl thinks she heard something."

Mangan looked out of the window, across the parking lot. It was empty, still.

"I don't hear anything," he said.

"No," said Patterson.

Mangan relaxed a little and perched on the edge of Pearl's bed. The girl was still rooting around in her pack.

Patterson went back to her bed, reached into her back pocket and took out her secure handheld. The screen came on, the silver glow throwing shadows on the wall.

"Anything?" said Mangan.

Patterson shook her head.

"Nothing. We're getting the silent treatment," she said. "Don't know what I was expecting."

Mangan turned to Pearl, who had gone very still.

"Pearl, it's okay."

She shook her head.

"Really, there's nothing there."

Pearl leaned forward and pushed something across the bed towards him. He looked down. In the gloom, he could barely make out what it was. He reached for it and found his fingers connecting with a stubby pistol. She fumbled in her pack again, and produced a spare clip and a box of ammunition.

There was a moment of silence.

"Well, aren't *you* full of surprises?" said Patterson. But Pearl was kneeling, very still again, looking at the door. Mangan followed her gaze.

And there it was, the faintest rattle of the ill-fitting door in its frame, and a tiny, fractional movement. The door was being tried, softly, from the other side. Mangan watched as the handle moved, ever so slowly, down a half an inch, an inch. He had a horrible, almost paralysing feeling of déjà vu.

Patterson went to the bed, moving very quickly, very quietly. She gestured to them—*shoes, things*. She picked up the car key from the side table and gave it to Mangan. Mangan eased his feet into his shoes. Pearl put her backpack on and stood, slowly. Patterson took the Ruger from Mangan, eased the clip out, checked it, slipped the pistol into her waistband, and with astonishing speed scooped seven rounds out of the box and filled the second clip, the rounds slotting in with the metallic *snick-snick*. She leaned in to Mangan and whispered.

"As soon as you see a chance, get out and run for the car. I'll be right behind you. Okay?"

"But—"

"*Okay?*"

"Okay," he said.

"You remember where the car is?"

"It's…it's…"

"It's off to the right, in the corner of the lot."

"Yes, okay."

"You take Pearl and you run. Got it?"

He nodded.

The door handle was depressed now, and the door was creaking, as if someone were leaning against it from the outside. He watched Patterson move silently across the room and take up a position. She stood, poised on the balls of her feet, hands hanging loose by her side. The door rattled in its frame.

Then silence. Mangan had hold of Pearl's arm; he could feel her terror.

And then the air ripped with the sound of wood splintering and the door was flying open and the room was filled with light which Mangan couldn't explain or understand. But he saw Patterson kick and the door flew back on its hinges but wouldn't shut because an arm, a torso was in the way, and there was a muffled grunt, and Patterson slammed the door shut on the arm a second time, and then she had hold of the figure's head, an ear, and was slamming it against the door jamb, and then she was bundling the figure out of the room.

And there was the gap.

Mangan pulled Pearl across the room, but she was resisting, leaning back, too terrified to move. He could hear the sound of the fight outside the door, a cry—was it Patterson? He grabbed Pearl by the shoulders and propelled her to the door, hissing at her.

"Move, Pearl. *Now*."

And then they were outside and the light was blinding, and he realised it came from a pair of headlamps trained on the door to their room. In his peripheral vision he saw Patterson. She was forcing the flailing figure back, and she seemed to be pushing him back onto a second man, and he saw her deliver a brutal knee to the flailing man's crotch. The man's knees just went out and he was down, and then Patterson was leaping over him, out of the light and into shadow.

Mangan staggered sideways looking for the darkness, but to the left—away from their car. Pearl was whimpering, but moving, and he tried to run and pull her along, his feet stuttering on the asphalt. Suddenly they were in darkness, but he'd been utterly blinded by the headlamps and couldn't see anything in the dark and was disoriented. Where the hell was the car now?

He changed direction and ran, Pearl keeping pace. He headed across the lot, towards street lamps, the highway, glanced back, trying to orient himself. An SUV was parked, its doors open, its headlamps lighting up the motel walls. He could make out shadowy figures, their urgent movements. Was Patterson still standing, or was that her on the ground, the others working on her?

Dear God, where was the *fucking* car?

"Use the clicker," said Pearl.

"What?" he said.

"The remote key thing. Use it!" she said.

Dear fucking Christ.

He fumbled the key ring out of his pocket, thumbed the unlock button, looked around. Nothing.

He did it again.

And there, behind them, the flicker of orange as the car's lights flashed. They turned, and ran, but there was someone there.

And the someone was walking briskly, but calmly, to intercept them. Mangan slowed to a walk, and so did Pearl, and the someone was ahead of them, his hand up to stop them, and he was speaking.

"Come on, guys. Hold up now, it's over." Male, speaking American English. It was too dark to make out his face.

"Fuck you," said Mangan briskly. "Get out of our way." He took Pearl's arm again and carried on walking.

"Um, nope," said the man. "I need you to stop now, and you're just gonna come along with me."

Mangan was only feet from him now, and could see his face. He was a black man, well-built, in a sweatshirt and jeans. He had close-cropped hair and a little beard. The car was about thirty feet beyond him. Mangan kept moving, ready to push past, Pearl keeping up.

"Sorry, dude," said the man, and laid hold of Mangan's upper arm with a grip of wrought iron. Mangan wrenched himself away and yelled, "Get *off*." But the man still had hold of him and was walking with him towards the car, talking to him in a reasonable tone.

"C'mon, man. You're not going anywhere, so please just calm the fuck down and chill a little and let's just take you and Pearl here over to talk to the boss lady, okay?" Mangan kept walking towards the car, the man pulling his arm to slow him. Pearl was looking at the ground. "C'mon, man, you're being crazy now."

They were almost at the car and Mangan reached to open the door, got it open an inch or two, but the man stepped quickly in front of him and slammed it shut. Mangan stood there, breathing heavily, his stomach turning over, hands shaking.

"Get out of the way." He could feel his own voice quavering.

The man made a regretful face and laughed knowingly.

"C'mon, man."

Pearl had eased herself a few feet away from them and stood by the rear of the car, looking on, transfixed. Mangan thought she might be readying herself to run. But then he was aware of movement by his right ear, and the man was looking too, at a spot just next to Mangan's head and the expression on his face changed from the *faux* regretful to the really quite seriously concerned. Mangan felt a flash of absurdity, as if he were at the centre of some comic scene, waiting for the reveal. He turned, slowly, and inches from his ear was the little Ruger. The hand holding it was glistening with what appeared to be blood. But it dawned on Mangan that the Ruger was pointed not at his own head. Rather it was being pointed over his shoulder at Mangan's assailant.

And the hand was attached to Patterson, and she was speaking, her voice unsteady, but determined.

"Move away," she was saying. "Move away *now*."

Mangan shifted his focus from the Ruger to Patterson's face, and registered that it was a mess, blood coming from her nose and mouth and a swelling starting over her left eye. And then he looked over to the man by the car, and the man was raising his hands and was moving slowly, carefully away from Patterson towards the rear of the car, towards Pearl. And Mangan knew that behind his own fear and disorientation he was thinking quite clearly.

"Wait," he said. He stepped towards the man, who

tried to back away from him. Mangan reached around behind him, searching.

"What're you doing, man? Get your hands off me," the man said.

"Shut up," snapped Patterson.

Mangan found a wallet, a set of keys, a phone. He took them.

"Who sent you?"

The man laughed.

"Oh, man, you're a kick. You think you on TV?" He chuckled again. Patterson stepped over to him and jammed the Ruger into his face, the tip of the barrel just under his nose.

"Who are you working for?" she said.

"Calm the fuck down, okay, I'm a contractor."

"Well, who is the bloody contract *with*, you idiot?" shouted Mangan.

"Jeezus Christ. I don't know, I just get instructions."

"What were the instructions?"

"Pick you up. Deliver you and the girl."

"Deliver us where?"

Patterson spoke. "Philip, we've got to go."

"Deliver us *where*?"

"Just an address. In Oakland."

"What address? What boss lady? Is she there?"

"What? No, she's in the car."

"*Philip.*"

"Is it Hopko?"

"What? Who the hell is Hopko?"

But Patterson raised her arm and brought the butt down hard on the bridge of the man's nose, and he brought his hands to his face and staggered away, breathing hard and cursing into his cupped hands. Mangan felt a jolt of shock, revulsion, and Patterson saw it and turned away from him.

"*Move*, Philip, for Christ's sake," she said. "There'll be others. *Now.*"

They drove fast, further to the north, and then turned off the highway and went west, towards the ocean. Mangan drove, Patterson tried to wash the blood off her face with a bottle of water and some tissues, and soon the front of the car was full of wads of used tissue paper, red and sodden.

"Do you think you're going to be all right?" said Mangan.

She turned and stared at him, the one eye badly swollen now, and his whole heart moved and lurched.

"Christ, I'm sorry," he said.

"So am I," she said. There was no rancour in it. Regret, maybe.

Pearl sat in the back, her knees drawn up, her eyes red. Mangan drove on. They barely spoke, and the sense of hopelessness in the car was palpable.

"What are we going to do?" said Pearl finally. Her tone was flat.

"We're going to put some distance between us and them and then we're going to figure it out," said Mangan. And as he spoke he tried to muster a conviction he did not feel, and he knew its lack showed in his voice but it was the best he could do.

"How, though?" said Patterson. "How did they get to us?"

"You have a phone," said Pearl quietly. "Or the traffic cameras, maybe. They're inside the system."

"But—"

Mangan spoke over her.

"Or they were Hopko's."

Silence for a beat.

"What?" said Patterson.

"Maybe they were Hopko's."

"No, that's absurd," she said. "That's..."

"Unless it's not."

He glanced over at her.

"He said 'the boss lady.' He had to take us to 'the boss lady.'"

"No, no. He means Nicole, for Christ's sake."

"You've been thinking the same thing, haven't you?" he said.

"What have I been thinking, Philip? Tell me."

He thought for a moment, trying to get it straight.

"That she's using us against a Chinese network, and protecting that same Chinese network at the same time."

"I do not understand why she would do that."

Mangan thumped the wheel.

"So why the hell doesn't she want the Americans involved? Why not hand the whole bloody case to the FBI? Why does she want Pearl back so badly? Because..."

There was another silence. Patterson sighed, then spoke.

"Because she doesn't want the Americans to roll up the network. She wants the network kept intact," she said. "She wants Pearl and Pearl's parents intact. She wants it all as it was."

"Go on," said Mangan.

"I don't know. She's protecting something." She paused for a moment. Mangan could see she didn't know whether to carry on.

"Bit late for secrets now, sweetheart," he said.

"Don't 'sweetheart' me." She dabbed at her eye and spoke in a monotone. "I think she's protecting an operation called BOTANY."

"Which is?"

"I think it's an agent in Beijing. A big one."

"But why would this agent—"

"I don't *know,* for God's sake. But this American network is important somehow, it's leverage or something. And it has to be protected. Maybe…"

"Maybe what?"

"Maybe if this network—Pearl, her parents, all the rest of it—gets rolled up, then BOTANY falls apart. And she loses whatever she has in the agent."

"Which means…"

"Which means, Pearl must be brought back under control. Which means *we* are now the biggest threat to the network. *We* are the problem."

Mangan was silent for a full minute, the road winding into uplands in clear morning light. They were nearly at the coast. He felt jittery, wired, his thoughts coming hot and unfocused. Patterson was clearly exhausted and in a lot of pain.

"I can't do this any more," Pearl said.

Patterson turned around in her seat.

"What does that mean?"

There were tears on Pearl's cheeks, and her face was puckered and raw.

"They'll find us again. They'll find us again."

"Pearl…"

"This is all my stupid fault. All of it." She had balled her hand into a fist and was grinding it into her own thigh.

"Pearl, stop. Please. It's not helping."

It was getting light. They were driving through rolling hills of alder and pine, the ocean off to their left. Mangan watched the mirrors.

Some distance further on, he saw a sign. It said SCENIC VIEW, and pointed down an unpaved track towards the coast. Mangan took it, needing to stop, to piss, to think. The track came out in a dusty parking lot atop cliffs, the ocean crashing onto rocks a hundred feet below, where the heaving slate sea ripped itself open, bled white spume.

Alone with his thoughts, feeling the wind on his face, Mangan contemplated the last two years of his life: his immersion in espionage, this weird ecology of manipulation and untruth. What exactly he'd imagined it would be like, back in that frigid Beijing winter, during those first moments. Then, the passing of a document, a hard drive, was a step into the thrilling dark, an affirmation. He'd stepped off the sidelines. He'd *mattered*.

And then, when he'd started to lie to the people he trusted, even loved, and his distance from them grew, he could justify it by resorting to his urgent, secret reason. *I can't love you, I'm afraid, because I lead a secret life and that precludes truth and honesty in my relationships.* He thought of the bewilderment on the faces of the people he had betrayed: his thoughtful, gracious lover in China, whose arrest was the direct result of what he'd done. And in Ethiopia, a brave and forthright Danish woman, who'd seen right through him before he'd crept away.

He turned and looked at Patterson, who was sitting next to Pearl on the back seat of the car, gentling her. Her eye was half closed and her lip was badly swollen, and when she moved, Mangan could see she was in pain, from what he didn't know and she wouldn't say.

He thought again that she was the only person who knew him, and to whom he told the truth. *My handler.* He looked out at the cold glitter of the Pacific. He could see a pelican out there, skimming smooth and low over the water.

"Philip," said Patterson, warning in her voice.

"What?" he said. He was still looking out at the sea.

And then Pearl's voice in a long, frightened wail. "Oh, God, no, no, no, no."

51

There were three cars.

One blocked the track, so there was no getting away. The other two pulled up about thirty feet from them and six people got out. Five men, one woman. A couple of the men were white, the rest of Asian appearance. The woman wore elaborate shades and an expensive quilted jacket and Mangan knew immediately it was her, the woman Patterson had told him about—Nicole.

The men spread out a little way and faced them. Were they armed? He couldn't tell. But they were professionals, not thugs. They had the lean, spare movement, the watchfulness.

Patterson pulled Pearl out of the car, grunting with the pain, her arm around her, but the girl was visibly shaking. Mangan went over, stood by them.

Nicole was going to do the talking, apparently. She walked out towards them, raising her shades onto the top of her head, so Mangan could see her eyes. She was striking, almost beautiful, her face ivory pale, slender, a pronounced chin. In it, Mangan saw intention, a ripple of cruelty. Her posture and her clothing made him think of some wealthy businesswoman, a fund manager or an investor, a citizen of the boardroom and the private jet. What was she doing here, rooting around in this shitty operation, hunting a terrified teenager? She spoke directly to Pearl, her accent an elegant American, touched by the coast of China.

"Pearl, you are to come with us. And I know you are confused and afraid. I want you to tell me what kind of assurances you need right now. Tell me what you need. Please."

Pearl didn't reply. Nicole tried again.

"Pearl, this is over, and you need to come with us. Really. The people you are with, these people," she gestured contemptuously at Mangan, "they do not have your interests at heart. They are not—"

"And you do, do you? You lying *bitch*," Patterson roared at her.

Nicole half smiled.

"Let's just calm down a little, all right?"

"Let's *not*, actually." Patterson was shouting. "Do *not* come any closer."

"Stop this." Nicole was standing about twelve feet from the three of them, and the others had started to move forward as well, as if to rush them. Pearl was backing away. Mangan felt the tick of violence in the air, saw them readying themselves. "Pearl, you are going to have to come with us. I'm sorry, but that is the way it is. Nothing is going to happen to you. We'll take you back to your mom and dad. That's all, okay?"

"No," said Pearl.

"I guarantee you will be safe." Nicole's voice was hard, demanding now. "I guarantee that you will be reunited with your family."

"You don't know what you're saying."

"Of course I know what I'm saying. What do you mean?"

"I can't be reunited with them. They're . . . I just can't."

"Why not, Pearl?" She was trying to moderate her tone, make it sympathetic.

"Because they are...everything is a lie." She was sobbing, her voice wobbling up and down like a child's. "They only want me so I can spy for them. That's all they wanted."

"Oh, Pearl, please, that's not true. They are your family. Your future. They miss you so much. And so does Cal."

Pearl looked up at her.

"You saw Cal?"

"Yes! Yes, we went to see him, and he told us how much he missed you. He helped us." She was trying to sound reasonable, but Mangan could see it was only a matter of moments now.

"What? Cal? He *didn't* help you."

"Oh, Pearl, he's just as concerned as everyone. He wants you back. You should be..."

"*No!*"

"...together."

Nicole was reaching out now, extending one hand to Pearl.

"Come here. Now. Please."

"*Get away!*" But then Pearl let her head fall and stared at the ground.

"Cal," she said, tears on her cheeks, her nose running, as if the loss of him were the loss of everything.

Nicole abruptly stepped forward. In a single smooth motion, Patterson whisked the Ruger out, pointed it upwards into the air. Mangan didn't know what to do.

"Trish," he said quietly. She gave a tight shake of the head.

"*Back* off," she shouted.

Nicole stopped. The five men behind her didn't move. Nicole exhaled sharply, as if impatient.

"There is no need...Just put it down," she said. And

as she spoke, Mangan felt Pearl take his hand, her fingers fluttering around his. Nicole went on, and Mangan heard her shading once again into threat.

"Look. We have been with you for a while now. And we're not going anywhere. So we will find you. Wherever you go now, we are going with you. So it's going to happen either now or later. Let's just do this now."

Pearl's fingers were pressing on his palm.

She was pressing something into his hand.

The five men were moving forward, slowly. One of them was sidling sideways, moving to get behind them.

"Get back!" shouted Mangan, whirling around.

But the man didn't stop.

"No!" Pearl screamed.

Patterson brought the Ruger down to aim it at Nicole, who turned her head away as if in disgust.

And now Pearl was pulling herself out of Patterson's protective grip, and moving.

Mangan thought for a mad second that she was going to give herself over to them, said "What the hell . . . ?" and grabbed at her, but she batted his hand away. She ran away from them all, towards the cliff.

"Pearl!" he shouted.

One of the five men, a white guy in a navy windbreaker, the one who'd been trying to get behind them, lunged for her, but Pearl lurched sideways and he missed, and Mangan was on him, trying to tackle him, and the two of them went down in the dirt. The man kicked at him and then seemed somehow to lift him and throw him off and Mangan hit the ground hard, the wind going out of him and a thick pain running up his back and through his lungs.

The man in the windbreaker was back on his feet, and Mangan struggled onto his elbows, gasping. Patterson was shouting, "*Pearl! Pearl!*" in her huge military bark.

And then the whole scene was frozen. All of them, stock still, in various poses of shock.

The man in the windbreaker with both hands raised as if in refusal.

Nicole with a hand over her mouth.

Patterson half-doubled over, one arm out, reaching.

But none of them moved or spoke. Mangan noticed how the wind moved their hair.

And as he lay there, he realised that he had glimpsed her go, just out of the corner of his eye, a smear of blue and pink against the sparkling sea.

52

The first thing he heard was a harsh whisper, something in Mandarin, a foul swear word, stained with disbelief. It came from Nicole, who seemed to Mangan to have shrunk, her whole being diminished.

And then a drawn-out yell from Patterson. She was on her knees, the Ruger at her side, her face contorted, blood trickling again from her lip. The five men were standing awkwardly, not sure what to do.

Mangan got to his feet and walked unsteadily to the edge of the cliff to look over, down towards the sea and the rocks. At first, he couldn't see her. She'd vanished, and he wondered if she'd been drawn under by a current. But then he saw a little streak of light blue, her backpack, he realised, and a pale arm breaking the surface. She was rocking back and forth, the sea drawing her out, then thrusting her back, beating her against the rocks, again and again.

And as he turned away, the wash of deep, black shame rose up in him, through his gut, his chest, his neck and eyes, as if every failure of his life were renewed and magnified in this moment. He thought he might faint. He bent over and put his hands on his knees.

Patterson was looking at him as she knelt there,

interrogating him with her eyes, as if she still awaited confirmation of what had happened. He looked down at the ground, swaying, tried not to black out. And then he heard Patterson speak, her voice soaked in revulsion.

"Oh, Jesus *Christ.*"

"Trish," he said.

"No, just... we need to report... this."

He stood upright, took a breath, tried to steady himself. He looked around and caught the eye of the man in the windbreaker, who just shook his head. But now Nicole was pointing at Patterson.

"You will take full responsibility," she said blankly.

Patterson looked at her, disbelieving. Then she stood up quickly and raised the Ruger, said nothing.

And suddenly everything was movement. The men were running for their cars, and Nicole was backing away, and Patterson squeezed the trigger, once, twice, and Nicole was running for a car, and one of the windshields had a white spider's web thrown across it. Mangan saw the little brass casings tumbling through the air and he wondered how hot they would be if he picked them up, and birds were rising from the trees. The cars were starting up and their wheels were spinning against the dust and he caught a last glimpse of the woman, Nicole, glaring out of the car window at him, and then the cars were tearing off down the track. Patterson, almost idly, squeezed again but Mangan didn't see where the round went, just that one of the cars wavered slightly, veered one way, then the other, steadied itself and picked up speed, and then all the cars were gone and everything was silent.

It was over, and the two of them were left there, the cool sun on their faces, the wind on their skin, as the great sea birds beat steadily away over the water.

53

They drove wordlessly away from the coast in the direction of San Francisco, stopping at a Motel 6 in the early afternoon. They took a room and lay on the bed and he put his arm around her and Patterson tried to talk, but cried, her broad shoulders heaving against him. Tears didn't come for him; he placed it all where he always did, deep in the fissure. And there it would sit, along with all the rest, lining his soul like a layer of hard, dried mud.

Patterson's secure handheld had died, and Mangan gently told her to charge it, because they were going to need to talk to someone, and soon. And Patterson nodded and got up and went to her bag and took out the charger and plugged it in. Mangan watched her and thought that she seemed very fragile.

"What will you do?" he said after a while.

"I don't know. Any suggestions?" she said.

"We have to talk to Hopko."

He saw her shudder, the dread on her face.

"We have to get away, Trish," he said quietly. "We have to get away fast."

She nodded dully.

"Who are we running from now, do you think?" she said.

"Oh, I don't know. The police, probably."

The phone had started to charge and was pinging as notifications came in, the tiny *ting* precise against the mutedness of the room.

"That's her, isn't it?" she said.

And it was only then that he remembered. He reached in his pocket. It was a little ball of paper, scrunched up and wrapped around with a light blue hairband. He thought of Pearl's fingers, fluttering around his, pushing her legacy into his hand, and for a moment thought he might faint again. He breathed deeply, steadied himself.

"What is it?" Patterson said.

"She gave it to me, pushed it into my hand. Just before." He sat on the edge of the bed, picking at it.

Patterson came and sat next to him. She held a tissue to her bloodied mouth.

Mangan untwisted the hairband and opened up the little ball of paper. On it, handwritten in pencil, were a web address and a password. He felt his thoughts quicken. Beads of possibility. And even as he thought it, self-loathing billowed up in him—beads, crystallised out of her self-erasure.

But the two of them still checked the room and drew the curtains. They sat in the gloom in front of his laptop. Entered the web address. They waited, watching the absurd little swirling circle on the screen.

It was a personal blog, password protected, and looked to have been set up in a hurry. Patterson read out the password, a long jumble of numbers and symbols. The blog had only a single entry.

It was a video, apparently recorded on Pearl's tablet. Mangan clicked play, and at first the screen was all moving shadow and the rattle and click of the microphone. And then there she was, Pearl, in the pink Hopkins T-shirt. She was in a bathroom, perched on the edge of

THE SPY'S DAUGHTER · 403

the tub, the shower curtain behind her, the light hard
and yellow. She looked at the camera. She seemed to be
preparing herself to speak.

Mangan knew that he wanted it all to end now, that
he was unequipped to manage whatever it was that
Pearl was handing to him, whatever judgement she had
arrived at. He reached for the mouse to turn it off, but
Patterson took hold of his wrist and stopped him. Her
eyes were locked on the screen.

Pearl began to speak, but her throat seemed to catch and
she had to start again.

"Philip and Trish. This is for you."

Her voice was drained of feeling. She held her hands
in front of her, palms together.

"To start with, I wanted to, like, say thanks. I, like,
know you guys have really tried to help me. And I really
appreciate that."

A pause.

"But, the thing is, I don't think you can. Help me.
Because, I am a scientist. That's who I am. Or who I was.
And I am a daughter. Or I was.

"And both these things have been exposed as . . . lies, I
guess." A shrug.

"I wasn't really a scientist. Scientists deal in hypoth-
esis and evidence and truth. I was a spy. I was dealing
in . . . well, I don't even know. But nothing was true. And
I wasn't really a daughter. I was a tool. So I was just one
big, fat lie."

Patterson had her hand at her mouth, and Mangan
heard her whisper, "*No.*"

She shifted her position on the edge of the bathtub.

"And so I don't know what I can do now. Science
won't have me. I mean, who'll ever trust a Chinese
ex-spy, right? And my family's gone. I mean, it was never

really there, right? And I can't ask Cal to be with me, not after all this. But I thought for a while that maybe you guys could help.

"But I don't think you can.

"So I just wanted to say goodbye, and thanks, and leave you a token of my appreciation."

She leaned forward a little, towards the lens. The yellow light caught her eyes behind the spectacles, and Mangan saw the glisten on them.

"So, the hard drive? From my dad's computer? I posted it to General Delivery, U.S. Post Office on Ellis Street in San Francisco. It's addressed to you, Philip. It should be there. I think if someone can get into it there'll be a lot of stuff on it. I mean, a lot. Like everything he was doing. Names, bank accounts, passwords, communications, everything. The whole network. And that's what you want, right? That's what you want. So there it is."

She sat back and wiped her nose with the back of her hand.

"Remember that poem, Philip? The Bai Juyi poem? About the slave girl? That's me. I'm, like, sneaking away, over the wall. Off into the trees, into the mountains. Looking for a new home. Because I have been a slave my whole life and I can't do it any more. I just can't."

She leaned forward and reached up for the tablet.

"Bye."

And the screen went black.

Mangan, numb with shock, looking for something to do, lit a cigarette and watched the smoke curl upwards in the half-dark. Patterson sat on the bed, her shoulders slumped.

"Was she right? Was that what we wanted? All we wanted? Some fucking hard drive?" she said.

"No," said Mangan. "She was wrong."

"Why? What were we going to do? *Save* her?"

"I wanted to . . . I don't know. I wanted to prevent that bloody woman from getting her hands on her, at least."

"Which bloody woman?"

"Either. Both," he said.

Patterson didn't speak for a moment, then got up and walked over to him. She stood in front of him, then leaned into him and put her arms around his neck, her forehead on his shoulder. He embraced her, still holding the cigarette. He was gentle, careful so as not to hurt her ribs.

"It's okay, I won't break," she said.

"I know," he said.

They just stood there, locked together for a while.

"I remember," he said, "you once told me not to expect endings. You said the stories don't end, they just hang there, unresolved."

He felt her nod.

"I think that's about where I am right now. It's over. But it's not," he said.

"Oh, Philip," she said, looking up. "They're not finished with you yet. Or me."

54

The message from Hopko was terse and angry. They were to meet that night in San Francisco, at the Marriott near the airport. Arrangements were being made. On no account were they to communicate with anyone. On no account were they to undertake any operational activity. The operation was stood down.

"Do not pass Go, do not collect two hundred dollars," said Patterson, her face lit silver by the screen.

They talked about it, and agreed on a course of action, despite Hopko's order. Or perhaps because of it. So Patterson took her secure handheld and dialled. She put it on speaker so Mangan could hear.

"Polk."

"Frankie, it's Trish Patterson."

"My oh my, it's the Disappearing Woman. What the bejeezus, Patterson, I thought we had a good thing going."

"Can you talk?"

"When my mouth's not full."

"Frankie, listen. Are you secure? I'm going to give you something."

"Really? Not humping me today? I'm disappoi—"

"Are you secure?"

"Okay, okay, I'm secure. Tighter than a gnat's ass."

"Frankie, get to San Francisco. Now."

"Shit, we eloping?"

"There's a flight in two hours from National. Get on it, Frankie."

"Uh, why?"

"I have something for you."

"You're a little vague there, Patterson."

"We have a proof. Proof of the whole network."

"FedEx it."

"Get here, Frankie. We'll be at the airport."

There was silence on the line.

"Frankie?"

"Jeez, Patterson, you're like a frickin' hernia. I can ignore you in the short term but you just keep—"

"Get here."

And she hung up.

This is it, Mangan thought. This is the last time, the very last time, I will ever do this. This is the last time I will ever be operational, the last time I will depend on tradecraft. He was back in the Tenderloin, standing on a street corner watching as Patterson trailed up and down Ellis Street in the late afternoon.

Was anyone there?

That filthy white kid in a sleeping bag, eating something out of a styrofoam tray, was he a watcher?

What about that strung-out old black guy on limbs like dry sticks, weaving in and out of the gutter? What about him? Or the woman in a pink wig and heels and tattoos idly smoking and staring at her phone? Was she static surveillance? Who owned her? Who owns any of us?

And the absurdity of the scene struck him hard, the ridiculousness of it all, a stupid contrived little story about spies and power aspiring to seriousness. The more dangerous the better, because danger means authenticity. When someone dies, it's *real*.

He couldn't tell if anyone was watching Patterson. He had no idea.

The General Delivery Post Office was a block away. They'd conducted a first pass earlier and the place was nothing more than a store front with a graffitied metal shutter, a window of bulletproof glass and a counter. Sod it, he thought, and set off up the block towards it.

Patterson was with him in an instant, flitting out of nowhere, gripping his upper arm.

"What do think you're doing?" she said.

"I'm going to pick up the bloody package."

She walked beside him, her eyes skittering across the street.

"We agreed I would go up there first, take a look, come back for you. Remember? We had a whole conversation. About fifteen minutes ago. Ring any bells?"

"I just want to get this over with."

"Don't lose the plot now, Philip. Not now."

He stopped, heaved a huge, exhausted sigh. She looked at him, a bright, brittle smile on her swollen face.

"Just...wait here," she said.

He nodded. She turned and moved up the street, jogging through traffic, swerving, sidestepping, ducking in and out of some store, and he glimpsed on her the deftness of the trained operative, before losing her from sight altogether.

He lit a cigarette, trying to push aside the leaden sense of failure, of pointlessness, that squatted at the centre of him.

She was back in minutes, coming from behind him.

"All right. We go," she said.

Just this one last thing, he thought.

They walked towards the post office.

* * *

In the event, it was easy. There was no one there watching them or waiting for them, and Mangan walked up to the window and presented his ID while Patterson stood there taut as a steel cable and watched his back. The woman went back into a storeroom and came out with a package: a yellow, padded envelope with Pearl's handwriting on it. And he walked away, back to the car.

The only difficulty he encountered came when he saw the handwriting. Its childish swirls and loops stirred it all up, and, sitting in the car as Patterson drove, he was soaked with shame all over again, to a point where he could hardly breathe.

Mercifully, there was no note, just the hard drive.

Patterson drove them out of the city and they holed up in a side street in Oakland for two hours, and then it was time to get to the airport.

Polk came off his flight rumpled and snappish, in a beige trench coat and a grey suit. Patterson carried a backpack with the drive in it and took him to a quiet gate with empty seating. Mangan stayed away.

Polk leaned forward, staring at her fat lip, her swollen eye.

"Jeez, Patterson, fuck happened to you? You walk into a door?"

"It's not important."

"Don't tell me what's important. Fuck am I doing here, anyway?" he said. He was quietly furious again, his eyes crystalline blue in his pale, pouchy face.

"Listen to me."

"Knock yourself out."

"There's a network. It's run from Beijing, through the Caribbean. A lawyer in Suriname. T. Y. Teng. Tango Echo November Golf. He's the money, carries the bags.

One of the network's assets is in your manor. Silver Spring, Maryland. Name of Tao. Tango Alpha Oscar. Given name Mitchell." She gave the address, waited a beat for a reaction, for a flood of questions, but he was silent, just sat there with folded arms. She pushed on.

"Their target is high tech in the Washington area—defence, corporations, government contractors."

Silence.

"Frankie, are you hearing me?"

"Um, yeah."

"Okay, well, next is one of the handlers. Chinese woman, name of Nicole, surname Yang. Her cover is fancy academic, she has a history at Harvard and Oxford. Taiwanese, but an asset of MSS."

More silence.

"We think the network included Jonathan Monroe, and Nicole was his handler, and his squeeze."

And there was a girl, she thought. No, a young woman. Short-sighted and pale and ill-favoured in all but the most important ways. And we lost her, and the knowledge of that loss is clattering around inside me as I speak to you, even as I don't mention her name.

"Frankie, are you with me?"

"I'm listening."

"Start with Mitchell Tao and his wife, and it will unravel from there."

He had taken a packet of gum from his pocket, and was unwrapping a piece. He put it in his mouth, began to chew.

"Frankie?"

"Patterson, you're freaking me out a little bit here."

"It's all true, Frankie. You can roll it up."

"On the basis of what you just told me? What am I, Chuck Norris?"

She took the hard drive from the backpack, handed it to him.

"Put that in your pocket, Frankie."

Polk exhaled.

"You gonna tell me what it is?"

"I think it's everything."

He took the drive, held it, feeling its weight, and studied her.

"Patterson, you seem like a nice person. You seem like you're not gonna shoot the Pope, or push opioids in trailer parks or whatever. So I'm going to give you one chance to take it back and we pretend like this never happened. Or you're going to explain why the fuck you are giving this to me and not to the weirdos who run your Washington Station."

"Personal preference."

He fingered the drive, saying nothing. Then he suddenly sat up, as if remembering something.

"Hey, Patterson, guess what? A little bird shat on my desk. Seems Jonathan Monroe was about to begin cooperating."

"What? He'd gone to the FBI?"

"Mm-hmm."

"He'd decided to confess?"

"Mm-hmm."

"But then he goes and tops himself," she said.

"Anything's possible. I mean, it's Washington, right? The city that eats and breathes paranoid delusion."

"You think he was killed as well."

"Do I?" he said.

"Don't you?"

"You coming back to DC, Patterson? Why don't you buy me a chilli half-smoke and ask me again."

"I'm asking you now."

"I think it doesn't matter what I think. It matters what the prosecutors think."

"It matters what you tell the prosecutors."

Polk made a mock-surprised face, his mouth an O. "Holy Toledo! Nothing gets past you." He smiled and held out a hand to her. "What do you say? C'mon back to DC with me."

She gave him a tired smile.

"You trying to recruit me as a source, Frankie?"

He looked at the hard drive in his hand.

"Uh, seems like I already did that."

"I don't think I'm going back to DC. "

"You want to tell me why that is?"

"I may have to go back to London."

"Is that right."

"It's become . . . complicated."

"I'm not complicated, Patterson. Look at me. I'm a lunk. I make seventy-two grand a year. My kids don't talk to me. I buy discounted shoes. You bring glamour into my life. Come on back east and let's talk. About all this stuff. Lots to talk about. Lots of people interested."

What?

"Lots of people?" she said.

"Oh. Lots and lots."

"You trying to tell me something, Frankie?"

"Ya think?"

Patterson blinked.

"Thanks, Frankie."

"Don't mention it."

"I won't."

"Right answer, babe."

And then he was gone, the hard drive in his pocket, and she watched his huge frame recede along the concourse, wondering if she'd ever see him again, and she if were to, if he would be putting cuffs on her.

Mangan was behind her.

"Well?" he said.

"They're onto it. All of it. And I just confirmed it all for him."

She frowned. "And I think he's just given us a minute to get out."

They went quickly to the car and left, Mangan driving, Patterson sitting stiffly in the seat, holding her ribs. Her eye had opened a little, but was coming out in a terrible bruise.

It was gone two in the morning when they got to the Marriott and O'Riley was in the lobby, waiting for them. She nodded at them and led them to the elevator without a word.

Hopko was waiting in a suite on the ninth floor, sitting on a straight-back chair in the middle of the room like a Cleopatra in jeans and a mannish shirt; her silver bracelets, her dark-rimmed spectacles. Her hair was pulled back, and she looked exhausted. The other three watchers—Harker, the Paulsons—were positioned strategically around the suite. Mangan had a ridiculous vision of them standing there wafting peacock feathers, like ancient Egyptian flunkies, with himself and Patterson as miserable petitioners. He caught Harker's eye, and the man raised his eyebrows and pursed his lips as if to say, *Watch out, shit storm coming in.*

Mangan and Patterson walked towards Hopko, and he noticed O'Riley move to cover the door. The tension was coming off Patterson like a heat lamp. He felt suddenly terribly tired, and his mouth tasted foul, and he could feel his own resentment starting to build at this fatuous room and its fatuous kangaroo court.

There were no pleasantries. Hopko had a file open on her lap. She began.

"The body has been recovered, you'll be glad to hear."

Mangan felt himself unable to react. He had no idea what was expected, or what he expected of himself.

"There'll be an autopsy, of course. There are tyre tracks all over the place, and apparently at least one empty shell casing."

"She just ... she jumped," said Mangan.

"And we failed to stop her," said Patterson.

"We failed to stop her," Mangan repeated quietly.

Hopko was silent for a moment. She adjusted her glasses.

"This is now a *flap*," she said. "You will leave the country in the next few hours. You," she looked at Patterson, "will fly to Mexico City and from there to London. The Paulsons will accompany you. You will be met at Heathrow by Service Security Branch and taken for debrief. Is that clear?"

Patterson didn't reply.

"You," she looked at Mangan, "will fly separately to London, via Costa Rica. You will be accompanied by Harker. You, too, will be met on arrival in the UK, and taken for debrief."

Hopko's gaze was utterly level. It had, he thought, the look of the inquisitor to it.

"Neither of you will attempt any communication with anyone."

Mangan took a breath.

"And what if I say no, Val?"

Her facial expression didn't change.

"No to what, exactly?"

"Just no. No to you. No to London. No to debrief."

"Philip, I am terribly sorry, but that is not an option you have at the moment."

"You'd force me?"

"I expect you to cooperate. Let's leave it at that, shall we?"

He was aware of a stirring in the room, Harker adjusting his stance.

"I'm afraid that may not be possible, Val."

She shot him a mock-offended look, which germinated a little flower of anger somewhere in him.

"It may not be possible!" she repeated. "And dare I ask, Philip, *why* it may not be possible? Do you have other professional commitments?"

This is it, he thought. This is where I acknowledge to myself all that's happened, all I've done, how wrong I've been.

"I think we both know—"

"Both know *what*?"

"We both know that this is finished for me. I thought I could do this, but I can't."

"Nonsense. You're a bloody natural. Didn't I say so, Trish? One of the best I've ever worked with." Hopko's voice dripped with derision. She looked to Patterson. "Didn't I say?"

"I'm not equipped for it. I thought I was, but I'm not," he said.

Hopko was half smiling.

"So it all ends with a whimper, does it, Philip? All right. You'll help us find Mitchell Tao's laptop. I assume you know where it is. And we'll see you home. Back to Blighty. We'll have a nice chat about all that's gone on. You'll sign a few boring pieces of paper. And then you'll be free. Free to go. Free to bugger off back to your career in journalism, what remains of it. Who knows, there might even be a little money for you."

Patterson spoke quietly.

"I wouldn't believe a fucking word if I were you, Philip."

"Good heavens, *it* talks," said Hopko. "Philip, if you stay here, the FBI is coming for you. A woman is dead.

Do you understand? You have a day or two and they will be on you."

"Two women," said Patterson.

"What? Two women?"

Patterson took a step forward. She was holding herself very straight, despite her pain, and Mangan was struck anew at the physicality of her, the way her physical strength emanated from her, dominated a space.

"You are responsible for the death of Molly Monroe," said Patterson evenly. "So, yes, two women."

"You are absurd," snapped Hopko. "Are you suggesting that British intelligence would commit a murder on American soil? That is unthinkable. Good Lord, woman, who do you think I am? Get a grip."

But Patterson had taken another step forward, and the Paulsons shifted themselves, moving away from the wall and closer to Hopko. The room was starting to seethe with intent.

"You were trying to *protect* Mitchell Tao, weren't you, Val? Molly Monroe could have brought him and his network down. And she died."

"You are embarrassing yourself," said Hopko.

"What about Jonathan Monroe? Did he kill himself? Really?"

Hopko got up from the chair and stood behind it. She's defensive, Mangan thought. And suddenly Patterson was bellowing at her.

"Come *on*, Val, let's have it. Tell us!"

Mangan realised that she was close to hysterical. Hopko took a wary step back.

"*You* are going to have to explain," yelled Patterson. "*You* have made us into murderers. That is *not* who I am, do you understand?" The chair now stood between her and Hopko; she batted it away and it fell over onto the carpet. "I am *not* responsible." The expression on

Hopko's face changed to one of concern. Genuine concern, it seemed to Mangan.

"Oh, Trish. I see what this is about. Really, I do."

"Do you hell."

"You are blaming yourself for a great many things."

"I'm blaming *you*." She was shaking.

Hopko stood with hands on her hips, and Patterson was close to her now, too close. Harker moved like quicksilver across the room to interpose himself with a sharp, "That's *enough*." O'Riley had left the door and was there too, her hand around Patterson's upper arm, but Patterson, in one fluid movement, turned fast, twisting herself out of O'Riley's grip and locking the woman's wrist and bearing down on it with her torso. There was a distinct cracking sound, and the woman gasped *For fuck's sake* and Patterson thrust her away and she stumbled backwards cradling her wrist. She hit a side table, fell backwards, knocked over a lamp, and the room was suddenly chaotic, with Hopko yelling at Patterson and Harker advancing on her, the Paulsons both positioning to get behind her and bring her down, and O'Riley moaning.

Patterson came around with an elbow strike that took Harker hard on the chin, saw his head snap back and his eyes close, a string of spittle in the air. And in the middle of it all Mangan saw her glance over her shoulder at him, her eyes bruised and bright and feverish, and mouth the word, *Go*.

That was the last time he saw her.

55

Philip Mangan ran. He ran from the room and every room like it, all the silent rooms in the safe flats and hotels and basements, the vile, silent rooms where the watchers leaned against the walls and the air was stale with mistrust. He ran down the corridor, unsteady on his long, slender legs, made for the elevators but thought better of it, went for the emergency stairs. He clattered down the concrete stairwell, eighteen flights, stopped at the bottom, gasping, pain in his chest. Then out, into the brightly lit lobby, walking purposefully, ignoring the gaze of the receptionist, sweat on his temples and his back, pushing out of the main doors, feeling the chill night air on his skin, and then he was running again, looking for the car. *Use the clicker,* Pearl said in his ear, and he did and he heard the horn start to go off, ran towards it. Here I am again, running for a car, he thought.

The Paulson woman was standing there, breathing heavily, between him and it.

"I don't think so, Philip," she said, and he saw her hips move in an elegant, fluid swing and the kick was aimed straight at his groin, but he was unbalanced and she misjudged it fractionally and the strike came at the point where his thigh met his pelvis, sending him staggering back.

She was coming at him and he shouted at her but no words came out, just an incoherent roar. He raised his arms to cover his face as she started to work on him. There must be other people here, he thought, people must be seeing this. But it was dark and deep in the most desolate hours, and no one was coming.

Paulson hit him several times in the torso, the solar plexus, and somehow the lower back, and the pain came hot and percussive, conjuring storms of white sparks in his eyes, and he knew he'd go down very quickly. He only had seconds, the shock coursing through him like a drug, dampening his thought, paralysing him—he knew he had to move on her or it was over.

Mangan shouted again and, bent double, he ran at her, trying to get his shoulder into her, but she was skipping away from him easily, backwards, down the narrow space between his car and one parked next to it.

Now there was about ten feet between them and she was still, waiting for the moment to move back in on him, and he realised he was standing right by the car door. She saw it at the same moment, and lunged for him, but he wrenched the door open and it thudded into the car in the next space, and he held it there, barring her way. She gave it an almighty kick, and the door bucked in his hands but he held it open.

Was it there? The Ruger? Was it under the seat?

He struggled into the car, holding the door open with one arm and one foot, and she kicked it again and this time he couldn't hold it and it slammed on his leg and the sound that came out of his mouth seemed not his own but the ragged voice of another. But now he had his hand under the seat, his fingers skittering through wadded, bloody tissues and dried leaves.

The door slammed again, and he drew his leg in just in time and he took the force of it on his shoe. Paulson forced her way around the door and was reaching in for him, her hand seeking purchase on his shirt, his neck, his hair. He could hear her breathing, smell a subtle perfume. She was trying to drag him out of the vehicle, but his weight was too much for her. His hand scrabbled in the detritus of the entire terrible day that lay on the car floor and there was nothing, nothing, just grit and the fibrous feel of the matting.

Until his finger nail grazed something hard and cool, and his fingers found the cross hatching on the grip and settled around it and he pulled the little weapon out and up and jammed it hard in her ribs.

Mangan remembered that he needed to work the slide and flick the safety off and he fumbled for it and heard the *chenck* as the slide snapped back into place and felt the safety make its short, smooth journey under his thumb. The woman had taken her hands off him and was standing there with a slight smile on her face because she knew, as he did, that he couldn't shoot her, that he wouldn't get a mile down the road.

For several seconds they just looked at each other. Then he swapped the Ruger to his left hand, easing down into the seat and aiming it at her face, jammed the key in the ignition, started the car and rammed it into reverse. Paulson realised what was happening just too late, her eyes widening as the car jumped backwards out of the parking space. The woman brought her arms up to protect herself but the open door hit her hard and dragged her with it. She went down and the lower edge of the door raked her back and smashed into the back of her head. She screamed and curled up into a ball.

Mangan leaned out, grabbed the door, slammed it shut and accelerated away.

He drove wildly in a direction he thought was south, until he saw signs to I-5 and Los Angeles. About eight hours to the Mexican border. Mangan found himself rigid at the wheel, his stomach and sternum churning with pain, shock. When he leaned down and touched his left shin, his fingers came up sticky with blood.

After two hours he pulled over, some speck of a place with chain-link fences and wizened palm trees bathed in sodium orange. He didn't even see its name.

He filled up the car, parked it and walked off the garage forecourt into the darkness. He was walking on hard, scrubby desert. He could make out hills against the night sky. There were houses up in the hills—he could see their lights twinkling.

He lit a cigarette, and then felt his knees all but go out from under him, and he knelt hard in the dust and great lurching sobs were rising up and he just let them come, giving himself over to them because there was nothing else he could do.

He had abandoned her. Patterson had cracked open a moment for him to get out, and he had just gone. He thought of the Venezuelan woman in the foul brothel, beaten and penetrated and abandoned, of how he paid her off. And then billowing up in him all over again, Pearl, the flicker of pink against the sun's glitter, her tiny body rocking on the sea.

He stayed that way for some time, kneeling there in the dark, letting it all play out. And for a while he thought he might not be able to get back to the car, to carry on. But in a while he forced himself to his feet, his breath still coming in great shuddering gasps, and retraced his steps.

He stopped, felt in his pocket.

The little ball of paper, Pearl's tiny, dangerous legacy, was still there.

He unfurled it, looking at her handwriting for a moment, the web address. He thought of her looking into the camera, giving her own eulogy, and how that consciousness in all its complexity and its subtlety and its pain and confusion was now extinguished, its moment as brief as a firefly's.

He held the scrap of paper between his thumb and forefinger, tore it into pieces, and let them flutter from his hand in the dark.

56

Chiang Saen, Thailand
Eight days later

Granny Poon's boys had set up a perimeter of sorts. They flanked their mother, facing away from the river, keeping their eyes on the Thai security men. Eileen, resplendent behind enormous shades, a fan in hand, sat on a little folding stool and sipped from a bottle of water. She wasn't sure what agency the Thais were from: something civilian, but nobody was talking. Hopko was stern and silent at her side, gazing at the river. She was angry, Eileen could tell, an anger born of something more than the usual failures and frustrations of intelligence work. Hopko, she sensed, felt betrayed, undermined. And to Eileen, Hopko's simmering silence reinforced her own sense that a chapter was closing, that their long partnership was at an end. Not such a surprise, given her own age, and Hopko's recent troubles. But still. A sad way for it to end, unresolved, silent.

Hopko grunted a dissatisfied *hmm* and took a drink of water from a bottle. The figure standing next to her—a hard, bulky man of Chinese appearance, his hair brush-cut, his eyes like sharpened flints, a Mandarin speaker—was familiar to Eileen, his face etched on her mind from the recent past. But he didn't know her, of course, and she said nothing. The man stooped and spoke quietly to Hopko, and she nodded, but the senior Thai officer waved him away, and he stepped back, deferential.

Eileen turned her face to the river, scanning its sluggish brown surface, all the way to where it disappeared in a welter of green. Eileen was a veteran of a dozen moments like this, defections, the wait in the heat for a blown and panicked agent to surface. Will he? Won't she? Are they even there? Are they alive? She'd watched them all—the traitors, drunks, narcissists, manipulators, crooks, and the occasional thoughtful volunteer—come blinking across borders, down ramps, out of car boots, to confront their fragile futures. And, sometimes, she'd watched the best-laid exfiltration plans crumble in an electrified instant of shouts and sirens and shattering disappointment.

Today, she had been told, it would be a boat. A long, fast, wooden boat with a shallow draft and a powerful long-tail outboard engine, laden with reeking baskets of fish. The boat would come down the Mekong River, skirting the Chinese patrol boats, lingering in the shallows.

And BOTANY? They didn't even know his name. Eileen thought of him only as the purveyor of White Rabbit milk candy in little twists of waxy paper. He had been, Eileen knew, Hopko's great hope. He was to be the penetration of Beijing's deep and secret canyons that would show them China's brave new world, would lay bare the intelligence operation that was scraping the insides of the world's corporations for every secret they ever owned. But—the rumours were a welter of metaphor—Hopko had called it all wrong, overplayed her hand, speared him and tried to reel him in, rather than playing him with a long line. She had threatened to cut off his legs, pressured him, ruined him.

Eileen waved away a mosquito, fanning herself. It had been an hour already, more. Would he come? Could he?

And just as the thought registered, she sensed a quickening of the moment, an increase in tension around her. A flat-bottomed boat had come into view, hugging the Thai bank, rounding an outgrowth of trees that overhung the water, two figures aboard, one at the outboard motor, the other at the prow. The boat seemed to accelerate a little towards them, the pilot glancing over his shoulder.

Hopko stood, and the senior Thai officer and the rotund, brush-cut hard man stood next to her, and all took small steps towards the jetty. One of the Thai security men held a nasty-looking sub-machine gun. The boat slowed as it came in, and the pilot threw a rope, and the Thai security man fumbled it and it fell in the water. The pilot had to pull it in and throw it again, wet, this time.

The man in the prow was in his sixties. He wore a blue polo shirt, a light tan golfing jacket and beige slacks, all of which were improbably immaculate. He sat very still, his hands in his lap. His hair was silver and was combed back from the forehead and Eileen noticed his soft, smooth skin, and thought that this was, indeed, a man who paid attention to his appearance, to his grooming: a spotless man.

No emotion registered on the man's face as he stood and clambered out of the boat onto the jetty. His eyes were black and hard as obsidian. Hopko moved towards him and held out her hand and he gave it a brief shake, but was looking beyond her. He started to walk down the jetty, as if this welcoming committee were a waste of his time, and he had places to be. Hopko was forced to turn and walk after him, which she did with ill grace.

Eileen watched her go, stocky, hard Hopko, trailing a twist of perfume, the jangle of silver bracelets and an air of endurance. She made Eileen think of a runner deep into the hard miles, or a boxer in the corner, waiting for the seventh round. As Hopko passed her, their eyes met for a moment, and Hopko gave her a tight smile, as if to say, *Well, that's that*.

But then her boys were next to her, murmuring, *Come on, Ma, let's go*. There was a safe house on loan from the Thais, about thirty miles away, with a team waiting to carry out an initial debrief. It was a big place surrounded by forest and fences, with airy, wood-panelled rooms. Fastidious Man would have his own room fitted with wireless microphones, and he'd be permitted to take short walks in the garden in the company of Service personnel. They'd flown in a cleared Chinese chef from Singapore to do the cooking. Hopko wanted Eileen there listening, checking the translation, picking up on the names, the connections, in the way only she could. So she'd go, be there for two or three days of it. But perhaps this would be the last time.

Eileen got to her feet, brushed away Winston's helping hand, reached in her purse and extracted a packet of beedi; she lit one, took a deep pull and felt it hot and astringent in her chest. Winston made a reproachful face but she ignored it. She walked towards the riverbank, looked out over the reeds to the brown water and felt the pull of home.

57

Mangan got out of the car and lingered for a while by the side of the road. Some soldiers had erected a make-shift checkpoint—three oil drums and a couple of branches—and he wasn't getting through. The soldiers stood around in the dry heat and hard, flat midday light, their fatigues faded, their boots covered in dust, their M16s slung. He noticed that the rifles were dull, unoiled.

Further down the road, someone had been hacked to death with a machete. Maybe two people. No one seemed sure who had been killed, or who had done the hacking. Was it the notorious martial arts gangs, fetid pools of toxic masculinity? Or the Revolutionary Council, a local dissident group prone to getting shouty and violent? Or an angry husband? Mangan tried to ask the soldiers, but they took his cigarettes and waved him away.

He walked back to the car and stopped for a moment. Clouds were massing out over the sea. The afternoon would bring rain, perhaps a storm. He wanted to be off the road before then. He turned the car around and headed back to Baucau along the coast road, slowing for goats, children, piglets. He stopped at a gloomy Chinese store and bought water and nuts and rambutans and a fresh packet of cigarettes from an unsmiling Hakka woman, before heading back into town to the guesthouse.

The kids were in the courtyard, Inacia, in a little blue flowery dress, holding her baby brother. She was walking him around, winding between the flower pots and the enamel basins and the wicker chairs. The air was sultry, the sky grey, low.

"*Elo*, Philip," she said. It came out *Pleep*. She ran over to him, her flip-flops *slap slap* on the concrete. "*Elo*."

She put the boy down on the ground. He wobbled for a moment but caught himself, a flicker of a smile on his face. Inacia looked up at Mangan and said something in Tetum, way too fast for him to catch, pointing, her brown eyes on him.

"*Favor repete*," he said. Please repeat. And she burst out laughing and gave him a playful whack on the thigh. She took his hand and pulled him across the courtyard, past the hanging cage where a lorikeet gabbled and whistled. Fernando, the bird was called. He'd bob and weave and follow your finger. Inacia motioned for Mangan to sit on one of the chairs. She had her pencil and her exercise book, its paper a gritty beige colour, the print smudged and uneven. He tried to read her loopy handwriting while she looked up at him eagerly.

I go to school.
My bird name Fernando.
I have brother. He is good. I love him.

A gentle, reproving voice came from the kitchen. Her mother peered out. Inacia looked up at him and he smiled and nodded to say it was okay. He sat there and helped her correct the phrases and she bent over the book, frowning, working an eraser back and forth.

"*Obrigada, Pleep.*"

"You're welcome," he said.

"You're welcome," she repeated in a whisper, mouthing the sounds.

He got up, crossed the courtyard and went up the stairs to his room, opening the shutters to the quiet street sounds, a bicycle bell, the rattle of a taxi, the children wandering home from school chattering beneath the banyan trees. The air smelled of dust, woodsmoke and leaves.

He'd found the place, the job, quite by accident. A half-drunk conversation in a bar in Ubud led somehow to an interview in Perth, then a flight, and here he was, producing reports for a group of Australian non-profits. There was some writing, some editing, some human rights monitoring, a bit of interviewing. It paid enough to keep body and soul together, no more. But it gave him a room in this quiet guesthouse on the furthest edge of Asia with its courtyard and peeling paint and squawking lorikeet and the little girl who brought him cups of instant coffee in the mornings and sought his help with her homework and laughed at his height and wild red hair and his long, pale limbs. It gave him some structure, some purpose.

From here, he'd thought, he could, perhaps, begin to rebuild, to reconstitute a sense of himself, examine where he'd gone awry, reconcile himself to the things he had been part of.

Espionage.

The word had lost its mystique, its soft, sibilant glitter, its promise entwined with threat. Now, to Mangan, it evoked a world that was hard, vicious even, yet in the end, banal. It meant murderousness, and loss. He wondered, as he sat there in his room with the first fat drops of rain spattering on the roof and the geckos patrolling the ceiling, if he would ever be able to expunge that image, the smear of pink and blue against the sea. It floated at the back of his eyes. Sometimes he fancied he saw Pearl's hair, too, flying in the wind. But memory reconstructs itself, remaking itself every time you summon it, so his every recall of that moment was each time a fresh horror, retold in a new way. Her hair, her hands, her voice would enter the narrative unbidden, pushing him to the very edge of coping.

He could, he had discovered, dampen the memory's potency with alcohol, and some nights he did.

Three weeks after his arrival, there'd been a visitor, of course, the type instantly recognisable to him. Young, white, clever in a university way, fluent in the calculating charm of English institutional power. He was down from the Embassy in Jakarta, and wore hiking boots and a T-shirt with a clever design on it. *We just wanted to say hello, Philip, touch base, make sure you're okay.* Mangan had nodded, resisting the urge to be rude and just send him packing. He knew that, if they were to leave him alone, they needed reassurances. So he gave them. No books, no splashy exposés in the Sunday supplements, no semi-fictionalised novel. Nothing. There would be silence. And the young man smiled and expressed relief and satisfaction, but looked at him with an expression that said, *We're watching.* Mangan was surprised at the amount of contempt he felt for all of them.

Except, perhaps, for Patterson, whose letter lay on his desk. She'd written on paper, believing it more secure, oddly. She gave her address as a poste restante in Accra.

So, Philip,
I hope this finds you well. I just wanted to be in touch with you, but I'll understand if the feeling is not mutual.

I don't know if you're aware, but I was dismissed from the Service. It was unpleasant. There was questioning, and a board of inquiry, and a lot of lawyers. I even had to talk to a psychologist at one point. It didn't take very long, but it was a horrible experience. I felt as if I had failed by every standard I ever set myself. I had become the unreliable, shaky woman, the one who lost her head, who choked when things became hard. I am the black woman who couldn't hack it. In their eyes, that is who I will remain. It makes me furious, and I try not to think about it. I am trying to put it behind me.

But when I walked out of VX for the last time, I went and stood on the bridge and looked out at the river. It was this beautiful day, crisp and cold, and I felt very alone. But even in my misery, I felt a sort of freedom, or maybe just the beginnings of it. I'm not much given to self-reflection, you know that about me. I'm not like you, constantly moping around examining my own motives. But I had a gnawing suspicion that none of it mattered very much any more, like I'd left something heavy behind.

Through some old army friends I've been lucky enough to get some contract work in West Africa, working security for aid organisations. We travel with aid convoys and set up perimeters in refugee camps, that kind of thing. It's boring and hot and the food's horrendous. But I can do the work and do it well, and maybe it means something.

Philip, you once said to me that ours was the only honest relationship you had. I took that to mean that all your other relationships had been corrupted by the nature of what we were doing, by the need to lie.

But I also hoped it meant that I deserved your trust. I feel the same way now. I feel that there is nobody in

*the world who can understand me except you. What
happened up on those cliffs changed me for ever, and I
am only beginning to comprehend how. And only you
know what happened.*

*So, I guess what I am trying to say in my very
clumsy soldier's way is . . . should we meet? I get leave.
And I hear the beaches are nice where you are. We
could go hiking or sailing, except I imagine you don't
hike or sail.*

Never mind. We can sit in a bar. What do you say?

*I hope you say yes. It would do me good to see
you. It really would. Perhaps it could be good for both
of us.*

All the very best to you,
Trish

He thought of her, in her soldier's stance, her straight
back, flinty expression, lecturing him on the stories that
don't end, but hang in the air, unresolved. He imagined
her in the forests of West Africa, pursuing her frantic
search for duty and integrity and meaning. He imagined
her in a bikini, on a beach. Maybe he could hike. A bit.

"*Pleep.*" There was a tapping at the door. "*Jantar.*" Dinner.

He let Inacia lead him downstairs, her hand tiny in his.
It was twilight now, and the rain had been nothing more
than a shower, and the concrete was already drying and
was cool beneath his bare feet. The girl's mother gestured
for him to sit. The little boy was in a high chair, his fingers
in a bowl of rice, probing, moulding it. Inacia served, her
mother looking on. Rice, a fish grilled crisp with lime and
basil, some corn and pumpkin stew, a great welt of red
chilli sauce. There was a cold Anker beer for him. They
ate together, the four of them, fumbling their way gently
through conversation in Indonesian, Tetum and English.
The weather, the market, school.

I can live in these moments, he thought. It is when I search beyond them that I make such terrible mistakes.

He said goodnight, and Inacia gave him a little wave. He went back up to his room, left the light off, and watched the street in the blue, darkening air.

He wondered what he should write back to Trish Patterson, the woman who was once his handler, but now had to become something else, something new.

He wondered what he could write about the day that had just passed, and everything that had gone before it.

ACKNOWLEDGMENTS

The odyssey of these characters, Philip Mangan, Trish Patterson and Val Hopko, has come to an end, but its telling was made far more vivid by the many people who helped along the way. Chief among them are my agent, Catherine Clarke, and everyone at Felicity Bryan Associates, and my editor, Ed Wood, and everyone at Sphere. Ed is a marvellous editor who reaches deep into the story, finds its innermost machinery, and makes it run more smoothly. I am very lucky indeed to have had such help.

At the FBI, Robert Anderson helped me imagine the position of the sleeper agent in America from the perspective of those who know whereof they speak, for which I'm very grateful indeed.

Pearl's flight was facilitated by Sarah Manello, whose knowledge of fugitives and how to hunt them would be chilling were it not for her great good humour. Pearl's mathematical prowess is entirely down to Ittai Baum, a very talented young mathematician who tolerated my ignorant questions with forbearance, and helped Pearl become who she was.

James Lawrence and Kara Wright first introduced me to the beauty of northern California, and have fostered my love for San Francisco over the years. A late night walk with them through the Tenderloin gave Pearl a destination.

Harmen Boerboom and Pieter Van Maele showed me Suriname and aided me enormously in the creation of Mangan's sojourn there. The two of them have the true reporter's eye, and the wit and insight that makes journalists such good company.

I have had help, too, from a small number of people who can't be named, because they are current or former intelligence officers. I'm very grateful to them. The failings and mis-imaginings of Philip Mangan's world are all mine.

I continue to trespass on the goodwill of the public libraries of Takoma Park, MD, and Takoma, DC. Long may they tolerate me.

None of my writing would be possible without my family. Susie, Anna and Ned, to whom this book is dedicated, keep me secure with their love and humour and perspective. They are the finest handlers that an operative, alone on the continent of writing, could hope for.

Adam Brookes, Takoma Park, MD. February 2017

MEET THE AUTHOR

ADAM BROOKES was for many years a journalist and foreign correspondent for BBC News. He reported from China, Indonesia, the United States, and many other countries, Iraq and Afghanistan among them. His debut novel, *Night Heron*, was nominated for the 2014 CWA John Creasey Dagger and appeared on best of the year lists in the *TLS*, *Kirkus* and NPR; its follow-up *Spy Games* was nominated for the CWA Ian Fleming Steel Dagger. *The Spy's Daughter* is his third novel. He lives with his family in Takoma Park, Maryland.